C0-DYE-783

BECOMING THE ENEMY

1 9 8 8

SAINT PAUL / 1988

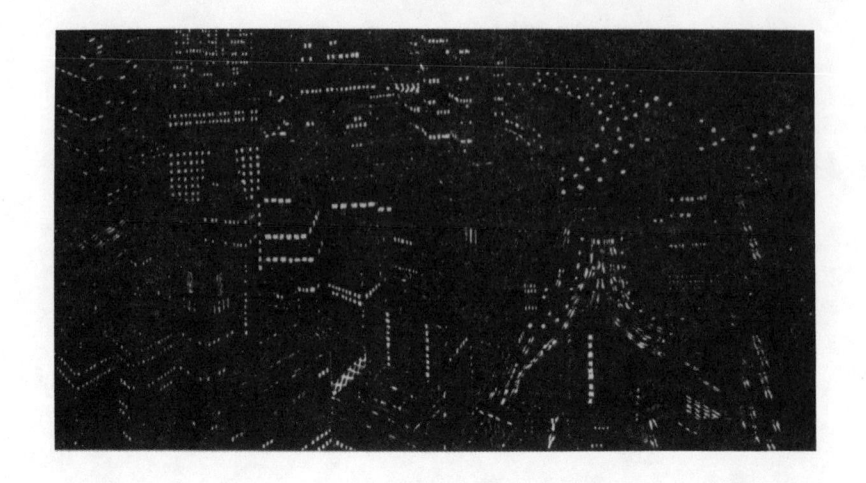

BECOMING THE ENEMY

A NOVEL BY

BRENDA PETERSON

GRAYWOLF PRESS

Copyright © 1988 by Brenda Peterson

Grateful acknowledgment is made to the editors of the following, in which portions of these manuscripts were first published: *Chicago Magazine,* which published "Mother and Maureen," and the 1985 PEN Syndicated Fiction Project, which published "Survivor" in participating newspapers.

The photograph of the woodcut on the cover is by Jacques Cressaty. Copyright © 1987 by Jacques Cressaty.

ISBN 1-55597-104-0
Library of Congress Catalog Card number 87-83083

9 8 7 6 5 4 3 2
First Printing, 1988

Publication of this volume is made possible in part by grants from the National Endowment for the Arts, the Northwest Area Foundation, and several generous contributors to Graywolf Press. Graywolf Press is a member of United Arts, Saint Paul. Publication is also made possible in part by a grant provided by the Minnesota State Arts Board, through an appropriation by the Minnesota State Legislature. The Minnesota State Arts Board received additional funds to support this publication from the National Endowment for the Arts. Graywolf Press is the recipient of a McKnight Foundation Award administered by the Minnesota State Arts Board.

Published by GRAYWOLF PRESS
Post Office Box 75006, Saint Paul, Minnesota 55175.
All rights reserved.

Library of Congress Cataloging-in-Publication Data

Peterson, Brenda.
  Becoming the enemy.

  I. Title.
PS3566.E767B4   1988   813'.54   87-83083
ISBN 1-55597-104-0

ACKNOWLEDGMENTS

In the long birthing of this book, I've had much support. Chapters of this novel were sponsored by an artist-in-residence grant from the Seattle Arts Commission, the Arizona Commission on the Arts, and PEN American Center. The book was begun with encouragement from Judith Geer, Pamela Stewart, Judith Fowler, and Paula Nechak. Along the way, there were careful readings by Deborah Wilner, Susan Pelzer, Judith Wilner at Viking/Penguin, and Karen Braziller at Persea Press; there were years of inspiring authors' lunches with Laura Shapiro, coffees with Kathleen Cornell Wallace, drinks with Gregory Bolton, nurturing meals with my second reader, Susan Biskeborn, and a harmonious home-by-the-sea with Lynettie Sue Kern and Alix Howard-Jones. There was also much support from Kathleen Beamer and REI, as well as Merrily Tompkins's safekeeping the manuscript in her own artist's studio.

Sara Vogan, my sister novelist, read and edited an early version of the novel, Rebecca Wells lent me good counsel, and Katherine Koberg offered sound editorial guidance. Throughout the labor of this book, I've had the abiding mental midwifery of Leslie Altschul, and in the final stages, close editing by Rebecca Haller, who along with my generous massage-midwife, Linda Boudreau Smith, helped me deliver this book to the publisher. Without all these minds and hands to bear, this book would not be what it is. Finally, I'd like to gratefully acknowledge the work of Graywolf Press, particularly Scott Walker, Tree Swenson, and Sheila Murphy.

CONTENTS

Part I

MIDWEEK, MIDTOWN, MANHATTAN

1. COMING TO THE CITY / 3
2. SOMEWHERE, A WAR / 21
3. WANTING TO BE A NUN / 39

Part II

WINTER

4. BOTTOM OF THE OCEAN / 65
5. TEA FOR TWO / 84
6. LIVING TOGETHER / 101

Part III

LIVES-IN-PROGRESS

7. MONEY MATTERS / 117
8. FELLOW CREATURES / 131
9. TO KEEP THE WORLD SPINNING / 144

Part IV

THE NEW YEAR

10. EVIDENCE OF THINGS NOT SEEN / 169

11. A SMALL BURG / 191

12. COMING TO THE COUNTRY / 198

Part V

SPRING

13. BECOMING THE ENEMY / 209

14. ONE ROOM, ONE LIGHT, ONE BODY / 224

15. LEAVES OF ABSENCE / 236

Part VI

BEGINNING AGAIN

16. SURVIVING ONE ANOTHER / 249

17. SMALLER THAN LIFE / 263

18. BETWEEN PEERS / 270

in memory of
RACHEL MACKENZIE
my friend and first editor;

for
BEATA SAUERLANDER,
whose long life has lent me light;

and for
PAULA PETERSON LESTER,
my sister, my first reader.

BECOMING THE ENEMY

"For what is lovable about any human being
is precisely his imperfections."

JOSEPH CAMPBELL
Myths to Live By

Part I

MIDTOWN, MIDWEEK, MANHATTAN

FALL, 1972

1

COMING TO THE CITY

OUTSIDE THE revolving doors of a proper brown-brick skyscraper, Lauren Meyer pulled close the collar of her new fall coat. She had bought it on sale at Lord & Taylor and its darkly woven tweed was so warm; she wished she could wear it during this whole interview. The coat had demanded the last of Lauren's little hoard. After six weeks in New York City, she'd spent the savings she'd hoped would last six months—that was the length of time she'd given herself to find a job at a publishing house in Manhattan.

As a man with a Danish cart pushed past her expertly to tuck himself and his metal wagon into the wedge of revolving glass, Lauren stood back and laughed. He looked for all the world like a baker folding himself into a perfect piece of pie. Others shoved and bustled by her, some using briefcases like battering rams, but Lauren didn't mind. She felt their weight as no more than the great wave of her own happiness.

Here she was; and here she would stay. So far, New York was a first love affair. Its brilliance buoyed her up, carried her along like the shooting electricity that ran the underground. In her last letter to her sister Clare, Lauren wrote, "I love riding the subway. It's speeding with my eyes closed, but knowing exactly where I'm going."

For a moment Lauren did close her eyes, then she opened them and caught sight of her own reflection coming and going in the gleaming glass doors. Yes, Lauren decided, it had been right to risk everything on this coat for the interview.

But as she stepped forward she suddenly remembered her father's admonition: *Nothing is so sad as a woman who shows all her beauty on the outside.* For a moment Lauren felt her confidence leave her and she hesitated.

Her father, a Harvard-educated, half-Cherokee Southerner, successful in his own right as the regional head of Fish and Game for the states of Virginia, North Carolina, Georgia, and Tennessee, was more a mother to his four children than was his wife. It was James Meyer who really raised his three girls and youngest son like a small tribe.

"Half of your people were here to meet the *Mayflower,*" he'd tell his children, "the other half were standing on the *Mayflower* deck when it landed, trinkets in hand. But you know . . . ," James would add with a dark look in those half-lidded Indian eyes, "it wasn't trinkets we wanted. It's never trinkets we want. It's something deeper and so beautiful you can't see it, can't hold it in your hand. And you never give it away, even if you love someone so much you let them share your heart, your land."

It was land that James Meyer believed really held people down to earth so they didn't just fly away. Land and God. Since he was himself closer to the land than to God, James Meyer believed that what he could best pass along to his children was his beloved acres. When Lauren announced after graduation from William and Mary that she was New York City-bound, James refused to speak to her until the afternoon she boarded the Greyhound bus with her two trunks and typewriter.

"You'll forget who you are up there," he'd warned, without meeting her eye. It was one of the first times she could remember her father's black eyes not settling on hers as if she were a small mirror. "Nothing grows up North really. It's dying, you can see it in the land itself. She's exhausted, all used up. People are so busy in their brains, they don't notice the earth beneath their feet. That's like not recognizing your own body . . . to let your land go like that." Her father did not return Lauren's embrace. His eyes rested on the ground; they were moist and still. "I know what I'm talking about, girl. After all our years wandering the world, I recalled us here ... home. You belong here, too."

Lauren had glanced hopefully to her mother, but Madeleine Meyer was lost in a lively conversation with the black bus driver about his past as a hobo; she barely noticed her daughter's leave-taking. Lauren stepped forward toward her father, instead kissed her sisters and brother, then boarded the bus. She felt giddy, with a fierceness in her chest. But as soon as she settled in her seat and stared through the tinted window at her father—both his arms outstretched like a great eagle to embrace the remaining tribe—Lauren's elation changed to longing. All she could think of was her father combing her hair every morning of her childhood. It had always been wild, her hair, he'd say, like the acres and acres of wilderness he managed, half for the government, half in memory of his first people—the ones who knew everything before they'd been managed, the ones who'd forgotten themselves.

With a deep breath, Lauren finally straightened her jaw and caught the revolving doors with a flat thump of each hand. Deftly she ducked into the glass triangle as it swung her inside a dark lobby. The moment she took off her knit cap, her curly black hair flew away from her face with static electricity; she felt little sparks pricking her numb ears.

"What floor, Miss?" In his musty gray uniform the elevator man nodded benignly to Lauren.

"Cowley and Pelzner please, Personnel." Lauren scanned the solemn row of polished elevators. They looked spit-shined.

"Number six or seven will take you to the editorial floors fifteen through seventeen ... just be a moment, Miss."

Lauren stood beside the elevator man and thought he looked like a general in the Confederacy. Taking heart from his genteel dignity, she stood almost at attention and watched the control panel, its red lights rising like mercury in a thermometer.

As she waited Lauren was seized with nervousness. This was, after all, the interview she'd anticipated for the past six weeks. Yet now as she faced the prospect of really entering so distinguished and venerable a house, whose commanding presence in the literary aristocracy predated her own birth by a full century, Lauren considered bolting. It wasn't just fear that prompted her retreat, it was the sheer weight of history; Lauren imagined she was like a manuscript of promising, but very recent, poetry stacked side-by-side the *Oxford English Dictionary* of this publishing house.

She'd first heard of Cowley and Pelzner when her American Literature professor devoted half his Melville lecture to a history of Bernard Cowley, an early mentor and publisher of Melville's work who would have published *Moby Dick* if Melville had not been honor-bound to another house. Lauren's professor described Cowley, a bookish young Boston sea captain, intimate of Joseph Conrad, Henry James, and Edith Wharton; how Cowley returned to Boston from his Oriental trading routes to begin Cowley House and publish his notable, if eclectic, books on American history, what he fondly called "sea fictions," and those odd, elegant Chinese rice-paper, handset leather volumes of Taoist poetry that would become the Cowley House trademark. After Lee surrendered at Appomattox, Cowley took a sailing trip down South and met Bailey Pelzner, whose fortunes the war had so scattered that Bailey was forced to trade his ancestors' land for the lease of a printing press and go into business. Pelzner, too, was obsessed with the sea, though he couldn't swim and only once ventured abroad by steamer. That was after his new partner, Mr. Cowley, agreed that they should search out the finest printers and study their bookmaking so as to bring it back to Boston for their own house. If it was Cowley who knew good writing, it was Pelzner who knew that a book must combine fine leather, paper, and the most classical typefaces. Together, Mr. Bernard and Mr. Bailey, as they came to be known in publishing history, introduced the best American writers abroad and the European classics to this, their war-torn and thus thoughtful country.

When Lauren first heard this Cowley and Pelzner history she'd fallen into the habit of trying to pick out a Cowley and Pelzner book simply by its classic design. The Cowley and Pelzner imprint, an open-faced book instead of a ship's model, adrift in a graceful sea-green bottle, never failed to adorn the books Lauren believed the most beautiful. So later, when her own professor was himself published by the prestigious house, Lauren was not surprised to find him one day in his office jumping up and down. She would always remember him that way, Professor Bartlett so happy to be accepted as a Cowley and Pelzner author that this most reticent of scholars sent his wall of bookshelves shuddering.

"Up you go, young lady..." the elevator man chivalrously tipped his cap, "number six."

Despite her reverence and fear, Lauren's feet moved purposefully toward the elevator. Like a horse leading herself to water, Lauren smiled inwardly, like one of those steady, willing Morgans her father raised, because they were workhorses and yet had perfect manners and presence. Summers they'd all sit in the field and watch his Morgans move through the grasses in animal reverie—Morgans always moving toward the water. *Be like water,* James Meyer would say, sitting mid-field and feeding his perfect mechanical pencil its long filaments of lead. He often scribbled in pocket notebooks. *Be gentle enough to follow simple curves in the earth.* He'd continue, *yet if water rises up... well, it was water once destroyed this whole world.*

In the lobby, the elevator man suddenly snapped to attention as a shambling gray suit lumbered toward Lauren and number six.

"Morning, Mr. Padgett," the elevator man called loudly. "How are you?"

"Terrible, Charlie. I have *two* colds."

Like a bear braving the first light after long hibernation, this Mr. Padgett seemed shrunken inside the lived-in hide of his woolen suit. Tapping the linoleum with his gnarled, walnut cane, Mr. Padgett turned slowly to Lauren and, as if in deep pain, extracted a courtly bow from his old body. Lauren was moved by the man's courtesy. As he thrust his cane toward the elevator buttons, Lauren was delighted to see Mr. Padgett punch the sixteenth floor button marked "Cowley and Pelzner: Editorial."

So he must be an editor, Lauren decided, but he was so dilapidated. For all his rotund Jamesian bearing, Lauren believed this man was obviously an omniscient narrator worn into decrepitude by all he had observed. Gazing sympathetically at the old man leaning so heavily on his cane, Lauren herself rested her full weight on the elevator bars. In the lobby Charlie was gesturing to the sixtyish woman whose bright green scarf billowed behind her like a spinnaker. Charlie's manner was all nervous solicitation as he inquired, "Will this one be all right by you, Miss Jaynes?"

The woman studied both Lauren and Mr. Padgett, her frown deepening. "Of course, *he'll* be no help." She nodded distastefully toward Mr. Padgett, then demanded, "And who's the girl? Another hopeful for Mrs. Holden? I don't know why Muriel keeps up this incessant interviewing. She's got her own talk show going on up there."

"Well, you could take number seven, Miss Jaynes," Charlie offered with the faintest grin toward Lauren. "I could certainly send you up alone."

"No, no," Miss Jaynes said quickly. "I'll just have to make do with these two." And with a grimace which Lauren realized was a sort of smile, she entered number six. She also punched the 15th floor button.

Though Lauren was thrilled to meet a woman she believed might be her first Cowley and Pelzner writer, she stepped back to allow Miss Jaynes the largest share of the elevator. Lauren knew that New Yorkers and some authors made a virtue of rudeness, but this woman's distrust seemed so pointed. It reminded Lauren of the way some churchwomen would dismiss her mother when Madeleine Meyer had one of her more imaginative bad spells. As Miss Jaynes dropped her overstuffed leather bag and let out a distinct sigh, Lauren lowered her eyes to avoid what she knew would not be a pleasant greeting.

But the girl intently studied Miss Jaynes's purse and shoes. Her flats were supple, red calfskin, unscuffed. She must take taxis, Lauren decided. Miss Jaynes's gaping carry-all was quite intriguing. There was an ancient pair of white PF Fliers with red rubber toes. Beneath the shoes was an impressively thick paperback—Lauren twisted her head to make out the title, probably one by Tolstoy, she thought. Instead, she saw it was *True Accounts of UFO Landings*. Research? In spite of herself, Lauren grinned. It was with this great amusement that she let go her guard and met Miss Jaynes's eyes.

Bloodshot was hardly the word for those eyes; they looked bruised. The woman's face had the blotched, puffy texture of an alcoholic's, as if there was lukewarm water sloshing under the skin.

"You think it's funny risking your life?" Miss Jaynes fixed Lauren, whose smile was promptly extinguished. "And you're so busy snooping you haven't bothered to check the inspection date." Miss Jaynes's voice dropped as if she were pronouncing a death sentence. "Nineteen seventy. It's been two years since anyone's even checked the cables. They can fray, you know, until they're no thicker than... than dental floss!" Miss Jaynes brought this last out with a tremor in her voice. "Snap!" She popped her fingers so loudly it made Lauren jump.

It was this woman who was about to snap, Lauren thought and immediately forgave Miss Jaynes her pique. After all, anyone in the grips of a phobia couldn't be expected to be polite. Lauren was not surprised at all when the woman grabbed her arm, holding on for life.

"Most people don't realize that force equals mass-times-gravity," Miss Jaynes confided in a breathless voice. Her eyes were riveted on the numbers above. "That's the formula for falling," Miss Jaynes continued between clenched teeth. Her eyes were furtively unfocused until she glanced over at Mr. Padgett. "This means a worse time for us with that gargantuan Padgett in here."

Lauren looked to see if Mr. Padgett was offended, but the old man seemed blissfully unaware of either their danger or Miss Jaynes. "Nothing will happen to us," Lauren found herself assuring Miss Jaynes. "We'll be perfectly all right."

Miss Jaynes made no answer; she only squeezed Lauren's arm painfully and kept her eyes on the elevator man who greeted two other morning passengers.

"*More* mass..." Miss Jaynes went white and whispered as a good-looking young man and his gray-haired companion stepped into the elevator.

They pressed the button for the 15th floor editorial offices. Lauren thought they were both ever so much more impressive than either Miss Jaynes or Mr. Padgett.

The older man looked foreign and sensual with his pale, wavy hair parted down the middle and his generous lips. This man must be French or Mediterranean, Lauren decided. His young companion frowned. His fine but irregular features reminded Lauren of her first boyfriend, a fiercely handsome fourth-grader who thought of himself as more Confederate than Jewish. Lauren noticed most this young man's tousled black hair; it was the luxurious hair most women longed for, a soft, shining thickness that people wanted to stroke and pet, even if it belonged to a perfect stranger.

Both men ignored Miss Jaynes and Lauren. It was obvious their elevator entrance had interrupted some engrossing conversation that now continued more deeply in silence.

From her vantage point close behind the men, Lauren saw that what the young man gripped in his right hand was a small, bound manuscript. What he held so protectively was his whole world, Lauren believed, and she studied him in earnest, as if she were invisible. He didn't seem to notice Lauren's scrutiny, so absorbed was he with some private struggle. His body showed a deep preoccupation—the way he bowed over as if he'd recently been dealt some blow to the chest, the heart. Lauren's own heart quickened to the young man's pain and at the same time she understood it was not a physical burden under which he bent, but a sadness.

Lauren found her head swinging like a radar scan to discover if the older man was the cause of his young companion's pain. No, Lauren decided, not the origin, but somehow part of it. When she glanced back to the young man she found him gazing straight at her. She was startled by the movement in his dark eyes—as if behind many veils, he still profoundly recognized her presence. In fact, he seemed somewhat startled by her, too. Then, just as suddenly as he'd opened them to her, the young man's eyes fell to the floor.

He reminded Lauren of a mourner at a funeral—lost, brokenhearted, and furious to discover how naked yet untouchable his grief left him.

"But Mr. Sorenson . . . " the young man began, "you *can't* cut that part of my book . . . my father would never have . . . "

"It's not I who'll change it, Joseph," Mr. Sorenson answered rather tenderly, almost as if he were speaking to a child, explaining some implacable passion peculiar to adults—like war or consciously cutting off what feels like part of oneself. "It's you." Then Mr. Sorenson added softly, "And it's not really your father's story anymore, is it, my boy?"

Joseph's face said it was. Watching him, Lauren felt that familiar mixture of sadness, envy, and awe she usually reserved for her men friends finally back from Vietnam. They were more alive, she believed, because they had so recently passed through death. Now here was another kind of soldier, Lauren thought, except Joseph was returning from his own war-torn interior to tell a story. Was it his father whom he mourned so deeply? Lauren wondered. Had this young man's father just died and left his son in such a shadow? Or was it worse—a disinheritance?

Lauren lowered her own eyes and her chest caved in on itself. *When you leave your tribe, it's the same as being dead,* James Meyer had taught his children. Lauren struggled with her own sadness. Last week Clare had written:

September 1, 1972

Father intends to disinherit you, *Behba,* if you don't come home by Christmas. Mother is in a bad way again and he needs you. We all do, of course; but then, it ain't the end of the world, is it? I think you should just stay with the Yankees until you've had your fill of them and *want* to hightail it home. Meanwhile, we be missing you, that's all. It don't kill us.

> Your solitary,
> singing-the-blues but
> all-for-you sister,
>
> Clare

Clare's words helped Lauren gather herself. How she loved Clare's sensible and loyal hand in her leavetaking. It was also Clare's hand that had sewn Lauren's briefcase of lightly scarred deerskin from a doe their father shot last summer. Clare's needlework showed the exacting, fervent stitch of the medical student asked to close a wound. Lauren's little clutch briefcase was Clare's way of answering their father's demand that she be the one to convince Lauren to stay home.

Gripping her briefcase all the more tightly, Lauren turned back to the two men in the elevator who were again locked together in silence. Lauren's intuition told her that Mr. Sorenson was in danger of losing his influence over this young man, about whom he seemed very concerned. She could tell this by the way the older man gave Joseph so much time to answer, as if that time were really an expansive physical space between them. Even though they were all crammed and impatiently waiting for this elevator, Lauren sensed Mr. Sorenson's spaciousness.

At last Joseph relaxed so deeply he looked drowsy. He stretched. "Well, I'll have to ask Ruth what she thinks of the cuts...." He yawned, and his complete surrender seemed to astonish even Joseph.

Mr. Sorenson's face changed, grew very still, even meditative. The agreement between the two men was so complete that Lauren relaxed, too. She felt a luxurious moment of welcome—imagining she was at a family reunion—before the elevator doors suddenly shuddered and slammed shut.

It was then that Joseph turned to Lauren with a sudden grin.

"I'll bet you'll be one of Mrs. Holden's girls," he said, and there was a playfulness in his voice Lauren hadn't expected. She was suddenly shy, lowering her eyes. "Just be sure you smoke her cigarettes all during the interview," Joseph added.

As the elevator at last lurched and heaved itself upward, Lauren had to admit that perhaps Miss Jaynes had cause for alarm; the lift, running on its antique set of pulleys like a dumb-waiter, jerked and stalled between floors.

"We're off," Miss Jaynes intoned between gritted teeth. She glared at the flashing floor lights and tightened her vise on Lauren's arm. "I don't believe in God," Miss Jaynes whispered. "Someone else pray."

Obligingly Mr. Padgett hunched over his cane, but instead of yielding to novenas, he gave way to a rhythmic fit of snorts and coughs. He was a one-man band of bodily noises and Lauren would have laughed if she hadn't noticed the reddish-blue flare of his cheeks and his eyes rolling back in their sockets. The next thing she knew, Mr. Padgett toppled off his cane, one arm reaching out, not to fall, but to levitate.

He was having a heart attack, Lauren recognized the signs. And just as she raised her arms, palms outward, to take the brunt of Mr. Padgett's fall, just as she began the CPR count Clare had taught her—Mr. Padgett fell backwards against the control panel, his padded elbow punching the red STOP button.

There were bone-jolting jerks, someone hissing, then an arm slapped Lauren's back and she fell, shoved from behind. Miss Jaynes's green scarf blinded Lauren and she hit the floor so hard, with both hands flat, that her palms ached terribly. It reminded her of the time she stuck her hand inside a hornet's nest. But what about poor Mr. Padgett? Lauren felt hardly in any shape now to administer CPR.

"Oh, hell." It was Joseph's voice. He seemed more annoyed than panicked. Lauren stayed on the floor of the elevator, dreading the moment when she would have to pull herself up and find Mr. Padgett dead, Miss Jaynes catatonic. "We're stuck."

"Between floors?" It was Miss Jaynes's thin, wobbly voice.

The woman spoke like an emphysema victim in the final stages of oxygen starvation. But Lauren was glad to hear her voice.

"No, Heather," Joseph answered, "we're stuck on the moon."

"What about the girl?" Daniel Sorenson bent down and, taking Lauren's arm gently, lifted her to her feet. Lauren steeled herself to look at Mr. Padgett's corpse. She'd never really seen a dead person before, but she'd survived many vivid descriptions of Clare's pathology classes.

Mr. Padgett was preoccupied with unfolding his checkered handkerchief; his sneeze ricocheted off every wall of the elevator. Then he neatly folded it. In the stuffy air of the enclosed lift—at close range—Mr. Padget's handkerchief seemed the size of a picnic tablecloth.

In the tight, hot fit of their stalled elevator each rider claimed a corner, leaving Lauren in the middle. Pinned against the bronze walls, faces taut with a terrible alertness, they reminded Lauren of repentant thrill-seekers, spun in an amusement park's antigravity machine ride.

Miss Jaynes was riveted to the blank numbers above, as if she had turned to stone. Lauren had never seen anyone go so still. Mr. Padgett seemed to be snoozing as he leaned against the control panel. Joseph was obviously irritated and punched first one button then another in a vain effort to communicate to the outside world their predicament.

When Lauren glanced at Mr. Sorenson, she caught her breath. Sweat stood in luminous beads on the man's pale forehead. His hair seemed whiter, his eyes splotched a yellow that Lauren recognized as the shade of a sulfurous sky. Once as a small child she had watched the March horizon divide into bands of iron-ochre and felt electrified as the sky zoomed down on her, its zigzags of black and light winding round and round her bare, wet feet. She planted herself in the pasture, arms clenched stiffly at each side, but the sky lifted her a foot off the ground where she balanced above a noisy, hot geyser of air. Her hair crackled and her body shimmered. Then almost tenderly the twister set Lauren back down and took the Langley's slim willow instead. Lauren heard the tree tearing inside the tornado, split white wood everywhere.

Looking now at Mr. Sorenson's eyes, Lauren felt again that coiled electricity; she wondered if he, too, were taken by another power because he trembled visibly, his skin ashen.

As if drawn out of himself, Joseph left his corner and took Mr. Sorenson's arm with the soft but attentive touch of real alarm. A current ran through them all, and Lauren knew with a flash of certainty—just the way she'd recognized, even welcomed that tornado sky before it struck—Lauren knew that this older man loved Joseph. He might take the young man up, lifting him aloft, but for how long could he, being old, bear Joseph's weight?

Turning to Mr. Sorenson, Lauren found that he was watching her with those golden eyes, as if he read her mind. Unaccustomed to being observed as intently as she watched others, Lauren could not hold the man's gaze. She moved her mouth to speak, although she had no idea what she might say, when suddenly a mechanical mewling sound began; it grew louder and louder, at last so insistent that the siren filled up what little space there was left in the elevator. This is what the end-of-the-world sirens would sound like, Lauren thought and for the first time felt physical terror. She, too, began shaking.

It was hard to breathe and Lauren felt a rush of blood in her ears; she gasped, felt guilty about her great intake of breath, then noticed with a terrible calm that one wall of the elevator was gently moving in, pushing Mr. Padgett's great weight against her. She also noticed that Miss Jaynes was exhaling rather frighteningly as if someone were pounding her on the back and she were choking.

"There *must* be a way out," Lauren heard her own voice saying, "I watched an elevator repair once... I think there's... there's a little door on top of the elevator."

"Oh, just what we need," Joseph said, and Lauren saw that his curly hair was wringing wet. "An escape hatch. Are you going to eject yourself up and out of here like a fighter pilot?"

Lauren was about to shout something at Joseph because his stare and the screeching siren made her head ache. But she would never allow herself to yell at anyone she didn't completely trust, even in an emergency. Yet something in her, anger or energy, coiled to meet Joseph exactly at his level. "And how do *you* suggest we get out of here?" Lauren asked in a low voice.

"Without heroics," Joseph answered. He nodded to Mr. Padgett, who slumped comfortably against the wall. "And no more life-saving. This is not the end of the world . . . we're just stuck."

Lauren flushed darkly. It wasn't her fault this elevator was stalled, but now that they were trapped, couldn't Joseph see the need for in-the-trenches support? Was he somehow blaming her for the whole thing? Well, she wouldn't say so to his face, but Lauren believed that Joseph's behavior showed a smallness, a *not rising to* this emergency like a true soldier. She was wrong to have given him the admiration she reserved for both anti-war activists and those doomed Vietnam vets. She bet that Joseph had probably filed 4-F, stayed here on the home front and hadn't even protested the war. What did he know about life and death situations anyway? If he hadn't done his part to protest or face the Vietnam war in the wider world, how could she expect him to play his part in this booby trap of an elevator?

"We just have to . . . to *wait* here?" Lauren asked. "For someone else to save us?" She had meant her tone to be hopeful, but it sounded forlorn somehow in this hot, airless box; and then suddenly Lauren noticed that Joseph's knuckles were white from holding up Mr. Sorenson. She hadn't until now noticed the young man's movement to take his mentor's full weight. The older man swayed, sweat streaming down his face, and Joseph swayed with him in a slow-motion dance of what Lauren recognized now as true concern and loyalty.

Sweat was beading her forehead, too, as Lauren glanced down at her watch—twenty minutes stalled in this elevator. It felt like hours. In her chest a heaviness settled; she could hardly breathe. Looking around at the others, Lauren saw everyone laboring to take in what little air seemed left.

"Shall I offer you my shoulders?" Joseph asked softly, and there was that unexpected playfulness again in his voice. He raised his eyes to the elevator ceiling where there was, indeed, a small rectangular panel—perhaps a little door.

"No," Lauren answered and took a deep breath in spite of herself. "I'll just fly."

Then they both burst out laughing and Lauren felt her breathing steady, deepen. She drew what seemed the fullest breath she'd taken since coming to this city, realizing that it was all mixed up with Joseph's clean, somehow familiar smell.

There was a sudden blast of wind rushing down upon them from above, a noise like the whoosh of wings, and the elevator man's oil-streaked face beamed down upon them. "Jesus, it's hot in here!" Charlie swore and crawled into the elevator, then swung himself down with a loud plop. His tools jangled against his leg; now he looked more like a telephone lineman than a Confederate general. He snapped open a metal box, tinkered with some steel innards, and slowly the elevator shuddered upwards.

Up seemed only about three feet. Had they really been so close to the 15th floor all along? As the elevator doors glided wide, they were met with a burst of applause that was restrained, yet heartfelt. Blinking, Lauren and the others stepped off the elevator. She was aware that Joseph had reached for her arm, too, and her dazed smile trembled with gratitude. The young man then let go of Mr. Sorenson who seemed to have perfectly recovered himself to walk steadily through the crowd. Everyone fell back for him. At last Joseph let go of Lauren's arm to follow Mr. Sorenson.

It was wonderful to be here at last, Lauren thought and would have said so except she realized now that it was not for her they all cheered and clapped—it was for their own. Glancing around at all the faces, Lauren felt a sharp longing for every detail of this place and these people who seemed more real than she because they belonged. This was their world, not hers. Ghosts must feel this way when they got stuck between dimensions. They hovered just above, aching for the living and still feeling the false pain and throb of life like a lost limb.

Abandoned, Lauren found herself in the tiny foyer with one table, two ashtrays, and one stiff chair. The room's only color came from a display case of current Cowley and Pelzner books. She hadn't expected the place to be so dingy, like a nineteenth-century newspaper office with darkly smudged linoleum and Gothic hanging lights. She had expected sheer intelligence and wit to shine out from every corner of the place. Instead there was one haphazardly framed sepia photograph of Herman Melville and an ancient, even yellowed collection of Melville memorabilia, as if the house had published no other author of merit in its century of distinctive literary coups. But no, just Melville and a receptionist behind her glass, seemingly bullet-proof, wall. This woman had astonishingly red hair and was smiling with obvious enjoyment as she studied a disheveled Lauren.

"What can I do for you?" the woman asked, still smiling.

Lauren felt utterly exposed and small standing there. "I have an appointment. . . . " She checked the clock that hung behind the receptionist like a giant, conquering planet, and continued, "I'm a little late."

The receptionist resumed her business-as-usual face—an expression of complete disregard and boredom. "Perhaps you might like to tidy up," she said, and there was no question in her voice.

Lauren looked down at her own shoes, as scuffed as the linoleum she stood upon. Her new coat was soiled and underneath it she'd sweated through both her blouse and sweater. Slumping, Lauren realized that she had no energy left for her interview.

"No, that's all right," Lauren murmured to the receptionist. She turned away and thought about running down all fifteen flights of back stairs to the street. But instead she pressed the DOWN button on this elevator—the only thing that would ever open for her at Cowley and Pelzner.

The doors to number seven dinged open rather dangerously Lauren thought, but she squared her shoulders and was about to step inside when a hand restrained her.

"Don't be such a little soldier," a familiar voice said, and she turned to see Joseph smiling at her. "Why don't you rest here a while before taking on the whole world again?"

"I can't . . . " Lauren began and then thought she might cry. "I look just . . . "

"You look just fine," Joseph said firmly. He took her arm with the same natural authority and care he'd shown in the elevator. "In fact, you look like one of us," he laughed and walked her with a wave of his hand past the receptionist's glass box and into the equally dingy, old-fashioned hallway.

He escorted her past rows of tiny cubicles like monk's cells. There was the rapid-fire sound of only one typewriter. Every other door was closed—barricaded, it seemed to Lauren. But against what? There were two people at the water cooler; they did not speak to each other in companionable tones. They addressed one another with the formality of perfect strangers. Lauren had the feeling she'd entered some monastic or contemplative order where the faithful had taken vows of silence and inner scrutiny. Yet she didn't get the sense of otherworldly serenity; everywhere she felt retreat not toward oneself and God, but away from threat.

Joseph noticed her glance at the editors circling the water cooler and he said quietly, "They usually only meet in the margins of page proofs—murder by memo, I call it." Lauren smiled and looked up at him, but before she could thank Joseph he halted and whispered, "This is as far as I can go. Right through that door is the ladies confidential lounge, off-limits to the likes of men. But with your sweet accent and manners the ladies will take you in. You'll be safe and can let down your guard. Be off-duty, for God's sake. Have yourself a cup of tea before you launch into Mrs. Holden's Harbor. And if Heather Jaynes is still in there, make her give you some gin with your shortbread."

Lauren was so surprised at this man's solicitude that she wondered if Joseph were himself in that twilight world between the sexes—but his hand on her arm was too conscious, too warm to be completely disinterested. His touch was distracted, perhaps, and even confused, but he did not have that sweet, immune intimacy of her gay men friends.

"Thanks so much," Lauren managed to say before Joseph was

off, signalling her to remember to smoke cigarettes during the interview. "I'm beholden to you," Lauren added, but he had disappeared around a corner, leaving her alone to enter the rather pink, faded door of the ladies' confidential lounge.

2

SOMEWHERE, A WAR

"I'LL PUT THE kettle on, Heather dear." An accented voice, thick with smoke, was almost drowned out by the rush of splashing water in the bathroom sink. "Calm yourself."

In the last stall of the ladies' confidential lounge, Lauren, too, tried to calm herself.

"Camomile?"

"Yes, Hella..." a familiar, shaky voice answered and Lauren recognized Miss Jaynes. "I'm afraid I made rather a fool of myself," Miss Jaynes began, and Lauren could hear she was crying softly. "And in front of a perfect stranger.... God knows what she must think of me."

Lauren was surprised at Miss Jaynes's concern over how she had behaved in the elevator. She had struck Lauren as most oblivious to others; but here she was, just as shaken and somehow ashamed as Lauren herself. As the women's footsteps came nearer Lauren wanted to bolt from the bathroom; but in a movement for which she would later scold herself, Lauren simply lifted her feet up so they didn't show under the stall.

"Daniel already thinks I'm mad..." Miss Jaynes continued crying. "As if my last manuscript wasn't enough to convince him of that already, I had to go make a scene in number six." Miss Jaynes paused and wept loudly. "It's just... it's just that I'm terrified really... of everything..."

"Tea's on," Hella answered calmly, and the women's footsteps faded to the end of the bathroom and into the little alcove Lauren had explored when she first entered.

In the last stall of this ladies' confidential lounge, Lauren felt silly and quite exposed. She wished she'd followed her instinct and left Cowley and Pelzner when she'd had the chance. Even a retreat would be preferable to finding herself in this predicament: if she tried to leave the lounge now she'd be recognized, not only as an intruder but an eavesdropper.

"Oh, Hella... here I am going on about the elevator when you've so much to think of after that terrible memo this morning. What will we do? Now that the new owners have in one move killed off so many of the older editors? That's like... why, like losing our memory."

"Camomile is my favorite tea," the older woman said in a deep, full voice. "Do you like it, Heather? Perhaps you'd pour me another cup?"

Lauren had to smile; she recognized the other woman's strategy—hadn't Lauren herself learned it long ago with her own mother? Give her a simple task, anything to stave off the dread, the despair, the demons. And there was in Hella's tone a soothing Lauren well recognized from having seen Madeleine Meyer through her worst spells. Nerves, her father called his wife's moods, and would not allow her to seek counsel from anyone except himself, God, and the preacher.

Now as the smell of camomile tea comforted Lauren and she relaxed as much as she could without losing her balance, she heard the gentle stirring of teaspoons in porcelain cups.

"I'll take honey, Heather dear," Hella called out.

More clink, clinking of tea service, then companionable silence. Lauren pictured the two women sitting together in their private tearoom alcove off the laboratory. One would be sunk deep in the soft blue reading chair, the other, perhaps Miss Jaynes, draped across the daybed with a pale chenille coverlet over her legs. Lauren had to smile—under the citrus-colored comforter Miss Jaynes might look as if she were dreamily floating in a dessert of peaches and cream. On a rickety table between them was that delicate rosebud china teapot with its built-in heating element. Upon first entering the ladies' confidential lounge, Lauren had peered inside at the teapot's copper heating coils and noted they gave off a phosphorescent blue-green glow like algae. Foregoing the chore of fixing herself tea, Lauren had instead sampled a shortbread finger from the silver tray. It tasted like sweet chalk dusted with perfume and smoke.

"Hella," Miss Jaynes asked in a low voice, "what will we do about the new owners? Thank God they haven't yet turned on you or Daniel."

"We'll do all we can," Hella answered, but for the first time there was a catch in her voice.

Lauren was curious about this woman Hella. She seemed older and her voice—did it have a German accent? Her tone was like a deep touch, a wide hand on a narrow shoulder. It was not maternal so much as mellifluous, and above all profoundly attentive. If this woman's voice was so much a presence, Lauren thought, her actual physical nearness must be extraordinary.

She certainly had that effect upon Miss Jaynes. Lauren could hear the other's breathing change from ragged and high to steady. In fact, the two now breathed together. There were only the sounds of tea being stirred, sighing, and the gentle chink of the shortbread tray.

This stillness was so complete Lauren closed her eyes and rested her feet back on the ground. No need for subterfuge. She felt safe, somehow accepted. Only then did Lauren realize that she hadn't felt this depth of privacy yet closeness, this meditative self-possession since coming to the city. Lauren smiled to herself. How odd that here, after such a debacle, she should find a resting place.

The murmur of two women's voices meant they'd now closed the tearoom door. Quietly Lauren stood, swayed a moment on her feet, then imagined that there were roots growing from the soles of them down fifteen stories, through the cement, and into the earth. Here she wanted to stay, to put down her roots. Lauren decided now to face-down that flame-haired receptionist and ask to carry through with her interview—even if they'd all forgotten her by now. She would not forget herself.

As Lauren unlatched her stall, the door to the ladies' confidential lounge burst open and in tapped two high heels followed by a slower, almost begrudging shuffle. Lauren's instinct was to duck back in her stall; she looked under and saw the heels were startling—stilettos—and the other shoes were sibilant Hush Puppies.

"Well!" the stilettos struck linoleum in an indignant tap routine. "As if that retirement memo wasn't insult enough, now I hear the new owners are appointing Lyle Peabody, that hack publisher of self-help books, to oversee Mr. Wolff as executive editor. It's insane!"

"Nevertheless, Muriel, it's... it's... it's... official." Those Hush Puppies tracked the heels rather doggedly, Lauren thought. Then she was struck by the woman's name. Muriel. Was this Muriel Holden, the woman to interview her?

"I'll tell you, Miss Crafton," Muriel began so firmly that Lauren took her hand off the stall latch and just stood there in a vaguely military stance of attention. "Retirement is simply out of the question for most of our editors. And Lyle Peabody should stick to selling jumper cables, not books."

"Nnnnnnnnevertheless...," Miss Crafton stolidly repeated, and Lauren realized the woman had a difficult stutter. Then her voice dropped so low Lauren couldn't make out Miss Crafton's words.

"Impossible!" Mrs. Holden burst out. Then she added in a hoarse voice almost as if she were making a threat over the phone, thinly disguising herself, *"He* will never leave us. Besides, he's not yet sixty-five." Muriel gave a little cry. "We'll fight that all the way," she announced. There was a pause during which Lauren heard lipstick tubes pop open. "I'll tell you, Miss Crafton," Muriel Holden finished in a low voice, "this is not the end!"

"One cannot say it is the end," Miss Crafton said softly, without a trace of her stutter, "if it *is* the end." There was real sadness in her voice.

"Who knows this?" Muriel snapped.

"So far only you and I and Hella and Mr. Wolff."

"Mr. Wolff will fight it, of course... until he can't stand it anymore and leaves himself."

There was a silence so long that Lauren wished Miss Crafton would say something, even if it were simply stuttering.

"Oh, my...," Muriel at last said, and it sounded as if all the air were knocked from her. "Wolff *will* play *King Lear*, at a time like this. He has to fight it, not abandon his kingdom and all his editors. After January first, Mr. Wolff will be just a figurehead. *Now*'s the time to fight. He can mourn himself later...."

"It's a tragedy," Miss Crafton said. Lauren thought her tone was one of grim reassurance.

"Nonsense!" Muriel retorted, and Lauren liked this fierce woman so much she almost cheered from her stall. "I don't believe in tragedy except in books. I don't believe there is tragedy in life, only silly, short-sighted people who don't know how to take care of each other or themselves. I'll talk to Mr. Wolff myself and the new owners *and* even Lyle Peabody. I've never claimed to recognize literature, but I know people and I know Cowley and Pelzner. Thirty-five years here should give me *some* say in what goes on!"

This proclamation was again met with a steadfast silence from Miss Crafton. The way this woman withheld support from the other angered Lauren.

At that moment the inner door to the ladies' confidential lounge opened and Muriel greeted Hella and Miss Jaynes with a cry of pleasure. "Oh, Hella, exactly the one I need to see."

"Will you excuse me to talk with Mrs. Holden?" Hella asked Miss Jaynes or Miss Crafton or both.

Lauren was excited. This Muriel Holden had already captured her loyalty and she must be the Mrs. Holden of Holden's Harbor. It was a sign, Lauren believed. Perhaps they needed her here? She was, after all, nothing if not loyal to her own.

The moment the tearoom door closed and the stiletto heels walked out with a sensible pair of European walking shoes—they must have belonged to Hella—Lauren threw open her stall and ventured out. Miss Crafton and Miss Jaynes were gone, too. Going straight to the mirror, Lauren washed her face. She washed away all her makeup. A woman couldn't wear all her beauty on the outside.

"I have that appointment with Mrs. Holden," Lauren told the receptionist, meeting her eye with a level look. She felt completely settled in here and the receptionist took one look at Lauren's wide, cleansed face before nodding with real courtesy.

"Of course, you do," she said. "Mrs. Holden will see you anytime you're ready."

"Now, please," Lauren said and felt again that wave of happiness she'd first experienced standing outside the building—was it only an hour, not days ago?

The receptionist walked Lauren into a large, clattering workroom of six desks where two men and three women bent over typewriters. "Holden's Harbor," the receptionist said, as if this were Lauren's subway stop.

This was the most activity Lauren had seen at the publishing house and it reminded her that she was here for a job, not a social call, as the comforting ladies' confidential lounge had promised. Yet the same Victorian courtesy of the ladies' confidential lounge held sway here because all the Harbor workers paused mid-keystrokes, gave Lauren polite nods, and then hit their typewriters like maestros not missing a beat.

In the center of the workroom was a glass-enclosed office in which sat a sixtyish woman in a sturdy, red-belted blue wool dress. She was wreathed in smoke.

"Come in, come in . . . ," Muriel Holden beckoned to Lauren. "Settle yourself." Lauren sat in the uncomfortable straight-back chair as Mrs. Holden peered at her intently behind bifocals that made her dark green eyes huge. But they were beautiful, the color of Kentucky clover grass. And, Lauren thought, like a young girl's eyes. This woman had not outgrown her capacity for wonder or outrage. "Now, then," Mrs. Holden took both of Lauren's hands and held them warmly for a moment. "Did you really think I *wouldn't* see you?"

"Yes," Lauren answered, "after . . . after what happened in . . . "

"Oh, *that!*" Mrs. Holden waved it away like so much smoke from her cigarette. "You were mugged, and by one of ours. I'm glad that Joseph made you come in to me. He told me all about it. Imagine! You ready to give CPR to Mr. Padgett!"

Lauren was startled. Joseph had preceded her with Mrs. Holden? Lauren was touched by Joseph's concern; her eyes welled up. Tears usually startled Lauren, coming upon her as they most often did when she received unexpected kindness. Mrs. Holden's kindness now unnerved her and Lauren found her body slouching of itself as if she were simply a cat being petted. Lauren disliked this about herself, especially now, because it felt like a surrender—an openness she was not quite sure it was safe to believe.

Mrs. Holden studied Lauren, who sat still in her rumpled coat with runs up her nylons. Muriel made no gesture to take Lauren's coat, so she wrapped it tightly around herself. Then Mrs. Holden surprised Lauren by reaching out and familiarly touching Lauren's hand. Mrs. Holden clucked and then shook her head. "Oh," she lamented with a sigh, "I'm sorry about that elevator. It's certainly not all in this place that regularly breaks down."

Again Lauren's eyes blurred. Now she remembered why she had not wanted to follow through. It was always *after* the crisis that she fell apart. While Mrs. Holden politely scanned Lauren's résumé, Lauren tried to summon all her reserves to meet the pressure of an interview.

Glancing past Mrs. Holden, Lauren imagined herself at home in Virginia. In the middle of the night, in hip boots, she stood, feet sucked into mud the color of dried blood. Resounding in the warm night air was the noisy throb of James Meyer's irrigation pump, an inherited contraption rhythmically beating and breaking. It made a sound like helicopter blades. To Lauren it was her father's heart, bursting with its own power and flow. All she had to do was divert, channel, help the reservoir's water seek its own level. *Be like water*, Lauren almost said aloud, and felt her own heart beat slow, strong.

Mrs. Holden looked back up at Lauren and thought the girl seemed quite self-possessed after her elevator ordeal. She was also attentive; this impressed Muriel Holden mightily. In these dark days at Cowley and Pelzner, young people needed to be both calm and concerned about their elders. It was, after all, quite alarming to be old and surrounded by successors.

"Poor Mr. Padgett... ," Mrs. Holden began, setting aside Lauren's résumé, "if you could have met him when he was your age... ," she fell quiet, then Mrs. Holden studied Lauren with a new sharpness. "A fine man, Thomas Padgett, no one better. The worst thing for him now is pity. You didn't pity him, dear, did you?"

"No," Lauren answered simply, "I thought he was an editor."

Mrs. Holden laughed, but the answer seemed to satisfy her for the moment. She sat way back in her chair and folded her arms, fixing Lauren with eyes that were at once kind and shrewd. "Well, here you are... ," Mrs. Holden said as if they might now drop the pretense of employer-employee and really speak their minds. The passion play was over, the outcome assured. This was like being backstage. Mrs. Holden's attitude even suggested that they might be conspiratorial, discussing the recent drama as if they themselves were not participants. "Would you like a cigarette?" Mrs. Holden offered with a soothing smile.

"Yes, thank you." Lauren took the strong Lucky Strike and leaned over for a light. Her hands were still slightly shaky, but she was beginning to enjoy the tension returning to her body. This was, after all, what she had come for—to be here, to be considered, to give herself over to something greater.

"I'm glad you smoke," Mrs. Holden said and blew out a stream of dense, gray air. "I always think of cigarettes as small celebrations—or consolations. You know... ," she gave Lauren a blazing smile, half-sympathy, half strangely confiding, "there are so few of you young people at Cowley and P., you're quite outnumbered. Most of us have been here since the war. That might be a burden, if you're terribly ambitious.... " Mrs. Holden stopped and studied Lauren again, this time making no pretense at intimacy. "Of course, you *are* ambitious, it goes with youth... but the question is, how are you ambitious?"

"I hope to support my own writing with a career in publishing," Lauren answered.

"That's like supporting your starving by starving," Mrs. Holden commented, but not unkindly. "I did read your little magazine story you sent along with your résumé. But specifically now, what do you want from Cowley and Pelzner?"

Lauren hesitated only a moment. All Mrs. Holden saw was a faint blush. "Anything," Lauren said at last.

"Oh," Mrs. Holden had to smile. "Just that." Then she leaned forward to lay her hand again lightly on Lauren's wrist. She eyed the girl intently. "But what if you never go farther than my typing pool? What if, after five years—and that's really the minimum here, you know, for any proper editorial apprenticeship—what if you are *still* right at that desk over there, pounding your heart out on the typewriter?"

"I've given myself all my life to become a writer," Lauren answered. "And I know there is a long apprenticeship to becoming an editor, too." Lauren couldn't help but glance at the cherished desk which Mrs. Holden had randomly pointed out. Right now a young man, ashen-faced, sat hunched over his red I.B.M. He looked like Raskolnikov as he scowled and glared at his typescript.

"Yes," Mrs. Holden cheerfully reminded Lauren, "but you might very well pound away here forever. There are some who've waited decades to get even an assistant editorship at C & P."

Lauren was not discouraged. "Well, then I will have at least lived out the life I've always imagined for myself, even if it doesn't exactly take the turns I'd expected." Lauren fell silent, then added thoughtfully, "No regrets."

"No regrets," Muriel smiled, "I couldn't put it better myself. They you won't be unhappy." Muriel Holden snuffed out her cigarette. "Unhappy people are predators. They don't mean harm, they're just so preoccupied with themselves they have nothing to give the world."

"Well," Lauren finished, "I've given myself lots of time to become whatever it is I'll become."

"Time," Muriel mused, "yes you do have that, dear. Time is

its own gift and burden." Mrs. Holden lit another cigarette and focused vaguely on Lauren. "Do you know, Miss Meyer, how long ago it was I had my first cigarette?" Lauren shook her head, then leaned nearer, listening to Mrs. Holden with a direct, open gaze. She seemed completely calm now, quite at ease. In fact, both women seemed to have forgotten the interview. "It was right here in this very office on V-E Day that I shamelessly had my first Lucky Strike. My husband was coming home from the war. I was working as the executive editor's secretary. That was Gregory Pelzner, the grandson of Mr. Bailey Pelzner, one of the founders . . . but of course, you're familiar with our history. Mr. Pelzner the Younger, as we privately called him. He was the first to break the Armistice news to me. Mr. Pelzner and I hugged each other and tore up old editorial memos to make confetti. Then Mr. Pelzner handed me that Lucky . . . " Mrs. Holden paused wistfully then continued in gruffer tones to imitate a man, " 'Here, Muriel,' he said, 'the war's not over for us. I want you to stay on and be my front line . . . stave off all the writers when they come back with their war diaries.' "

Lauren laughed and Mrs. Holden Holden leaned forward, cocking her finger in deeper confidence. "It's like what Mr. Bailey himself used to say—'Somewhere, a war . . . usually right outside my office.' "

Lauren nodded, as if in recognition. This put Mrs. Holden slightly off. Lauren was so young. What did she know of wars? Of the whole world gone mad? Her generation had only that shameful guerrilla war in Southeast Asia going on now.

Mrs. Holden straightened. Gone now was her conspiratorial air and any intimacy as she announced in a sad, formal tone, "Well, more to the point now, Miss Meyer. We really *don't* have any job openings, dear."

Lauren gave way to an inward collapse. She was more startled than sad. Nevertheless, she felt herself again near tears. How had she been foolish enough to let herself hope? Lauren looked down, shoulders hunched. She wondered perhaps if she had practiced all her life for this one moment of defeat.

Mrs. Holden saw the droop of the girl's shoulders and felt a familiar regret. She *did* hate breaking such news to these daily hopefuls. But it was her duty and usually she was quite diplomatic about it. Today, however, she really did mind this dismissing chore more than usual. Perhaps it was because even before Lauren Meyer had walked into her office, somewhat shaken but stalwart, Mrs. Holden had liked her. She did not like Lauren Meyer because of her résumé, though it was impressive; she certainly did not like her for her well-thought-out clothes (any Smith or Bennington girl would win that fashion show hands-down); nor did the personnel director like Lauren for smoking her Lucky Strikes. Mrs. Holden was predisposed to admire anyone who could be so naively wrongheaded as to try and save someone like Thomas Padgett—a man obviously doomed.

Muriel allowed herself a gentle smile as she offered the girl a last cigarette. "I'm really very sorry *not* to hire you," Muriel said, lighting the Lucky Strike. The smoke seemed to sting the girl's eyes, and for the first time, Mrs. Holden was struck by them; they were so clear and light a gray that the pupils looked drilled into the center of each iris like those of a stone sculpture. Lauren's curly black, rather wild hair seemed at odds with the delicate features and astute expression of the face it framed. Mrs. Holden paused, then said, "You see, dear, these are our dark days. In many ways Cowley and Pelzner is robust . . . ; reviewers still give our books first and most careful attention. But so many of us in editorial here are . . . well, older. In fact, there are only about fifteen people here under thirty-five, so it might be quite shocking to you at first." Mrs. Holden stopped and lit another cigarette. She thought of all the frequent black-bordered eulogies on the 15th floor bulletin board: Gregory Pelzner had been the first to die, followed by his favorite writers, Fowler and Cain, then Howard-Jones. And just that morning as Muriel sailed past the bulletin board, spilling her coffee on the ancient linoleum that curled and crackled underfoot, she was stopped short by another black-bordered notice. But this time it was not announcing just one death:

THE MERCER CORP. ANNOUNCES A POLICY CHANGE: BEGINNING JAN. 1, 1973, THERE WILL BE MANDATORY RETIREMENT OF ALL C&P STAFF OVER SIXTY-FIVE YEARS.

In all Muriel's decades at the publishing house, there had never been an official retirement age. No one left until they chose to or died. But since last month when the ailing publisher's nephew took over and sold the major share of Cowley and Pelzner stock to a corporation whose main interests were oil and automobile parts, Cowley and Pelzner's editorial staff had begun dreading this very policy change. This morning as Muriel stared at this notice, her eyes had clouded over. It was just like the new owners to make so momentous a decision, then run to tack up their stark, poorly written prose on the editorial floor.

For over 120 years, Cowley and Pelzner had kept its polite, respectful distance from the indignities of the marketplace—their formidable backlist assuring them a steady, but not immodest, profit. Literature, unlike a fortune, was not made in a day or even a decade, Mr. Bernard and Mr. Bailey had always said. Nor was literature ever lost. These dictums had been passed down to Muriel Holden by Pelzner's grandson himself. It was Gregory Pelzner who sailed his stately way through the Great Depression and war years by investing in young authors instead of the stock market. He was a kind of conscientious one-man WPA for struggling novelists. After the war these authors came into their own and maintained their loyalty to Cowley and Pelzner. And their new works were the basis for Gregory Pelzner's move to publish literary paperbacks for the post-war masses.

Muriel herself had been on these fictional front lines and remembered that era as a high point of her career. And now to have the very editors who had ushered in this solid, even profitable, wave of classics themselves dismissed like so much flotsam on the sea by the Mercer Corporation's efficiency experts and market analysts—well, Muriel thought, it was the same as the shipwreck of Cowley and Pelzner itself. The irony was that in his bid to acquire instant culture (like counterfeiting old wealth) Mercer and his ilk would destroy the very vehicle that might carry him into respectability.

All morning Mrs. Holden had watched the older editors wander the halls, stricken by the morning memo. Kern, Wilner, Biskeborn, and Bolton.

She turned back to Lauren and said softly, "So many of us are retiring these days. And there are... well, changes in the air. We'll all need to pull together."

Lauren listened so intently that it gave Muriel some comfort. The girl seemed malleable, sympathetic, unlike some of the other young people here who waited with the withering desire of servants standing in line, not only to inherit, but also to watch the master's death throes.

But this girl had tried to save poor Mr. Padgett. Mrs. Holden sighed while she snuffed out her cigarette in the pink lung ashtray. Then she said softly, "You're not a cynical young thing, are you, dear?"

"Ma'am...?" Lauren leaned forward, confused, struggling to follow Mrs. Holden's logic.

Then Muriel found herself smiling. "No," she murmured, "I think not." Mrs. Holden hesitated, then asked, "And can you really type 110 words a minute?"

"Oh, yes!" Lauren replied, her confusion gone.

"Would you consider it beneath your literary aspirations to take a typing test... I mean, just for form's sake?"

Lauren fairly jumped up from her chair, already removing the small cameo ring from her finger. The girl's fingernails were cut to the quick, her tapered hands surprisingly strong. Muriel gave Lauren a rather difficult, heavily edited chapter on archaeology that was one of Hella Steinhardt's new titles. Then Muriel opened the office door and led Lauren to a typewriter.

All firm resolution, the girl pulled the red plastic cover from the I.B.M. Selectric, snapped it on, slipped the Cowley and Pelzner special cream copy paper around the roller with a flourish that struck Mrs. Holden as something between reverential and perfectly self-assured. Then she began typing, head bowed, leaning over the I.B.M. with a slight sway. She was obviously in her element now, her movements a meditation as the keys chanted.

Muriel exchanged a nod with one of her workers, Cassie, and then went back to her own office. She was careful to close her door; Cassie, with whom Muriel had worked thirty years, despised smoke.

Muriel lit another cigarette and watched Lauren through the streaked glass. In every movement of the girl's head and hands there was such expectation. Muriel wished she could justify what seemed like the girl's infinite hope. But the truth was that at her age, it made Muriel weary. For such hope carried the same burdensome gift as time. And the tragedy of it was not how much time or hope one offered others, but how very little those others could truly receive.

Mrs. Holden spent much of her time holding back the flood waters in her harbor; she had discovered the best precaution against young ambition was to channel it inward. Hence her encouragement even to these lowly editorial assistants to read all the manuscripts they typed and mailed back as rejections. One never knew what one might discover even in returning the slush-pile manuscripts to their authors. Muriel was fond of telling the story of a young Holden's Harbor worker who, in mailing back a book that his editor had rejected, read the manuscript and decided to champion it to the executive editor. The book turned out to be a classic bestseller and the editorial assistant became the youngest assistant editor on staff.

Such stories kept hope alive in her Harbor. One might hope forever, if one had a mind to distract oneself from the reality that though one was part of the stately flow of the Cowley and Pelzner river, one was not in the mainstream.

Watching Lauren Meyer's rhythmic performance at the typewriter, Mrs. Holden had to smile. Where was the rest of the symphony? In the girl's head, no doubt. This made her truly worth considering for the Harbor. Mrs. Holden liked to think of her Harbor as always open—to the right vessel. But since the new owners took over Muriel anticipated a freeze on all new hiring. Perhaps now was the time to get all the loyal recruits into the fold?

Mrs. Holden tapped on the glass to signal Cassie, who was openly watching the young woman's headlong typing. It was so fast, yet also its sound was a comforting reminder of the old days when everything at Cowley and Pelzner was flourishing and self-possessed. Mrs. Holden nodded to Cassie, who would not yet commit herself; after all, this new girl was a smoker. Cassie shrugged as if to ask the question, "Where to put a new one?"

There was no room right now in Holden's Harbor. Several of Muriel's workers would soon be back from temporary, roving assignments to the other staff members in other departments. Then Muriel remembered the encounter she'd had this morning with Miss Crafton in the ladies' confidential lounge after that death notice went up. Of course, Muriel didn't believe the gossip, only filed it away as more wishful thinking on the part of the sharp teeth. But this had come straight from the Executive Editor's secretary.

Holly Crafton was hardly a loose talker. Mrs. Holden suspected that the woman was hired 40 years ago because her speech impediment was so pronounced, she rarely opened her mouth. Miss Crafton also didn't answer her phone, which was a continual irritation to Muriel. Anyone who wanted an appointment with Mr. Wolff had to put in a supplicating appearance and brave Miss Crafton's monosyllabic reception. It certainly spared Mr. Wolff many interruptions, but it was hard on the aging staff who labored up and down the stairs. Mrs. Holden herself had taken sometimes to wearing sneakers in the office as a respite from her stilettos.

It would be weeks before Miss Crafton opened her mouth again, Muriel knew. But that was cold comfort—the words were out. And the words reverberated in Muriel's mind: Daniel Sorenson had been asked to leave.

Muriel picked up her phone. "Sally," she interrupted the switchboard operator mid-sentence. "Give me Daniel's office . . . " Muriel expected Ruth Littlefield, Daniel's assistant editor, to answer; but when Daniel did himself, Muriel took it as an omen that she was on the right track.

"Hello, dear," Daniel said when he heard Muriel's voice.

Muriel loved this man. He might be critical—that cutting edge hadn't even spared her on occasion—but Muriel had worked with him for over thirty years and her respect for Daniel as an editor had never eroded.

"Daniel. . . . " Muriel tried to keep a consoling tone from her voice. "First of all, I'm sorry to hear about that elevator incident this morning. Miss Meyer was just telling me all about it."

"I liked the young lady," Daniel said. "I thought you would, too. And Joseph seems quite taken with her."

Muriel smiled. "Well, perhaps Miss Meyer is a bit . . . dramatic. But I was wondering if now Ruth might need some temporary help."

Daniel interrupted Muriel and for the first time his tone was somewhat cool. "You've heard, then?"

"Hearing is *not* believing," Muriel said staunchly.

"Thanks for that, dear." Daniel's voice was muted. "You're such a loyal old goose."

"*I'm* so old?" Muriel snorted. But it was the wrong thing to say. There was an awkward silence on the line, then Daniel added slowly, "Hella and I are going to take it up with Mr. Wolff and Lyle Peabody, as well as that new owner, can't remember his name. . . . "

"You know it very well, Daniel. We all know it."

"Yes, Mercer. . . . " Here, Daniel broke for a moment. There was a whoosh on the telephone line and then Daniel continued in his normal, calm tone, "But meanwhile, I'll be giving Ruth many of my writers—for safekeeping; and she, in turn, will be needing someone to help her with the chores of . . . " Suddenly Daniel's voice broke. Far off was the sound of Sally's voice on the line. "Oh, do come down to me, Muriel." Daniel was annoyed now. "Bring the girl's résumé and anything of hers you want Ruth to read. We *could* use some help just now."

Muriel frowned, lit a Lucky Strike. Then she jumped up from her desk and waved at Lauren, who barely seemed to notice her as Mrs. Holden streaked by, making for the door and down the back steps. Who was listening on the phone these days? Muriel wondered. Oh, everyone was used to Sally, but she was so obvious about her eavesdropping; you could hear her breathing, smoking, even eating potato chips on the line. But these days Sally was in the distance and that whoosh of air was a signal that someone else was there with you, between you, listening. Would the new owners really go that far? Muriel wondered, spying? After all, this was still a gentleman's business. Yet Muriel was worried. It would be good to have allies in this strange war of old and young, of management and editorial, of the present and the faded but glorious past.

When Muriel next climbed the back stairs, an hour later, she was even more troubled and her feet in these stilettos ached. What Daniel had told her—oh, what he had told her. And his eyes, so old and full of pain.

Well, Muriel resolved, she would do what she could; she would do her part, however small. As Mrs. Holden strode back into her Harbor, she obliviously passed Lauren Meyer, who was still typing. Muriel closed the door to her glass office, lit up a Lucky, and it was a full five minutes before she remembered the girl.

"Miss Meyer, dear . . . ," Muriel called and waved her inside the cubicle. "You don't have to break your head over it!"

Lauren's face was flushed, her fingers red, as if the sheer effort of all that typing made her blood circulate in little torrents. She handed Mrs. Holden twenty pages of typescript. No wonder the girl seemed faint, Mrs. Holden thought, taking the manuscript.

Muriel felt by contrast her own fears and failures—her divorce, her feud with her only daughter. Today they seemed particularly physical, as if her old arteries had grown narrow overnight. Muriel wondered if now she could finally stop smoking. Or maybe she'd wait until she was sixty-five and Cowley and Pelzner finished her off, too, as implacably as the smoke that had been stealthily filling her lungs all these years. Sorrows and regrets and fear would kill her, Muriel thought, not cigarettes. And she, like this young girl, had never expected to have regrets.

Looking at Lauren, Mrs. Holden felt a familiar itching in the bridge of her nose. She gave a sigh and said sadly, "We'll just have to find you a desk, dear."

Heartily Lauren returned Muriel's handshake. The girl's physical exultation ran through Muriel's own body like a strong current.

Muriel watched Lauren's happiness illumine her face and the older woman found herself smiling, too. Passion was never old, Muriel thought; and a joy remembered, even for an instant, felt fresh, immediate—it happened to you all over again.

"Oh . . . ," Lauren seemed to have to struggle to keep herself from levitating, "that's so . . . well, it's just . . . it's . . . "

"Wonderful," Muriel finished for her and was met with a radiant nod.

They both plopped back down in their chairs. "We'll discuss salary and other details later, dear . . . ," Mrs. Holden said lightly. Then she offered the girl another Lucky Strike. "Small celebrations, small consolations . . . ;" Muriel added softly, "because there's always a war on somewhere."

Lauren nodded, but she was staring past Mrs. Holden. There was no brick wall outside this woman's window. Only an expanse of bright sky so dazzling it hurt Lauren's eyes. She stood now on the 15th floor of the Cowley and Pelzner building, *her* publishing house, gazing way down at streets where women who all looked a lot like a young Muriel Holden were kissing strange men in uniform and lighting Lucky Strikes under a rain of confetti, made of old memos.

3

WANTING TO BE A NUN

Ruth Littlefield was reminded of her childhood catechism, *First snow forgives everything.* Sister Margaret Magdalene had taught her this and Ruth still believed it. This chilly October morning she stood at her office window sipping her first cup of English Breakfast tea as she stared down fifteen stories to 57th Street. The snow, falling since last night, was still soft and new; tomorrow it would be slush, Ruth thought, sooted and too familiar underfoot. But this morning its peculiar hushed whiteness left the city still and changed. Ruth gazed up at the flurries against her window and tried to follow one flake down, as she had all her childhood in her parents' Park Avenue apartment which she now shared with Joseph Girard. Ruth imagined she was inside a paperweight where snow lay in drifts. Then she was shaken—snow swirled, white whorls everywhere.

This first snow and last night's lovemaking with Joseph brought Ruth a luxurious, settled warmth. Had she not been at work, Ruth would have wrapped one of Joseph's fisherman sweaters around her shoulders and knelt to fit her back against the clanking spines of her office's radiator, letting its whoosh and whisper lull her. Instead she stood, one palm resting on the chill glass window. Below the snow was so deep its gentle glow lent a nimbus even to garbage cans and taxi cabs. Ruth smiled, remembering how last night she had shifted carefully under Joseph's weight to study his face as he slept. In the reflection off the luminous snowlight, Joseph's cheekbones shone so high that even asleep, he seemed to smile. Holding his head between her breasts, Ruth had lightly counted the faint freckles on each eyelid with her fingertip.

"What ya doin' to me, girlie?" Joseph had mumbled softly and twirled a strand of her dark blonde hair around his finger. "Your hair always gets curlier after we make love," Joseph said, and she could feel his smile against her neck. "I could save you some money at the beauty shop."

"They don't have beauty shops anymore, Joseph," Ruth laughed. "They're salons."

"Yeah?" He raised himself on one elbow to stare down at her. "Maybe uptown they're salons, but in Brooklyn they're beauty shops. I know, there was one on the corner near Tata's house called..." Joseph fell quiet, gave Ruth a tender look, then rested again on her breast. "Oh, I don't remember what it's called."

Ruth stroked his damp head and said nothing. So often since Joseph's father died last summer his sorrow would catch up with him. Just when Joseph seemed to have found a respite from his mourning, something would remind him of Tata. Then he'd fall into himself with the extreme awkwardness of a man usually quite graceful. So his stumbles over himself were quite noticeable. Or perhaps, Ruth thought, she cared for him so deeply, she noticed everything.

Ruth ran her fingers lightly up Joseph's back; she meant it as a comforting stroke, but instead this roused him.

"So... I asked, what ya doin'?" Luxuriously he shifted and lay alongside her, wrapping one leg around her hips.

What I'm doing, Ruth thought as she clasped her hands around Joseph's neck. His skin smelled sweet and dense like mid-summer grass. She rested her chin gently against his thick hair. *I'm doing what I'm doing*, she thought simply.

For once in her life, Ruth believed, she wasn't trying to prevent pain, to control or defend herself against a lover like an enemy or outsider. She was instead letting Joseph deeply inside, giving herself over to him and trusting she would survive even his loss, if it came to that—just as she'd survived her own father's death last

December and as Joseph would survive Tata's. She knew now she would not lose herself; and what, after all, might she find? This was what women must feel when they decide to bear a child, Ruth thought. No matter the consequences: a body that bloats and stretches painfully to embrace another's. The physical weight of love she would gladly carry. Let it open and live and move through her as the nuns had taught Ruth that God's love would do. Hadn't Sister Margaret Magdalene said the body was holy, every cell with its own memory and fate? In loving Joseph, Ruth at last believed this.

But along with the body's beauty, there is the terror, Sister Margaret Magdalene had also told Ruth before the nun left the Church to marry. Twenty years later she was back in an upstate New York contemplative order. Ruth had always wanted to visit Sister Margaret Magdalene, but she was afraid. Already the nun was too much with her; and it was enough that as a child Ruth had wanted to *be* a nun. Some things, Ruth firmly reminded herself, some things were better left in childhood.

"Ruth . . . ?" Joseph had asked, his voice muffled by her hair. He startled her by suddenly rocking her back and forth. "You're hogging all the covers!" Joseph tickled her sides from hip to underarm and she burst out laughing. "My Park Avenue Baby," Joseph sang in his perfectly tone-deaf voice that always delighted her. "She shares her bed, she shares her body . . . but she doesn't share her comforter. It's down . . . and I must go down . . . to the very bottom . . . " He tickled her stomach and thighs. " 'They call it Bottom's Dream because no man hath dreamed it to the bottom' . . . don't ya know?"

He cupped her small bottom in each hand and lifted her up to meet his mouth. Their lovemaking was not exotic, but so familiar that when her body shuddered, she felt throbbing in the exact center of her head, and the warmth expanded until her whole skull was filled with a liquid light like snowmelt.

When she lay still, her sweat trickling down Joseph's face, he turned to gaze out the window. With one finger he traced swirls in the clouded glass.

"Look," he laughed softly, "we got sssssssssssteam heat."

"Yessssssir," she murmured, half-asleep already.

They lay side-by-side, sharing the comforter, except Joseph's feet stuck out slightly. He didn't seem to mind; he lay quietly, still running one finger in circles on the window.

"Ruth?" he asked when she was floating somewhere just above their bed, almost flying, almost a bird above a blanket of white.

"Yes... ?" Ruth's voice came as if from a little distance.

He laughed and was quiet a little while longer. Then he began in a deep voice, "Did you ever read that believe-it-or-not story about the newlyweds who went hiking on their honeymoon in the Alps?"

"No," she sighed and snuggled against him. "Tell me."

"Well, on the hike there was an avalanche and the bridegroom turns around to see that she's suddenly *disappeared*. His wife, I mean. Just dropped off the face of the earth. Probably into a crevasse."

"What?" Ruth roused herself, but she was so content that she wrapped one leg around Joseph's waist and hugged his back. "Oh, yes... she disappeared..."

"Terrible... ," Joseph continued softly. "Anyway, decades pass. So at last he decides to go back to the same Swiss inn where he lost his love years before. He's very old, very weary; he's never loved anyone else. So he goes on another hike thinking that it might be good to just stop walking and lay down and sleep in the snow. You see, he's very old. Did I say that?"

"Yes... ," Ruth murmured, "very old."

"He doesn't want to die, I don't think, just to rest. Forever. And not have to keep looking... for her, for what he lost. But just at that moment, the old man does look and sees a slab of ice. And inside is a young girl, perfectly preserved in the ice. *Perfectly preserved* like the last time he ever saw her...."

"Really?" Ruth sat up and gazed at Joseph. She leaned her head on her elbow and smiled at him. "That *is* hard to believe, love."

"Well, believe it or not, his bride is right there frozen in front of him, saved all those years like some sort of dinosaur."

"Long before man," Ruth said gently and touched his cheek, running a finger up to the small dent in his temple. That dent was made so long ago, Ruth thought, long before she knew him. This private hollow where she watched his pulse trembling was made at birth when he was very small, so small he could fit inside her, as he just had in their lovemaking.

Leaning over, Ruth kissed him affectionately. "What did he do, the old man, when he discovered his bride again?"

"She was so very beautiful," Joseph said in a low voice, with some awe to it. It was the awe that caught Ruth's attention; she'd never quite heard Joseph take this tone before. "And he was so old—he'd lived too long without her."

"So," Ruth found her voice quavering; she was strangely moved. "What did he do?"

"Do?" Joseph turned to wrap his arms around Ruth, then he laid his length atop hers from head to toe; he rested on her as if she were a snowdrift—valleys and bone-deep crevasses—but he wouldn't fall far. He would simply accumulate over her like the snow. "What do *you* think he did?"

"Let her be," Ruth guessed. "He left her where he'd lost her long ago?"

"Yes," Joseph had lifted his head to gaze at her and his eyes were dark, but there was light encircling each iris like rings around a distant planet. "Yes, he let her be."

"But she survived in her own way," Ruth said. She could feel that Joseph was very moved and she didn't quite know why. His body fit so closely against hers and it was so warm and fragrant that she just let him be. Someday he might tell her what the story really meant to him.

All he said was, "Yes, they both did. They both survived."

Now in her office, Ruth gazed down the fifteen stories to the street below where people struggled in slow motion, heads ducked under a blizzard, dense and muffling as goose down. Clasping her teacup between her hands, Ruth went back to her desk and picked up her red pencil. She was just leaning over the manuscript of a new book by a young author she'd discovered and, with Daniel's encouragement, signed to do a book of essays, when the door to the older editor's office swung open. Daniel walked past her to the tea table.

With his back to Ruth, Daniel Sorenson said softly, "I'd like to ask you, my dear, to take on Wells, Vogan, and Patrick Stewart."

Ruth felt a sudden chill. "But Daniel," she protested, "those are your best authors."

"That's why I want you to take them on for me," Daniel replied, his back still to her. He poured himself a cup of Earl Grey.

Ruth was dumbstruck. "I don't understand, Daniel . . . ," Ruth began, but he interrupted her, his face smooth and old as a mask.

"Think of it as just an insurance policy against the unnatural acts of the new owners and other catastrophes," Daniel said. His frown deepened. "It's the only way I can think of to protect my writers and their future work." He turned to Ruth and his face was grave; it made her catch her breath, looking as he did so like her own father as he lay last year in his hospital bed. Ruth closed her eyes for a moment and saw again that green hospital room, Lawrence Littlefield's spindly body under white sheets. He wore blue silk pajamas and stared at a golden honeydew melon that he could not eat, but only hold in his hands. Now Daniel gave her a direct look. "You'll help me protect them . . . my writers, won't you, dear? It's only temporary, until we can ride out the rough times here with this takeover."

"Of course, Daniel," Ruth answered. "I'd be glad to take them on." She hesitated. "But can you tell me what's wrong?" Ruth asked. "Has there been another Mercer memo or an editorial policy change?"

Lyle Peabody's first editorial act was to suggest to Daniel Sorenson that he begin "scouting for more commercial fiction," and that his fellow senior editor and vice president, Hella Steinhardt, launch a new series of books by noted mystery writers. It was laughable, Ruth thought, if it weren't for the fact that it was true. Office politics had never really interested Ruth, but now that the fate of Cowley and Pelzner was itself at stake, Ruth found herself vigilant and aware of every office nuance as never before. She'd even caught herself eavesdropping on a group of messenger boys gossiping in the mail room. This kind of behavior mightily embarrassed Ruth. She looked back to Daniel, who seemed chagrined, too.

"I don't like it one bit, Ruth, all this subterfuge. I just want to make sure my writers survive at Cowley and Pelzner, no matter what happens to their editors. As I said, it's just a temporary safeguard."

Daniel moved away from her toward his own office. "Another thing, Ruth. We'll be having some help for a while, a young woman from Holden's Harbor. Here... " he picked up a file from his in-basket and quickly crossed the room to hand it to Ruth. "Her name is Lauren Meyer... yes, of the infamous elevator incident." Daniel smiled. "She's an aspiring writer and Muriel says she types like nobody else, ever. Here's her résumé and a magazine excerpt from something she's working on, if you're curious." Daniel was at last recovering his usual calm. His smile broadened. "I'll be even more *curiouser*, as my grandson says, to see how you like having your own editorial assistant, my dear." Then Daniel went back inside his own office, and his door quietly closed.

The man had the most amazing way of announcing to Ruth her promotions, Ruth thought, and shook her head. When he'd chosen her as his assistant editor from her first reader job, Daniel had simply said, "Instead of red eyes from reading, Miss Littlefield, you might want to try a red pencil."

Nevertheless, this did call for a celebration. Ruth was about to pick up the phone and call downstairs to Joseph who was Clifton Butler's editorial assistant, but an instinct stopped her. She was not quite ready to talk to Joseph before she figured out what might be going on with Daniel. Joseph was so keen that he'd sense something amiss if she called him now. And he was already nervous enough these days over the fate of his own manuscript at the house.

In a rare act of in-house patronage, Daniel Sorenson was proposing Joseph's first novel as an addition to his noted list of *Amer-*

ican Voices. This series of modern fiction from new writers had been Daniel's most cherished brainchild. For the past five years it had steadily built a loyal following. It was welcomed by critics, too, though it had not achieved the wide commercial success Daniel had hoped would justify the further development of his *American Voices* imprint.

Ruth bent over her desk and stared at the snowflakes melting as they fell against her window. She had to wonder, was Daniel somehow asking her help in a deeper way than he or she even knew? If so, Ruth certainly wanted to offer it, if she understood what it was the man really needed. She tapped her non-repro blue pen against a stack of galleys and found herself giving way to an odd happiness. After all, she realized, she'd just been assigned some of Cowley and Pelzner's finest authors. It would be wonderful working with Wells, Vogan, and Stewart, authors she'd long admired before coming to this house.

Ruth did feel somewhat guilty that her own opportunity should come at any personal expense to Daniel. But he'd assured her it was a temporary assignment; she could perhaps settle back and enjoy this unexpected offering—an experience she might have waited many more years for if there had not been this takeover. Ruth wasn't exactly grateful to the new owners and their editorial meddling, but she was aware that in their wrong-headed housecleaning there might well be some unforeseen and on their part, unintended benefits. She only hoped that whatever came her way did not harm Daniel himself. For who wanted to inherit a fortune if it came from a father's death? Ruth knew only too well the weight of that inheritance.

With a faint smile, Ruth cleared a space on her desk for the folder Daniel had handed her on Lauren Meyer. It would, indeed, be interesting for Ruth to have someone working for her. Many times over the last seven years here at Cowley and Pelzner, Ruth had sworn that if she ever had the chance, she'd treat editorial assistants with more regard for the indignities of so long and often antiquated an apprenticeship. Now she would have that chance.

So Ruth fixed herself another cup of tea. All she wanted now was for the tea kettle to keep boiling, the snow falling—and most of all to lose herself in her work. She picked up the literary magazine excerpt in one hand, her notepad and red pencil ready to make notes. Now she was in her element as she steadily began to read:

Mother and Maureen

by Lauren Meyer

When I was eleven and my mother just turning thirty, we took an unexpected trip.

"We'll go by train, of course," Mother said. Her voice came from the closet, where she searched out her old-fashioned plaid suitcase. She flung it open; the silky pink lining smelled of lilac sachet.

"What will we do with the others?" I asked. "The others" was what we called my sisters, Jo and Clare, and brother Daniel, who at this moment toddled into Mother's bedroom with Father's missing galoshes.

"Oh, them...." Mother waved her hand distractedly and then seized upon a tiny blue satin ball that was the stale sachet. "Here, Danny," she said, tossing it to my brother, who delightedly stuffed it into the boot, buckled it, and then carefully arranged it on my father's empty shoe rack.

Mother straightened and gave me a conspiratorial glance. "We'll leave them with some church ladies. They're always after me to go away."

This seemed like a good idea at the time, though I was afraid to leave my little sisters and brother with strangers—especially the fussy spinsters and grandmotherly Women's Missionary Union ladies who, harpy-like, followed local funerals and insinuated themselves into the dim homes of shut-ins or backsliders or the "not well," as they discreetly classified my mother. She had made top ten on their prayer list for as long as I could remember. "Witnessing" was what these women called their swooping, unannounced descents on the sick or grieving or unusual. My mother told us bedtime stories that always began, *One day your mother died, and then there was no one to keep her children from them ... from The Ravens, with their red claws and big black Bible beaks.*

"And what about Father?" I asked sensibly, helping Mother fold her long blue nightgown like a clean sheet; we snapped it to hear the air go taut with static. "Will we tell him?"

We were, all of us, always forgetting our father because he traveled three and a half weeks out of every month; he worked for the Fish and Game Department and we imagined he spent most of his time leaning intently over spawning streams, counting tadpoles or salmon or whatever it was the government kept so sharp an eye on.

That he couldn't keep so sharp an eye on us and Mother troubled us only when Mother had her migraines. Of course, we did not think it unusual those days to hide in closets or the laundry chute while Mother stomped around the house talking to her own Furies, or, upon discovering us amid the dirty clothes or in her basement fallout shelter, whacked us with whatever was in hand. We thought of our mother as much like a fine-blooded family dog that had been too closely bred, so was high-strung—and sometimes even attacked the ones it loved.

We were fiercely loyal to our mother's moods. "Ups and downs," we called them, or "bad spells," or our favorite explanation had something to do with the concept of humidity in the head that made Mother's mind swell into savagery, then fade into the most playful fondness. I had read about this in a book called *The Moon and Menstruation*, which I'd stolen from the Fairfax, Virginia library and hidden in my own closet. There, while Mother raged like a thunderstorm overhead in her room, I would read aloud. Clare held the flashlight and nodded earnestly over lines like " . . . due to this hormonal imbalance, the ebb and flow of estrogen, and the peculiarities of the feminine pituitary output, menstruation is a radical moment in the mystery of reproduction." Jo was most excited by the colored charts and graphs that used Greek goddesses for illustrating chapters such as "Diana's Descent: The Egg into the Sea." We dreaded growing up into this mythic cycle and pitied our warrior mother. After all, she bravely went before us into this underworld where women were abandoned not only into the arms of their distracted husbands but also to the Man in the Moon.

During these readings my brother sometimes laughed out loud and in the wrong places. Then we would scare him, warning that his lot was much worse: he must spend his manhood staring at the ground, poking into moldy fish ponds and tacking little metal tags onto see-through gills. Most terrible, he would always be leaving his children, just as the fish were always swimming upstream, away from Father.

"And where will we say we're going on our trip?" I watched my mother packing her shapely perfume bottles, swathed in underwear. "They won't let us just . . . leave, will they?" Always I approached Mother as one does a sleepwalker —with an extreme and wondering attention. Even I, who had watched her from the moment I opened my eyes, could not always read her mind.

"We'll just say someone is dying and needs us," Mother laughed out loud.

"Who shall we make die, *Behba?*"

She always called me that—*Behba*—because it was what her immigrant mammy named her and what I called my little sister when I was two and she, my first doll. But my real name was Amanda, the name of my mother's character in the first and only novel she ever wrote. She had written it while pregnant with me, living with a group of wives and meandering men up on a fish-and-game reserve in California's Sierra Nevada Mountains. Every day the men trooped off to their streams and wildlife; the women, bovine and tribal, tended to their small circle of cabins and children.

I'm going to have a baby AND a book, Mother had written then in my white satin-covered baby book. It was meticulously kept for the first three months of my life—anecdotes, my every twitch and start told, as if I were the most fascinating creature alive, and all hers. When I was four months old the doting photographs and narrative stopped. Mother had just learned she was pregnant with my sister and her novel had been returned by every publishing house in far-off, indifferent New York. The fact that it was rejected with encouraging notes from several editors didn't matter to Mother; for all her disregard of personal rejections, she always accepted an authoritative "no" on official letterhead with absolute clarity. She even seemed calmed by these rejection slips, as she was by the formal responses from her congressmen, senators, PTA chairmen, and local newspaper editor. They all set her straight, she said. So purposefully she put away both her novel and my baby book, devoting herself to playing ragtime piano and writing long, fervent letters. Along with her political correspondence, Mother began writing her railroad friends, who still couldn't fathom that she had gotten trains out of her blood and married some myopic fellow who counted fish all day. She also wrote Maureen.

"Now . . . counting train cars," Mother told me wistfully as we sat at the crossing, a red ball clanging, the Fairfax Depot so near that we could smell rail grease and corn-dogs, "that's something I could have loved your father for. I think I just got mixed up, *Behba.* He was very handsome, you see, and I wanted so to be like other girls. In Sunday school I saw them raise their hands to answer questions they didn't even know . . . just to show off their wedding rings."

"You have a nice ring," I said to see her smile and break that reverie. Also, cars behind us were honking and I didn't want to miss our train.

We both knew it was a lie—the ring Father gave her was so small that its diamond looked like a speck of dust that light falls upon, but graciously, to hide the meanness of the fifty-two-dollar chip. I looked upon my lies in much the same way as that light: while pretending to illumine, its shine hid the shame.

"Well, I bet Maureen's ring is much bigger." Mother snapped back to herself, shoved the gear into a grinding first, and we sped over that crossing, racing everyone. It was Mother's favorite trick at stoplights, too, that pause until the line of cars behind us believed we were in trouble, then that bolt out of the starting gate, leaving them bewildered, "in our dust," as Mother called it.

In the station, where everyone sat as if in pews waiting to stand up and sing benediction, Mother bought me a red plastic package of pistachios; she cracked each green salted shell with her lipstick-smudged front teeth before handing me the sweet nut inside. "But . . . " she continued, as if we had not just broken our previous conversation to buy tickets, treats, and a paperback medical-miracle novel called *Daybreak*, by Frank G. Slaughter, "but, I still have my coat, and Maureen may not. They're twelve years old by now, older than you."

I had wondered why Mother wore her favorite coat on this trip. It was July, and in her leopard-skin, knee-length coat she did get a few curious glances. My response to these gawkers was much the same fierce, protective glare that I gave The Ravens on their visits. If my mother wanted to wear a winter coat in summer to take the train to see her best girlfriend, what business was it of anybody else? Besides, I loved its feel, the soft and intimate drape of real animal fur. My father, when he was home, told us stories of the forest, how wolves and wild cats were really brothers and sisters under the skin. If those curious passengers only had eyes, I thought, they would know it made perfect sense—my mother embraced by leopard.

"You know the story of this coat," Mother said softly, "but I'll tell you again because we're waiting for a train and you know I hate riding like a passenger." She opened her hand to reveal a whole palmful of red, yellow, and black Dots that I hadn't seen her buy. Greedily I took them, but they were harder than the pistachio shells.

With her free hand Mother tapped out Morse code along the sleek, soft hide of her coat. She always sent imaginary messages as she talked, because she believed there might be someone else listening in. Clare thought it was also her way of praying.

"Well, Maureen and I were the best telegraphers on the line," Mother began with great spirit. "We were heroes at home—they called us that because we kept a great railroad running."

I loved to watch Mother's face change when she told her story of being seventeen and working a man's job on the Wabash Cannonball.

"It was not so very long ago," she said, "though it must seem so because I used to dream about having another me somewhere inside. You see, I had so much then—so much life—more than just for one person. So, let's say, *Behba*, that you were there and that's why this story seems familiar."

"I was there," I agreed instantly. I was happy to think that before I was born I did things like jump trains and spend a night with a hobo, drinking Sterno and staring at a shanty campfire. I was elated to remember that Maureen and Mother and I traipsed around to every expensive furrier in Chicago with the amazing five-hundred-dollar apiece bonus that the stationmaster, Mr. McCaffey, awarded us for Secret Duty: carrying an unsuspecting hero, a corpse, to Washington, D.C. and the Tomb of the Unknown Soldier.

"When Maureen and I stood there side by side in all those fancy dress-shop mirrors—there were millions of us. We bought the same exact leopard-skin coat, new black heels. Spikes, we called them. The only difference was that my seams were crooked. Oh . . . !" Mother clapped her hands, not at all distracted by the salt from the pistachios. Absently, she wiped her hands on her dress, then stroked the leopard coat like a pet. "Oh, *Behba*, we looked swell, just swell . . . ."

"Still do, Mama," I said. It was my second lie so far that day. First the diamond ring, then to say that my mother's face, sunken and frayed by her own fidgeting hands, was still like that photo I'd often seen of Maureen and Mother in their elegant coats. Then they had looked lithe and racy, like cats really, prowling those streets with the old men and boys left behind by war, patrolling those empty train yards, guarding war goods—and always their fingers tapping, tapping out secrets.

"I haven't even told Maureen we're coming," Mother said suddenly, and stopped her telegraphing.

"She'll know," I said with the quiet authority I always used when I thought something terrible might happen. What if we arrived to an empty house, a deserted town, a place that existed only in Mother's mind? Of course, I knew Maureen was real from the picture. But she might have died in childbirth, as Mother's main character in her novel did, or maybe she had lost touch with Mother and Mother had lied about the letters. "She's still your very best friend, isn't she?" I asked Mother, imitating my Sunday-school teacher's no-nonsense tones. "She'll know we're coming."

And then I felt convinced that we would be perfectly all right. I remembered that among my brother and sisters and me was a telepathy that we found not at all disconcerting, just handy. I could be in the schoolyard and know that Mother was about to have a sick migraine; that Daniel was making too much noise and Jo and Clare were having a hard time getting Mother to bed. At that moment I could simply direct them not to fret over Mother, but to hide Daniel. Then I would dash home, find all fixed, and fetch Mother's whiskey. This would knock her out while we napped, so one of us might stay up the rest of the night watching, while the others slept toppled over one another in bed like a litter.

To believe that Mother and Maureen might have this same communication did not seem a bad thing. Besides, the loudspeakers were announcing our train, Mother was halfway down the platform, forgetting me and the bags, and there was no stopping her.

"Who's the girlie here?" A porter beamed on me like a black sun. We were sitting high up in the Vista-Dome. "She's got railroading in her blood, too?"

He and my mother had been carrying on a conversation about Mr. McCaffey, the Wabash stationmaster in St. Louis, an alcoholic who once crashed two trains on a bet. Mother had left the house without a word once when I was five; only when she returned did we find out that she had attended Mr. McCaffey's funeral.

"Well, I recognized your mama here right off as a railroader... knowed by those hands," the porter continued with a sweetness in his voice as if he were talking to a child. It seemed like the first thing I knew, those hands so scarred and agile. "It's the sparks done it, child." Then the porter insisted on explaining. "Sparks off train wheels while your ma was decorating the platform. That's railroad talk...." He droned on. I shut my eyes. I didn't need him to tell me about Mother perched high on a crane so near the tracks she could feel grit pock her face, sparks making light at the end of her fingertips as she gripped the mail bag on a hook-pole and, in a breathtaking moment, the bag soaring from Mother's pole to that train speeding by.

But the story the porter told about my mother, as if she and I weren't sitting right there, pleased her. So I opened my eyes, smiling as the porter passed on.

"Someday your ma here will run off to the trains again, girlie," he laughed. "Just you watch out for her."

He didn't even know my mother, I thought savagely. It was unusual for me to lean against her or take her hand. I left this childish habit to other people's children. It was a nice coincidence, then, that at the porter's words my mother grabbed hold of me with an unfamiliar, possessive grip and didn't let go until it was time to visit the dining car.

We decided, gazing down over chasms as we sipped our coffee, to steal the one perfect rose swaying on the white linen tablecloth. I watched for suspicious diners and at my sign (a big blink), Mother snatched that red rose from its prissy cut-glass vase and it was only later that I found it, uncrushed, in the hidden inner slit of her fur coat.

"That's why they called me Fast Fingers," Mother whispered, and we both giggled over our big square napkins.

During dessert, of which we had two apiece—pecan and chocolate-cream pie, with two peach cobblers—Mother began to fret again about Maureen.

"You know," she began in that tone that scared me most; it was thin, birdlike, and it signaled the onset of her headaches. "Maureen and I were so close—like you and Jo and Clare. We swore we would always be together, riding the rails. Then the war ended and I was transferred to that small burg...."

I smiled now, because nothing could hurt Mother so much while she used her hobo slang. Just the words themselves put her in a better mood. "Well, the boys came back from war and, you know, we were... sad. Isn't that horrible? I've never told your father, but when Maureen and I stood there on that St. Louis street, heard the bands playing and saw our boys—they looked swell in their uniforms—march right back and take over the town...." Mother stopped and stared at her hands. One held a fork and was poking little holes into her minute steak. Then, abruptly, she smiled, "Your father was wild about his navy whites. They were just dazzling. I couldn't see anything else... not for days, or months, or.... On the honeymoon, you know, we took a train. And that's where we dreamed you up, *Behba*. I know exactly the night, because Maureen and I were always a little confused about sex. You see, she told me the wrong days for lovemaking. Isn't that funny? There I was on my honeymoon, convinced I was safe, and it was the exact days when I shouldn't have...." Mother was talking so quickly now that she didn't stop to breathe.

"Don't you think we've had enough coffee?" I asked her. I had not remembered to bring the little flask of whiskey and knew it would be hard knocking her out that night, what with the train and Maureen either there or missing at the station first thing tomorrow morning.

"Sometimes I wonder if Maureen did that on purpose," Mother said softly. "You know, she had just found out she was pregnant and I was gaily going off with your father to the mountains to write my book. Maureen *had* to get married, of course—she was like that. But what about me? A baby born nine months to my wedding day?" Mother burst out laughing. " 'A baby instead of a book'—that's what I wrote Maureen, and she wasn't sad, not like me. She wrote back and said wouldn't it be nice to be old and visit each other, watch our children play?"

"Well, you're doing that now," I assured her. But I couldn't stop her face from falling, her hands from fiddling with her hair. At that moment I didn't care if we ever saw Maureen; because it was she, certainly, who made Mother so fretful, pulling her hair over her eyes and swatting her face, little slaps as if flies buzzed there. Of course, I suspected even then that I should really be angry at the small baby who had taken up so much space inside my mother. Well, I told myself, I might have come along at the wrong time, but it wasn't me who hurt Mother—just my body, which was only something like me.

"Do you think Maureen will meet us, do you really, *Behba?*" Mother asked, after she checked her face in the mirror of her compact. I knew she did this so often to assure herself she was still here; sometimes when she stood very near me I would make my eyes wide like tiny mirrors so she wouldn't have to fish around in her great purse for that compact and ruin her good mood.

"Well, if she doesn't come, we'll send her a telegraph," I answered. I did not count this as a lie; it was more like whiskey or Mother's head pills. I did, however, feel some terror myself that night, sitting beside my sleeping mother, my legs dangling over the berth. Rarely had I been away from Jo, Clare, and Daniel. None of us liked sleeping with Mother because she stole all the bed.

We had never seen exactly what it was our father and mother did when he came home to sleep in her bedroom; there were those books' stick-figure illustrations, but they didn't satisfy even Jo's curiosity. We did agree that it was a direct threat to us, our parents being together, because we did not want any more reproduction in our house. That's when we began to read novels, and finally, in an old, broken-spined book called *The Fountain of Love,* we read about the "Two-Headed Beast," when a man and a woman joined bodies and souls, but were still separated by their heads.

It was the same thing with Mother and Maureen and their leopard-skin coats, I realized that morning when Mother stepped from the train almost before it stopped at the tiny mid-Missouri station. ELMO: the sign slid by and I looked up, expecting to laugh with Mother over the town's awful name. But she stood, tears spilling down her face.

Here I am, I knew she was thinking as she pulled her coat closer. *I'm here and Maureen's not here.*

And suddenly I thought I might cry, too, because maybe we were lost; but it wasn't our fault. It was Maureen who had lost us. I saw the hysteria working its way from Mother's hands to her head. This was what I dreaded the most. Someday, I feared, Mother might not come back—even to herself or those who loved her. Then The Ravens would pick her apart, shut her off in one of those homes where women sang hymns for breakfast in small, croaking voices. Once I had been Christmas caroling in a place where an old woman with two blots of rouge on each cheek politely chose one of our Three Magi cupcakes and smashed it atop her head like a go-to-church hat.

"Maureen's probably just home fixing us a big supper," I suggested, but even I could hear my voice shaking.

Mother then did something I've thought very brave and sensible. She said, "Of *course* . . . Maureen didn't know we were coming. In a nothing little burg like this, you lose touch with everybody. Come on, girlie, I'll show you a thing or two."

Into the tiny station we strode. I didn't like the station man's face when he first looked at Mother, but suddenly his expression changed and he practically waltzed her inside to let her use the telegraph set. It was those secret scars, I thought, like a password between railroad hands. I sat contentedly, listening to my mother tap our messages. Surely Maureen would know now. I did notice the station manager used his old telephone and spoke in a whisper. Maureen arrived in less than half an hour.

She was a lot older-looking than my mother, and harsher, with lines around her mouth like animal bites. Her hair, too, was short, bobbed, as if she couldn't be bothered anymore with those black waves that once covered her head. Firmly, as if by old habit, Maureen took my Mother's arm and gestured for me to tag along with the bags. She said not a word about the leopard-skin coat, and she certainly was not wearing hers. Maureen had on a faded, obviously home-made print dress that fell below the knees. There were pictures of red birds around the shoulders and dress hem and I believed they made noise when she walked. I was horrified to turn in the front seat of the pickup and find four sets of eyes staring at me as if I were something killed along the road.

Only in the truck did it strike me that Maureen had not greeted Mother with a hug or any sign of real pleasure; and I felt invisible, which was not bad considering all the eyes looking at the back of my head. I stole a glance at Mother, who seemed to be thinking very deeply, as if she had hitched this ride from a stranger and now must make polite conversation. At last, regaining her strange calm, my mother turned to Maureen and said, "Did you like all my long letters?"

"You always wrote well, honey. . . . " Maureen seemed to adjust her mood as she changed gears—with a certain grudging purposefulness. "How's Stuart? Still working for Fish and . . . "

"I put you in my book, of course."

At this Maureen turned sharply and stared at Mother's face. I knew Maureen turned in surprise or fear, but when she saw my mother's smile—that distant and radiant expression we children adored—Maureen, too, suddenly gave up her gruff distance. "Even the part about our stay in that boarding house and the army boys who hitched on at Cincinnati?"

Mother burst out laughing and Maureen at last greeted her. It was just a smile, but Maureen looked then like her photo.

"Oh, that was swell, wasn't it? With our new fur coats and the look on those smalltown boys when we told them we were just in from Paris?"

"I even spoke French all night, didn't I?" Mother asked.

"You were a wonderful foreigner, Sissy." Maureen's laugh was full and low.

It surprised me that she did not call my mother by name. When I thought of it, even my father had a nickname for her, Hotshot. Only The Ravens called her Cordelia, but usually they said "dear," which we, for the longest time, thought was "deer."

All the way to Maureen's farm they chattered on. I hardly had time to notice the countryside, in case I had to find the way back because Maureen lost us again. The stories they exchanged were familiar, but it was wonderful to hear Maureen's gleeful contradictions.

"No, now that was Joplin, Missouri, when you telegraphed our parents that we were missing in action, Sissy. I'll never forget my mother's letter telling me that she wished I were dead for all the grief I'd caused her."

This did not strike me as funny, but Maureen and Mother laughed and laughed.

"Can't you speed this old heap up?" Mother slyly glanced at Maureen. "Anyone would think we were hicks on this old back road. Why, I'd fly right past you in my new red convertible."

Maureen glanced at me. "So you've got a red roadster?" she demanded, and I just rolled my eyes. "Well," Maureen brightened, relieved, "someday we'll all have to take a ride in it. Did your mother tell you about the engineer, Rick Barnes, who let us drive a six-locomotive train?"

"Oh, yes," I nodded, and repeated the story word for word, except for a few places where I'd livened it up.

"Well," Maureen laughed, "I don't remember all of *that*, do you, Sissy?"

When Maureen looked at Mother I saw that expression—at once fond and indulgent—that they both wore in their old photo. I, too, listened happily, as Mother took up the tale, because her stories ended differently every time. I was pleased that Maureen didn't correct Mother when she put me in the story before I was born.

I had a chance now to watch Maureen more closely. She was smaller than Mother and nowhere as pretty. I thought that without Mother near, she might just be an ordinary lady. More than anything I longed to see Maureen back in her leopard-skin coat. When we finally arrived at the prim but ramshackle parson's cottage next to the Rose of Sharon Baptist Church, I thought I might sneak away and search the closets.

But I was distracted by the four children who piled out of the truck and made straight for their backyard. It was trimmed with woe-begone rosebushes, but suddenly I caught my breath. Because there—almost like a miracle—was a wonderful thing: a weatherbeaten trampoline. And because I had ignored them in the truck, Maureen's children excluded me from their play. They sailed high, almost touching the roof, and the oldest boy made a face at me, midair. I was hurt for a moment, but then Mother called me in.

Maureen's kitchen was warm and messy, as if she spent too much time there to bother cleaning it up. I loved the sticky Formica table and the feel of crumbs under my sandals. Mother could feel it, too, and she and Maureen could do a soft-shoe dance.

"Why didn't you ever let me read your book?" Maureen sat down from Mother and suddenly she looked pretty, as if she had put on mascara when I wasn't looking.

"You were everywhere in my book," Mother said simply. "You didn't have to read it."

"You were *there*," I added, just to see Maureen's wonderful smile; it changed her face and she looked at me as if for the first time.

"You're the spitting image of your mother, Amanda," Maureen said softly, and then turned back to Mother. "Remember, Sissy, how we used to talk of this day when we would watch our children play together?"

"Well, Maureen," Mother said with a frown, "in France when a woman is thirty she comes into her own. She has affairs and starts a new life...."

"If that what you think you're doing, Sissy?" Maureen suddenly reached over to push me firmly from the table. "Run out with the others, dear, and let us talk."

I took my time getting out, sliding my shoes along the gritty linoleum. I just had time to hear my mother laugh and say, "We both ran away from home once, didn't we...?" before Maureen called, "Don't let the screen door slam!"

I sneaked around to the front, but these rooms had been tacked on and I couldn't overhear what was going on in the kitchen. So I decided to check out Maureen's children's bedrooms to see if they, with a minister father beholden only to God, had fared better than we with our father and his government. I was surprised to see how untidy their rooms were, how poor and haphazard. There was something about the disorder that frightened me, as if these children were allowed to show something that we dared not make visible—some chaotic play and clutter.

When I came back into the kitchen I found my mother and Maureen gone. It did pass through my mind that they had run off on the railroad, and I pictured them in an empty freight with army boys and whiskey. But then I heard voices from the bedroom and crept very stealthily to peer in the doorway.

There was Maureen sitting on the bed, her big rough head bent over a ratty old coat; it was moth-bitten and there was even a big patch cut out.

"I made a muff for my Sarah," Maureen said in a soft voice. "You live near a city, Sissy, and can wear your fur out any time, but do you know when I wear mine?"

"Revivals," Mother said helpfully, with the chirping quality of her voice that I recognized as a warning sign. "Summer revivals! And I'll bet you just wow them..."

"Early in the morning, Sissy. I wear it when everyone's sleeping... and I go outside and hang my wash for all to see."

At this Mother bent over and kissed Maureen on the head. She whispered something that made Maureen laugh suddenly and jump up, wrapping the coat around her as if it were a famous cape. They strode out of the bedroom, right past me. I felt the short silky fur cross my face like a caress, and delightedly, although I was still worried about that tone in Mother's voice, I followed them outside.

Without so much as a word, Maureen's own children cleared away. They didn't behave as if this were something they often did for their mother. But what did this mean?—Mother and Maureen clambering atop the trampoline, falling, laughing, helping one another up.

"One—two—three—" Mother called gaily, and the two began jumping up and down, up and down, singing:

> Why are the stars always winking and blinking above?
> What makes a fella start thinking of falling in love?
> What puts the kick in the chicken, the magic in June?
> It's just Elmer's Tune.
> What makes a lady of eighty go out on the loose?
> What makes a gander meander in search of a goose?

I, of course, felt proud of my mother and explained to the gawking children that this was how our mothers lived before they ever dreamed us up. The littlest one began to cry noisily, but was hushed by the oldest boy, who had a cowlick that fell backward, not over his face but over his ear. I liked him because one hip stuck out as if he was used to carrying the baby. But then I saw his face take on a slow, disapproving frown. "Hope Dad doesn't come home and see this. He'll think they've gone off!"

I resented the boy for his lack of imagination, though I appreciated his worry. I had mine, too. But I needn't have worried. Just as suddenly as she had opened up to Mother in the truck, Maureen now turned back into her solemn, haggard self. She stopped jumping, calmly took Mother's hand, and though they fell through the springs a time or two, both climbed down safely from the trampoline.

"Amanda," Maureen called me. "You can stay overnight. God knows if your father has figured out where Sissy is, and I won't be the one to call him. He never did care a fig for me. My Clyde has service tomorrow and won't be happy to find your mother here. She played the organ at our wedding so fast, we practically had to foxtrot down the aisle...." Maureen stopped for a moment, ran a hand down the rotted pelt, then took it off. "Hang this somewhere, sonny," she told the boy, who promptly put the baby down and, as if carrying a dead thing, slung the coat over the clothesline.

In the kitchen we finished our tea. Maureen said nothing, but stirred the lemon rind around and around in her china cup. Her face was frozen in a dazed smile. She tapped code on the faded Formica top.

"Your mother has always been like this, Amanda," Maureen said, and I looked up, suddenly afraid of the flat tone in her voice. I couldn't stand the way Maureen stared down at Mother as if she were far off and high up.

Mother didn't even glance at Maureen, but stirred her tea until it sloshed onto the saucer and all over the table. Her smile widened, fingers tapping. "And you, Maureen Bradly, you were always *small-town*," Mother laughed.

I thought Maureen might slap Mother, just slap her silly. But instead she leaned near Mother and I saw an expression I'd never understood until now—when Maureen, someone I was completely convinced loved my mother as much as I did, said, "You were crazy to come here." She was shaking, furious. "You never cared about anybody, Sissy. You can't."

I didn't move, but instead turned to stare with Maureen. It was as if suddenly Maureen and I together were looking at my mother and thinking: *Here is a crazy thing. I love something so not right, so sly and sick and mean.* I felt nauseous with the betrayal and remembered that German shepherd dog I saw my father kill without a blink, before I could even try to pet it.

Mother shrugged and stood up. She made straight for the cupboards and began rummaging around.

"Do you have whiskey?" I asked Maureen in a whisper.

"There," she directed me. "In the cookie jar. It's Clyde's ... medicine."

The jar was round like a colorful little drum and its handles were blue elephant heads. I took out the pint of unlabeled whiskey and handed it to my mother, who just wandered off.

Neither Maureen nor I followed her, but sat back down at the table. I felt frozen solid and wished my mother had left her fur coat behind. Maureen seemed like a sleepwalker, as if she had been the one drinking.

Suddenly she focused on me and I felt trapped, my face reflected in her little eyes, as if I were now as small and ordinary as Maureen. She leaned over and touched my head. "Maybe your mother shouldn't have had kids," she said.

Then I was free and could move quickly away from her touch. "But I was already here," I firmly reminded her. "Before I was born."

Maureen hesitated, then at last nodded. She looked around at her kitchen as if there were something she must cook or tidy or stitch tight. Maureen began fluffing her frilly curtains, staring outside the window. "You should ask your mother to make you something nice, Amanda," she said quietly. "I'm going to make my kids furry mittens from that old coat."

"What?" I demanded. I hated her for looking so dead and dazed, like an animal you see shot but not killed with tranquilizers. "You're crazy to do that. It belongs to you."

"The way you belong to your mother . . . ," Maureen said so softly. I thought it was a question and answered her by flouncing away and outside—there to watch Maureen's children flying higher than their house.

The rest of the evening I played Monopoly with the older boy and we knew to be very quiet. Maureen was in the study with her husband. I never saw him, not even in the dead-end hallway where I waited to watch in case he made his way from study to bathroom to bedroom. But he never came out, not once.

Next morning, my mother was very tired and did little except sip her breakfast tea and lay her head on Maureen's shoulder every now and then. Mother whispered that she would write Maureen long letters. Maureen never did look angry again, but she didn't look pretty, either.

I had to make up another face for Maureen in my story and I never told anyone what happened when Maureen and I suddenly looked at Mother like a mean Two-Headed Beast. What I told The Ravens, who swooped down on us the minute we returned to Virginia, was all about the floral arrangements at the funeral. What I told Clare, Jo, and Daniel in bed that night was this: Early a.m., in Elmo, a small Missouri burg, Mother and Maureen hung out laundry in their leopard-skin coats. Then they wore them in a top-down red roadster and Maureen traveled with us like that, all the way to the depot.

RUTH **L**ITTLEFIELD was just making her last reader's notes on her yellow legal pad when she sensed someone in the doorway. Ruth looked up distractedly, then greeted Muriel Holden and an attractive young woman who stood shyly beside her.

"Ruth, dear, I've brought your new assistant—Lauren Meyer," Mrs. Holden said in her usual no-nonsense tone. She was particularly proud to present Lauren Meyer to Ruth, noticing as Muriel did the girl's story open on Ruth's desk and the look in Ruth's eyes as she shook hands with Lauren. Mrs. Holden recognized this delighted and yet far-away expression as Ruth Littlefield's "discovery" look. Muriel had also keenly noted that crease of concentration between Ruth's hazel eyes, the absent tapping of her red pencil against the desk, and the full teacup of English Breakfast gone lukewarm on her typewriter stand: all spoke of Ruth's loyal attention to the writers she particularly liked.

"Thank you, Muriel," Ruth said, and invited them both into her office. "We do need help. . . . " Ruth gestured for her visitors to sit down. She put the tea kettle on to boil. Then she laughed and spoke directly to Lauren. "I'll bet you like riding the subway trains," she said.

"Oh, yes, I do," Lauren answered happily, then glimpsed her manuscript on Ruth's desk. She blushed and gave Ruth a faint, frightened smile.

"Of course," Ruth said. "And sometime, we'll go by train—you and I—uptown for lunch. I know a wonderful little tea room . . . "

"We'll charge it to the new owners!" Muriel added, taking up their tone as if it were a Revolutionary rallying cry.

Ruth hesitated and felt again her mixed emotions about this takeover. Of course, Muriel would never admit this might be a change for the better. That would be outright mutiny. Instead of echoing Mrs. Holden's war cry, Ruth politely turned to her new assistant and gave Lauren a warm, welcoming smile.

"When I first came to Cowley and Pelzner as an editorial assistant right out of college," Ruth said, "I worked in Holden's Harbor, too. And on my first day assigned to this department, I was given copious written instructions for serving the editors tea." Ruth laughed. "I want you to know, Lauren, that now we all take turns serving tea."

"That's progress," Muriel Holden nodded to Lauren as Ruth offered her English Breakfast—full, brimming cups—all around. "Ruth's brought her little realm of C & P kicking and screaming into the nineteenth century."

Part 11

WINTER

4

THE BOTTOM

OF THE OCEAN

THIRTY YEARS after what he now with wonder and surprisingly little detachment thought of as his first "affair," Daniel Sorenson sat in his office on a snowy day in November and asked himself the same question he asked then: Should he tell Hella? This time?

That long summer after the war he hadn't told Hella. Certainly, Daniel thought, these thirty years might have taught him something, or at least protected him. But was it really from Hella now that he needed protection? Hella had never been an affair; she was his mate. This time, then, couldn't he tell her?

Daniel stopped his pacing long enough to listen to footsteps outside his door. He hated his body for listening, the old, painfully tough body that would pause of its own as if his senses were still those of a hunter, alert and listening, never alone as long as there were sounds, movements in the high, musical grass. Daniel heard voices, treble-cleff and good-humored. He listened intently. No, Joseph Girard's voice was not among them. It was Ruth and her new assistant Lauren Meyer getting ready for this morning's editorial meeting.

Only Daniel and Hella knew this meeting was probably his last. Hella had gone to Lyle Peabody this morning to fight for Daniel. He sat back now in his kid-soft leather chair waiting for her. He lit a cigarette and stared at the smoke hanging in his steam-heated office. Daniel tried not to think, but when he closed his eyes his chest tightened.

"Tired, love?"

The voice didn't startle him. Daniel opened his eyes and smiled wearily at Hella Steinhardt who stood in his doorway, her presence as quiet and near as if she were not there at all.

"Shut the door, will you?" Daniel said, and stood. She leaned against the heavy wooden door to close it and remained standing there, arms crossed, regarding him. "Hella . . . " Daniel said with a sigh, and she joined him on the couch.

They no longer had to lie together here. These dented leather cushions were so like their own bodies left behind. Hella and Daniel sat shoulder-to-shoulder, she smoking her hard-to-find Chesterfields and he his Dunhills. They held hands loosely and stared out the 15th floor window. Daniel had often imagined, sitting like this with Hella, that they were on a slow, undulant porch swing, arcing out over the city, calmly, fondly, as if they were the most forgiving of ghosts. This was their old age, this mild swinging. When Hella and he were young, their swing was wild and soaring. They weren't above it all. They *were* it all.

"You already know what I have to tell you, don't you, dear?" Hella's voice, though thickly accented, was throaty and soft from years of smoking and years of comforting.

Hella's voice still thrilled Daniel, its cadences like those of a country that was somehow his now, too. He smiled at her. For a moment their eyes met and Daniel felt her devotion. "Yes," he said finally. "I know now."

"What will we do?"

"It's not *we* anymore, my dear." Daniel held her hand more tightly.

"But, of course, it is," Hella took up her most persuasive tones that Daniel usually enjoyed teasing. But this time he was silent.

Hella stood up and moved across the room to sit directly facing Daniel on the edge of his desk. "Mr. Wolff says the new owners will accept our resignations whenever we feel . . . "

"*Yours* wasn't asked for," Daniel said sharply, giving her a look that years ago was what Hella first loved in him. It was what she called his "eagle" glance—the golden, relentless eye, that sudden downward turning toward the truth, the prey. But Daniel didn't kill; he simply lifted the small, running rabbit so it didn't have to run anymore. By his talons, Daniel carried others aloft.

Hella threw back her head and laughed, a full, deep sound, almost a pleasurable growl. "And it's not you who must accept *my* resignation," she reminded Daniel. She came back to the couch and laid her head on his shoulder. "My dear, we always wanted to retire together."

This made Daniel growl. "You know that's a lie."

"As a piece of fiction, then, how would you judge it?" Hella murmured.

"The worst kind of fiction," Daniel said, then put his arm around her and leaned his cheek against her head. "There's no truth in it." Hella's hair was white-blonde, fine and ashen, fragrant as if she washed it every hour. He cupped her head with his narrow hand. "And sweetly wrongheaded," he finished.

"No, we never wanted to retire," Hella finally admitted.

"*You* won't," Daniel said just as softly, and when Hella moved her head to look over at him, he kept it down on his shoulder with a stern pressure of his hand. "You'll stay on for the books . . . for the writers."

She escaped his hand and stared directly at him. Her eyes were as old as his, and as fierce. Like sonar, Hella's eyes listened rather then watched. But she was listening to herself now, not to him. She asked, "But how can I stay without you?" Daniel saw the words bounce off a vast, unchartered emptiness within Hella herself. She gazed at him and her eyes filled.

Daniel said in a low voice, as if they were not alone, "Stay for yourself. Stay for me."

"And where will you be?"

"I've told you," he answered, "not far away."

In her eye Hella felt a stinging, like a gnat under the lid. She thought she might weep. Well, that was not so terrible. What was terrible was this sudden ache in all her joints—a weariness down to her marrow. This was how it was to be an old, soft-boned woman, Hella reminded herself in her most severe inner voice. Why fight it? Only accept decrepitude, only understand and make it your daily companion. Certainly it was easier to comprehend and much harder to accept old age when the softness was in the body, not in the mind.

Hella shifted her weight on the couch, feeling Daniel's arm draped heavily around her shoulder. She crossed her sturdy legs and saw the purple veins broken or bulging beneath her flesh-tinted stockings. Once, during the war, when all the American girls were rubbing tan make-up onto their legs and drawing seams from ankle to mid-calf with eyebrow pencil, a sailor had stopped her on the street to stare at her legs. "You got silk for skin, baby," he'd said, and was too overcome even to wink. The thought now made Hella smile. She uncrossed her legs and surrendered to their soft, shapeless need for stimulation. As she leaned over to rub her calf, Daniel stood up again and began his pacing.

She could not take her eyes off him, but watched Daniel with all her senses heightened to an animal awareness. This physical keenness had been Hella's childhood affliction; her psychiatrist father had dubbed her *la petite sauvage*. With his mild, preoccupied smile, Herr Doktor Rosen lectured his only child that while it was good to think with her body, someday he wished his daughter to be admitted to university. She must not confirm the general theory that women are capable of anything except education.

Sitting here in another country, over half a century later, Hella Steinhardt told herself she was still a primitive, and glad of it. It had been a primitive's instincts that alerted her family to flee the Nazis. A month before the infamous Crystal Night, Hella—studying medicine in Italy—had a terrible dream. Because of it, she persuaded her parents and a distant cousin to meet her on holiday in London. From there the Rosens found passage to France, so that on the night when the Nazis shattered storefronts and skulls, the Rosens were steaming somewhere mid-English Channel. Her cousin did not get deported with the Rosens the moment they landed in France. He did finally manage to get his relatives out of the displaced persons camp, and together they all set sail for New York. Throughout the war years, refugee artists, bankers, singers found a way station, if not a home, with the Rosens in upstate New York. Her second year in America, Hella promptly fell in love with a Czech tenor, but instead she married the cousin who embodied her entire childhood as well as her homeland.

Like a close childhood friend, Hella had lived amiably with Samuel Steinhardt all during her years at Cowley and Pelzner. A contemplative translator and amateur astronomer, Samuel never intruded on Hella's love for Daniel Sorenson. Hella had not the slightest desire to live with Daniel. They each needed a home for privacy and to rest from their work with one another. Since neither had ever planned to retire, Hella had been quite certain that things would go along as they had for 30 years—she in her companionable solitude with Samuel and Daniel with his harmless wife Myrna and five married, but still devoted, daughters.

Only once had Hella and Daniel discussed what they might do should this rather European arrangement be disrupted by death or the unexpected. They had decided that continuing their work would be the first priority; and just five years ago when Hella's mother died, Hella and Daniel had quietly pooled their resources to buy Mrs. Rosen's house in Binghamton. Daniel at last sat down again on the couch. Wreathed in his own smoke, the hand that reached out for her seemed to stretch from a dense and forlorn fog.

"Not far away?" Hella repeated. She took his hand.

They sat in silence. Why didn't Daniel say, "Yes, you and I could begin again . . . "?

Hella rubbed his hand between both of hers, feeling the heat as of a tiny fire. "And what about our work?" she asked.

"I don't know," Daniel answered softly.

Hella took a deep breath, her heart aching. "And, my dear, what about you and me?"

Daniel did not answer. After another moment of silence, Hella was up, abruptly straightening the manuscripts on his desk. Daniel watched her—those long, well disciplined legs once so elegant, now all but hidden beneath thick support stockings. As he watched her, Daniel remembered every detail of the first time she had, on quite a different impulse, tidied up his desk.

It was that summer 30 years ago. They were in his office arguing over a manuscript on Russian history when suddenly Hella stood up and straightened his desk. A "tidy attack," he'd teased her. But when she touched his blotter, his coffee cup, his manuscripts, his stapler, Hella had touched his body. They'd lain alongside one another on the slim day bed that late August night and made love until the cleaning lady clanked down the office hallway with her buckets and mops.

Daniel was about to join again with Hella this morning, many years later. He wanted simply to cross the room and claim her with a hand on that familiar shoulder. But he did not move. Heaviness overtook Daniel in the very moment of rising. He told his body to stand up; it sat. He asked his legs to walk toward Hella; they crossed casually, revealing two thin ankles under finely woven socks.

Hella stood on the opposite side of his desk, witnessing his effort and his collapse. In this moment she knew he had resigned. It left her with a sense of separation made more terrible by his presence. As she stared at Daniel from across his office, their distance might as well have been that ocean which first divided Hella from her homeland. Without Daniel, Cowley and Pelzner would be an unknown country, Hella thought. Yet even at this moment she recognized that she was better off than Daniel in this uncharted territory. Hella had the heart to explore, to make and map a new world. Daniel had never lost his homeland before and so he didn't know he was an explorer. And there was something else, Hella sensed, that Daniel feared would happen if he didn't leave Cowley and Pelzner.

"My dear . . . ," Daniel said at last. "I'm . . . I'm ashamed."

She listened to him as if her eyes were sounding his depths.

Then he took a breath, "You know what I'm talking about, don't you?" Her eyes were level with his. "I'm not talking about Cowley and Pelzner or Lyle Peabody or the Mercer takeover. . . . I'm talking about myself."

Hella folded her hands and looked down. Then she came over to sit beside him. She looked very old. "Yes, Daniel," she said in her throaty voice. "Yes... and you didn't think it could happen again, did you?" She looked at him, her eyes full. "This is what becomes of the Stoics—you succumb like all students of the Greeks. You surrender because you have held out too long. You don't bow down to necessities or tyrants. Beauty bends you, brings you to your knees."

"No, I didn't think it could happen again," Daniel repeated in a low voice.

"With Joseph Girard?" Hella studied him for a long time, not critically, not as Daniel would have studied himself. But Hella looked at Daniel with a gentle gravity like a woman who hasn't seen her lover in a long time and who, before she can remember how much he has hurt her, remembers how much she's missed him. At last she said, "Ashamed, Daniel? There is no shame if you love him...." Then she gave Daniel one of the few brutal gazes he'd ever felt from her. It was so powerful, utterly authoritative. "I would be ashamed of you, my friend, if you pretended *not* to love him."

Daniel looked down. "And is this how you felt all those years ago... about Gerald Newland?"

If Daniel had glanced up at Hella, he would have seen her face fall, as if in following Daniel she had unexpectedly stumbled over something in her way—something she only now recognized as herself. For a long while she was silent, face full of some inner struggle. Only when Daniel did not look up at her could Hella master herself and shake her head. "No," she said in her low, angry voice, "not then."

"And now?"

They exchanged a long, meditative look in which each watched the other with all the power of unconcealed scrutiny.

They were interrupted by Joseph Girard himself. Had they heard him knock? Had he simply entered of his own accord, drawn to this door and opening it with the intuitive power of one who hears himself called?

"Ruth asked me to tell you... to tell you that it's almost time for the meeting...." Joseph stopped as if someone had a hand on his throat. Looking from Hella perched on the desk to Daniel below her on the couch, Joseph flushed deeply. "Oh," he said, backing out the door, as if afraid to turn his back on this woman who was one of the people at Cowley and Pelzner whom Joseph most revered. Joseph dropped his eyes, turned, and closed the door quickly behind him.

After the boy's retreat, Daniel said softly, "He didn't even look at me, Hella. He doesn't see me at all."

Hella came to sit beside Daniel on the sofa. She shook her head and sighed. "My dear," she said with a rueful, sympathetic smile, "that's exactly why you have to look so hard at him."

Hella sat back on the couch, lighting another cigarette. Again they began their swing. "It is as it was with Gerald. I saw it that first evening in Rossellini's. Do you remember?" Hella didn't have to turn to him; she knew Daniel remembered. "While you were at the bar, this boy walked up to our table . . . as if he belonged or as if he'd been invited. He *was* beautiful, Daniel. . . ." Hella turned to him and laid a hand on Daniel's knee. "Did you think Myrna and your five girls would protect you from his beauty?"

At this Daniel could smile, "I thought *you* might."

Hella shook her head. "I didn't even try. I wanted to be part of you, but not every part."

"So you asked him to sit down?" Daniel continued for her. "So you knew that first evening?"

"Of course," Hella said quietly. "Gerald ordered white wine, and I remember thinking that it was oddly attractive—his long, fine fingers smeared with printer's ink and wax under the nails, while he held his wine glass as if it were the most precious objet d'art." Hella turned to Daniel and fixed him with her softest gaze. "And then I understood all your trips to the printer's." Hella paused and took a breath. "But the boy wouldn't let you hold him, would he, love?"

Daniel hesitated. *Only here,* he wanted to tell her. *Only here on the same couch where you and I sit and have loved, too.* But instead, Daniel said, "Not really."

"Yes," Hella nodded as if she'd heard everything. "You were, after all, only together when you made love."

He registered her words by a slight flinching. "Only then, yes . . . ," Daniel said.

"That's why . . . finally, I could endure it," Hella murmured, and held Daniel's hand with a sudden grip that surprised him. "But that first night when you came in from the bar, Daniel, you were walking so straight, so purposefully. It was the way you usually walked when coming to meet me . . . " Hella's voice dropped, then she continued, "but I knew you were not there for me that night. I saw your face. Gerald had his back to you. You stopped mid-step. You smiled to yourself, Daniel . . . " Hella stopped, then forced herself to go on, "and oh, my dear . . . that smile was *mine!* Yet you were giving it away to this awful boy. I glared at Gerald who had his back turned to you; he didn't even sense your nearness. I hated him at that moment. I hated you. But then you joined me—you were so happy, so abandoned. . . . " Hella snuffed out her cigarette. "Then I couldn't hate you anymore, because I saw you'd given yourself to a boy who was more impressed with his crystal wine glass."

"I remember," Daniel said shortly. "There were many wine glasses after that."

Hella nodded and they both fell silent. Then she said, "Do you know, Daniel, that when young Joseph came in the room a moment ago, I saw that face again?"

"Gerald's?"

"No, my darling . . . yours." Hella answered.

Daniel took a deep breath. He turned to meet Hella's eyes. "You can't forgive me, then," he said, and it was not a question. Abruptly he stood and again began pacing back and forth before the window.

"It's you who can't forgive," Hella said softly.

Daniel halted and gazed at her across the room. "I'm an old man," he said, but without conviction, as if it were something he had to tell himself everyday because it didn't make sense. " 'Bodily decrepitude is wisdom?' Well, look at me!" Daniel gestured to his narrow body, his skin drawn and taut, the pale ridges of his face and hands. Finally he offered Hella one of those splayed, age-splotched, powerful hands. He offered it as if it were all in the world he had to give, and it also belonged to her. "Look, Hella... I can't see that my wisdom keeps up with my decrepitude."

Tenderly she drew him to her again side-by-side on the couch. She held his hand in hers, which was so well-matched, so equally powerful and ancient that they could have been hands from the same body. "Maybe...," she offered simply, "maybe we're not yet old *enough*."

Daniel would not be put off by her faint smile. He shook his head. "Old age should naturally prohibit at least some humiliations, some of your lower forms of foolishness..."

"Like love?" Hella laughed out loud. "And why else do you think we're here, Daniel, if not to learn how to love?"

Hella was very still, not smiling now. She studied Daniel with a strange leisure, as if by traveling up and down his body her eyes might heal him and lend him new skin. "Oh, my dear...," she said so softly that he leaned very near, "the tragedy of being old is that you're not old. You're young. And so you love with that same pure, unstinting and grateful passion of first love. It comes full circle finally: first and last love."

Hella and Daniel gazed at one another, but this time the intimacy was so full and quiet it was as though between two old people drowned, bodies entwined, but still breathing—breathing at the very bottom of the ocean.

This is what Ruth Littlefield thought when she opened the office door to remind them that it was time for the editorial meeting. She noticed they were holding hands; but they barely took notice of Ruth. Hella and Daniel nodded absently, as if Ruth called them from another world.

As Ruth closed the door, Hella said, "My dear, we still have time...." But Ruth did not know if Hella were talking to her or to Daniel.

Frowning, Ruth gathered the file of readers' reports for the editorial meeting. Her hands, Ruth noticed with an uncomfortable detachment, were shaking. Was it because of what she had just interrupted between Hella and Daniel? It certainly wasn't discovering the older editors holding hands that unnerved Ruth. No one here at Cowley and Pelzner had ever assumed they were *not* lovers. In fact, as Ruth gazed down at the readers' report file with its familiar checked initials—D. S. and H. S.—Hella's and Daniel's names seemed to Ruth more symbolic of this publishing house than the Cowley and Pelzner logo itself.

Perhaps, Ruth tried to tell herself, this editorial meeting felt like none before it because Joseph's manuscript was one of the books being discussed today. And Lyle Peabody as executive editor had not, so far, in his first few editorial meetings proved himself open to new writers. Yes, Ruth decided, that must be why her hands shook. Hoping no one would notice her trembling, Ruth handed out the readers' report to each editor who now strolled into Daniel's office for the morning meeting.

Daniel's office door closed after the editors who filed in like monks. Everyone took his or her seat at the round oak table. Ruth looked to Hella for some sign. The older woman avoided Ruth's eyes, and busied herself with her papers. Daniel sat next to Hella, whispering something to which she nodded a brief assent.

"*Ja*, right," Hella answered shortly.

Then Ruth felt true alarm. When Hella Steinhardt was most upset the only sign was her accent slipping so deeply into its first language that it seemed for the moment she'd never left the old country. Daniel looked defeated, yet remained somehow determined. He reminded Ruth of her own father, who, after the discovery of his bone cancer, drove to his summer house in Amagansett and—legs bowed, trembling, crumbling—played two days of polo.

The editors busied themselves with tea. As long as Ruth didn't look at Daniel or Hella she was able to pass off her rising fear. Ruth closed her eyes and listened only to the pleasant social buzz. It comforted her like white noise.

At last Lyle Peabody, a bony man in a beautifully cut suit,

began the meeting abruptly by tapping his strong fingers on the table and saying, "Before we start, I'd like to announce that Mr. Wolff here and I have decided to discontinue the *American Voices* imprint until such time as it can prove itself a more commercially viable part of the Cowley and Pelzner list."

Ruth sat bolt-upright in her chair. Around her editors shifted nervously. Mr. Wolff himself seemed lifeless and wooden as any figurehead. Only Hella and Daniel seemed calm.

Daniel countered in a dry, flat tone, "Then, Mr. Peabody, I have no choice but to ask your discretion on behalf of the Mercer Corporation to grant me a leave of absence from Cowley and Pelzner until you do see the viability, indeed the value, of supporting and developing new talent such as those writers Cowley and Pelzner has committed to in the past."

"You *will* come back to us, Daniel. . . . " It was Clifton Butler leaning over the table and gruffly grasping Daniel's arm. He was often Daniel's editorial adversary. But now this ruddy curmudgeon looked as if he might cry if his carefully carved pipe weren't clenched between his teeth.

"Your decision is unfortunate," said Lyle Peabody. He seemed not unkind, simply efficient. "But understandable."

Ruth looked away, more to avert her own burning eyes than to avoid Daniel's face as he gingerly patted Butler's thick hand. In her mind, Ruth escaped the room—not by the door but by the window. This was not really happening, she told herself. This was a shock so unexpected, Ruth didn't bother feeling the fool for not having suspected. How could she have known that the Mercer Corporation would cut the imprint and editor everyone assumed —if only because Daniel Sorenson's *American Voices* was a steady critical and modest commercial success—were beyond their cull? It was like abandoning the house's bottom-line altogether, Ruth thought—now anything was possible. And what about the *American Voices* authors? What about Joseph? Now Ruth understood why Daniel had asked her help in protecting his writers.

As the meeting went on by sheer force of habit—this

manuscript, that concern, this reader's report, that editor's hesitation, this editor's newest project—Ruth wondered at how they could all just keep sitting at this table after Daniel's dismissal. Shouldn't someone make a scene, walk out, cry out?

The minute they broke for tea, Ruth herself stood up and strode to the window unaware that she still clutched her readers' report file in her hand. She glanced down at the file with the initials *D.S.* and *H.S.* and tried to imagine Hella's initials alone from now on. Or perhaps Hella, too, would leave? Ruth couldn't bear the idea of being so orphaned here. She gazed out at the window box where someone had once planted a miniature garden. For a while last spring Ruth had watched a gangly assortment of midget vegetables: tiny stalks of corn and patio red tomatoes bravely leaning out toward gray light. Finally the soot and the winter had strangled them. Now all that was left were stubs and one tangled black shoot that resembled a withered hand.

People died, Ruth thought, and they just never came back. You could not ever touch or smell them again, never meet their eyes. Last year her father had gone and Daniel would now go. She wondered whether Daniel, like these window plants, would wither as soon as he was put out of his office. Winter would get him.

Then Ruth heard herself called back by Hella. "'*Kinder*, come," the older woman was imploring. "Come back. We've still much to do here."

Ruth nodded, glancing down the fifteen stories to the 57th Street intersection where tiny people hurried, heads bent, leaning on harsh winds off the East River. She was sick of the snow, Ruth thought, sick of winter. And it was just beginning. As she stared down, Ruth did not see Joseph and Lauren, bundled below in their overcoats.

Nor did Joseph or Lauren look up to see Ruth in the window high above. Joseph wanted to get far away from this place where the fate of his manuscript was being decided.

Joseph turned to Lauren as they crossed the street. "We could drink or we could shop," Joseph said.

"Which distracts you most?" Lauren laughed, but Joseph

noticed that Ruth's assistant—about whom both he and Ruth had come to care a great deal—seemed uneasy.

"You look like *you're* the one who needs distracting," Joseph observed. Lightly he took her arm. They marched like two grown-ups bundled in snowsuits down the frozen slush ridges of the street. "Do you have a bad feeling about it all, Lauren?" Joseph had to ask.

"Yes," Lauren admitted, "but not about your manuscript. Ruth says your book is awfully good. It's... it's something else... oh, probably just an earthquake somewhere."

"Earthquake?"

"Yes," Lauren explained with a laugh, "I get spooked like this before an earthquake... runs in my family."

"The Cherokee side?" Joseph asked.

"Maybe." Lauren shrugged and quickened their pace. "I'm sure everything's just fine. Let's windowshop."

"Do Cherokees windowshop?" Joseph asked. But Lauren didn't hear him. She was lost in the crowd outside Brentano's, whose windows were already decorated with books for Christmas.

Watching Lauren in her disarmingly out-of-fashion knit cap, Joseph thought she looked delicate, childlike. But she was no child, he decided; Lauren was too aware of others for that. She was also something even more engaging and perhaps dangerous to him— she was profoundly open. Her openness was remarkable enough to distract him, even at this moment, from himself.

In fact, Joseph found himself hardly thinking at all, and this delighted and freed him. As he and Lauren darted in and out of the human traffic he was aware only of his boots flapping against the brown, salty slush of last Sunday's snow. Crunch, crunch, lean and push through the bitterly cold, unsated Christmas shoppers, narrowly missing the pretzel wagon with its chestnuts sizzling, split wide.

"Oh, look!" Lauren pointed to the window at F.A.O. Schwartz. "We could get a sled."

"How would you get it back to the 'Y?' On your beloved subway?" Joseph asked.

"Why not? We've seen much stranger things on the I.R.T."

Suddenly Joseph had a picture of Lauren, red American Flyer under her arm, on the uptown express. The image filled him with pleasure. Standing there on the sidewalk in front of the toystore where his own father had brought him on rare holiday expeditions from Brooklyn, Joseph thought for the first time since Tata died that it might be possible simply to be happy again—that the mourning which had held him in its deep vise might sometime ease and let him be, let him breathe and make love and eat heartily without remembering his loss. It was like a fever breaking—but Joseph didn't feel cool; he felt luxuriously warm.

"Lauren . . . you ever seen Brooklyn Heights?" he asked impulsively.

She turned to him, her gray eyes translucent in this winter light. "Never," she said almost solemnly. "What's there?"

"Everything," Joseph answered at once, and had to smile at himself. "Or, at least, everything that meant anything to me for years and years."

Suddenly Joseph wanted to carry Lauren down into the warm tunnels, those depths of the I.R.T.; she'd be his stowaway as he brought her to his old home. He'd show her Brooklyn Heights, where he grew up with his father—that working harbor which had held all his hopes. On a chilly December day like this Joseph as a boy would have leaned out his bedroom window. Everything seemed magical then: the harbor metamorphosed into a murmuring expanse of dark water, brief gleams of portholes, and the forgiving foghorns that called men in black watchcaps back to ship. Everyone was going somewhere, oblivious to the boy above in the window. Those days Joseph had been a stowaway in his heart. And he'd believed that growing up would be like simply leaving someone behind on the dock—someone who waved, crying out, but you were already far away, under sail, smiling back at yourself with vague tenderness and pity.

But it was he who had been left behind, Joseph thought now and felt those familiar waves of sorrow overwhelm him right here on the sidewalk. It could happen anywhere, the strong flow of grief, as if he were bleeding somewhere so deep inside no one could see, no one could help staunch the flow.

"Brooklyn...." Joseph repeated more to himself than to Lauren. "I'd like to take you back there."

"Do we have time?" Lauren asked. "I'd love to see where you lived."

Joseph's mind seemed to work in slow-motion. While Lauren was gazing at him, he felt himself physically step far back from her, though his body didn't move. He looked at her, at the toy-store window, at the crowds as if he were completely separate, an alien dropped here and wondering how he might best pass for human. It was like getting lost right inside your own body, feeling at once utterly without skin and yet trapped.

Joseph tried to remember where he'd felt this before. It was long ago. When he was in first grade he'd somehow gotten himself lost on the same subway he took home every day. How? It hadn't made sense, but there he was, a little boy standing in a freezing phone booth, its windows covered with red graffiti. Fingers trembling, Joseph had made a terrified phone call to Mrs. Shreiber, the housekeeper, who had summoned his father.

While Joseph had waited for Tata's voice, his feet began dancing. Soon he was jiggling, holding his crotch, whimpering in confusion, thinking *I'm lost. I'll never get home. I'll never get out of this phone booth!*

He'd tried to calm himself with the memory of Tata sitting at his workbench; his father smelled of fine watchmaker's oil and old purple felt from jewelers' cases. In those days Tata smoked Camel unfiltereds and his hands were fragrant with fierce tobacco, metallic coils and copper. As he stood in that booth, Joseph had wanted more than anything in the world to feel the old man's big, ruined hands on his head again. He wanted to smell Tata's breath, not because it was sweet, but because it was so *known*. This physical need for his father seemed deeper than anything Joseph had ever felt since for a woman.

Then Tata's familiar voice on the phone, *"Tak?"*

Joseph's foot stopped jiggling—he had cried and pissed in his pants at the same moment. Warm wetness pooled in his shoes, trickling down his thigh as he wept, barely managing to get out, "Tato, I'm here! I don't know where.... Come get me!"

"Read the signs to me, Yoncle," Tata answered in his hoarse Polish accent.

"Atlantic... Atlantic Avenue and... I can't see it... there's a Stefan's Ice Cream on the corner..."

"*Tak*, you are very near me. Stay... *dobrze*, my Yoncle."

Tata was there in minutes and fairly had to pry his small son out of the phone booth's folding glass door. As they had walked to their battered duplex, Tata reached down, picked up his boy and rubbed his big, warm hands around and around on Joseph's stomach. "How did you get lost so close?" Tata asked softly.

"I scared myself," was all Joseph could say.

And Tata's answer had been a deep, throaty laugh as he threw back his head, acknowledging, "Yes, Yoncle, sometimes it is myself I scare, too."

"Brooklyn...." It was Lauren leaning near him and eyeing Joseph with concern. "If that's were you want to go... if that will take your mind off all this, I'll go with you."

"What?" Joseph tried to focus on her and felt a chill through him. "Oh... that... oh, no, you're right. We don't have the time. We should get back."

Without waiting for her, Joseph started off down the street. Lauren caught up with him and took his arm. She was surprisingly strong for one so slight and small.

"Joseph," Lauren said softly, "everything will be all right."

They strode quickly the blocks back to Cowley and Pelzner. Joseph's ears felt solid, numb, swollen large as a prizefighter's. And when he put his gloves to his ears he heard a crackling as if any minute his ears might burst with the fever of frostbite. His lungs ached.

As if his shivering ran through her body, Lauren said, "It's so cold. I didn't know it was so cold."

JOSEPH AND LAUREN rounded the corner of 57th Street and then stopped. Ruth and Daniel stood outside the building on the sidewalk. They were talking, heads lowered, not looking at one another, but staring down at the brown, rigid slush; its miniature valleys and mountains were like a topographical map they studied intently because they'd lost their way. Ruth was disconsolate, her body clamped against the cold, arms wrapped around herself. She was in her streetclothes, but Daniel wore an overcoat. It looked as if Ruth had run outside after him. Now she stood near Daniel and shivered.

Then Joseph understood; they wouldn't take his book. Joseph felt Lauren's hand, her mitten loosely knit and soft like a paw, patting his shoulder. It took all his courage to gently shrug her off, because he wanted her touch. Walking quickly ahead of Lauren, Joseph came upon Ruth and Daniel, who turned to him as if they had been discussing something that had nothing to do with him. For a moment Joseph thought perhaps he was wrong and they had accepted his manuscript.

Then Ruth said in a low, husky voice as if she'd been crying, "It's not fair."

Ruth took Joseph's arm and on the other side Daniel touched his elbow, guiding both him and Ruth across the street. Lauren caught up and Ruth included her with a sorrowful nod as they all ventured into the cozy darkness of Rossellini's.

As if by feminine telepathy, Lauren and Ruth disappeared into the ladies' room and left Joseph alone with Daniel. The old man said nothing until he had hailed a waiter and secured them both a table in the bar. Automatically Daniel ordered them both the same drink, a double martini straight up. Then he ordered Ruth's standard champagne cocktail.

"What will Lauren have, do you think?" Daniel asked Joseph, as if this were the only question between them.

"Bourbon, maybe?" Joseph guessed.

They waited for their drinks and when they arrived, Daniel stared at his martini without touching it. Very softly he at last said, "Please, my dear boy, don't give up on yourself—or me."

Daniel's voice was so heavy and his face so altered that Joseph could say nothing. "You see," Daniel continued, "I haven't given up."

Joseph lowered his head and felt as if Daniel had touched him, though the old man made no movement, but seemed lost in a stillness so dense that Joseph dared not move or speak himself.

As Lauren and Ruth returned to the table, both seemed to Joseph subdued, but as if they at last fully shared some secret. Daniel took the elegant menu and studied it a long while, his hands worn thin, transparent. "This is my treat, my dears. And you . . . ," Daniel made a gesture to include them all, "each of you may have whatever you want. Anything on the menu. . . . " Daniel stared at Joseph and the editor's face was very sad, white and abraded, like stone under water. "Anything."

5

TEA FOR TWO

> Am I blue? Am I blue?
> Ain't the tears in my eyes
> Telling you?
> Am I blue? You'd be, too,
> If each plan with your man
> Done fell through...

"WHAT A silly band," Ruth Littlefield whispered to Lauren as they stood in the long line at the hors d'oeuvres table.

Every Christmas Cowley and Pelzner traditionally gave a lavish party for its design and editorial staff; but this year Ruth was keenly aware that that holiday tradition was no real balm for the Cowley and Pelzner editors faced with a New Year's mandatory retirement date.

"No wonder no one's dancing," Lauren agreed as she piled her plate high with Swedish meatballs and black cod pâté. "That band belongs on Ted Mack's Original Amateur Hour."

They exchanged a faint smile, then Ruth gazed out across the ballroom and her smile faded as she sensed the whirling darkness among those retiring few. Standing around the bar, the editors stared at the gleaming, empty dance floor as if surveying a wilderness of what was unknown about themselves.

The bandleader, Jimmy Klein, swung his Dyna-Tones erratically through "Waltzing Matilda" and "Twist and Shout" in a desperate effort to tempt the party-goers into a dance.

"At least Heather Jaynes has found a partner," Lauren laughed and helped herself to three desserts. She and Ruth watched as a tipsy Heather Jaynes lead an editor to the floor and began a wildly original fox trot. It looked like the couple wobbled on stilts.

Ruth couldn't help but wonder at Lauren's appetite; she herself hadn't eaten all day. Nervously glancing around, Ruth saw no sign of Joseph, Daniel, or Hella, who were supposed to meet up with her and Lauren after they finished a meeting.

"I've just never seen so many different kinds of food on one table!" Lauren topped her plate with a taco and piroshki. Then she was off, deftly weaving her way through the crowd to the table Ruth had reserved for all of them.

Mid-dance floor, Lauren was hailed by Mrs. Holden and a lively discussion ensued, with Lauren balancing her plate in one hand, her bourbon in the other. Lauren was trying to figure out how to have a cigarette with Mrs. Holden and still juggle her immense plate. Ruth smiled; Lauren would manage it, as she had managed everything Cowley and Pelzner had asked of her these past four months.

Finding her own way back to the table, Ruth nodded to a few passing messenger boys and then turned to the task of eating. She tried the piroshki and found it too doughy; the taco was hopeless, but the Italian sausages were actually edible.

>We will thrive and
>Keep alive on
>Just nothing but kisses,
>Just Mr. and Mrs...

Ruth put her fork down and frowned. There was too much on her mind to eat anymore today. Last year when she and Joseph had attended their first office party together, thus announcing their affair, she had ended up dancing a drunken Bunny Hop with a line of messenger boys and women from accounting. Ruth could still hear the tipsy rustle of their chiffon; it puffed out in pastel colors like flavors of ice cream. Last year it had seemed like a carnival; this year all Ruth could think was that women hadn't worn chiffon in decades.

Ruth stared across the room and caught sight of Daniel Sorenson entering with Joseph at his side. Where was Hella? Ruth wondered. From this distance Ruth studied Joseph and Daniel and felt a fear of losing this man who had been her first mentor. But Joseph was Daniel's protégé now; Ruth was chagrined to feel jealous of Daniel's continuing patronage of Joseph as a writer when she was left at Cowley and Pelzner so bereft. Of course, that wasn't completely true, Ruth had to remind herself. Working this past month with the writers inherited from Daniel had lent Ruth an exhilaration akin to that of her first days at Cowley and Pelzner. It almost, though not quite, made up for losing Daniel.

Ruth frowned now as she watched Joseph greeting some of the other editorial assistants who were his friends. In some way Ruth couldn't yet fathom, she was also losing Joseph. When had *that* begun? Closing her eyes as the music ricocheted around the room, Ruth tried to pinpoint the exact moment when Joseph finally withdrew from her. Of course, there had been Tata's death, but now it seemed a deeper desertion on Joseph's part. All winter Ruth had noticed little things: Joseph keeping more to his side of the bed; Joseph not visiting her office anymore for their midmorning coffee; Joseph eating more and Ruth eating much less. Maybe, Ruth told herself, it was just the changes and departures at Cowley and P. bleeding over into their own daily life together.

> Every now and then
> In my lonely, lonely reverie
> When I think of you,
> Do you ever think of me?

It was Jimmy Klein with his falsetto again. Ruth noticed that now the chiffon-clad women were clustered right in front of the dance band. They swayed, eyes closed as if in the throes of a romantic but solitary interlude. Ruth had to smile—it was like watching a Gothic novel gone amuck.

"Want to dance?" Joseph was suddenly standing near her. He had the habit of appearing like that lately, just like Ruth's cat. "I heard you call me across a crowded room." Rather tipsily, Joseph sat down and Ruth pushed her plate away. "Actually I came because it was the first time all night I'd seen you smile. Are you still very angry with me?"

"I'm not exactly thrilled," Ruth heard herself say, and was surprised. She'd meant to say nothing more about their lunch together this afternoon.

"I can see." Joseph popped up again, taking this as his dismissal when she'd meant it as an invitation to talk. "I can see you're still not hungry. And you haven't forgiven me." Then he was off, lost in the crowd.

Though he wasn't dancing, Ruth reflected, Joseph was dancing. He was exhilarated, over-the-edge. Last year this had attracted her; this year it made Ruth wary. She watched the rosy bitters rise up in her champagne cocktail as she remembered this afternoon's scene with Joseph.

They'd met at the corner Chock-Full-of-Nuts, but it had been quite crowded.

"I don't see how we can talk here, Joseph," she'd said as they stood shivering outside the orange and purple eatery. Ruth watched the lunchtime bustle through the blue-tinted windowfront. It was like watching a silent movie.

"There's nothing really to talk about." Joseph had taken Ruth's arm and led her toward the door. "I just wanted to tell you that I'm taking a studio apartment—I need a separate place to work."

Ruth had turned to him, open-mouthed, as he eased her inside the heavy glass doors. Even if she'd wanted to say something, she would not have been heard above the din of this soundtrack: clanking forks in the corner, a coffee machine's percolating, voices raised, yelling as if everyone had the same lisp, "Miss... Miss... Miss..."

Ruth had sat down next to Joseph just in time to avoid the crush of customers behind her. Her stool tottered; slashed in the center, its orange plastic seat pinched her thigh. But perhaps, she thought, it was the pinch that kept reminding her she was indeed awake. This was no nightmare; Joseph was telling her—wasn't he?—that he wanted to move out.

"Want to have what I have?" Joseph asked, staring up at the soup-of-the-day sign. To the waitress, he said, "How about two cups of beef barley, two hot dogs with sauerkraut, mustard, and catsup, and two coffees... "

Ruth had watched a waitress smear mustard, relish, and catsup into a glob on a paper doilie and slide it, oozing, across the counter to a burly man who smelled like hair spray and sweat. She felt her stomach tighten. "I'll just have tea," she told the waitress.

Joseph turned toward Ruth with a sigh. He put his hand on her coat sleeve. "Look," he said, not unkindly, "I didn't expect you to be happy about it—but there's no need for fasting. Come on, join me, what d'ya say?"

Ruth had found it hard to talk there, with the fumes of hot dogs left boiling for hours in their own pink juices, with the flat, sweet scent of stiff meringue pies in the air like cheap perfume, with the clatter and call of feeders whose bottoms stretched and jiggled over stools the color of popsicles. Next to Ruth was a woman whose forearms were flaccid and white like plump guinea pigs perched on the counter. Turning toward Ruth, she reached right over her shoulder for the salt shaker.

"I hate this place, Joseph!" Ruth burst out, under her breath. "How can anybody eat here?"

Joseph had dropped his hold of her. "They do it every day— they just eat." Slowly Joseph shook his head. After a moment, he added, "You can't eat in Chock-Full; I can't really write on Park Avenue."

"But I *like* it when you work around me, Joseph," Ruth said, "That's one of the things we used to do best together... "

"But this is different," Joseph insisted. "In the office... ," he shrugged, "sure, we worked well together."

Ruth had been hurt by his casual dismissal of their early days together at Cowley and Pelzner. She remembered them in every detail: waiting for galley proofs, they had talked on and on, drinking bad coffee in the slovenly kitchen behind the office water cooler. Sometimes they had argued over a typeset absurdity that survived on a proofreader's long battlefield of a galley.

In the lamp's harsh light, Ruth would rest her eyes on Joseph, his generous lips, his black hair curling at the nape of his neck, his beard's dark, blue shadow that crept along his jawbone, measuring the hours.

Ruth would often be startled by her impulse to cup Joseph's bowed head. It would be so natural. But there was often another longing, one Ruth knew was not natural for her: she wanted to reach over and touch that private hollow in Joseph's throat where she saw his pulse beating. It awed her, this heartbeat like spirit made flesh, made visible. For the first time Ruth had understood why Sister Margaret Magdalene had left the convent for a mere man.

"It's hard for me to do my own work with you around, Ruth." Joseph himself had seemed bewildered. This was not the pain of recent death, Ruth knew; this was pain that belonged deeply to Joseph—yet it had the same effect of separating him from her as had Tata's death. "I talked to Daniel about it and he understood, even offered to try and find a writer who'll let me use his studio when he's not in the city."

"You talked to Daniel first? Was this studio his idea?" Ruth had asked. Her heartbeat was suddenly strong and she felt a hot flush of anger in her cheeks. "If you want to leave me, Joseph, then leave me. But don't let's lie about it and say it's because you need a place to work."

At this Joseph had put his arm around Ruth's shoulders. He held her close to him. "Look, honey, I'm not leaving you. I just need a place where *you* aren't all the time, that's all."

Ruth barely heard him. "Everyone's leaving," she said. "It's . . . it's too much."

"We'll manage something about the rent," Joseph assured her. "Daniel will help me sell my book to some other house and I'll use the advance to . . ."

"I wasn't speaking of the rent," Ruth had said, and felt frozen solid like winter earth. She had the oddest sensation that any minute she might disappear. And then she understood—this was it, the Ice Age; the woman disappearing into the glacier crevasse.

But she hadn't dropped away from him; it was Joseph who was frozen and disappearing. Or perhaps he had pushed her into that crevasse? "When?" was all Ruth had managed to say.

"Soon," Joseph answered, and Ruth saw his relief at what he must imagine was her agreement. He didn't know she was closing herself to him, that she was willing his every movement and gesture not to touch her.

She tried to pretend that Joseph was just anybody sitting at this counter—that she could get up and walk away from him as if he were a stranger. "Studios are cheap in bad neighborhoods," he grinned at her.

"Yes," Ruth heard herself saying from a great distance, "you've always been partial to bad neighborhoods."

Instead of showing hurt, Joseph had burst out laughing. "I'd get a studio in Brooklyn Heights if I could afford my old bad neighborhood these days!"

How could he be so good-natured? Ruth had wondered. *Because he was happy*. This thought hit her with the sound of something cracking open in her, like ice along the Hudson. It was so simple: Joseph was happy to be free of her. He was wide open again, but not to her. And she was closing down.

"How often?" Ruth had begun, and faltered. The huge woman nearby shifted and nudged Ruth with her elbow as if for encouragement. Now Ruth was grateful, not repulsed by that touch. "How often will you go to your studio?" she asked Joseph. But she wanted to ask: *How many nights will I be without you?* It was then she had realized that she had not slept alone in almost seven years. The thought astonished her; how could she have let herself count on another body next to hers? She, an only child. Had she learned nothing from her past?

"Well," Joseph answered, "I'll work there any chance I get... weekends, of course."

"Of course," Ruth said, but now her outward numbness was giving way to a hard, inner rage. "And weeknights?"

"Not that much during the week... maybe Thursday nights..."

"Thursdays," Ruth repeated softly, "of course, Thursdays." Her rage had changed into a curious detachment. My, how much careful thought Joseph had given this idea. She wouldn't be surprised if the studio were already rented.

"Oh, listen, Ruth." Joseph at last had met her eyes. "It'll be kind of fun, don't you think?"

"Fun?"

"I mean, we'll never know . . . "

"Know what?"

"Whether we'll sleep together that night or not. It'll be . . . well, kind of like a little suspense in our lives. Every night we'll have to keep *choosing* one another."

Ruth had turned open-mouthed to Joseph and seen that he was perfectly serious about this idea of a nightly seduction. "I don't want to make being with you a daily decision, Joseph," Ruth had said quietly. "There are some things . . . ," she faltered, and began again. "There are some people one should be able to count on. Even rest on."

"Don't rest on me, Ruth." Joseph's voice was softer than her own. "Please . . . don't." Abruptly he stood and tossed down some money for their half-eaten lunch. He made an effort at smiling, "I can't take the weight." Then he was out the door.

There had been pain in Joseph's voice, and he'd looked almost as if he might cry. Ruth realized this only now as she stared blindly at the suddenly crowded dance floor. Where had all the dancers come from? So much activity, movement, but Ruth sat very still trying to remember the exact expression on Joseph's face when he'd turned away from her this afternoon in the restaurant. Was it really sorrow she'd seen in his eyes as he left? Ruth wondered now. Or was it some deep regret? She wished she knew Joseph better. Ruth wished she understood more about his past, his father, his upbringing. But maybe she needed Joseph too much now to truly understand him, Ruth decided. Maybe she needed a friend herself.

"Everyone's dancing!" It was Lauren, returned from her own long tête-à-tête with Mrs. Holden.

"What happened?" Ruth asked. "It can't be the music."

Lauren looked around the ballroom, taking everything in. At first she said with a shrug, "I think everybody at Cowley and Pelzner is finally drunk or just tired of being unhappy." Lauren turned to Ruth and was quiet a moment, then asked, "How about you?"

"Oh," Ruth smiled faintly, "I'm just settling into it."

"The music?" Lauren asked. "Or the misery?"

This time Ruth's smile was real. "Both," she said, and felt somehow lighter. It must have been the champagne. Ruth sipped another long draught of her cocktail. For a moment she felt quite giddy. "Well, what did Mrs. Holden waylay you so long about at the buffet?"

"She's on a rampage about my still living at the Y," Lauren answered. "Seems she thinks I should find a studio."

"Joseph did," Ruth blurted, and then was embarrassed. Though she'd grown close enough to Lauren to feel a kinship, she'd rarely talked about her personal life. Confiding was difficult for Ruth, and yet she felt that perhaps soon she might try to take someone else into her confidence.

"Didn't you tell Muriel that a studio is out of the question on your salary?" Ruth asked. "No, Lauren, you were probably too polite to mention money."

"I told her I was fine where I am for a while longer."

"And are you?"

Lauren hesitated. During her first weeks in the city the exuberance she felt for the subway extended to her lodgings in the 92nd Street Y. As the only *shiksa* in this co-ed Jewish dormitory on the elite Upper East Side, Lauren believed herself somewhat chosen. After a childhood of Southern fundamentalists, it was an adventure to find herself so ensconced with the offspring of Scarsdale and the brilliant alumni of Brandeis or Columbia. But lately the Israelis on the 11th floor had taken to tearing down Lauren's *mezzuzah* to protest her using space meant for another refugee.

Lauren faced Ruth and tried to make light of the uneasiness she felt in her living quarters. "Yes, I'm just fine at the Y... for now." Lauren quelled a momentary wave of melancholy that rose up in her. Really, she scolded herself, she had no right to be sad when so many people around her at the publishing house had to mourn. The sorrow was contagious, Lauren told herself, and tried to brighten. "Do you know I'm picking up Yiddish?"

"How useful for you," Ruth smiled.

Lauren urged herself on. More than anything she wanted to cheer Ruth. When she herself was sad, the solacing of another helped Lauren though it wasn't as deep a comfort as grieving herself. "Listen," Lauren laughed. "I called my sister Clare last night and told her our Mama was a *meshugana,* and that except for my missing everybody at home, New York was a *makiah!*"

Ruth laughed. "My, I don't think I've ever heard Yiddish with a Southern accent!"

She was indeed distracted and seemed to forget momentarily her woes. For this Lauren was grateful; in the past month of working with Ruth, Lauren had learned so much from her. While only five years her elder, Ruth seemed so mature in her sophistication and her sense of her own presence or power. Yet Lauren had noticed that in other ways Ruth Littlefield seemed much younger than she was, in need somehow of protection, or perhaps loyalty.

There was also something generous and compelling on Ruth's part. Ruth's light, expert editorial touch to Lauren's own writing had seemed an affectionate mirror held up to Lauren and made every exchange—even their delicate, daily teas—for her a deep pleasure.

"So you'll stay in the Y a while longer?" Ruth asked Lauren.

Lauren felt the drunken, insincere swirl of dancers all around her. "Honey, I'm as happy at the 92nd Street Y," Lauren confessed flatly, "as you are here tonight."

Ruth met Lauren's eyes and gave her a long look of recognition, perhaps of greeting. Then she relaxed and her expression was one of relief. "I know," she said simply.

They each turned to stare at the ballroom dancers. Heather Jaynes had corralled two messenger boys, whether as dance partners or crutches, it wasn't clear.

Ruth said with a smile, "You remind me of someone, Lauren."

"Who?"

"My dear cousin George," Ruth replied. "He never let me get away with much. And he never let me get far away from him or myself."

"Where's this cousin now?"

"He's here in the city; he's a priest."

"Oh," Lauren laughed delightedly, her words softly slurred from the liquor. "So he don't let nobody else get away with much neither."

"Actually, I think it's himself George is hardest on. With others he's quite sympathetic and loyal."

Lauren nodded thoughtfully. In a silence they found as comfortable as their companionable quiet in the office, the two women sat watching the Christmas ball.

"Lauren...," Ruth asked some time later. "Perhaps you'd like to stay with us for a while... until you can find a place of your own? With Joseph's extra studio, we could both use some help on the rent."

"Gosh, I don't know...," Lauren began.

"I'm sure it wouldn't be long; you could post notices on the bulletin boards and there are always writers who sublet their places for the winter. I have lots of room."

Lauren was quiet, but smiling. "I wouldn't just be crashing in on you and Joseph?"

"You wouldn't be intruding, believe me," Ruth assured her. "Except for boarding school, I've never lived with friends, only a husband or lover. You'd be adding to us. Having you with us would be like," Ruth stopped and smiled, "well, like a little family, like the time I lived with my cousins when I was a child." The idea made Ruth brighten. "At least keep the offer in mind, Lauren... until you can find your studio."

"How long before Joseph found his?" Lauren asked and felt the deep well-being she'd first found when coming to the city return two-fold. Ruth was offering what Lauren had missed most of all these past months—a sister, a brother, a small tribe. Lauren felt her eyes welling up: she shouldn't drink any more bourbon tonight, she told herself firmly, happily. Her accent was getting so deep, she felt like she was home.

"How long did it take me to find what?" It was Joseph again, standing right behind Ruth's chair. Ruth could hear how drunk he was by his slurred words; for the first time since they'd become lovers, Joseph reminded Ruth of her ex-husband. "Are you joining us, Joseph?" she asked, unable to keep a certain coolness from her tone.

"I'm asking you for this dance, Miss Littlefield," he announced and made a mock bow. Then he turned to Lauren with a nod, "I've been trying to get this woman to dance with me all night. But I think Ruth would rather be swooning over Jimmy Klein up there with all the other accounting department dreamboats." Joseph grinned and nodded playfully to Lauren. "Yup, she did the very same thing last year."

"He's lying." Ruth stood up and gave him a brief smile.

Lauren's expression of politeness seemed fixed, for she was watching them both very carefully. Lauren's alertness somehow calmed Ruth. It was as if with Lauren observing so closely, Ruth didn't herself have to watch. She might even rest a bit.

Rest now in the dance, rest against Joseph's shoulder the way you did when you slept together. She would rest on him now because soon she might not have him near. As Joseph swung her onto the floor Ruth felt all the anger and resolve drain from her.

> Picture you, upon my knee
> Just tea for two
> And two for tea.
> Just me for you
> And you for me, aloooone, dear...

The Dyna-Tones seemed as drunk as the dancers and if not for the drummer, Ruth believed everyone might simply slide to the floor and sleep it off. But the drummer kept four-four time with his muted bass drum thud. It was like being inside someone bigger and being comforted by another's great, rhythmic heartbeat.

Ruth and Joseph said not a word as they danced. But their bodies were close, familiar. Was it just because she knew his body so well that she could ignore everything else about Joseph? Ruth remembered someone telling her long ago that touch was everything, that even wars were about that—touch and territory.

There was another touch on her shoulder, but not Joseph's. Ruth turned to find Daniel cutting in. He, too, was dulled by drink. But where was Hella? Ruth wondered. Joseph passed Ruth off to the older editor and made his way past a flailing Heather Jaynes, who was doing a Martha Graham imitation. Then Joseph disappeared and Ruth settled into Daniel's arms.

"You dance well to these old songs," Daniel said, and his voice was so like her father's that for a moment Ruth had to look up to see if Lawrence Littlefield had not, for an instant, come back to her, just to take his daughter in his arms, to claim her for one dance. "And these songs don't even belong to you."

Tears filled Ruth's eyes as she looked up at this man who led her into a more difficult dance. "I don't know these steps, Daniel," Ruth said softly, still looking up at his face.

"You can learn this," Daniel said, and Ruth saw that he avoided her gaze, but apparently with some effort. "Watch my feet, my dear," he whispered and then executed an intricate series of steps. "My *feet*, Ruth," Daniel beseeched Ruth as she kept staring at him.

And she did. Ruth finally gazed down at Daniel's perfect steps, trying to follow and, after a moment, succeeding so well that everyone watched the old man and his protégé glide across the ballroom.

"Look at them," Lauren marveled from her table. Joseph sat next to her, his eyes glued to the floor. "I've never seen such a complicated dance."

"A regular Fred Astaire and Ginger Rogers," Joseph murmured, still not looking. Then he turned with a lopsided grin. "We could try it ourselves, you know."

Lauren looked doubtful. "No, I've had too much bourbon...."

"Oh, come on!" Joseph was up, taking her hand.

He looked hapless and shy, and this charmed Lauren because she was not expecting shyness from Joseph Girard. Or maybe, Lauren reflected, for him there was a direct ratio between drunkenness and charm.

> You go home and get your scanties
> I'll go home and get my panties
> And away we'll go
> Oh, oh, oh...
> Off we're going to shuffle
> Shuffle off to Buffalo...

As Lauren and Joseph attempted to dance to the music, they noticed a commotion near the bandstand. Jimmy Klein was helping a heavy-set woman in orange chiffon up onto the stage. Lauren and Joseph paused, panting slightly as a woman from accounting took possession of the microphone.

She whispered something to the band. The bass began its walk, the snares their whisper. Without Jimmy Klein, the Dyna-Tones seemed seized with self-respect as they swung into a bluesy dirge. On the dance floor even the most drunken staff members were motionless, embarrassed that one of their own had thus displayed herself. There was a general hush, and then everyone stared straight down at their feet, shoulders hunched as if awaiting a blow.

The big-bosomed woman gave a heave, her chiffon flounced and shush-shushed right into the microphone, and then she sang:

> Maybe I'm right and
> Maybe I'm wrong.
> Maybe I'm weak and

> Maybe I'm strong—
> But nevertheless,
> I'm in love with you...

"Thank God, she's decent," Joseph breathed to Lauren. "I was afraid she'd sing 'The Days of Wine and Roses.'"

Lauren said nothing. She felt transfixed by the woman's voice. It was deeply luxurious, as if within her were many other voices she might summon at will. Her voice was so low, it resonated in the cymbals and the snares and the silverware. For the first time all evening, Lauren noticed that all the musicians were black. And now she heard the difference as the Dyna-Tones backed up the wide, white woman.

"Why hasn't she been on stage all her life?" Lauren asked wonderingly. She was so oblivious to anyone but this singer that she actually leaned against Joseph, as if he were no more than a post.

"No matter," Joseph responded, himself caught up. "She's on stage now."

> Somehow I know in my heart
> The terrible chances I'm taking.
> Fine at the start, then blessed
> With a heart that is breaking...

And then everyone began to dance, slow, intensely, as if the woman's music were recognized first by the body. Joseph pulled Lauren closer to him, but Lauren was so carried away by the woman's song that she had to keep correcting herself from taking the lead.

Then she did forget to let Joseph lead; Lauren swept him around the other dancers in grand, feline movements. This thrilled him—that for a moment he might change roles, and rest, simply rest.

Lauren seemed oblivious to him as they moved, her eyes closed; but her body automatically settled into his. This was an intimacy more unnerving to Joseph, to feel Lauren's body blend into his like a cat settling onto his lap, imperious and intent only on its own luxury. It seemed that now he could let her have him, because she did not really want him.

The moment the woman let out her last throbbing note, Jimmy Klein reclaimed the microphone. "Thank you, thank you, Mrs. . . . Hilleschiem, for that lovely rendition of an old favorite."

"God," Joseph said savagely, as if they'd all been propelled from a dream and into broad, brutal daylight. "Klein sounds like a cross between a rooster and Lawrence Welk."

Lauren was quiet, but she shook herself all over as if throwing off cold water.

Then Jimmy Klein forced his band into a silly, upbeat "Yellow Submarine" rendition. The floor emptied and Joseph stood side-by-side with Lauren, his hand still resting on her. As he stared at her sloped, lovely back he had the distinct memory of having once before unzipped this same long, violet silk dress—all the way from the low back to the full bottom.

Joseph shook his head. How could women switch around like that, playing dress-up, borrowing one another so easily? You didn't see men lending their clothes to other men. It was too intimate an exchange, a bond. Joseph didn't want to try and figure it out. He was too drunk. He wanted another drink. But instead he found his hand resting again on Lauren's back, as if he had a right to be there. Joseph decided it was logical: it was Ruth's dress; Ruth was his lover—so he had a right to touch this long, silken back.

Joseph glanced across the room to see Ruth and Daniel, arm-in-arm. Ruth's attention was riveted on the woman from accounting who stood now surrounded by chiffon ladies who bobbed and fussed and embraced her. The woman from accounting accepted this flutter with the dignity of a tribal leader.

It was Daniel who met Joseph's eyes across the dance floor, Daniel whose glance made Joseph drop his arm so quickly that Lauren turned to him with her easy, preoccupied glance.

"Ain't she something?" Lauren asked, still under sway of the performance and the alcohol.

"She was . . . " Joseph said, and felt an odd pain in his chest. "She was . . . something."

Lauren smiled at him and Joseph realized that she was well accustomed to being touched; she was so used to it that she hardly felt him. Placing his hand on her was like approaching what one believed was a closed glass door, plunging one's hand through that door and expecting shards of glass, only to find that the door was wide open.

The band was spinning on the stage and so was Joseph's head on his shoulders. Spinning, almost separated from his body. He was aroused, but who was it he wanted? Joseph tried to steady himself. If he weren't so drunk, Joseph told himself, he would be deeply confused. He found himself wondering about Daniel.

Joseph did lean now on Lauren, but he made a pretense of taking her arm to protect her from the besotted crowds. In his mind he felt himself falling through level after level of himself. There was no foundation in him, Joseph thought in a panic, no real final resting place. He was continually changing. Anything could happen. He might do anything. He might even change so completely he wouldn't even recognize himself.

> And we live
> Beneath the sea.
> Everyone of us
> Has all he needs . . .

Walking toward them was Mr. Padgett, wheezing all the way, his cane tap-tapping the dance floor. He and his slim wooden partner were the only ones dancing now. Then Joseph saw Daniel leading Ruth back across the dance floor, but they weren't dancing anymore. As they crossed the ballroom toward him and Lauren, Joseph wondered if Daniel wanted to exchange partners.

6

LIVING TOGETHER

EVER SINCE Ruth could remember, coffee was holy. It was the one thing her mother never allowed Cook to make for the family. Mornings, Edith Littlefield awoke early. After washing her face with almond soap, she walked straight into Cook's kitchen. Here her daughter would discover Edith with the coffee—but not her face—fixed. Ruth had loved her mother's cleansed face; it seemed as wide open as her pores.

In those days, Edith Littlefield looked like she had never stopped believing—in her marriage, in her Catholicism, or in herself. She was to Ruth like a scene from the illustrated Bible that had belonged to Ruth's cousins in which two radiant women stood in flowing blue robes outside a tomb. Even Christ was crying, but he returned Mary's anointment, Martha's faith. Their brother was not dead; he was beloved. And Lazarus, in tatters, leapt forth, his death just a dance. Mary didn't smell the grave on him; Martha didn't feel his rags like rotted skin. The sisters didn't care that their brother's breath was foul and musty from the tomb. All they knew was that Lazarus was too thin and they must feed him. He danced, graveclothes unwinding, on the way to their kitchen.

Ruth imagined that in Biblical times kitchens were cool, stone chambers smelling of olive oil, ripe figs, and sweet wine. This was before they had coffee, of course; because if Mary and Martha had coffee this is what would have been offered Lazarus first: you've come back from death, from sleep; and those you love hold out arms and the stronger coffee.

Ruth liked to think of this story when she awoke early to find her way to the same apartment kitchen that had been her mother's in the mornings. For the past two months Ruth and Joseph and Lauren had been living together and Ruth loved making their morning coffee. After a year of living with Ruth, Joseph had learned to drink his coffee black. Ruth suspected that during the day he might ruin good coffee with two-percent milk or that ghastly white talc the editorial assistants kept in their metal nook. But when Lauren sat down for her first breakfast she politely asked for cream when Ruth passed her a brimming black cupful.

"Oh, just try black," Ruth said. "It'll be the first time you've ever really tasted coffee."

Lauren smiled agreeably, but Ruth noticed that she concentrated on her croissant and let the coffee stand cold. After two weeks of sadly emptying Lauren's full, lukewarm cup, Ruth made what was for her a grand concession. On the way home one night, instead of taking the uptown bus with Lauren and Joseph, Ruth took a cab to the Richgold Dairy and bought cream. Not half-and-half, not one of those petroleum powders, but heavy, raw cream. When she offered it to Lauren, Ruth said, "If I were still a practicing Catholic, we'd call it communion."

Today Ruth glanced down the nine stories from her kitchen window to the white, ploughed Park Avenue below. She had all the time in the world to wait for the kettle to boil. Settling comfortably at the breakfast table, Ruth glanced through the *Times*. More snow predicted. There had been too much snow this month, even for late February. But there also had come a kind of hiatus between herself and Joseph since Lauren moved in. Before Christmas Ruth had truly believed Joseph was leaving her; but things had settled into a liveable schedule and Joseph was only absent on Thursday nights when he saw Daniel Sorenson for their weekly writing conference.

Ruth sang to herself while waiting for Lauren and Joseph to come down. Her expression was blank and her usually pale face was flushed; it had a look of desire, though none of Ruth's lovers would recognize it. Singing was something Ruth would never do in company. One of Ruth's secret fantasies was of being sung to sleep. It seemed the most sensual of intimacies and one that she had never experienced. Her mother would have clucked her tongue with mild but unmistakable reproach had Ruth ever asked her to sing; and Cook was practically deaf. So Ruth sang to herself in the mornings under cover of the coffee grinder. It was most always the same song, one her cousin George had taught her:

> My father was the keeper of the Birmingham Light
> and he slept with a mermaid one fine night.
> Now from this union there came three: a tuna,
> and a porpoise, and the other was me!
> Yo ho, yo ho, the cold winds blow,
> Hurray for the life of the ro-lling sea!

"Morning," Ruth greeted Lauren as she padded barefoot into the kitchen.

"My God, I'm glad it's Sunday," Lauren said, and set about pouring half cream, half coffee into a big breakfast mug. Ruth's eclectic collection of pastel mugs in pink and azure made Lauren happy simply to look at first thing each morning. They were more like jumbo soup cups for children than adult coffee cups, and were a pleasure to hold. Lauren had expected delicate British porcelain from Ruth Littlefield's kitchen, but the first morning when Ruth served coffee in these absurdly pink mugs with hand-painted carnival scenes, Lauren knew she was privy to a side of this rather formal woman that most people at Cowley and Pelzner would never suspect.

"You know what?" she said. "I'm beginning to feel at home here. I mean, in New York."

Ruth laughed and looked up from the *Times*. "We'll start hiding the classifieds from you each weekend. Joseph and I can hardly think of your leaving us."

Lauren smiled as she reached for a rhubarb tart. It was her treat; she'd gotten them last night especially for Sunday breakfast at the Puerto Rican bakery on the corner. "I've decided what the best thing about living together is," Lauren announced, chewing contentedly on her pastry.

"What's that?"

"Well, when you live with others you catch yourself saying to no one in particular, 'Think I'll just take me a shower . . . ,' and someone answers back, 'All right.' It's not like asking permission or because you have to report your every little move and quirk. . . ." Lauren paused and sipped her coffee. Then she said softly, "It's more like call-and-response . . . you know, like what they do down south in tent revivals. Someone calls out, someone up and answers."

"Yes." Ruth nodded. "And when you live alone, you say, 'I'm going to take a shower . . . ,' and there's silence. Some people like it better that way. Not I. Sometimes I think the whole world can be divided into those who like to live alone and those who like the sound of someone else stirring about in the next room, not demanding attention, just nearby, a life alongside your own."

"Tribal versus solitary," Lauren agreed. "I'm tribal." She hesitated. "But my father believes that when you leave your tribe, you might as well be dead."

Ruth was quiet a while, then commented, "I'd say I'm a solitary, in search of tribe. It comes from my training as an only child. You know," Ruth rested her chin on her hand and propped both elbows on the breakfast table, her voice took on a tenderness, "once I lived for a while with my cousins. That changed me completely."

"Do tell . . ." Lauren, too, propped herself on the table, listening.

From down the hall came Joseph's voice. "I'm going to take a shower!" he called.

Lauren and Ruth exchanged amused glances, then Ruth called back to Joseph, "Easy on the hot water, there's two of us in line."

"Okey dokey," Joseph called back.

Lauren laughed and turned back to Ruth. "So you were saying . . . about your cousins?"

Ruth smiled and waved her hand. "Another time," she said.

"Joseph will be here soon and he's heard the story a million times. He thinks I'm still in love with my cousin George and is jealous. Imagine!"

"Are you?" Lauren asked.

"Coffee is my first love." Ruth stood up. "Want seconds?"

Lauren shrugged good-naturedly and let Ruth fill her cup. Then she went back to studying the classifieds; but her eyes just skimmed the ads. She was more aware of Ruth, who was already cleaning the kitchen, scouring the sink. Lauren suppressed a smile everytime Ruth donned her pink plastic gloves, yanked up to and cuffed at the elbows.

"Can I offer you some help?"

"No. Remember, this is my way of meditating," Ruth said.

"Oh, well...." Lauren helped herself to another tart, shaking her head with a smile. She was glad to be living here with Ruth and Joseph. It had been good timing, Mrs. Holden's calling her back to the Harbor to work on a manuscript with Hella Steinhardt. Ruth had hired a permanent editorial assistant. Their separate office lives had left Lauren and Ruth free to pursue a more egalitarian friendship and home.

Lauren jumped up from the breakfast table announcing, "Think I'll run a load of whites. How about your dishtowel?"

"Thanks." Ruth tossed her it over to her without missing a beat in her cleaning.

As Lauren walked down the hallway, she smiled to herself. This city and these new friends were civilizing her. After her childhood, Lauren often wondered if this was really how other families lived. Without emergencies, without subterfuge, without making themselves into a small militia as she and her siblings had done all their lives. Some people, Lauren had to reflect, some people just lived, like civilians.

In his shower, Joseph was barely surviving his own civil war. He sang at the top of his voice, head thrown back to take the full, throbbing brunt of the shower he'd turned to the dial marked *massage*. Water stroked and probed his neck and back. Joseph imagined he was getting a good talking-to, only a stern warning this time. He was aroused, though he did not touch himself.

Staunchly he took the sandalwood soap and, ignoring his erection, sudsed his arms, his flat belly, his buttocks. But even this stalwart denial felt much too erotic. Maybe there *was* something to the Catholic insistence on celibacy, Joseph considered. He bowed his head beneath the shower. Maybe those crafty Jesuits had discovered the most profound of passions: Look away from what you most desire, shyly at first, but then with a discipline so intense it becomes a kind of abandon. There was so much pleasure in *not* eating the apple. Why hadn't Jews, with all their suffering, discovered the sublime agony of this repudiation? Why did Catholics have all the fun out there in blazing deserts and gloriously empty caves, while Jews built up their lives like stockades? Why simply survive when there was so much pleasure in denying life?

The life that throbbed in Joseph now flowed without his touch. He leaned against the hot tile and let the shower cleanse him. Its pulsing fingers were no longer sensual, but brisk and efficient as an old nanny. It was all right now; he had not thought of Lauren or anybody else—not once. He'd thought only about a monk's cell, the low, male murmurings of disapproval, a white flash of flesh that Joseph hoped was some remnant of his feelings for Ruth.

Now he could almost forgive himself. But he was spent, realizing that *not* being unfaithful was a full-time job. Leaning his face against the warm shower tileworks, Joseph found himself crying.

At a knock on the bathroom door Joseph straightened so quickly he knocked the metal soap dish off its suction cups. It clattered loudly in the blue shower. He wished it were Lauren wanting in, wanting to be with him.

Joseph's heart beat fast. He wasn't sad anymore, he told himself, he was aroused. Then he calmed himself and reached for a towel. He punched the faucet to the wall and the silence startled him. But of course, it would not be Lauren at the door. She would never share the bathroom with him. Lauren didn't even intrude on Ruth in the sisterly way Joseph imagined women did when they lived together—obliviously bumping elbows at the mirror as they put on mascara. Or one chatting from the john while the other read *Cosmopolitan*—no, *Vogue*—and bathed, borrowing the other's razor.

Joseph smiled to himself. He suspected that Lauren had once borrowed his razor to shave her legs.

"Be right out!" Joseph called.

"Coffee's getting cold..." Ruth's voice faded down the hallway.

"All right!" Joseph yelled.

He must be efficient now, busy. Busy body. Then he could show up at breakfast and take his place between the two women like Lazarus returned from the grave of desire and denial and death. *La petite morte*, the French called orgasm—and now he understood why.

"Morning...!" Ruth called down the hall to him.

As usual for these past few weekends, she was in a fine mood. Fondness and even a bit of mischief now made up Ruth's moods. Joseph liked her more lately than he ever had. She was more fun. At first with Ruth, Joseph was astonished by a well-bred, intellectual woman discovering her first real physical passion with him. Ruth believed her passion belonged to Joseph and for this naive generosity he was still grateful.

Joseph slipped into his chair at the breakfast table. "Thank God it's Sunday," he said.

He gave Ruth a brief kiss as she leaned over to offer him coffee. "I smell Comet cleanser," Joseph said, thinking that Ruth really did look lovely in her black silk bathrobe and elbow-length pink dishwashing gloves. He wished he really did love her faithfully, like a brother or a priest. "Say, Lauren," Joseph began, "did Ruth ever tell you about her cousin George, the priest?" Smiling, Joseph helped himself to the heavy cream for his coffee.

"Now don't start in on George," Ruth said from the sink, where she was unrolling her plastic gloves with the precision and satisfaction of a heart surgeon.

"You were going to tell me about George," Lauren said, and Joseph saw that she'd noticed his return to using cream in his coffee. For his part, Joseph noticed Lauren's soft, plaid flannel bathrobe that was so worn and comfortable he wanted to reach out and run his hand along her back. "Tell me more," Lauren asked.

"Well," Joseph continued with a smile, "I suspect that Cousin George was Ruth's first real love."

"Joseph!" Ruth protested, and shot a spray of Windex his way.

"If not first, then what would you call it?" Joseph demanded playfully.

Ruth considered this a while, then said softly, "George was the first person I really trusted to... well, to truly love *me*." Ruth smiled to herself.

"You know," Joseph took up, settling back luxuriously in his chair, "I read some scientific report which said that if you can figure out what the first moment of attraction to someone is, you'll see it's the same with every one of your lovers. So if someone figured out this pattern, he or she might replicate it and *bingo*... you'd fall flat in love. I think Ruth first fell for George because..."

"Because he told me the truth when everyone else was lying to me..." Ruth said quietly, "including myself."

Joseph was surprised at the depth of her response. Her usually cool hazel eyes were fervent now. They shone like the eyes of a true believer. This must be the expression Ruth wore in mass, Joseph thought, though she never went near the cathedral of her childhood.

"Ruth," Joseph said softly. "Don't get me wrong. I *like* your cousin George. I even like the fact that he's a priest. You don't have to protect him from me."

"What are you talking about... protecting?" Ruth asked, and finally focused on Joseph.

"You have the look of Joan of Arc," Joseph said, then admitted, "it's scary... especially across the Sunday morning breakfast table."

"So it's *you* who need protecting," Ruth said.

When she meet Joseph's eyes he felt the truth of it. He managed a grin, then glanced to Lauren. "Well, enough about Cousin George," he said.

Lauren smiled rather nervously; she took a great step back from the table, although she remained very still. Joseph threw up his hands. "Look," he said. "I'm sorry I brought it up. Love is never a safe subject, even at breakfast, even if it's long, long ago. It's like handling radioactive . . . well, radioactive rhubarb tarts!" Then he helped himself to seconds, as if making a show of finally silencing himself.

Ruth began again, "So if I figure out exactly what it was about George I first loved and then look for a similar pattern in all my lovers . . . then I'll be much more conscious about what makes me fall in love?"

"Yes," Joseph nodded, relieved that Ruth was taking this in the light spirit he meant it. "For example, I noticed right off that George teases you mercilessly. . . . " Joseph grinned at Ruth. "So do I."

"Yes, and he's also got beautiful hair like yours, Joseph, and a little bit of a wall eye that wanders when he's tired, and freckles, and he squirrels away at the seminary writing his books. . . . " Ruth paused and seemed somewhat surprised at herself. "When I stop to think of it, there *are* many, many similarities between all of—"

"Except Cousin George is celibate," Joseph reminded her. Then he knew if was exactly the wrong thing to say. Lately he'd been shying away from Ruth in their big bed; fatigue or worries about the office or working too hard on revisions of his book for Daniel—whatever it was, Joseph simply had not found himself reaching out for Ruth as much as he had before. She still aroused him, but not so much anymore that he forgot himself. Forgetting himself was something he only did these days when he was writing, or when he endured those grueling editing sessions with Daniel Sorenson. He realized with a little jolt that he'd settled into loving Ruth the way he mourned his father—as if they both were somehow daily shadows that were part of him, that followed him but were not part of his body.

"How about letting me see the Book Review section, if you're finished with it, Lauren," Joseph tried to retreat. He felt a rising desperation, as if right here at the breakfast table he was shedding layer after layer of dead skin, and he feared becoming raw, absolutely vulnerable between these two women. They meant him no harm. If Ruth noticed he'd shed a skin, she would simply take a broom and whisk away his shimmering old lengths like so much translucent trash. Lauren might ask to keep the skin to study it with her passionate attention.

Joseph stood up abruptly from the table. "Should I make a second pot?" he asked from the safety of the kitchen counter. Ruth had moved under the sink and was refilling a furniture polish bottle with some new product the super had peddled to her. Lauren, her elbows propped on the table, head bowed over the classifieds, began. "I guess I fell in love with my first boyfriend when I finally saw him backstage." Lauren pushed aside the classifieds with a little frown. "He was the star of every high school play... Tony in *West Side Story* and Tevye in *Fiddler on the Roof* and Curly in *Oklahoma*. He was handsome in an oddball way with his black eyes and pale skin. But I paid him no mind when he was on stage; later he said he'd had a crush on me since we were second- and first-chair clarinets in the eighth grade symphony. Then, one night, I ran into him at a dinner party. Well, he was the life of the party. Honey wouldn't melt in his mouth, as they say. I wasn't very taken with him until I suddenly looked up from my sherbet and saw him coming back to the dinner table from the bathroom, where he must have combed his hair because it was slicked back perfectly except for one cowlick over his eyebrow.

"Well, as he walked back toward us I saw him pulling himself together for the next act; he summoned up his persona to please and dazzle and seduce: But what really moved me, what took my breath away, was his vulnerability. How ordinary and small he seemed without his performance personality. He was so . . . well, imperfect. My heart went out to him when I saw how ordinary he was. How human. And every lover since him has been the same—they certainly had the power to dazzle, but it was the backstage self I most loved."

As Joseph measured the coffee beans into the grinder he noticed his hands shaking. Was he moved, he wondered, or terrified? As he turned on the coffee grinder and the kitchen buzzed with its insistent, obnoxious noise, he remembered: Daniel's hands trembled like this. Just last Thursday when they sat together in Joseph's narrow studio, when the older man had reached across to show Joseph a page he'd slashed with his red pen.

Usually Joseph was too unnerved by Daniel's editorial presence to notice anything about Daniel Sorenson the man. But when pointing out that excised paragraph, Daniel's hands shook visibly. Perhaps it was Daniel's age, but that tremor in the man's hands had moved Joseph. Daniel's hands were nicked and grooved and criss-crossed with papercuts—working hands, but full of energy. Joseph had felt a moment of childlike reverence. Then the moment had passed. Daniel had again taken up his pen, his criticisms, hands firmly holding the manuscript.

"If I were you, Lauren . . . ," Ruth was shouting above the noise of the coffee grinder. "Joseph! Can you please turn that thing off?" Ruth was laughing.

"Sorry," Joseph said and busied himself with the Chemex paper filters.

"Well, if I were you, Lauren," Ruth continued, "I'd be very careful about spending any time in the theater district. It's just crawling with actors who are backstage— and none too happy about it either. You'd be in danger of loves at first sights."

"Should I wear blinders going to and from the theater?" Lauren asked with a smile. "Just as long as they stay on stage, I'm safe."

Then Ruth turned to Joseph. "And what about you? What makes you fall in love?"

Ruth watched him very closely as he turned from the steaming kettle with a look of intense preoccupation. He'd been like this so often lately that Ruth knew it to be a hazard of living with a working writer. Carl, her ex-husband, had been the same when he was at work on a manuscript. And certainly Ruth had seen her own writers in final throes of a book do everything from walk into walls to fall down their own front steps. When Joseph turned to Ruth with a strange look, she found herself smiling fondly at him, waiting for his answer.

"Well," Joseph began slowly, "it's bad etiquette, at least in Brooklyn, to talk about old lovers when your True Love is standing right across the kitchen from you—especially when she's near the iron skillets and knives. But I think what really does it for me is anyone who sings to me. My mother used to, you know, she was an opera student and that's all I remember about her. She used to sing to me *The Magic Flute*, and though I think opera is silly now, whenever I hear that one opera, I feel..." Joseph stopped so abruptly he seemed to collapse into himself.

Ruth watched him with some concern; he looked for all the world as if he might cry. But, she recognized with a pang, this was also the way he looked sometimes making love with her. It was an expression of openness, yet fear, as if any moment he might be overwhelmed. She wanted to cross the kitchen and take Joseph in her arms, but something in Joseph held her back. Or perhaps, Ruth chided herself, it was she who was unable to reach out to him.

When was the last time they'd made love? Ruth wondered suddenly. But she said aloud, "What else did she sing to you, Joseph?"

"Don't remember," Joseph said softly, and poured himself a cup of fresh coffee.

Between them, her head bowed over the classifieds, Lauren felt their distance, she smelled their loneliness, as if it were the sharp scent of the sea.

This smell was familiar to Lauren; and her own response to it equally familiar—to watch, to protect, to solace. Now she knew what she had only sensed when first living with Ruth and Joseph:

the couple might be in love, but they didn't instinctively want to be near one another. Lauren had noticed how Ruth touched her possessions more than she did Joseph. Only when Ruth placed her hand on her mahogany desk or ran a finger along the dustless glass coffeetable did she really seem to rest in her own home. When Ruth touched Joseph, Lauren had seen them both flinch slightly, as if they received a little shock from static in the carpet. At first Lauren thought it *was* the carpet, but in the kitchen, too, on placid tile, Joseph and Ruth seemed to startle one another.

"Let's go for a walk in the Park?" Lauren suggested now, and was relieved to see Joseph's faint smile.

"It's freezing outside, Lauren. How about we catch a matinee? Don't worry, we'll blindfold you when we walk through the theater district."

"Why don't we all just stay in and build a fire?" Ruth countered.

"Backstage, you mean?" Lauren smiled, pleased that the tension between Ruth and Joseph had passed.

"Yes," Joseph answered softly, and poured the two women more coffee. "Dangerously off-duty. Ordinary life."

Part III

LIVES-IN-PROGRESS

1950S AND 1960S

MONEY MATTERS

The year the Meyer family lived in Boston, Lauren realized that the enemy was not Yankees or money. The enemy was people who pretended to give, then took it all back, and more, by force.

"Parasites!" Madeleine Meyer would dismiss their latest form threat. Before she could crinkle the letter into a wad, Lauren marshalled all her third-grade reading skills and made out:

DEAR CARDHOLDER:

BECAUSE YOU HAVE REPEATEDLY IG-
NORED OUR REQUESTS TO PAY THE
MINIMUM BALANCE DUE EACH
MONTH, WE HAVE NO OTHER CHOICE
BUT TO TURN YOUR ACCOUNT OVER
TO OUR COLLECTIONS DIVISION.
PROTECT YOUR VALUABLE CREDIT!

PAY NOW!!

To Lauren, who had never quite caught on to cursive, who was held in a primitive's thrall by the authority of print, each angry letter thundered across the page like a stampede of Jumbo elephants. There seemed no escape—just as there was no escaping Mrs. Pritchett's remedial Earth Science class, held during recess at the Carl, Willard, and Maybee Elementary School in run-down Revere Beach, Massachusetts.

"You see," her mother pointed a bright Mimosa Glow Orange fingernail at those ominous capital letters, "now they're shouting at us." Then she'd sound the rallying cry, "No manners up North!"

Madeleine Meyer acted as if "up North" were an afterlife where Yankees continued their everlasting Civil War humiliations, and the Meyers were on the losing side. But upon finding themselves in this neighborhood north of Boston while James Meyer was on a graduate fellowship, Lauren decided that "up North" was more like a detention hall the family had to go to after the South. It would end; they would eventually go home. Besides, sometimes Lauren even liked this Yankee-reconstructed place. But she never breathed this to her mother.

Lauren liked living across the street from the striated white and blank-gray winter beach where she and her little brother and sisters dug for clams at ebb tide; after dark, they patrolled the rocks with pocket flashlights looking for lovers entwined in secret crevices like seaweed or crabs. Every morning on the way to school, they passed a battered amusement park and once witnessed a man falling off the roller coaster. He was a sailor, drunk, and he stood up to read a sign that said "NO STANDING." In deepest winter, the children could walk, slipping up and down, atop the gleaming snow drifts that froze high into hard humps like white camels' backs, all the way to school. The schoolhouse itself had heavy tin slides for safety escapes that slanted down from the second-story windows like vertical wind tunnels. Lauren lived for fire drills and low tides.

But her mother maintained her staunch resistance to Boston, bill collectors, and the Yankee neighbors who, she said, spoke like cement mixers. Lauren supposed all this was her mother's way of seceding from the Union. These days, she might simply have divorced Lauren's father. But in Madeleine Meyer's family, divorce —like paying impolite creditors—was not done.

Pinching the latest Filene's or Jordon Marsh statement between her forefinger and thumb—the way Lauren had seen her pick up a limp bluebird that had flown into their kitchen window and broken its neck, as if this bill, too, had those invisible cooties that instantly attach themselves to dead things—Mother would drop the letter into her credenza's secret drawer. "I'll never pay," she'd declare, closing the drawer on the only stick of furniture James could afford to transplant with his family.

Madeleine Meyer never did pay. Bills piled up like a weightless white jungle. Lauren had nightmares about that credenza drawer where elephant letters trumpeted their intent to bolt out of the woodwork and trample the children as they slept. But this nightmare was nothing compared to the creditors' daily calls.

Like so many monkeys chittering, that's what Mother said as she hung up on them. Every creditor had the same voice, like a drill instructor or a disk jockey on a Southern religious station. Lauren believed they all went to the same school to learn their insistent, self-righteous, one-step-away-from-a-good-slap inflections the way she had to learn a foreign language as part of her school district's experimental elementary school program in speaking (but not reading or writing) French. In Beginning Spoken French, Lauren was taught to let her inflection rise on the question mark, like a high note plucked from the air or bright red balls balancing on the crest of a water fountain, that's what Mrs. Pritchett said; but the bill collectors always bore down on every question.

"Where does your father work?" they'd demand, with so much emphasis on the last word—a heavy hammer-blow to the ear, a death knell, the weight of the whole adult world—that Lauren knew long before she was ever to punch a time clock, or sit attached forty hours to a typewriter, that *work* was synonymous with being put in one's proper place and being punished.

The Gray Ghost Brigade had to be on their toes when the bill collectors closed in on Father. Just as Mother was too high-spirited to have to deal with the bill collectors' army, Father was too busy studying. James Meyer was the most bewildering person the children knew. All the adults, even Mother, maintained that it was Father who held absolute sway over the Meyers' lives. Like fate, he could move them north, south, east, and west; but once there, James Meyer disappeared. His children figured that perhaps, like God, their father's absence lent him more authority.

But there were times in the day-to-day when the Gray Ghost Brigade wondered just who was in control here—certainly not them. And yet that was the way they often eerily felt. An even greater mystery was that Father somehow needed their protection. The children sensed it. What did it mean that this acknowledged power needed his children's help? Also, Father never answered the phone, because he was on-duty, burning his way through piles of books like Sherman going through the South.

Sometimes Lauren was afraid that her mother might take her children back where she bought them. Once Madeleine Meyer had confided to Lauren about the wondrous department store where she'd gone on a shopping spree especially for each one of her children. Her offspring were not discount items, look-alike on a table, Mother said. They were luxuries, like the pastel-pink silk sheets Mother bought for Father before his final exams or the bright red lobster Father brought home when he got his first set of straight A's. Lauren didn't mind being compared to sheets or hardshell animals; what she minded was that only half of the children were paid for.

Around Christmas, things did get a little better; Father stayed home for winter vacation. He even answered the phones once or twice and gave those bill collectors a piece of his mind. Father never raised his voice, but was as earnest and reasonable as General Robert E. Lee negotiating a dignified surrender. For one solid month, the phones stopped ringing. Father only reprimanded Mother once, telling her that while he appreciated her generosity, she couldn't give away what wasn't hers. Then he told Madeleine to look up the meaning of the word *credit* in his fat, unabridged dictionary. Always, in speaking with Madeleine, James was restrained and gentle as if he spoke to his children. Sometimes he seemed sad and would gather the Gray Ghost Brigade and say, "Be careful with your mother. Don't push her. She has only two speeds: full speed ahead and stop."

Of course, the children agreed. But they were amazed, even

slightly offended, that their father was explaining what they already well knew. The children forgave him because they recognized it was the way adults often talked to themselves, by pretending to talk to their children. Mother's response to Father's lengthy-Christmas-break attention span was to behave as if she were countermanded to the barracks by her commanding officer. She didn't like it one bit, sitting around listening to Father talk in his soft, sometimes grieving voice. "The James Meyer Lecture Series," she called his talks, and often she complained that she would rather James just hauled off and hit her than administer these "psychological spankings."

Why James then continued to let his wife handle all money matters was a great mystery of Lauren's childhood. It was especially hard to understand, considering James Meyer's own nightmares from his Depression childhood, in which the Poorhouse Bus, like an Appalachian poltergeist, lurked around every bend in the road.

Lauren imagined that the Poorhouse Bus belonged to the Collections Division; it was probably yellow and black with red lights flashing *STOP!* like a school bus, but it had more in common with those St. Vincent de Paul Thrift Centers run by Catholics: it pulled up to the curb and carted away just about everything. Sometimes Lauren wondered if James Meyer didn't somehow *want* his wife to drive them all into the Poorhouse, where he knew his kind really belonged. But such suspicions were bewildering to Lauren and she never confided them to the troops.

In those days the Gray Ghost Brigade was afraid of everything —the bill collectors' threats, Father's capture in the prisoner-of-war camp of his college, and Mother's increasingly bad spells. Sometimes Mother acted as if her children were the enemy and slapped them away like so many creditors. She was confused, they thought, by the barrage of impolite calls. The children tried to keep her off the phone because the creditors filled her head with soreness and pain. Despite her migraines, Mother still went off on her shopping sprees. She bought things as if she were starving and could only eat lampshades or miniature Japanese radios. There was a wildness in her eyes and hands and she was always moving back and forth restlessly from room to room, from shop to apartment. In one day, just like the ocean, she could be high and majestic; and by night, at low tide. Father didn't see this much because he'd taken tutoring jobs to cover expenses and now was gone nights and many weekends. The children wondered if he slept at the library, stretching out on the empty shelves every evening in the dark.

One day in early March, the Gray Ghost Brigade, mistaking him for a neighbor, opened the door on a strapping but meagerly tailored man who beamed down on them.

"How are we this bright morning?" the man asked in a voice with not an unpleasant lilt. He was Irish, but since his inflection rose with the question, Lauren suspected he might be a kind of Frenchman.

Later Lauren admitted to the Gray Ghost Brigade that she was completely caught off guard by Mr. Potts's fresh, ruddy face and pretty green eyes. She should have looked instead at Mr. Potts's teeth: they were crushed together and brown.

One minute he was in the doorway, the next he'd scuttled over to perch right next to their mother on the velvet sofa.

Mother, at least, was suspicious of him. Madeleine Meyer thought Mr. Potts was a Yankee or a Jehovah's Witness. It turned out he was from California, which wasn't even old enough to enter the Civil War, and he was a lapsed Catholic. But this they found out much later. What the children thought that morning was that Mr. Leonard, as he insisted they call him, wasn't a worthy enemy.

For the longest time Mr. Potts just studied Madeleine Meyer, who ignored him and kept reading *I Led Three Lives*. Lauren herself had read a story of love-at-first-sight—a girl at a great ball fell in love with a soldier. Lauren recognized that morning that even Yankees could fall in love. Look at Mr. Potts this very moment.

"I said, it's a *bright* morning," Mr. Leonard repeated, and his voice was different, as if he couldn't breathe.

It wasn't bright at all. In fact, it was about to pour rain and the ocean was lunging toward shore. It was one of those days when one really *thought* about living across the street from such a large body of water. But Lauren could understand why Mr. Leonard believed it was bright. Mother loved lamps, and the Meyer living room was a luminous center. Also Mother herself was a dazzling creature. Her tastes ran not to the primary colors, but to the primitive. Fuschia was her favorite. Much later, back in the closed circles of a Virginia high school, Lauren would overhear in anguish her mother's taste described as "aboriginal." But back in Massachusetts, Madeline Meyer's fancy for giant red polka dots and Yubange-like earrings that looked like tiny plastic radar dishes dangling from each side of her head lent her all the splendor of an otherworldly creature. She was the children's own alien, and they marched proudly behind her dramatically flared lavender or translucent yellow skirts.

What they couldn't march so proudly behind, that dark spring, was Mother and Mr. Potts. Wearing a Yankee-blue coat and her fuschia scarf, Mother walked arm-in-arm along the beach with Mr. Potts, never suspecting that he was the owner of the only department store in Revere Beach—and a bill collector. By the time he had declared himself—and his love—Madeleine had already surrendered to him. And he had taken it upon himself to reconstruct her like the carpetbaggers did the South after they lost the war.

In the late afternoons Mr. Potts and Mother would walk the dilapidated boardwalk with the Gray Ghost Brigade marching behind. Lauren watched her mother gaze longingly into windowfronts and Mr. Potts correcting her as if she had a wall eye. One of Lauren's most vivid memories of this time was watching Mr. Potts guide Madeleine Meyer's hand as if they were slicing a wedding cake while they snipped her credit cards in half with pinking shears.

Lauren decided the attraction between Potts and Mother was that he had high spirits to match hers. But he was her backwards: Mr. Potts delighted in *not* spending money. He never bought anything on credit, saying that was just another word for organized crime. Mother and Mr. Potts also shared a lively interest in the underworld, spies, Mafia, and what Mr. Potts, with barely suppressed enthusiasm, called the Criminal Mind. Daily they strolled along the boardwalk, longing for McCarthy to come back from the grave and rout the Communist agents in Congress. Though they often went into thrift stores, they never bought a thing. When the Gray Ghost Brigade returned from school, Mr. Potts and Mother would be walking along the ocean looking disturbingly like those nighttime lovers who hid in the rocks undetected except during the children's low-tide patrol.

Lauren wondered if maybe her mother was allowing Mr. Potts to spend so much time with her as a way of paying back that $316.52 she owed his store. Whatever she was doing, it seemed dangerous.

"Poor people got to live poor": this was one of Mr. Potts's favorite sayings. He'd say the words so good-naturedly that no one really bothered with their meaning.

Mr. Potts had just said this for the hundredth time one summer day when the apartment door swung open and there stood Father, right in the middle of the afternoon. Mr. Potts's expression didn't change when Father walked into the living room. The bill collector just kept on staring at Mother, his lips slightly open to show those crushed, dark teeth. Mr. Potts had a way of looking at Mother as if he'd just eaten and was still ravenous.

In one glance, even without his spectacles, Father saw this expression and went ramrod stiff. Lauren saw his hands tremble as Father carefully placed his books on the radiator shelf and folded his arms across his chest.

"Potts' the name," the bill collector said pleasantly, but did not extend his hand. He stayed right there on the velvet sofa next to Mother. "Leonard Potts . . . you know, Potts Store on the corner of—"

"Yes, I know." James Meyer cut him off the way he bit down on words in a book. But he was staring straight at Mother.

"We owe him quite a lot of money, dear," Mother said almost

gaily, and Lauren saw she was strung tight like a high-wire act in the amusement park.

James Meyer was very quiet. He never looked at Mr. Potts directly that whole time, but Lauren could feel a part of her father that was thin and sharp as an iron dagger poised at the throat of the sturdy businessman. The Gray Ghost Brigade thrilled at the prospect of their father finally doing his part in the war. He'd massacre Mr. Potts, then bury him on the beach at low tide—a strategy that even Mr. Potts with his penchant for the Criminal Mind might admire. Lauren herself was poised for action; she would certainly help rout this enemy once and for all.

But James Meyer did not move. He just kept gazing at his wife. Maybe it was the first time he had noticed her gray flannel dress from St. Vincent de Paul's racks, her pale skin with blotches of high color under each eye like she'd been socked. She had lost a lot of weight, even though Mr. Potts was always buying her purple cotton candy and submarine sandwiches.

Madeleine Meyer looked poor—a poor man's wife, an Appalachian woman who rode the Poorhouse Bus that Father had thought he escaped when he left the North Carolina mountains. Whatever Father saw, it was terrible, a wound no one could see, only feel. Maybe this was what Mother had meant about psychological spankings? Inside you ached, although no one had hit you.

"Madeleine . . . ," he said, and in that one word all the fight went out of James Meyer's body. His chest caved in and he did something the children had never witnessed. He stood absolutely still and quietly wept.

It was terrible, those tears, from this man who was supposed to protect them all, a man whom they'd tried to protect and had failed. After all, here was the enemy right in their living room. He'd repossessed Mother, defeated Father—would he now demand the children themselves as payment for the Meyer debt? Mr. Potts could do anything he wanted, Lauren realized. No one would stop him; he'd gotten through every line of defense.

As she watched her father try, and fail, to gather himself, sitting down at last with his head between his hands, Lauren felt a great dizziness. In a plumb line from her throat to her toes, something inside her was falling—maybe an apple, she thought crazily, like Mrs. Pritchett and Isaac Newton had discovered. Earth Science was Mrs. Pritchett's favorite topic. But until now Lauren had never understood it. *Now* she made the connection: everything on earth was subject to gravity. People, too, were prisoners of gravity, and everyone—man, woman, child—fell at the same speed, hit the ground together, like that man on the roller coaster, like Mr. Potts fell in love with Mother, like the way Father was falling now into his own sorrow.

Lauren looked at her father and clenched her fists, her own eyes blurring. Even if she ran to him as her sisters and brother did now, fluttering around him, it would do no good. There was no comfort. And there was no protection. Grown-ups couldn't even protect themselves, much less their children. Gravity got them all; it spun everyone around like so many hapless tops; and when you fell—in love, in debt, in battle—there was no stopping yourself, no one to catch you, only the earth.

At last James Meyer looked up and said in a weary voice, "I can have the money to you next week. How much is it?"

"Mr. Potts doesn't want his money," Mother said in a clear, high voice like going up on a French sentence.

Then their father did another thing the children had never witnessed before; he reached into his wallet and wrote a check. Without a word he handed it to Mr. Potts. Then he looked around the room at each of his children as if even with all his straight A's he'd somehow flunked. "I'm sorry," he said softly, "for your trouble." But he wasn't looking at Potts when he said it; he was looking straight at Lauren—who would not return his gaze. She stared grimly at the floor, one foot kicking a tear in the old carpet.

"No trouble," Mr. Potts said with the bright enthusiasm that announced him that first day. This was the last the Meyers ever saw of him, and they would have celebrated, except it was also the last time they saw their mother for a year. The moment Potts left, Mother locked herself in the bedroom and did not come out until the next morning—when James Meyer announced he was taking his wife to the bus station where she was bound for North Carolina and his own people.

Once, in what seemed a past life, Lauren had heard her mother making fun of the Meyer clan. They were so pig-poor, Madeleine said, they didn't know credit existed. But that morning when Madeleine was whisked away, the Gray Ghost Brigade sat on the beach without a word. They didn't have to talk. They all knew what was happening with Mother: Gravity and the Poorhouse Bus had got her.

James Meyer explained only vaguely that the reason he hadn't sent Mother to her own family in Virginia was because he needed Grandmother Mason to come up to Revere Beach and be with the children.

Grandmother Mason came, a gentle, never-go-out woman who was in her own way surprisingly spry. Though she was a widow and quite genteel, she played a reckless and shrewd game of Chinese Checkers. She also knew French, both to read and write. When she finally wrote down the words Mrs. Pritchett had taught Lauren in Spoken French, Lauren was so shocked at how funny and wrong was her idea of French-on-a-page, that she despaired of ever learning it right.

Grandmother Mason explained other things to them now that Father was no longer giving his lecture series. Father was awfully quiet, and so was the phone. Father was paying the bills, Lauren supposed, or else he was referring the bill collectors to the Science Research Center that had bought what was left of the Meyer family because Father finished first in his class. After graduation, Father said, they would all move halfway around the world to another ocean where money would be as natural and flow as regularly as the waves across the street in the Atlantic. They'd learn yet another language and forget what happened in Revere Beach.

"Think of it," James Meyer said, his glasses shining. "We'll travel round the world, then all go back South and settle sometime."

Lauren wanted to tell him that it was too late to settle them after abandoning Mother and dragging his children around the world. The roots, like all their fighting, would just be pretend. Besides, Lauren wanted to remind her father, poor people got to live poor, just like his people. But the only thing Lauren could say was that she didn't want to learn another language because everything she'd learned in Spoken French was wrong.

James Meyer heard this from his oldest daughter with a stern face. "Nonsense," he said. "You're good students and you'll understand another language in no time at all."

Lauren shrugged; why should she try to lecture him? Besides, she understood so much less about the world now that Mother and the creditors were gone.

Some things were the same. They were all still in school for the summer at Carl, Willard, and Maybee. Father had enrolled them to give Grandmother Mason a daily rest. But she never seemed to mind her grandchildren. She even joined them on their low-tide patrols, except she looked for crabs and conch shells and razor clams. The Gray Ghost Brigade was relieved not to search for lovers in the rocks. After all, Mr. Potts was probably one of them.

One evening, before the Meyers left Revere Beach forever to move to the Mexican gulf, Grandmother Mason looked up from her prowling among the sea anemones and cucumbers. She called to her grandchildren, "Look you here!"

They all held back. No telling what she'd discovered.

"Here's a surprise!" She bent down, even though she had bad hips.

"It's a baby something," Clare said. She'd inherited Father's passion for marine biology, and the exact slant of his studious jaw. "Jellyfish, maybe?"

"It's dead," Lauren said, and tried not to show much interest.

"It's a big blob of nothing." Jo took up Lauren's tone.

"No, it's something you see every day," Grandmother continued, "but in a different form. Can you guess?"

An ex-kindergarten teacher, Grandmother Mason was always making them guess. But there were things they didn't want to know anymore. Besides, they knew that adults eventually answered their own questions. "It's a crab," Grandmother said with an air of tenderness and awe. "A crab in its soft state. You see, it shed the hard shell—"

"Exo-skeleton!" Clare piped up proudly, using her father's lecture voice.

"Right, indeedy," Grandmother smiled, and wouldn't let them touch the gooey pale glob clinging to that rock. "In its soft state, the crab is in danger from predators. So they search for a safe place to change."

"You're lying," Lauren said, and suddenly hated Grandmother Mason—hated them all. They were all so helpless. Anything could sweep them away: a wave, a bus, someone they loved. "You're just pretending to protect us. It's already dead!"

Lauren touched the thing with her toe and stared down at its shivering, white mass. It was all soft inside with no way to hold its shape. Lauren then had the overwhelming urge to step on it. It wouldn't fight back. Without its shell, it didn't know how. That was just another fact of Earth Science.

Grandmother Mason knelt down so her eyes were level with Lauren's. "They stay like this only a while," she whispered softly. "And it's natural. Then they grow back their hard shell. Things right themselves," she watched Lauren closely, "when they can."

Then Grandmother Mason did something strange. She reached down and very gently touched the molting crab with one finger, clucking her tongue the way she did when patting or rocking Daniel to sleep. "Don't you see?" Grandmother looked up at Lauren. "We're all so brave. No one, not even grown-ups, knows what's going to happen from day to day—but we just believe the earth will take care of us . . . like she does this little crab here."

"Can we take the crab home?" Clare asked. "Please, please!" Her eyes were bright, alert, clear as science in Mrs. Pritchett's class. Father had promised Clare a microscope when he graduated.

"No," Grandmother said firmly, and covered the crab gently

with some seaweed. She gathered the troops around her. As they walked on down that stark black-and-white expanse of beach, Grandmother Mason touched Lauren's head and murmured, "We are not predators."'

8

FELLOW CREATURES

As a child, Ruth Littlefield held formal tea parties for her friends, who were dinosaurs. They barely fit their scaley tails and folding, irridescent wings into the bedroom the maid cleaned with Catholic zeal. Ruth invited the gentle, bland Brontosaurus to carefully bend and forage over her windowbox of geraniums that perched twelve stories above traffic, up in her parents' Park Avenue apartment. Across her lush green comforter Ruth watched Tyrannosaurus Rex gratefully flop as if her small bed were an island, a floating escape. Here, high above the street, Ruth entertained her guests, whose flaps and squawks and caws went unheard for all the city noise below. Serving tea to them was an art, for the tiniest nod of a massive head, the pleasurable flick of a mastodon's trunk, made an echoing whack mid-air; it might break the sound barrier, the vanity's mirror, even her glasses. While it was nice to have such great presences for tea, Ruth did not want to see her room toppled in a Jericho of jagged white wallboard and plaster. Ruth loved her room, so she had earnestly trained these, her fellow creatures, to be polite, disciplined, and, above all, smart. This was their second chance and she meant them to survive.

Ruth was eight, and very serious in her tortoiseshell spectacles just like her father's. Like him, she loved melons, books, microscopes, and twirling the stand-up, illuminated world globe with one finger. Her father's degree was in archeology, but with his graduation he came into the family inheritance and Lawrence Littlefield now spent most of his time managing the Littlefield grants to the arts.

The Littlefields' live-in maid and cook, Katherine, who was simply Cook to the household, was more a mother to Ruth than Edith. It was Cook who first explained to Ruth that even though her parents were agnostics, they had enough sense to see that divorce was a sin. That's why they wouldn't leave their daughter or each other, no matter how much they argued. Cook was always reminding Ruth how she might turn her mother's moods to the good. When Edith would forget for evenings on end to tuck her daughter in, Cook gave Ruth a tiny Virgin Mary whose benediction, Cook said, was better than any just-mortal mother's kiss. Ruth loved Cook, although she was careful to hide her affection, just as she hid her little vial of holy water and the plaster Mary. Even then Ruth knew the difference between gratitude and devotion. Ruth was devoted only to her father, her dinosaurs, and her cousins. These were all her equals and they were sometimes better off than she.

Her father was better off because he was grown-up; even Cook admitted that for a man who didn't believe in God, Lawrence Littlefield was remarkably good. Ruth's dinosaurs were better off because they could disappear when her parents quarreled. And like Ruth's dinosaurs, her cousins had one another, but they didn't have to disappear.

Ruth's cousins belonged to her father's sister, Laura. There were four of them and together they formed an inner family against which, it seemed to Ruth, their parents had little chance. Laura, a lapsed Catholic, was happily married to a music professor at Columbia. He was a distracted, amiable flutist who rarely talked, but was always nodding absently, his head cocked as if he listened to a high, fine frequency above the ordinary babble. Ruth imagined her uncle had a whole orchestra in his head and that explained his lively eyebrows working up and down like a famous conductor's. He gave music lessons to all his children, who adored him, except for George, the eldest, who feared that his father was slightly mad. George was even more embarrassed by his mother, who spent her time and money on wayward mystics and ex-Jesuits with expensive experimental social reforms. For all Laura's own doubt and financial flounderings in the faith, she still insisted that her children receive a firm religious education.

How Ruth envied her cousins their parochial school, Sacred Heart of Mary. Set at the tip of Manhattan, the school was in the shadow of the solemn Cloisters, and yet the neighborhood was boisterous with alternating Irish, Puerto Rican, and Jewish blocks. On weekends, Ruth often visited her cousins' house in Inwood. It hardly seemed like New York up there next to the park, the wide, dark Hudson, the old Dutch apartment house in which her cousins took up an entire floor. George, who was nine, sometimes let his siblings tag along when he took Cousin Ruth to see the unicorn tapestries in the Cloisters. He knew the woven story by heart, and if asked correctly, he confided it with a mixture of condescension and world-weariness, as if to say, *Just wait until you're in fourth grade.*

One weekend George acted very strangely, when Ruth asked him politely to explain the unicorn tapestries story while they were touring the Cloisters. Instead of his usual lecture, George gave Ruth an angry glance. "I've told you a million times," George said. Then he pinched Ruth's arm, but this time it hurt. "The unicorn is a virgin; and a virgin can't have babies. That's why they killed her and she went extinct. See?"

This was not the usual story. Bewildered, Ruth had to think about this for a while. At last she suggested to George, "You'll always be a virgin then, won't you?"

Sisters tittering behind him, George scowled. "Boys are never virgins. Only girls . . . and unicorns, and nuns."

"*You* can't have babies," Ruth countered. She narrowed her eyes behind her glasses, aware that this always disconcerted her cousin.

"Mary was a virgin and she had babies," Marrie piped up, holding onto Ruth's elbow for support against her glowering brother.

Exasperated, George walked away from the cool stone chamber

that held the unicorn tapestries and out into the Cloisters' herb garden. It was June and the courtyard air smelled of oregano, rosemary, and tarragon.

"Mary was a miracle, stupid," George told Marrie. He took a swipe with his cap at a wasp buzzing around the honeysuckle, then stomped away and sat down heavily on the stone bench. He ignored his sisters and brother so completely that Spencer began snuffling and wandered over to George rubbing his eyes. The sisters followed, but Ruth hung back, pretending to study a gnarled tree. She couldn't quite read the label's horticultural name. Ruth knew it was a fig tree, and she loved figs, but she wouldn't pick the succulent purple fruit. It must be a mortal sin to steal from a monastery's garden; and even though Ruth was not baptized, though her parents didn't even believe, she suspected Catholics were right about hell and holiness. Ruth was shocked, then, when George jumped up from the stone bench, strode over, pinched off a ripe fig, and stuck it in her pocket.

"George!" Marrie said in a furtive whisper. "You're going to get it!"

"Ruth wanted it," George explained in his most matter-of-fact voice, "but she was too afraid to pick it. The nuns say if you think something, you've done it. Ruth's already a sinner . . . I was just making sure she got something out of it."

Ruth listened very closely to George, following his logic as if it would finally give her the key to her cousins' mysterious religion. This did make sense: you think something, it's done. Ruth had simply thought of her dinosaurs and they existed. The Virgin Mary had prayed and found Jesus inside her. God gave people power to create what they most wanted. What Ruth most wanted was for her father and mother to stop fighting. Perhaps in the same way that she had saved her dinosaurs from the Ice Age, Ruth could save Lawrence and Edith from freezing one another and her out. Ruth closed her eyes, imagining her parents gazing gently at one another from across the breakfast table the way Professor Smythe looked at Aunt Laura some mornings; it was the way George had once looked at Ruth when she offered to lend him her microscope; it was the way Ruth herself often watched Bronto and Rex—fondly, indulgently, delighted.

When she opened her eyes, Ruth saw George was somehow angrier with her than before, and when he said, "You're really in trouble now," and shook his head, Ruth realized she had half-eaten the fig, and she was frightened by George's fear. It was barely discernible through his anger, but it was there. Ruth smelled it. Sometimes she had smelled fear like this on her dinosaurs when they thought she would banish them outside on the streets. Fear smelled like cold, like winter air hurting all the way down your windpipe. You held your breath and the cold closed in. Even though it was summer, Ruth shivered. She dropped the fig on the wood chips and saw her cousins quickly kick mulch over it, furtively glancing around.

"But you said . . . " Ruth protested, as George roughly grabbed her arm.

"I didn't say to *eat* it!" George growled.

Confused, Ruth let herself be pushed along through the museum, past a wooden madonna, two marble carved lions guarding a coffin in the exact shape of a knight, a silver basilisk. Then her confusion changed to shame and nausea. How could she have been so hungry, so *obliviously* hungry? The greatness of her sin overwhelmed Ruth and she began to cry. Here she was, not even a Catholic, but by this one act she was forever damned.

There was only one penance, Ruth decided: she would become a nun. After all, Sister Margaret Magdalene had first entered her convent at the age of sixteen. Sometimes Sister Margaret Magdalene spoke to Ruth about her dream of leaving teaching and entering a contemplative order. Ruth could still visit her, the Sister promised. But the idea of Sister Margaret Magdalene becoming God's hostage and talking to her visitors behind bars made Ruth shudder. Now, after Ruth's great sin of eating the forbidden fig, she thought perhaps she should plan to enter a convent and pray for everybody for the rest of her long life, if only at last to forgive herself. Safely she could shut herself away from husbands and babies and especially her cousin George.

Yes, Ruth decided right then as George hauled her through the Cloisters by the collar of her new dress, that's exactly what she would do.

"Hurry up... hurry up!" George dragged Ruth past a bronze beast on their way out of the museum. His brother and sisters sailed behind him like little birds.

Ruth knew George was rushing because they were late but also because he was still afraid and felt he or someone else should take control. She wanted to stop and tell him that he didn't have to worry anymore. She wasn't afraid; she was happy.

Ruth dug in her patent leather heels that squeaked against the stone tile; she stared up at the bronze giant that looked like a cross between a water buffalo, a hippo, and her own friendly mastodon.

"Look like someone you know?" George teased. He'd forgotten they were in such a hurry.

"Yes," Ruth answered, without thinking.

George let go of her and bent double laughing. His siblings imitated him, though they didn't know what the joke was. "Know why he's a virgin?" George whispered. "He's so ugly... nobody to *you-know-what* with! That's why he died out!"

Ruth dropped her mouth open; she could only stare at George, who did a little hop in front of her as if the floor was hot. She had never seen her cousin so agitated. "George," she said, and her voice seemed grown-up, at least to Ruth. "Stand still." He was so surprised he stopped his little jig. "George," she continued solemnly, "I'm going to be a nun."

"Oooh," the little girls squealed, crowding around Ruth, admiring her as if their cousin already had the black wings of a wimple descending upon her head. "Then you'll really be our sister."

"You can't be a nun," George said flatly; "you aren't even Catholic."

The little girls looked across at Cousin Ruth and burst into tears at the thought of her so lost to them. Ruth herself stood very still thinking of a vast and lonely life excommunicated before she'd even joined the Church. She looked at George and her bottom lip trembled.

He tossed his head. "You can find your own way home," he snapped and strode off.

George disappeared around the corner into the Cloisters gift shop. For a moment Ruth panicked. If George left them, could she find the way home? Then she remembered the money her mother had folded into her pocket. Well, she'd never taken a taxi before by herself, but she could certainly do it to make sure she got herself and the little ones to safety.

Squaring her shoulders, Ruth walked into the gift shop, where George was studying a row of stained-glass-window slides. "I'm taking everybody to my apartment with me," she informed him, and was about to walk off when he grabbed her wrist. George pinched her so hard, she cried out.

"You can't," he whispered, and again she smelled his fear. "Nobody's there."

George stared at her with a guilty smile as if he expected to be punished, but couldn't keep himself from saying, "You aren't even going home yourself, stupid! You're coming to live with us now. Mom told the maid. Your parents are breaking up—Mom calls it separation trails. So, smarty, you're stuck with us . . . and you better do what I say, because—"

"Liar!" Ruth screamed. But she knew he wasn't. She jerked away from George and began running. She took the steps two at a time, not even looking, not caring if she fell down and rolled several flights—maybe even down the hilltop onto Dyckman Street. Ruth's shoes tapped the stone as she ran, hearing the staccato of other small shoes behind her.

"Ruthie!" the little girls wailed.

"Come back!" George shouted breathlessly as he closed in on her. "You can't go anywhere . . . "

Even as Ruth increased her speed, heart bursting, she knew this was true. She hated her parents. She hated them for not telling her, for pretending this was just another weekend away, for leaving her with her cousins as if she were hand-me-down clothes.

Behind her George lunged, his arms thumping her back, and they both went down, rolling on the sidewalk. Wind knocked from her, Ruth gasped and then was crying. She hated herself for crying in front of George. Ruth rubbed the tears from her eyes with her fists.

When she looked over at George, he was smiling at her. "It won't be so bad . . . ," he said, and pinched Ruth very gently on the shoulder. "It really won't."

It wasn't so bad. She fit into the same room with Grace and Marrie, sharing a double bed, went to mass and on summer field trips with the nuns, and was taught the oboe by Professor Smythe; it wasn't so bad. But it wasn't really hers. In the same way Ruth had been deposited here, she could be swooped away. Along with this knowledge was a deeper fear: what would become of her dinosaurs?

That fall Ruth entered Sister Margaret Magdalene's class in the Sacred Heart of Mary School. Mid-lesson, Ruth would turn to see the radiator steaming and remember that there was no heat in her parents' apartment. They had not sublet it and so Ruth's room was a frigid, white space—an Ice Age. On Park Avenue, winter would freeze her friends out. They would leave her room, shivering, helpless on the city streets, hiding in alleys, and like bag people, be moved around by doormen and cops. Ruth had seen people living in subway tunnels. She pictured her Brontosaurus and Rex and her dim but loyal mastodon hustling down the stinking stairs of the I.R.T. Feeling their way for warmth, they would smile gratefully when they saw the electric tracks, sparks humming in the dark caves. No warning—an express train with its bright, glaring eye would bear down on her startled beasts. Just a bump, a brake screeching *Out of the way! Die out, why don't you?*

Even though Ruth daily mourned her dinosaurs, sometimes a strange reprieve came over her: cuddling up close to Marrie in the big four-poster, or impetuously hugging George when she won at Parchese, or exchanging a quick glance with Grace when Professor Smythe's eyebrows worked like a metronone, Ruth felt the hard, distinct lines of herself slipping away. Briefly she would *be* Grace doing her fervent Hail Marys or George studying for his World History exam. Ruth became responsible for them; and everything mattered as if it happened to her. Then Ruth would imagine George being struck by a subway train or little Spencer freezing to death. Terrible things could happen. What if Ruth couldn't save them anymore than she could her fellow creatures?

One night, in February, when only the fireplace lit Professor Smythe's music room, Ruth lay sprawled between George and Grace, playing Scrabble. Just as Ruth glanced up at George to protest his spelling "jenuflect" and claiming a triple-word score, she was struck by two things: George, now in the stratosphere of fifth grade, had very pretty eyes, and the other thing Ruth noticed was that the door next to the professor's piano was ajar. Ruth distinctly remembered having closed it with a conspiratorial giggle when they had all sneaked in here, past the teen-aged babysitter who now slumped over her millionth snack, snoozing on her Latin grammar in the kitchen.

Ruth gave George the signal—twitching eyebrows. Immediately the other children huddled, waiting for Ruth to reveal her secret. She picked up Scrabble letters and spelled out, "S-P-Y A-T D-O-O-R."

Pretending to yawn, George stretched back, checking the door. "Anyone want cocoa?" He jumped up and ran for the door. "I'll just ask... ah-ha!" He jerked open the door, then fell back, startled.

The little girls saw the woman before Ruth did. They touched Ruth gingerly, then fled the study. George wavered. His eyes alert and full, he gauged Ruth's ability to protect herself.

"Why don't you see about that cocoa, George?" Edith Littlefield said.

Ruth stood up, trembling, as her mother walked into the music room. She smiled and held her arms out to Ruth, who didn't move.

"We don't want any cocoa," George murmured defiantly, and stood by Ruth.

"It's all right," another voice gently dismissed George.

Lawrence Littlefield held back, penitent, smiling sadly at Ruth from across the room. "We've been away from you for too long," he said simply, and sat down on the piano seat.

Ruth noticed that his face in this half-light was tired and he had his overcoat on as if he were still cold. This made Ruth shiver. She ran for her father, but she did not embrace him; she sat beside him on the piano bench where she had often watched Professor Smythe teach Grace or little Spence their scales.

"You got our letters?" Ruth's mother asked in a bright voice. She came to sit down on the other side of Ruth. "Didn't you adore that little scrimshaw we sent you from..."

"I gave it away, Mother," Ruth said.

Edith considered this, opened her mouth, then sighed. "You'll see," her mother said in a soft voice, "it will be much better now. Your father and I..." Edith faltered only a second, "well, you see... here we all are together again."

Ruth glanced from her mother to her father. Her father's face was shadowed, thinner, his eyes veiled. Her mother spoke in a quick, assured cadence, but Edith's eyes darted back and forth as if she were reading. It made Ruth dizzy to look at her.

Edith chatted about their travels. Ruth said nothing. She looked down at the piano keys, concentrating on the chipped middle C where Spencer had once dropped a paperweight. That paperweight had a white desert of sand dunes inside it and when the children shook it, the miniature world changed: sand settled in new hills and smooth, quiet ridges. It was a beautiful paperweight; and it hadn't even broken when Spencer dropped it on the keyboard.

Ruth wished she could shake both of her parents and, like Spencer's paperweight, they would just change and be beautiful, different, brand new. So you couldn't even remember the way they used to be.

She looked up at her father. "Are you going to take me with you?" Ruth asked, and her glasses slipped down on her nose.

Lawrence pushed the tiny tortoiseshell glasses back above the bridge of the nose that looked so much like his own. "We would like to, yes."

"Where?" Ruth demanded.

"Home, dear," her mother said.

"The apartment . . . " Ruth began slowly. How many times had she dreamed of walking into her old room and finding her dinosaurs, her bed perfectly made, Cook cleaning her drawers? If her parents had just come back a little sooner; if they had warned her; if they had arrived looking as if they really had been together all this time—then Ruth could believe again. But now she could only stare at her hands in her lap and say, "It's probably empty now."

"Not for long," her mother said gaily.

"No!" Ruth suddenly cried, and grabbed her father's hand. "I won't go back there. It's the loneliest place in the world now."

"Well," Edith said, "we could all go back to London. I've always wanted Ruth to—"

"We've done our traveling," Lawrence said in a low, steady voice. Lawrence met his wife's sulking stare with an expression Ruth had never seen before. It was the way George looked when he would meet up with Grace and Marrie in the hallway at school and pretend he didn't really see them, that they didn't belong with him. Ruth's father was staring like this at Edith. For the first time Ruth could remember, she felt a tiny bit sorry for her mother. Edith wasn't a virgin, she certainly wasn't ugly, she had a child—but her father was looking at his wife as if he didn't care whether she died out or not.

"All right," Ruth heard herself saying in a breathless voice. "We'll go back . . . home." Only by the sound of her own voice did she realize her fear; but she didn't feel it. Paralyzed, for the first time in her life, Ruth felt dumb. Yet, she found her lips making a smile.

That smile was the most powerful thing Ruth had ever discovered. It moved her parents closer together, with her between them; it stopped Ruth's feeling that someone invisible in the room was breathing all their air.

Ruth held on to that taut, fixed smile as she said goodbye to her cousins, helped the babysitter pack some of her things, nodded to Grace and Marrie, who clung together whimpering. The babysitter looked slightly nervous, as if she expected, upon the Smythe's return, to find that this elegantly dressed, vaguely foreign-looking couple were, in fact, part of an international kidnapping ring.

"What about your microscope?" George asked.

"You can keep it," Ruth told him, and suddenly her smile fell off her face. She hid inside the taxi and would not look at George, who stood waving from the apartment steps. Edith chatted on, and Lawrence reached a tentative arm around his daughter. At first she did not respond, but at last, because it was too dark to see the look on Lawrence's face that would make Ruth pity her mother, Ruth leaned into her father's shoulder and closed her eyes.

She was not surprised to find Cook bustling about the kitchen when they entered her parents' Park Avenue apartment. Neither was Ruth surprised that everything looked exactly the same. In her father's study, Ruth was surprised to find a day bed made up with red wool blankets as if someone slept there. A visitor? Then Ruth realized no, that must be where her father slept now, in a separate room. That's the way it was going to be from now on—the happy lie. They were together. Through all of Edith's elaborate soirées and Lawrence's earnest arts board meetings, through all the years Ruth would now spend at the Nightingale private girls' school, through the next ten years the Littlefield family would live together in that spacious apartment; they would all wear those polite, cramped civilized smiles that showed they were, indeed, together.

Poised outside her own room, Ruth took a deep breath and swung open the door to emptiness. It took all her courage to enter this chilly place. Quickly Ruth undressed and crawled into bed. She put pillows on either side of her and pretended to sleep between these barricades when her parents came in to say goodnight. As Edith and Lawrence Littlefield walked down the hall,

Ruth heard her mother say in a hushed voice, "Why not sleep with me tonight, Lawrence? Now that Ruth is—"

"Fine," Lawrence said in that clipped, light voice.

Ruth waited forever—until the light went off in the hall. Then she abruptly pushed both pillows under her stomach and lay atop them, rocking herself back and forth. But she couldn't sleep. Only when she lifted her nightgown and put a pillow underneath it—small and warm bulk against her belly—could Ruth rest. Sometime in the night she felt it moving, the secret baby she was dreaming up, just like Virgin Mary. Maybe in her own way, Mary was a nun, Ruth thought as she cradled herself and rocked. And maybe this baby that she would have the first thing when she grew up would be as holy as Sister Margaret Magdalene said the body was, as holy and dear as her friends. Maybe her baby would have Bronto's sweet temper and the fierce loyalty of Tyrannosaurus Rex.

At last Ruth slept, and when she awoke it was still dark. Shivering, she crawled out from the covers and tiptoed down the hall. Outside her parents' bedroom, she found their door was left ajar, as if they meant for her to find them together and believe it was because of her. But Ruth gazed steadily at the gray wool covers that lay on the bed in a great mound like a big, familiar creature—and she was not fooled. She had not saved them. Buried side-by-side, her parents were also extinct.

TO KEEP THE WORLD

SPINNING

THE YEAR JOSEPH Girard grew three inches taller was the same year his father gave him an unofficial *bar mitzvah* and the same summer Joseph met his first friend. At thirteen Joseph was an aspiring biologist; he studied this science with a fierceness born of his own freakish growth. Molds, frogs, the insides of cats, anything that he might watch grow, reproduce, break down into basic structures of life—it all strangely moved him. Joseph believed that he might become a scientist, the first man of science in a family devoted utterly to the arts. Dr. Girard: the name matched the stature that his sudden biological spurt seemed to embody. Yes, Joseph decided that thirteenth summer, he would devote himself to the science of life. Perhaps if any Girard before him had done so, his family might have survived.

That summer Joseph also grew into quite a scholar. He was allowed to take an anatomy seminar at Hunter as part of their program for the top prep science students. A tall, slim junior-high Joseph walked among the older students as a physical peer. Those summer school days Joseph ignored the sunshine and Far Rockaway beach of his cronies and chose instead the dark cool of his anatomy lab. It smelled of formaldehyde and Borax soap crystals, a piercing perfume to cover up the flensed animal skin and laid-bare tissue that to the young boy looked somehow so vulnerable beneath whispering rows of fluorescent lamps. The lab became almost a holy place to Joseph, a workshop of mysteries made up not only of flesh, but spirit: sinew and bone; elegant gut, long, layered, and gleaming; all were sacrificed to this scholarly tribe.

There were more than a few avid students in his anatomy seminar. Among them was Stephen Cornell, whom Joseph would remember as his first consciously chosen friend. Stephen helped Joseph grow painfully alert to the intricacies of these small, dead bodies. They were no longer dislocated parts of animals; they were alive and in Joseph's mind, each had its connection, its life.

Because they looked so hard at things, Stephen reasoned, they could see these invisible connections—like what happened to a rabbit when energy shot across its synapses and it seemed to bound across the steel expanse of their lab table. Look again: and it lay absolutely still, skin pinned back to reveal rosy innards. It was all how you looked at things that made them dead or alive, Stephen said. Then he explained the theory of physics, stating that by gazing at something, you could completely change that object.

Stephen talked the way some people prayed, Joseph thought as he listened to his friend. This tow-headed, tall Manhattan boy with tortoiseshell glasses, who years later sometimes stared out at Joseph from Ruth's eyes, would surely be the first teenager to win a Nobel Prize. Of this Joseph was convinced, though he kept his schoolboy hero worship to himself. After all, Stephen was a year ahead in his private, Jesuit-run high school, and Joseph's devotion might distance him.

In Joseph's neighborhood Stephen Cornell would have been sneered at as a straight arrow; in Stephen's neighborhood, Joseph would have been snubbed as a lower form of city life—not even lower Manhattan, but Brooklyn. It was a statement of Stephen's influence that he convinced Joseph to join his Upper East-side Explorer troop. Joseph joined grudgingly; it was the only way he could figure to continue so unlikely a friendship once the anatomy seminar was over.

So that August, Stephen and Joseph celebrated their A's in anatomy by each piling into a bus loaded with boys all older than Joseph, and headed off to a camp in the Catskills. No one questioned Joseph's age, since he and Stephen were among the tallest in the group. They did question his borough accent and lack of decent camp clothes. Joseph didn't even have a uniform until midmonth when Tata mailed him one. It was brand new but already a little small. Joseph knew what it had cost his father and he wore the badgeless uniform like a proud soldier.

He wasn't broken by the other boys, but neither was he immediately accepted. Though he was good in games, Joseph felt his own lack of camaraderie; Stephen, on the other hand, was a favorite. Although not a natural leader, Stephen was a natural listener. He also had the strongest body among the boys, but for some reason he was perfectly disinterested in using this physical power over them. Applying brute force, Stephen said, was surrendering to inner weakness. The only sport, if you could call it that, in which Stephen was really interested was yoga. And yet when he was chosen (always among the first), to be on a baseball or soccer team, Stephen played with abandon and was among the highest scorers.

Stephen Cornell was the most complex person Joseph had ever met, except for his father. Joseph studied him as if he were a science. What really moved Stephen? Joseph wondered. For example, at night when Joseph and all the other boys in his tent stood on the edge of the platform and competed to see how far they could shoot the exuberant arc of their sperm, Stephen, with his typical aloofness, didn't join in the general boisterousness. He laughed amiably and ignored them all.

"Back at school I'm going to put mine in a jar and bring it into the lab," Joseph exulted one night after he'd won the contest. "I'll put it under the microscope and do a sperm count."

"Little boys . . . ," Stephen said good-naturedly, with an emphasis on the first word.

Joseph was too caught up in the fierce playfulness of these midnight Olympics to pay much attention to Stephen's remark. In fact, he felt an exhilarating sense of his own separate self, even while all the boys around him moaned with pleasure. Joseph felt like he was standing on the edge of the world; he didn't feel floorboards bending, talking back. Joseph rocked himself, his eyes tightly closed, his new hardness all that thrust out into the dark, encircling forest; he was his own little tree, a sapling.

In the final days of camp, all minds were turned to the closing ceremony. It was then that the elite among the troop, the Order of the Arrow, chose its few new members. The Order of the Arrow formed a sacred circle within the scouts. It was their initiation that some faint souls, though chosen, couldn't pass through.

The last Thursday night of summer camp began this initiation. All the boys stood blindfolded in a circle around the campfire. They shifted from foot to nervous foot while Order of the Arrow boys fervently beat tomtoms. Joseph could hear the leaders quietly walking within the bigger circle, but his blindfold doubled the blackness so that inside seemed outside. While Joseph had no hope of being chosen for the Order—he had earned no badges, had no other camping experience—his sexual prowess and his friendship with Stephen gave him expectations. Of what, he didn't know.

In the dark circle the boys stood, knees locked, not touching. The only sound was the drums and the soft footsteps like Indians barefoot in the dirt. At any moment a scout might be hit in the chest. He must not cry out in pain, but must fall backwards in blind trust to be spirited away into silence, solitude, two days of secret rites.

Joseph listened with his blacked-out eyes. A noise just to his left; yes, a thump to the chest, a boy's breath knocked from him. The fall, that soft scuffling. The circle instinctively closed. Every fiber of Joseph's being was alert, as if he were stalked by the most dangerous, most desired of night creatures.

Take me, take me, Joseph felt his heart beating to the drum rhythm. Thump, thumping, those palms on animal skin pounded inside him. And he was no more than a sacrifice, a small animal given up to this tribe.

Me, choose me—and then it happened: the sharp blow to the breast-bone, the thrust back into emptiness as Joseph fell down through the night into arms like branches, then to earth again. Dragged backwards through the woods, someone's powerful arms locked under his armpits. Joseph had never moved so fast, his feet barely skimming ground; blindfolded, it felt like flying or falling through space.

Joseph had never felt so afraid, so aroused. Suddenly his captor tripped and did fall. Joseph landed on top of the boy, his head hitting the hard ground of another's muscled stomach. But somehow it felt soft and for a moment Joseph remembered being very little and lying on Tata's belly. His father's great, ruined hands cupped Joseph's head as Tata breathed, buoying his boy up. To rest like that again seemed impossible, and yet here was another belly, another boy so like himself.

The drums murmured far away as someone gently removed Joseph's blindfold. It was Stephen, of course. Some part of Joseph had known already, had recognized his smell. Joseph smiled at his friend though there were no lights to see in this darkness. But after so much blindness Joseph didn't miss seeing.

Stephen struck a match. "Well, as long as we're here, we might as well stay. But you're supposed to stay here alone." Stephen stood up but made no move to go. He towered over Joseph, as if he'd grown in the night. "Here's a knife and sleeping bag. Tomorrow you'll work in complete silence. Alone. You'll know if you break the rules by talking—even to yourself. Be back here tomorrow night. There'll be no food except for what you forage." Stephen paused. "Goodbye."

It sounded final, but still Stephen lingered. Far off those thudding drums, and Joseph saw the faint glow of the big campfire like a haunting. Joseph had never felt so alone. Fear or joy aroused him. Then Stephen was very near, his gaze steady. And for the first time Joseph felt truly seen, and changed.

But at the end of that summer, Stephen Cornell was sent to boarding school; Joseph stayed behind in Brooklyn, and never saw his friend again. He mourned Stephen. When school started, he stayed away from his former cronies and devoted himself to a new passion: no longer science, but sculpture—working his hands in wood. In the basement of Tata's duplex, Joseph spent every evening and weekends carving, sanding, finishing. The projects were all his own, except for the one he was making for his father's birthday in early January.

This project was an oak chair that Joseph was sculpting to exactly hold and fit his father's body. For years his father had not been comfortable in his own body, the old man said. His arthritis, complicated by a recent diagnosis of diabetes, made it difficult for Tata to climb up and down stairs. Joseph worked in the cellar where Tata could not descend, carving the oak chair that would take Tata's weight.

But one winter night as Joseph labored late on the chair, he looked up, surprised to see his father easing himself down the basement stairs, hand over hand on the rickety banister.

"Don't come down, Tato," Joseph called out, "you'll fall." Not only that, he'd discover Joseph's gift before it was ready, before Tata's birthday.

"*Tak*," Tata kept on coming, "so this is where *you* work?"

At the bottom of the stairs, Tata stopped and waved a hand to include the sweet-smelling oak shavings, the metal plane Joseph had stolen from his woodshop class, the open can of lemon oil and varnish that awaited Joseph's brush like tiny, dark wells. Into them he dipped his fine bristles and slaked the sanded wood as if the chair's arms reached out not to hold, but to drink.

Tata surveyed the dim basement and Joseph knew his father was comparing his son's workshop to his own upstairs—a workshop that was now the old man's hobby since he couldn't make a living at it anymore. A Polish watchmaker before the war, Tata had tried to teach his son the trade of perfect mechanical worlds—maze-like gears and golden wheels that fit in jeweled casings. But Joseph fumbled or broke everything he tried to fix. Often he flew into a rage over Tata's workbench, but only when the old man was out of the house. Joseph tried to make excuses for himself, saying it was impossible to inherit a skill that Tata, too, had lost. For Karl Girard's hands had been ruined in Auschwitz. How they had been ruined, Joseph couldn't imagine. Tata never talked about the camps, except to say that Joseph's middle name, Erich, was after his closest friend there.

Joseph couldn't imagine his father young, having friends, going to school or summer camp. Joseph couldn't imagine Tata doing anything normal. And though his father never mentioned Auschwitz, Joseph felt that somehow Tata had spent his entire life there. When he mustered the nerve to question Tata about life before the war, Tata would respond, "That was then . . . , this is the new world." Then he'd fall silent and repeat, spitting out each syllable with scorn that was just as strong as his expectations of Joseph, "The New World. . . ."

When Joseph imagined his parents arriving in New York with their brand new baby, he felt an amazement that was the closest thing he'd ever experienced to religious feeling. The photograph of both his parents showed them holding their only child between them like a precious vase that at any moment might slip through their hands and shatter. Or be stolen from them; but it was his mother who was stolen. Measles killed her, not her baby.

Now, years later, Tata stood in his basement and eyed his growing son in his little workshop. Finally the old man spoke, and his voice trembled. *"Dobrze,* Yoncle," he said softly, "you make good with your hands."

There was pleasure in Tata's voice, and this outweighed Joseph's disappointment at his father finding out about the sculpted chair before his birthday.

For a while they were both still. Perhaps it was because the old man had discovered, here in the bowels of his basement, a secret that was also his son's gift—perhaps that discovery is what made Tata then turn to Joseph and offer the one confidence his son had always wanted, though never asked. Perhaps it was seeing Joseph's handiwork that made Tata reveal the history of his own shattered hands. Joseph never knew. All he knew was that for this one night Tata wanted his son to know his story.

"You have *my* hands, Yoncle," Tata began in a subdued voice. He sat very near his son on an ottoman that Joseph had rescued from sidewalk rubbish. Stuffing puffed out of it like dusty, gray clouds. There was a moment of stillness so complete that Joseph thought perhaps Tata's heart had stopped, as the doctor often warned. Joseph listened for his father's breathing and heard only the furnace belch, as if pleasantly satisfied, filled.

"I do?" Joseph said encouragingly. And when his father still did not respond, Joseph repeated, "I do, don't I, Tato?"

"*Tak*," Tata roused himself, and his voice was so worn out it was as if all this time he had been really talking and now his throat was frayed. "I never did think to see my hands again, to see them work... but then, who would think a son is born from a dead man?" Tata shifted on the green hassock, cleared his throat and began in a stronger tone, "Those of us who got such hands must use them to make something work. Izakitus taught this to his apprentices. He said there are two virtues to any invention: beauty and usefulness. Balance them and you have the world. Inside a watch, you see, there is gold. The eye does not see it because it is there to do work. On the face of this watch, too, is gold. But it is only truly beautiful if, inside, the watch works."

Here Tata turned to Joseph and held up his hands. Each thumb was twisted into the forefingers. It hurt Joseph physically to look at Tata's hands; he cringed at the misshapen, rigid fingers poking up like thick, numb antennae. The Nazis should have hacked Tata's hands off at the wrists, rather than leave a man's life dangling and dead at the end of each arm.

In that moment Joseph wanted to take Tata in his smaller arms, to embrace him with stronger hands. Sometimes in Joseph's own hands, he felt heat lightning. If he put each hand together there was energy and warmth enough for Tata, too.

Joseph felt he could heal with his hands. But as Joseph moved forward to embrace Tata, the old man jerked away, saying, "I *used* to believe all this. When I was only a little older than you." Joseph fell back, afraid of his father's eyes. "But I know now," Tata continued, his voice flat. "Nothing beautiful binds people together. Our inventions are more perfect than we are. What does this say about a God?" Here Tata broke off with a hoarse laugh that hurt Joseph's ears. It was a terrible sound, his laugh as broken as his hands.

Joseph did not turn away but instead faced his father and used an old trick from childhood: in his mind he covered Tata's mouth as he would a wound. He didn't hear a word. Joseph looked only at his father's eyes and hands; he leaned into the smell of Tata's warmth, his scent of delicate, golden watch oil. Now the body-longing, the closeness, the bigger arms that once held him. This was a bond that even Tata's words could not betray, as long as Joseph silenced his father's voice.

"You know, Yoncle," Tata said slowly, "that it is work for me to get up, to go through day and night. It is the hardest work I ever do. Tell me, why should I move from one side of the room to the other. Why should I ever climb those stairs again—because *you* love me, because *you* will it, because a God is stingy and will not give me the one thing I ask?" Tata sighed and said in a monotone, "Again and again I ask to die."

The old man buried his face in his hands, only his shoulders slightly trembling. Joseph sat as he so often had during his father's ritual. Long ago he had given up trying to touch Tata when he wept like this. Joseph imagined it was just because his father's skin was so raw he was flayed alive. The slightest touch was another wound.

Joseph bowed his head, trying not to hear. How Joseph hated himself for sitting there uselessly tapping his feet—as if his father's grief were music.

At last Tata looked up, his face resuming that smooth, absent mask that was his usual expression. "I did not ask for you," he said simply. He gazed at Joseph with a mild, almost casual eye. "I did not ask God for a son."

Joseph kept his head down. He felt nothing. But if he had felt anything, he would have gotten up right then and smashed that chair into a thousand splinters. This thought made Joseph clasp his own hands and hope that Tata could not read his mind as the old man sometimes did.

Tata was quiet a while, then said in a voice that was unexpectedly tender, "But you did ask me, Yoncle. You ask me all the time without saying. You ask me for what I can't give ... just as I ask God for what he won't give...." The old man hesitated, then went on as if forcing himself, "What do you want from me, my son?"

Joseph looked down immediately. "Nothing," he said softly. "You don't have to—"

"You're thirteen," Tata interrupted gruffly, "you're a man now, too. And you want what?"

Joseph still kept his eyes lowered, but he said in a small voice, "What happened to your hands, Tato? What happened to . . . ?"

Tata settled his weight on the ottoman. For a long while he was very still, then he lowered his head, staring sideways at the furnace. He seemed to be listening very intently before the words found their way from him. At last he began:

"The story is long. It begins in a café in Budapest. Erich Schuchmann and I sit drinking good beer that my money from working apprentice watchmaker for Izakitus brings. The old Greek loves me like a son, though I am a Jew. A Jew with false papers who works hard with his hands." Tata turned to his son with an expression that was unfamiliar in its wistfulness. Just for a moment Joseph caught a flash of what his father might have looked like all those years ago—before the war.

"How I love that man who teaches me," Tata continued. "When I come to Izakitus my hands are train only to play violin, but I am never good like Erich. Erich manages to find work in the Budapest symphony, what there is left of it after deportation and the army making its soldiers. The Hungarian army are never friends to Jews, but it is only after the Nazis invade Hungary that the army assassinates its own Jews. In the early days of war—before the 1941 relocations when Erich loses his whole family and flees to find me in Budapest—I have believe that as Jews we might volunteer for the army. But Izakitus talks us out of it; he gets us the false papers and tells us to hide—in the symphony, in the back of his shop.

"We live with his Greek Orthodox cousins who grumble, but even they do not know we are Jews. We go to their mass with them and pray to their God to protect us, since our own is deaf. We have heard the rumors that the family camps are really for killing, but as free men we don't believe such fairy tales. We argue, Erich and I, that killing Jews is not efficient for the Nazi war machine. They can take our belongings, our houses—but don't they need our bodies to fight their war? We cannot imagine, you see, a military mind that wants ashes, bones and soap before soldiers and slaves."

Tata stopped, musing for a while. So Joseph sat very still, waiting.

"The café. . . . *Tak*, I was telling you," Tata took up again. "It begins so simple. A man, Czech, in Erich's symphony, is jealous. I don't know whether he is worse as a violinist or as a man, but Petrouchak hates Erich. He won't follow his bow directions, must believe he is better. Often this Petrouchak complains to the director that Erich gets first chair through deceit, not talent. Erich treats Petrouchak as no more than a fly, some little thing you flick away without breaking the movement of your bow. We call him *Le Moustique* but we do not mean him harm."

Again Tata stopped and was silent. "No, we mean Petrouchak no wrong. But what can Le Moustique be thinking when he turns Erich in as a Jew to the SS? Does he think this makes *him* a great violinist?" Tata shook his head contemptuously. "Well, we sit, Erich and I, in that Budapest café. I have just order potato soup—I remember because it is the last time I ask for food and expect to get it. A car pulls up with two boys, SS. They look like kids out to play, hardly old enough to drive such a big machine. They know us in a minute, the way the predator recognizes food. They are hungry. It is simple.

"I, too, am hungry. In the corner of my eye I see the waiter hesitate, my potato soup on a tray above his head. I want to eat, just like the little boys dragging Erich want to eat. No one says a word to me, as if I am not also here with false papers. I watch Erich's feet bump along the sidewalk as he is drag backwards between two little boys. And suddenly I am moving, too. Because that day in Budapest I have not yet lost myself and Erich. Because I believe then that Erich is part of me, just as my mother and my sister, already in the family camps, and Izakitus belong to me. I believe then that God makes this world work like a master's clock.

"And so I find it is true. There *is* order. There *is* usefulness. There *is*, even, beauty. In the killing factories every bone and bit of hair, even our fat is put to use. They crush our bones to fertilize the beautiful SS lawns and flowerbeds, and for factories; they scalp the corpses of women for hair to make slippers and beds. That lovely, long hair shines and dries in the sun. I watch it swaying in rows, some blonde, some curly and dark like gypsy hair . . . like your mother's. . . . " Tata reached out gently to wind Joseph's locks around his bent fingers. "Beautiful . . . ," Tata murmured, "and useful. . . . "

Joseph's heart was beating so fast, he wondered that its violence didn't make Tata shudder. But the old man just petted his son's head gently, then sat back. He was quiet, resting.

Then he began again in his flat voice, "They will tell you brave stories; they will tell you in history book about how we sing and chant and pray on the trains or walking into gas chambers. But my story is not brave. Oh, in the train Erich and I at first make light of it. There is a mistake, we say; we will escape, we plan. We are together, we say. What could be so bad? And Erich plays an invisible violin for the children. He sings all the different parts of "Peter and the Wolf" and the children like most to hear the oom-pah-pah tuba and the trumpet Erich makes with his mouth. It makes them laugh.

"But after three days with only two cups of water the thirst is so great on those trains that we cannot even speak. The children are dull like dolls and their heads loll about without sense. One baby has died and the mother must hold it in her arms and it grows black, stiff at her breast. Still she nurses it. She doesn't bother to weep. There is no water for tears.

"Beside me Erich faints, but he is holded up by the crush of others. There is no place to fall; so I drape him like a cat over my shoulder, his head down so he will not die standing up. Everywhere sloshes women's blood and vomit. There is one can for waste. It is never emptied and the smell is like a slaughterhouse. So you see about brave. You see how we stop singing long before we come to Oświęcim—Auschwitz, as the Germans call it. This is how we come—train of Jews, bounded together for three days without food in the dark and stench of ourselves.

"When they open the sliding doors and sun and cold rush in on us, no one even moves. Thirty of us in my car are piled up dead, so the rest can sit. Erich and I use a child's corpse for a pillow the last night. It only takes three days to make us do that. Is that brave? Three days and two cups of water. No food. The SS jump into the cars and prod us out with canes. But is very organized in their shouts and in so little time we line up on the Oświęcim train platform in neat rows of men and women. Like gymnasium. We are told, 'Hold up your cups and the Oberstleutnant gives you drink when you pass by....'

"Can you imagine our thirst? My lips are two blisters, swollen shut. When I look at Erich I see he is fainting again. He licks his lips always like a dog and his eyes are full of mucus. This mucus makes me thirstier. I want to lick his eyes; I want to throw myself off the platform and lick dew on the grass. I will, if I don't know the SS man next to me speaking clear and calm is there to whack my skull with his stick.

"Such is the stupidity of a man dying of thirst, that I still do not believe the Nazis are to kill me.... So we wait our turn to drink and the line is no end. They sort through women first. Striped men in uniform with shave heads move about us like ghosts stripping us of bags, rings, watches... I think these men are Jews, too... but they say to us nothing. When a woman asks in Yiddish a striped ghost near me *What will we do?* he says nothing, does not even move to her whisper. Walking shadows in stripes...." Here Tata paused and glanced at his son out of the corner of his eye. Without warning, Tata demanded, "'Canada?' Do you know the name?"

"I... I know the country," Joseph responded, confused.

"*Tak*... full of riches, the country. But the walking shadows in stripes are called *Canada*, too. Think why!"

Joseph was silent. He had not expected Tata to interrupt his story with such questions. At last he said hesitantly, as if answering a question in school, "Maybe because those men were taking away all you owned... so they were rich, too."

Tata sat back and laughed without mirth. "My Yoncle," he said, "always he is the good student.

"You are right. The Canada Jews are good prisoners. They tell us nothing for fear they will be killed alongside us. And they are rich, because they are still alive. That's what I think, then, when I see them move among us on the platform.

"At the end of the platform lines are moving. There is the Oberstleutnant at the head of the line. He flicks his finger this way and that, sending some in a line to the left, others to right. He is bored, you can see. There is no logic or thinking in his decisions — except that he makes sure there are many more children on the left than the right line. For one moment I feel happy standing there because I am glad the children go with their mothers. I do not yet know this is the line that goes first into Birkenau and Number One Killing Factory.

"We can see its chimneys from the train platform and we think it is for baking bread. They will feed us here, we think, as soon as they give us drink. Erich stands next to me and he murmurs to himself. Sometime the night before he had a fever and is not right in his mind. But now he makes perfect sense when he suddenly laughs and says, very calm, 'Ah, there is a pattern here, look at the Oberstleutnant's choices.' Erich tells me, 'He thinks he is directing our fates like a great maestro. But he is a man of no imagination. Look, the way he never changes tempo. He is only a mathematician — a human metronome. He has no ear. Look, there... he counts off three, then one to the right. Three left, then one right....' Erich begins to laugh and then shouts in Hungarian to the others, 'Three against two. Three to die, one to live! But if Herr Oberstleutnant had a better ear, he can make music out of us. He can make a death march!' Then Erich is slammed in his ear with a rifle butt and he falls against me. I have more weight, yet I am weak, too. I cannot carry him. But I see that Erich makes sense.

"Most in the line pay no attention to Erich's warning. I listen. I give a man near me a beautiful watch that Canada has not find on me. I ask the man to hold up Erich and then I take my place four men down. Here I wait and when it comes Erich's turn he sudden stands straight without help, eyes the Oberstleutnant and gives him a smile, though the side of his head is smash and blood everywhere. It is the smile, I think, that saves him.

"The Oberstleutnant pauses, lights a cigarette, then nods to himself like he is remembering his rhythm. So, *tak! Dobrze!* He flicks Erich to the right and then, after three men, it is me he sends to stand beside my friend.

"I am happy! I am happy because they give us water then and when I drink I am still beside Erich.... "

There were tears streaming from Tata's eyes and Joseph wondered how these eyes had ever, for a moment, frightened him. And though Joseph had seen his father weep all his life, this seemed the first time Tata had ever really cried. Or perhaps it was the first time Joseph could ever comfort.

Reaching out to take Tata's wrists, Joseph breathed, "*Bądź spokojny* ... shhhhh, Tato ... " then Joseph shook his head, startled at his own words. How could he have remembered words that he no longer understood? Who had first taught him such solace?

Tata took the words within, without question, and he let Joseph keep hold of each wrist. When at last Tata spoke, the old man's eyes rested on his son's face as if recognizing a countryman. "Ahhhh ... ahhhhh.... " For a moment Joseph thought the old man might call him 'Erich,' but then Tata hesitated and said, "Ahhh, Yoncle, if you know me then ... before the war ... you will love me ... not pity ... not this.... " He looked down at Joseph's hands, then his own wrists. Then Tata tenderly disengaged himself. "You are hearing me?" he asked.

"Yes, Tato ... ," Joseph answered, "I hear."

"I tell you that I am still with my friend, but that is a lie. That day on the platform is the last that I am with Erich Schuchman. I never see him again."

"But what happened to him?" Joseph asked, feeling a prickling at the nape of his neck. There was something not right here; he could feel it. Tata did not answer, so again Joseph asked, almost demanded, "What happened to Erich?"

Tata looked down at his hands. At last he said in a halting voice, "I do not know."

It was a lie, Joseph could see it in Tata's every movement and expression. "You know!" Joseph burst out. "Tell me!"

"Maybe... ," Tata began slowly, still not meeting his son's eyes, "maybe he did evil things."

"It was an evil place," Joseph said and leaned toward Tata. Nothing had ever seemed more important—no fact of history or schooling. Joseph lowered his head and said in a low voice, "You named me after Erich; I have a right to know my namesake...."

"He'd dead," Tata said, "and you are alive."

Then Joseph was furious. He stood up, yelling, "Yeah, I am! And I'm real sorry about that. I'm real sorry you had to put yourself out like that!" Joseph coughed, then couldn't stop coughing. When he found his voice again, his anger spent, he sat down, saying in a subdued tone, "You're lying to me."

"Yes, Yoncle," Tata said quietly, and looked at him directly. "I lie."

"Don't," Joseph asked. "At least... at least tell me... "

"If I tell you," Tata said, "do not be afraid... "

"Afraid?"

"Of me," Tata finished.

And Joseph could not tell his father that all his life he had been afraid of him, for him. Instead, Joseph nodded and waited for Tata to continue.

"I do not want you to be afraid," Tata began, his voice as empty as Joseph felt—empty and expectant. "But Erich is not afraid that day on the platform when we are send to showers. These showers do not kill us, only lice. In the water running over us, Erich turns to me and says, 'We must imagine, Karl, that you and I, we each will live without the other. Just as we must imagine—when we practice only our own parts—the rest of the orchestra.' Those are his last words to me before they take him to another camp." Tata said nothing more.

"What did you say to him?"

Tata seemed stunned by the question, so stunned that he answered automatically, *"Ja Kocham Ciebie,* Erich... I said."

"What?"

"You know the words."

"No, I don't, Tato...," Joseph said, "I don't remember what it means."

"You remember," Tata said softly, and dropped his chin on his chest.

Then Joseph did. It was what his mother used to say to him in that soft, lullaby voice. *"Kochamie..."* It sounded like *ahem*—the lyrical clearing of the voice, the heart. Joseph let out the breath he had not realized he'd been holding and said, "You loved him, Tato. Of course, you loved him..."

"I let him die." Tata raised his head and his face was absolutely blank, as if all features were washed away.

"People die, Tato," Joseph said, "whether we let them or not." Joseph's voice was strong and full, but then he doubted himself. Of course, Tata knew about death. He knew everything about it; and his son knew nothing.

"Will you let me die, then?" Tata asked.

Joseph was confused. He shook his head vehemently, "Of course not, Tato... I would never..." Then Joseph could say no more.

Tata, too, said nothing. There was only the sound of the furnace throbbing. The basement was very warm, but Joseph had begun shivering. He waited; he didn't know if Tata would stand up and leave now or if he would finish his story. There was nothing at all Joseph could do.

After what seemed like an hour, Tata said in the softest voice Joseph had ever heard from the old man, *"Sonderkommando...* tak, remember this word—*Sonderkommando.* It is the only German word you must ever learn, because it is another name for your father."

Joseph caught his breath. It was not because he knew the word; it was because on Tata's breath it sounded like the softest, most terrible blasphemy.

"*Sonderkommando*—we were worse than the walking shadows of Canada. They, at least, just take possessions. We who work in Killing Factory Number Two at Birkenau take possession of bodies, souls, the last cries. We are devils who say nothing as we drive the trucks to that circle of white birches, or walk with women and children to showers. " 'Hush,' we say in soft voices. 'There is nice soap for you inside. You will be clean . . . no more sores. . . . ' " Tata spoke as if it were increasingly hard for him to breathe, and Joseph felt a rising panic. But he was not afraid for his father; he was afraid for himself. Suddenly Joseph didn't want to hear anymore, and he raised a hand but could not say anything to silence Tata. Tata's voice went on like a chant, an incantation. "*Sonderkommando*. We *are* special. We are Jews who walk into the crematoriums and gas chambers. We walk out with bodies, not souls. The other Jews leave these places with their souls, but no bodies. Their bodies are being sorted by the *Sonderkommando*. Sorted and burned and what is not human saved—gold teeth, jewels women hide inside like their babies and men swallow in the death showers." Tata stopped, changed his position on the ottoman. This made little puffs of gray push out of the upholstery. Joseph stared at the escaping stuffing and felt his own panic center in his belly. But then his father continued.

"I am here in this Killing Factory Number Two for two years. I am walking dead, walking with living Jews to their death. I feel and see and hear nothing. I am not human. Only my hands work. I do not remember myself. I do not remember a time when I play violin or make watches or drink beer in a café. I do not remember my mother or sister or Izakitus or Erich Schuchman. I know I am an orphan and alone of all my kind. One day I forget even to get up and move from one side of the factory to the other. I sit still in the yard and pick my sores, half human, like ape who preens. Another man in the *Sonderkommando* comes to me. I see him sometimes look at me across our crematorium; he sorts bones and gold and says nothing. But when I just sit down in the yard to die, he kneels beside me and says, 'What are you doing?' I say nothing. 'Do your work,' he says and, though he is like stick, puts his shoulder under mine. 'Why?' I ask and just slump. He lets me lean, says, 'We're keeping the whole world spinning here. You must do your work.'

"I laugh and push him away then. 'We're killing the whole world here,' I tell him and think for a moment I might hit him down. Then this man takes me by the skin of my neck and shakes me hard. He tells me he is anthropologist and before this war spent time digging bones—why should he not do the same work now? He says that there are Indian tribes in some country that believe to dig and bury bones makes us human. He says that these rituals—rattling bones and picking teeth and scalping the hair—spin the world. If we ever stop, so will the world.

" 'The world *is* stopped,' I tell him and yell, but I keep standing up and do not fall down in the yard again like a ape. 'The world is stopped spinning for one minute only,' he tells me, 'like you.' "

Tata paused, took a sharp breath, then continued, "So one day I am still spinning the world . . . it is maybe a year later and it is only two weeks before the Russian army will reach us. The Nazis speed up the gassing to destroy evidence. They will kill us *Sonderkommando* as soon as we finish. But I don't know this. I know only that I must do my work.

"I am walking a group of women from the typhus infirmary to the gas chamber. On the death march I sometimes count in my head—three-against-two, three-against-two. Syncopation. . . . " Tata turned to Joseph and asked absently, "Do you know syncopation . . . how it sounds? Tah-tah-*tah-tah*. Tah-tah-*tah-tah* . . . do you hear it, Yoncle? It is the rhythm in my head and hands. . . . *Tak!*" Tata nodded to himself. "On this day I am marching and suddenly it is Erich beside me as we go into the gas chamber.

"It is Erich who recognizes me first. He lets out a little squeak. But he says nothing. And I see that my friend is not really there inside—only a reflex of remembering. He can do no more than notice that I am somehow important to him. But he cannot remember why. He is all bones and eyes and sores and when I look at his hands they are broke in bits. There is one moment when I think I can pick Erich up on my back and run—run somewhere they'll see us and shoot fast. I even know the SS man who shoots the best. But what do my hands and feet do?

"They do their work. I walk toward the showers and carry my friend who feels sharp already like bones and so light he is ashes in my arms. 'Erich,' I say to him in a voice as I call a child, 'Erich, I am glad you come to me now,' I say, '... now, when I can help you.' I see him smile, an idiot smile. And then I begin to pick filth from his face. I rock him until he is very little. 'My son,' I call him, 'Bądź spokojny ... shhhhhh.'

"I wait until they have send all others into the chamber. At last I lay Erich on top of two women who are unconscious already from typhus. Their breathing is so hard it rocks Erich. I want to sing and make him to sleep before gas; but no song I remember. I remember nothing but *my* hands are last to touch him, *my* body carries him to die. When the guard closes the door and screams begin, it is Erich's voice I hear above all others—his high tenor. But he is not singing. He is screaming my name...

"Only then do I beg the guard to open again the door and let me die with my friend. The guard tells me, 'Nein, du habst starke hände ...' and they need strong hands here...."

Tata touched his son on the shoulder and Joseph flinched and fell back. "So, it wasn't the Nazis who...." Joseph began.

"On the day the Russian Army reaches our camp," Tata continued as if he hadn't heard, "... on that day when they gasp to see us through the barbed wire and we gasp to see them outside..., on this day when many of us die for joy, just topple over, our hearts burst—I stand in front of the trucks as the SS men from my killing factory make their escape. I kneel down in mud and put my hands under the wheels of their truck. And when it spins its wheels deeper and deeper into the ground it is my hands under those tires. I hear bones breaking, but it is far away. Mud sucks me up to my armpits. I feel nothing.

"When the Russians march into Birkenau they see my hands and curse my enemy and take me to hospital. It is there I meet your mother. It is there, sometime later I don't remember . . . that we make you." Tata stopped and yawned. As he yawned he stretched and then sank into himself. After a while, Tata added, almost absently, "So you see to what use I put my hands."

"But you made me," Joseph repeated dully. He said it the way a child repeats a litany learned from a dead language—like Latin or Yiddish.

And Tata's response was as much by rote. "Yes, Yonkle," he sighed, "such as you are, we made you. Your mother and me."

In the belly of Tata's house, the only sound was the furnace, its rumble like the eerie gurgling of a great whale, gap-mouthed, as it moved through the deepest waters. Tata seemed preoccupied with the noise, as if it were another presence.

At last Tata spoke. "When you are born, Yonkle, I believe . . . I think that it is Erich come back to me. But then your mother dies and I know better. Erich is dead; Elena is dead. And me—I cannot die because I have this baby . . . I have to carry him." Tata gazed at Joseph as if he weren't there. He stared, then dropped his eyes. "So . . . maybe I think Erich does come back—to punish me. Because I must carry you, Yonkle, like I do Erich." Tata stood up, finished. "The years," he said. With great effort he began climbing the basement stairs, hand over hand over hand. " . . . All the years I carried you—I carry you both."

Joseph turned away from his father. He did not watch to make sure the old man made it upstairs. If Tata fell, he would not die. Death would be the real gift. That would be what Tata wanted for his birthday.

Not this stupid old chair. Staring down at its wide, wooden slopes, Joseph wondered how he could ever have imagined that anything he made might hold Tata's full weight. He couldn't carry his father; he could hardly bear even to hear the old man's story. So why was Joseph here? And why did the old man have to live on in his son?

This was what his father was telling him, Joseph realized as he laid down his woodworking tools. He should return the plane to the woodshop and accept the consequences of his theft; he should forget becoming a sculptor and working with his hands. He must find some other skill, some other way to survive. After all, to hear Tata tell it, every Girard before Joseph was a genius at something.

Except living!, Joseph wanted to shout up the stairs after the old man. But instead he was very still, listening to the belch and rumble of the boiler. Did the killing factory furnace make this contented noise as Tata carried all those frail bodies inside its steel womb? Thinking of Erich like a child in Tata's arms, Joseph lowered his head—and at last the tears came.

He was not to cry like this for another sixteen years, or to hold another man's hands, or to carry the weight of another man's body. From that night on Joseph knew he was not made to carry anyone else but himself. And he would only do that because thirteen years ago in a Prague displacement camp two survivors had made him, and he would not fall through their hands to break.

The night of his unexpected *bar mitzvah* Joseph resolved that when Tata did die one day, he would bodily carry the old man to his grave. The second vow Joseph made on this, the threshold of his manhood, was very simple: he would never have children. Joseph would not make them carry him, carry his name, carry on.

Part IV

THE NEW YEAR

1973

10

THE EVIDENCE

OF THINGS NOT SEEN

Lying on opposite ends of the dark leather couch, Ruth leaned forward, tucking her childhood comforter around their legs.

"Cold?" she asked, shivering slightly herself. "I think March is always the coldest because you want so for winter to be over." Over her white silk camisole, Ruth pulled Joseph's rough robe close across her breasts. "Winter has a way of wearing one down."

"I'm just right," Lauren said. She luxuriated in a stolen pair of hospital-green scrub pants her sister had sent her for a Christmas present. She was almost too warm in her little brother's wool sweater—a hand-me-up, as Lauren's siblings often called their shared, vaguely military wardrobe. Joseph called this frayed sweater, with its hundreds of tufted fuzz balls dotting elbows and sleeves like an alien life-form, Lauren's "starving writer sweater."

Earlier this evening, Lauren had offered her sweater to Joseph when he was looking for something to wear for his weekly meeting with Daniel Sorenson.

"Maybe I *will* wear that old ragamuffin thing," Joseph said, and took Lauren's favorite sweater with a confused, flustered expression. He hardly noticed the hurt in her eyes. "I get tired of dressing up for him."

Ruth stood by the stove supervising the brewing after-dinner coffee. She shot Joseph a reproving glance, but said nothing. Then she noticed Lauren's expression, the way Lauren always looked whenever Ruth and Joseph came close to squabbling. Ruth dropped her voice. "Don't be late for him, Joseph," she said, and gave him a fresh cup of black coffee.

Joseph went to the refrigerator and swung it open. "No cream, dammit!"

"I'll get some," Lauren hurriedly volunteered. "Just be a minute." She was lunging for her coat and knit cap when Joseph roughly caught her arm.

"No," he said, and again his face was flushed, confused. "I'm sorry, just forget it, all right? Besides, I don't want coffee now. I'll have to drink potfuls to stay awake tonight." Then he ripped Lauren's sweater over his head and tossed it angrily on the kitchen table. "And I don't need this either!"

As he strode down the hall, he called back to Ruth, "Where's my new shirt?"

"I took it to the cleaners," Ruth answered.

"Naturally!" Joseph yelled.

Lauren picked up her sweater from the kitchen table. She lifted it to her face.

When Ruth handed Lauren her coffee, Lauren accepted it with a hesitant smile. "I can drink it black," she offered. And as if to prove it, Lauren drank half a cupful in one gulp.

"Don't try to make up for Joseph, Lauren. He's being a perfect ass."

Joseph walked into the kitchen in his finest trousers and a gray cotton shirt. Without meeting their eyes, he pulled on his overcoat and muttered, "See you in the morning." He closed the door softly behind him, but with the finality of a slam.

Ruth and Lauren listened to his footsteps in the lobby. It was Joseph's habit to forget something he needed to face these weekly editorial sessions with Daniel.

And he did again, and knocked. Lauren opened the door and Joseph entered. He turned to Lauren and gave her a direct, penitent look. "I would have ruined your sweater, kiddo, the way I sweat in the subway. But thanks anyway...." Then he crossed to Ruth. He took a deep gulp from her coffee and shook his head. "Sorry," he said. "Sorry I'm such a pain in the ass. You know I'd rather stay here."

Ruth nodded and smiled at him sadly. "I know, Joseph."

And then he was gone again.

Both women listened to the ding-ding of the elevator, the doors shuddering shut. Then, letting out her breath, Ruth said, "At least he didn't pretend to forget something."

"He acts as if what he's forgetting to bring with him all the time is us," Lauren commented quietly, and sipped her coffee. "Or maybe he's trying to forget us."

"Maybe he has to leave us and everything else behind when he works, don't you think?"

"Perhaps," Lauren said slowly, "but I think he'd be better off to bring his own world and balance it with his work, not abandon his daily life in order to write." Lauren was thoughtful a moment, then added, "But I really don't think Joseph's mood tonight has much to do with his writing. I think it has to do with Mr. Sorenson."

"Perhaps so," Ruth said, and dropped the subject.

It was only hours later, when she and Lauren were installed in their comfortable places on the couch, that Ruth again brought up Joseph.

"I'm trying to be patient with him," she told Lauren. *Patient*, Ruth repeated to herself. Even though Joseph's recent moods made them distant, meant they hadn't made love in ages. In their bed Ruth felt Joseph's real distance. They didn't argue—at least they didn't argue aloud. Neither wanted Lauren to overhear.

"I'll fix us both a hot buttered brandy," Lauren offered now. Slowly she unravelled herself from the comforter and walked in stockinged feet to the kitchen.

"Rum, please," Ruth called out. "You haven't made a Southerner of me yet, Lauren."

When Lauren returned with their drinks, she settled in at her end of the couch with a great yawn. "So . . . ," she asked, "where were we?" Then she noticed that Ruth herself had drowsed off, head thrown back against the comforting leather arm of the couch.

Smiling, Lauren used her foot gently to shake Ruth awake. "Want me to sing you a lullaby?" Lauren asked. During college she had earned money by opening a lullaby service on call all hours. School seemed to make insomniacs more than it made scholars. Lauren began humming to herself a lullaby her grandfather's mammy had taught him which he, in turn, had willed to her.

With an undignified snort that Lauren regarded with generosity, Ruth awoke.

"Well, honey," Lauren laughed, "for a moment there I thought you was dead."

Ruth smiled. "Couch death?"

"Otherwise known as Sudden Adult Death," Lauren giggled. "S.A.D.!"

Ruth took another sip of her brandy and felt quite silly. "I wonder if what they diagnosed as neurasthenia in Victorian women was really a lingering epidemic of Sudden Adult Death?"

"Oh, Victorian ladies were the original couch slugs," Lauren said as if she'd researched the subject thoroughly.

"No, I think it started long ago."

"In the Garden of Eden?" Lauren asked, laughing. "Look, here's my theory: the Victorians were imperfectly trying to remember an ancient feminine art form—*being*, not doing. But during an Industrial Revolution, who could respect the simple, quiet and particularly physical art of just being still?"

"Lauren, those Victorian ladies weren't being still," Ruth argued, her face rosy from the fire in the Victorian fireplace. "They were only quiet because they were strait-jacketed! I mean, corsets choked the life from them. They couldn't even breathe. What you see as bucolic feminine Buddhas were really women wasting away."

"I wonder . . . ," Lauren said, and leaned back, sipping her brandy. "I think they knew something about surrender that we've forgotten, with our competition and our trying to be better men than most men."

"Yes," Ruth said with a snort, "they knew about giving up . . . just like caged animals understand self-containment and self-control, after a life running smack up against the walls of their cells."

"Well, we're not in cells now," Lauren laughed. "So maybe we can just give up every now and then . . . secretly. Don't let the world know."

"I call this resting," Ruth said. "Not giving up."

"And I call it settling in, giving up the good fight. We can pitch our tents right far away from the battle and get ourselves some real R & R."

"Now that you're a civilian you've taken your off-duty time to an extreme," Ruth said. "I wouldn't want to be this way all the time," Ruth said, "would you?"

"No, ma'am," Lauren laughed again. "But it sure ain't bad. And it feels kind of old and female. Might be some wisdom to it."

"Don't you get afraid sometimes when you're just doing nothing, like this—especially in a place like New York City where everything is swirling around you, and seems so alive, even *without* you—that if you stay still for too long you'll just . . . " Ruth paused and knelt down to poke in the fire. "You'll just rot or die."

"Maybe that's what we're really afraid of," Lauren said softly. "Lots of times at home when I was supposed to be hoeing a row in my father's huge garden, I'd just sit down in the dirt and stare. At nothing. It felt right. . . . " Lauren smiled and dropped into her deepest accent. "I felt right fertile. Like I was growing alongside them vegetables."

"That's how gardens grow, my friend." Ruth now was laughing, too. "Not, I suspect, people."

"It is how we grow on the inside," Lauren corrected her gently and with, Ruth thought, an expression of authority that showed she was taking her full place beside Ruth as a friend. Ruth realized that this must be the way Lauren talked to her sister Clare at home when she knew she was safe, accepted, family.

"Perhaps you are right," Ruth smiled, and clambered back on the couch. "Right fertile." She picked up her drink and swirled it in front of the firelight. "Let's go back to those Victorian ladies," Ruth said. "What would you have done in that century?"

"Well," Lauren declared, "No way would I be a governess.... " She sat up, insisting to the chair across from her as if someone sat there proposing the very idea. "And no prostitute neither." Lauren turned to face Ruth. "Those were the only choices for women who wanted to do anything besides just *breed*."

"You say that with so much respect, my dear," Ruth commented. "What's wrong with breeding? According to your waxing eloquent about the fertile feminine way, breeding should be greatly honored."

Lauren fell silent a long time, then began thoughtfully, "That's right. Hellfire, I guess I'm confused.... "

"And I never am," Ruth laughed. "How difficult it is for me to truly understand human imperfection!"

Lauren laughed now, too. Then she sat up and said, "You know, Ruth, I really used to fall for all that stuff about the ideal—art is better than life—Plato's spiritual children. I used to believe that making a book or a painting was much higher than just birthing a baby. But now, honey, I don't know. My mother used to say she was going to have a baby *and* a book. She had me; then, she stopped writing."

"And so which would you rather have?" Ruth asked, her face half in the shadow of firelight.

Lauren shook her head vehemently, "But that's just it! Why choose one over the other? *Both* are human creations—the baby *and* the book. Both are flawed, but you can still hold them in your hands. Each give back mightily, a hundred-fold, 'showers of blessing,' as my Grandmother says." Lauren lowered her voice, "And dammit all to hell, men don't have to choose between babies or books."

"Oh," Ruth interrupted, "but they have already chosen. It's the masculine mind that rates spiritual or artistic creation over simply giving birth to a child."

"Why, that's because they can't *do* it!" Lauren laughed.

"But it's not really just men," Ruth said shaking her head, "it's the masculine part of all of us that has contempt for the real, human creations."

Both women fell silent for a long time, sipping their hot buttered drinks and staring into the fire. "So what's the logical extreme of that kind of contempt... ," Lauren asked softly, "contempt that we all have, men and women?"

"I don't want to think about it," Ruth said.

"Well, look at it," Lauren continued. "The logical extreme of that masculine contempt we all have for just plain birthing, the reward for always choosing spirit over body is transcending that poor, little body itself—and so abandoning the whole wide world. 'This world is not my home, I'm just apassin' through... ' " Lauren sang the gospel softly. She fell silent. At last she began again with a frown, "You know, if we really believe our masculine God only wants our spirits, then isn't our greatest act of love, and of creation to destroy our bodies, to just blow the world sky high?" Lauren turned to Ruth with a strange look. "Why, honey, that must be why they call it *The Rapture.*"

"Oh," Ruth said softly, as if the wind had been knocked from her. "So even eroticism is based on death."

"Surely not all of it?" Lauren suggested. Then they both fell silent.

Perhaps it was the hot buttered liquor, the flare of the fire, the bulk of the childhood comforter—but Ruth felt suddenly heavy and constricted, as if even her skin were too much weight, and she needed desperately to escape the dense prison of her body. It didn't matter, Ruth thought suddenly, that she wasn't a corseted Victorian governess held back by her times; she felt physically as limited, captured and corseted. This thought made her head pound; then she felt that dreaded, familiar ache at the base of her skull. Pain jabbed her temples, pushing to her forehead and her eyes.

"Oh, no," she breathed softly as if not to disturb herself.

"What?" Lauren asked, leaning near.

"I'm either very drunk or this is the aura of a migraine coming on."

Another bolt of pain between her eyes made Ruth sit back as if struck by a fist. "Ohhh. . . . " She tried to laugh, but couldn't. "I'm getting punished for all our sacreligious talk about a God who wants human sacrifice. He's declared war on my head."

"But you forget," Lauren laughed softly and took Ruth's bare feet in her hands. Slowly she began rubbing them with her calm and deliberate hands. "Tonight we're off-duty. R & R, remember?" Her touch communicated the same authority with which Lauren had addressed Ruth once before tonight, and Ruth, for all her pain, relaxed. Often Lauren had rubbed Ruth's feet; it was something her grandmother had taught Lauren, an old midwife's massage passed down along with the family's lullabies. Lauren taught Ruth this foot massage too, and they traded Grandmother's cramp cure during their periods, which now, of course, coincided. But Ruth had never suspected the foot rubbing might release a headache.

"That feels good . . . ," Ruth said, surprised. "Helps some."

"Oh, yes," Lauren said, completely absorbed in her massage work. "Do you think the headache is too far gone for me to work directly on your head?" Lauren asked.

"You know another grandmother massage?" Ruth asked, but already her vision was splitting in two and she felt her stomach turn. "Oh, I shouldn't have drunk that . . . "

"It wasn't the hot buttered brandy."

"Rum," Ruth quickly corrected, and she felt the fury that always accompanied her migraines. It was as if, in spite of herself, she turned into a hag or a witch: her native sweetness disappeared. This dark side of her, exposed, was what Ruth dreaded most about her migraines. Usually she would retire to her room claiming a need for quiet, but it was more a need to hide this terrible part of herself.

"Yes, rum," Lauren said. "Come, turn around and put your head in my lap."

Ruth resisted. Sticking her feet in Lauren's lap was familiar enough by now, but to put her head there, for another's hands to hold—that seemed too vulnerable and too childlike. Why, Ruth realized, she had never allowed even lovers to cradle her head. It was like some part of her body still kept its virginity, had been kept aloof from touch. It would take too much trust. Ruth was about to say *no* when a firestorm exploded in the exact center of her skull and she gasped. Her body turned itself around instinctively, the way a baby knows how to move from breech to birth position.

The strange thing was that it didn't seem unfamiliar to lay her head in someone else's open hands, though Ruth was quite certain her mother had never held her this way, nor Cook, nor her father. So what was the memory of it, almost an instinct? It felt very old, like a dream. Ruth at last closed her eyes.

On the left side of her head she felt the warm glow of the fire, but when she felt that same glow on the right temple, Ruth realized the warmth was radiating from Lauren's hands on either side of her skull.

"What were you thinking, right before the migraine hit you?" Lauren asked, voice very low, almost like a lullaby.

Ruth realized that her friend had never before seen her this raw and open, but she felt no fear, only a deep calm. "My body actually felt too tight, heavy, like I was trapped inside my own skin and I wanted to . . . to . . . "

"Explode? Blow up, get out of your body?" Lauren suggested softly, and when Ruth nodded, Lauren added, "That's what The Rapture will really feel like. There's really nothing erotic about blowing ourselves up. Not when we feel what that means in our bodies."

"No," Ruth answered, "it . . . " she grimaced as pain like an ice pick stabbed the base of her skull over and over. "It . . . "

"Hurts," Lauren finished for her. "Shhhhh, now you hush; honey. Be still."

"Be still and know," Ruth said, and felt a great dizziness overwhelm her. "It's what Sister Margaret Magdalene taught us."

"Forget about knowing.... Just be still."

"She also taught us the body was holy." Ruth thought she might cry. "But it doesn't *feel* holy, not now."

"Your body's afraid, that's all," Lauren said and, her hands clasped under the back of Ruth's skull, gently pressed upward, stroking the tight, long tendons running from neck to base of skull.

"Afraid?"

"Your body's afraid you want to leave her, desert her, blow her up. That's why you're in such pain. It's your body's way of going into mourning...." Lauren cupped Ruth's head now tenderly between her hands and rocked it back and forth very slowly, first one side, then the other. "At least that's what my grandmother used to say when she rubbed our bodies. She used to say, 'Body's got feelings too, children. You treat your barnyard pets better than you do your own bodies. So they squawk back sometimes, just begging a little of your time.'"

"Did your grandmother teach you this?" Ruth asked, and already her head felt softer, like a sweet summer melon held reverently between the hands, allowed just to stay on the vine in the sunshine and slowly grow.

Ruth lay back in what she imagined to be Lauren's grandmother's great summer garden. Wasps buzzed along the dense yellow corn squash tendrils and curling vines. Everything growing smelled musky and ripe. Her skull was simply a succulent pale rind, lush and sweet as honeydew. Fingers could press, stroke, and probe as Lauren's did now and Ruth's skull would gladly yield, malleable and tender as a newborn's head conforming to the curve and flow of the mother's birth canal. Born with bone supple and safe, the whole skull as responsive to touch as the vulnerable spot that stays open in the top of the head. Ruth had read once that the Hopi Indians believed this compliant circle in the center of the newborn's head was a door, the gods' and goddesses' entrance to our bodies.

Now her own head was wide open, shaping itself in someone else's hands. Ruth gave way to the deepest pleasure—not as if she'd abandoned her body, but more as if she had finally entered it through some physical doorway that was before left open only for God. This was what Sister Margaret Magdalene must have meant about holiness: the spirit finally takes up full residence inside its shining, soft, astonishing skin. Ruth felt the stretch of it, miles of skin from head to toe, half a continent at least, luxurious, expansive, *breathing*.

Skin moved with her, expanded wide with her, narrowed if she needed; every inch of it was erotic, attuned to touch, to sunlight and cool shadows. It was, in fact, here that she belonged. Here, right here inside her own skin. Within this world of skin, bone, blood, and long muscle she did not have to explode; her body opened naturally to breathe, to bring within, to give birth. In the ripeness and wisdom of the body's time, she let herself open out at the top of her head and let her belly grow soft and round like a baby's skull. Then the doorway between her legs, like the door in the top of her skull, was wide open for the gods and the babies to go in and out, like prayers, thoughts, creations.

As Lauren's hands clasped Ruth's skull, fingers finding the bony ridges and sutures, moving her skull as if it were the tectonic plates of the pulsing earth itself, Ruth remembered once her yoga teacher, Rebecca, confiding in her a secret of Rebecca's own birth:

This is what my mother told me when I was eighteen, Rebecca had said, *and she told me she'd kept it secret all this time because I should be the first to know. I was her eighth child of eleven and during my birth my mother suddenly felt all the pain stop; and there was this wide, gaping sense of wonder, not in her mind, but right there in her body, in her belly. She couldn't believe it. There the doctors and nurses stood around watching for the baby's head to crown and my mother was doing the usual screaming and protesting when all of a sudden those cries changed to pleasure. My mother said she realized the doctors couldn't tell the difference, so she just screamed her head off in ecstasy and gave way to the deepest, most erotic movement within her. She was so astonished she thought perhaps she'd died and was in heaven, but the pleasure kept growing and right there on the operating table at the moment I was born she had the most complete orgasm she'd ever felt before or since.*

Now, what do you think of that? my mother asked when she told me. That was you, baby.

And I said, I guess I was glad to be here.

Ruth was glad to be here, too, she thought, and at last opened her eyes. Lauren was bending over her, face perfectly composed. She looked as if she might be asleep or in a trance.

"Know what?" Lauren asked, her voice deep and very distinct.

"What?" Ruth smiled.

"In some tribes, when a loved one dies, women take his skull and set it out in the sunlight to be scoured clean until it's bright white, dazzling. Then they seal the ridges and sutures and use the skull for a drinking gourd."

"For rituals?"

Lauren laughed. "No, for just everyday. Every time you take a drink it's from the skull of someone you loved."

"I'll will you my skull, Lauren, you've done so well by it."

Lauren laughed and said, "Thank you. I'll take it."

"Then we won't be bloodsisters, we'll be bone-sisters. How about that?" Ruth felt her own laughter resonate inside her skull and she stretched long like a cat.

"No more pain," Ruth said simply, "only pleasure. I suppose that means you'll have to stop?"

"No, ma'am," Lauren said. "Grandmother taught me not to stop—the real healing happens on the other side of pain . . . in the *pleasurin'*, that's what she called it."

Ruth's laugh was a rumbling in her belly that ran up her spine and echoed between her ears. "Go on. Be my guest." She smiled to herself, imagining that the door on top of her skull was opening for Lauren, too. Whomever Ruth wanted she could take in; through either door, Ruth realized, and whatever she wanted to birth could also come forth from her, through whichever door. Both creations came from love—and all who entered her she would love.

Lauren's hands rubbed circular patterns now in Ruth's skull;

light finger-tapping to forehead and temples, thumbs warm and massaging on top of head, ears, then into the little dents, like holes in a coconut, at the base of the head. At last Lauren pulled Ruth's head straight out from the neck and Ruth's entire spine gratefully released. Lauren's hands held Ruth's skull in a deep clasp, as if Ruth's skull between her hands were a prayer. Suddenly there was a vibrato in Lauren's hands, at first subtle, then electric, a trembling passed from hand to head. It was like heat lightning following the nerves and synapses inside Ruth's skull, a warm, human vibrato following the pathways where only pain used to go.

"Oh," Ruth breathed. "You'll have to teach me this, your grandmother's summer-garden way of growing."

Lauren laughed ad finished the massage with a brusque and refreshing scalp rub.

Ruth sat up cross-legged and shook her head. "Do I have to get a migraine to have another head massage sometime?" she asked.

"Course not," Lauren said, and leaned back on the leather arm, finishing her hot buttered brandy with one long swallow. "My grandmother rubbed our little heads all the time. Not a big deal. We got her hands whenever we wanted."

"How lucky you were to have summers with her," Ruth said. "You know, I believed it *was* summer there for a while. Are you cold?"

Lauren simply smiled and held out her hands for Ruth to see; they were ruddy and warm from their work.

"I have to tell you a secret," Ruth said, but then fell silent for so long that Lauren at last got up from the couch and squatted in front of the fireplace, tending it as if Ruth's reverie were really a way of resting.

"You know, Lauren," Ruth at last began in her soft, musing voice. "Sometimes I think this apartment is too big, even with all of us here. All my life I've tried somehow to fill it all up, all this space."

"Maybe it's just that some part of you still feels small here?" Lauren suggested.

"Yes," Ruth said slowly, "there's that. But I've always felt I had too much just given me. The more money I give away, the more I seem to have; it accumulates somehow, you see... wealth does. My father even *made* money off the Littlefield Arts Foundation. It hardly seems fair."

"Makes perfect sense, honey," Lauren said. "Some tribes, the important people were those who could give the most. Now it's who *gets* the most."

"I would like to give more," Ruth said, her voice almost a whisper. "Or maybe I'm deceiving myself. Maybe I want something. Maybe I'm lonely in a way that you can't imagine, Lauren."

"How?"

"Imagine that you were an only child. Can you?"

"Nope," Lauren said slowly, "not really."

"And imagine that you've always wanted a child, yet a child is the one gift never given you."

"Gotten to the part about the father yet?" Lauren asked. "Or is this a gift you're giving yourself?"

"Carl couldn't have children," Ruth explained and stared down at her hands, wrapped in the comforter as in a muff. "Joseph doesn't ever want them."

"What'll you do?"

Ruth was quiet, then her expression changed from a distracted frown to a defiant, direct gaze. "What I'm doing," she said, smiling. "I'll do what I'm doing."

Lauren smiled, too. "Just how long have you been... well, Doing It?"

"We haven't much," Ruth answered simply, "not for a while."

Lauren nodded gravely. "Not because I've intruded?"

"No, if anything, Lauren, you've kept us together," Ruth admitted. "It's not you or Joseph. It's me. I've not been at all sensible about this."

"No, course you ain't," Lauren murmured.

"About six months ago—I think it was the first snowfall—when Joseph and I made love that night..." Ruth broke off, her voice full of feeling. "Oh, there's no reason for it. I just threw away my diaphragm, just like that." Vehemently, Ruth shook her head. "I can't make any sense of it, of what I'm doing, what I'm trying to do."

Ruth watched her friend make the mental calculation: six months of lovemaking with no protection. Still, Ruth wasn't pregnant. Lauren gazed at her friend, who shivered and pulled Joseph's robe more tightly around her. "It's cold in here," Ruth said. "And just a few moments ago I believed it was summer. Aren't you cold?"

"No," Lauren answered with a look of tenderness. "There's the fire."

"Yes," Ruth said softly, "and if we were in some primitive tribe we could sit drinking our liquor from the skulls of people we loved . . . ; then I might not be so cold."

"Time for a toast," Lauren said, and was halfway to the kitchen when Ruth murmured.

"What if I find out I'm barren, Lauren?" Ruth's face in the firelight was very old and very new as she waited for Lauren to speak.

"Listen," Lauren spoke after a time in a calm, clear voice. "There's no such thing as being barren. *We're* here, ain't we? My grandmother used to say—and she should know, being a midwife —*everything,* even a thought, even a lullaby, even a daily cup of coffee offered in love, is some kind of birth." For a moment longer Lauren stood in the kitchen doorway, empty mugs in hand. "So I'll teach you the lullabies I've inherited," she said.

"Just in case I need them?"

Lauren gazed at Ruth from across the room, then said very quietly, "You'll need them. Every man, woman, and child needs lullabies, Ruth." Then she disappeared into the kitchen.

After a moment, Ruth threw off her childhood comforter and knelt before the fire. Idly she knocked wood ash against the glowing grate. She squatted on her haunches the way Ruth had watched Lauren sit for hours at a time. Once Ruth had thought this posture unfeminine. What would her mother have said to find her daughter squatting before a fire as if she were not in a living room but in the desert? Yet now Ruth felt so very comfortable this way: knees tucked tightly against her breasts, bottom supported by bare heels, and her belly unclenched like a hand within her opening—a small eternity, an open door of skin and bone that could stretch to embrace another's body or simply shape itself deep and full, imperfect and complete.

JOSEPH stretched his full length onto the sofa. There was no time to make it to a bed. On his belly, he thrust and twisted, bare bottom high and urgent. Daniel's cupped palms lifted him. Daniel, more dressed than not, shivered. He stood still above the boy who, pumping and driving his body into the sofabed, was lithe, living energy. Its power would not release Joseph, but wave after wave shook his frame as he writhed, raising tiny dust storms in the rough upholstery.

When it would begin like this, Daniel told himself that he was just going to watch, that these young, long legs with sweat glistening on tight, flexing calves could run on and on without the weight of Daniel's body. Daniel feared for his heart. He imagined it was paper-thin; that it was narrow, dried up, the color of dead leaves. When his heart beat too fast he felt a brittle rattling like his body was no more than a pile of leaves that Joseph high-kicked through, just on a jog.

But then came a pounding in the center of Daniel's chest. It started slow, yet soon it was a gallop. Daniel's heart thudded like hooves against some soft center. Daniel felt he might die. But the impossible always happened: he didn't just watch. He didn't watch now. His heart pounding in exact rhythm with Joseph's thrusts, Daniel knelt, lay the side of his face against the boy's skin. Joseph's heaving, muscular ass seemed another heart. It opened, not far, but Daniel was not that big. He was light—a leaf, a shadow, a rider whose bones were at last hollowed out by living, by riding. Here was bone and marrow and more life. When Daniel was within that small, open chamber of another's throbbing heart, he wasn't old, Joseph wasn't young. They were like spirit and body, spirit flowing in, body barely containing.

Daniel knew now, as he began his own slow writhing, that he had never completely fit inside his own body. He had always wanted out. Yet all his life he had reined himself in. Even now, at sixty-three, he still checked himself. But now Daniel remembered this: the dangerous ride, this trampling over the body to get out. He was outside himself in another body that gripped him fiercely. It seemed the only other place, besides himself, that Daniel could ever be. Once or twice he'd felt this tight, stroking grip when Myrna had been a girl and he a boy masquerading as a man. Five daughters later, his wife seemed simply open and vague, a warm, unboundaried pool.

Hella's openness was different; she was another world, one that Daniel could trust Hella herself to explore and chart. Daniel could wander in Hella, but she would always bring him back. Geography, as she always told him, was her strong suit. Hella predicted she would die in a traveling accident or, if she really lasted like Methuselah, during her morning treck to work. Hella's stride, even in her sixties, was headlong and sure.

But even Hella's heart and body could not take Daniel's passion like the narrow, tight boy below him now, who let Daniel ride over himself. Daniel clenched his teeth, biting his lips, and the blood tasted bright and full-bodied. He felt strong, young, limitless. He was running the way electricity runs along any body, any conductor. And Joseph supported him effortlessly, as if he were no weight at all, as if—Daniel smiled and gripped Joseph's buttocks with his hands—as if Daniel were not really there.

The big horse loves to run, Daniel repeated as if it were the only sentence in the world, the only words he knew. *The big horse loves to run.* And he was here, riding this body like its own driving spirit. He was here and he was not here. He was out.

Joseph heard a faint, bleating sound. It reminded him of a rutting deer that had seen and once startled Joseph in the forest. This was Joseph's only thought before he felt Daniel pierce him and the pain take over, but only for a moment. As Daniel moved, Joseph felt the pain grow smaller and smaller in him, as Daniel grew bigger. Then there was nothing but the rough, textured scratching of red sofa against Joseph's own thrusts, as the crack in the cushions opened, took Joseph, and Daniel bore down above. Dust in Joseph's nostrils smelled wet, like woods in the heavy rain. Daniel's breath at the back of Joseph's neck smelled clean and white—scoured bone.

This old man had more power in his hands and worn-out body than Joseph ever believed. The first time it happened—was it only weeks ago?—Joseph was stunned by the sheer force of Daniel Sorenson. It was not his body, but another authority. Joseph had no choice but to take the force that moved through him, brutal and breathtaking. It was the most powerful thing Joseph had ever felt; and it was not his own.

Now as Daniel drove him into a wide, astonishing expanse where all Joseph could do was run, run with his arms outstretched, breathing so heavily his dry mouth stretched into a smile—Joseph cried. This was not how he expected to love; and yet this was how he loved. He was so hungry for this. It felt utterly right, as if all his life he'd waited for one certainty to rivet him. It was the most powerful thing Joseph ever encountered besides Tata's pain. And it was not his. He hoped it would never be his. He hoped it would one day be his. It might be Joseph's only possession, this love. It might belong to him, if he could keep it.

Daniel at last disengaged from Joseph, but he didn't stand up abruptly as was his habit. Instead he lay atop the boy and, reaching out his arms spread-eagle, took Joseph's hands in his. Tears eased from Joseph's eyes. It had been fifteen years since another man had held his hand.

Daniel never spent the night in Joseph's studio; but this evening he wasn't scrupulous about keeping to their schedule, which had included lovemaking and an editorial critique. Now Daniel stood up and walked across the room, keeping his back to Joseph. Daniel was fully dressed. He turned to Joseph.

"I don't feel like working with you tonight, my boy," Daniel said, and forced himself to look away while Joseph sat up on the day bed, his eyes dazed, darkly irridescent.

Beneath the one bulb that hung in this studio, the two of them exchanged a glance. It was not intimate; it was candid. Joseph saw no dazzling mentor smoking his slow Dunhill, staring down at him in doting blindness. Joseph saw a slender, elegantly dressed man, so ashen-faced that it seemed one touch might disintegrate him. But the force was still there in those golden, penetrating eyes. Daniel would not have to wear glasses until the day he died, Joseph thought. Even squinting under the harsh glare of this single bulb, his eyes were the most powerful source of light in the room.

For his part, Daniel did not see an adoring lover glancing across at him. He saw clearly a warrior; he also saw that Joseph's enemy was Joseph, not himself. Indirectly, others would get hurt, but it was Joseph who would take the brunt of his own battles.

Daniel allowed himself to smile as Joseph lay on the sofa, not bothering to replace his clothes. Naked, he gleamed even from across the room. Daniel smelled his sex. Daniel smiled in frank appreciation, but also because it occurred to him now that though Joseph spent much of his time being self-protective, he never suspected himself. Just as he had never expected he might want to love this way.

"Did you used to like double dates?" Daniel asked, with that edge to his voice that, in spite of himself, aroused Joseph.

"I never went to your fancy boys' schools, if that's what you want to know," Joseph shot back. "That formal, finishing touch must not be what you see in me." Restlessly Joseph ran his hand down his flank.

Daniel noted the gesture with a raised eyebrow. He nodded to Joseph. "No," he said, and there was that sudden drop in Daniel's voice that made Joseph's stomach plummet, and pleased him somehow, "what I see in you ... is *you*." Daniel paused, then continued, "But what I meant was, when you used to go on double dates, whom were you with ... in spirit? The other man or the women?"

Joseph stretched back onto the sofa and stared up at the dim ceiling. He was lost in thought, not even noticing Daniel's unreserved stare.

"I don't know," Joseph finally began slowly. "Mostly the man, I guess. Studying how it was all done. Sometimes the woman . . . sometimes back and forth. Anyway, why?"

"Curious."

"I'm curious or you're curious?" Joseph asked, and now he was on guard again. He dropped his head.

"Curious, that's all," Daniel smiled. "One can be impersonal, after all, in one's curiosity. . . . "

Joseph sat up and crossed his legs, the black hair curling from his crotch all the way up to his throat, like a mane. "This seems pretty damn personal to me," he said.

Daniel nodded coolly, but his eyes changed. Their gleam lost its focus, softened. Joseph, in response, almost relaxed. This was the way Daniel looked before lovemaking, not afterwards. This clear and naked fondness was the way Daniel first seduced Joseph, how the old man tightened Joseph's groin and heart; it was not usually what he allowed Joseph to see after lovemaking.

Tonight was different. Daniel was softer, showing something Joseph had not seen before. Joseph did not recognize it. So he kept watching Daniel, at once moved and suspicious.

"And who did *you* watch, . . . Daniel?" There, he'd said it. *Mr. Sorenson* was what Joseph usually called him, up until the moment he was seduced or he seduced—Joseph couldn't really remember which it was. *Sorenson* was what he called him when talking to others. He would say the word disparagingly or nonchalantly, the way a child will call his own parents by their surname—if he's given permission. Daniel, Hebrew for *Chosen of God*. Daniel, Chosen of God.

"I watch you, Joseph," Daniel answered in his grave, low voice. "I watch you."

Joseph could say nothing. He had counted on Daniel's reserve, if not his own. Tonight, Daniel was not aloof, and Joseph was scared. What did the old man want now? Why then did Daniel keep watching him with an expression which showed, for the first time, more than pleasure, more than simple physical possession?

"Why?" Joseph heard himself asking. He got up quickly to put on his clothes. "Why do you want to watch me?

Daniel felt a familiar weariness wash over him. It was like suddenly growing very sleepy right in the middle of the day, the middle of your life. So this was what it was, then, to be old: at the very moment when one's passion and bone-and-marrow call— one gets sleepy. One's body wants to curl around itself like a full gray cat, seeking warmth. The cat doesn't want the fire; it only wants near the fire.

Daniel yawned and his eyes filled. He looked down. If he were younger, if he had talent instead of the talent to recognize talent —he might have been able simply to write this scene: a single bulb burning above two lovers who do not touch except in passion. A man looking for an heir, a son, a second self; or the lover he lost thirty years ago. He could write: *An old man's love must be mostly grief, rage, much regret. When he loves, he mourns everything he has ever lost.*

"Did you know, Joseph . . . ," Daniel began, his voice so bleak that Joseph stopped his restless pacing and settled on the couch again, impatient and fully clothed, "that on his deathbed, Balzac kept asking if his characters were happy?"

Joseph frowned. He disliked Daniel's sudden literary lectures, especially after Daniel had been so personal a moment before. "No."

"Did you know that Henry James, as he lay dying, dictated sentence after perfect sentence? An hour later, he was gone—but his hands still moved in spasms, as if he were not dying, but still writing, still creating."

Joseph sighed. "No, I didn't know that, either." Wearily, he added, "You said you weren't going to criticize me tonight, Daniel. . . . "

"Did you know. . . . " Daniel began again, so softly that Joseph couldn't make out his words.

"What?" Joseph asked, leaning toward Daniel from his place

across the room. "What?"

"... that I'm not criticizing," Daniel's voice was an old man's murmur, "I'm loving."

And from this distance, they might as well have been in the dark, because Joseph couldn't hear Daniel's voice, hushed as it was, or read Daniel's face, bowed as it was. He could only watch the old man's hands, which were moving toward him.

11

A SMALL BURG

LATE THAT Easter afternoon, they barely slipped through the shuddering metal doors before the subway bolted down the tunnel and shot into the dark. In wavering underground light, Ruth leaned against Joseph and closed her eyes, swaying, one with the crowd. Though she had ridden the subway often in her life, Ruth had never felt this communal blur, as if her body lost its hard edges, was buoyed up by a greater body breathing in darkness. To find this flowing openness within her while here in the underground didn't surprise Ruth; it was simply another sign that inside her now was wide and spacious movement. Ruth was convinced she was pregnant. She was three weeks overdue and she could only rejoice.

Everyone else on this Easter/Seder express was rejoicing, too. They were embraced by the smell of a hundred hand-held meals: mince pies and strawberry-rhubarb turnovers; dill beans and shivering Jello molds in red and luminous lemon. A black woman carried a Dutch oven and Ruth saw a perfectly browned turkey tucked under a Chinese man's elbow like a football. Ruth smiled and leaned against Joseph, who held the stirrups above them.

"Now I know why you and Lauren love the subway," Ruth said and settled against Joseph in their slow dance and sway.

"It doesn't scare you anymore?" Joseph smiled down at her, his eyes half-lidded as if he could sleep on his feet like a cat.

"Nope," Ruth said simply, "not scared. Happy."

Joseph had to admit he was oddly happy, too. There was no reason for it at all; in fact, there was every reason to be worried: he was sleeping with Daniel, he wanted to sleep with Lauren, and he hardly slept with Ruth. Why, then, didn't he feel utterly bewildered and bad? Perhaps, he decided, it was just because he was bound for Brooklyn, his boyhood home. He hadn't been back since Tata's funeral last summer and he was happy to know how childlike was his desire simply to be home.

When the Steinhardts invited Joseph and Ruth to their small Seder, Joseph was surprised to learn that Hella and Samuel had lived in Brooklyn Heights since the fifties. And just last month, Daniel Sorenson had rented a studio-office two blocks down from the Steinhardts. More than anywhere else in the world right now, Joseph wanted to be in Brooklyn. His pleasure even outweighed his concern over seeing Daniel with everyone else around them. Maybe, Joseph reflected, he was so happy just because everything at last seemed so out of his control.

Last week Joseph had gotten a note delivered to his studio on Thursday saying Daniel would not be seeing him for their regular meeting because of family holiday obligations. This hurt Joseph, but in a way he was relieved; it gave him time to figure out just what he thought he was doing in this commute between various parts of himself, his body, and his own underground. So when Ruth announced their Seder invitation, Joseph accepted it as fate: part of Daniel Sorenson's family obligations now seemed to include Joseph.

"I wish Lauren were with us," he said now as the train lunged into Grand Central.

"I think she's excited about Muriel's Seder," Ruth laughed. "It should be quite an affair with all the others from Holden's Harbor there. And Lauren can practice her Yiddish."

As he bumped lightly against Ruth's body, Joseph caught her scent. Suddenly Ruth smelled of a hundred different countries he might travel—on this train, across her familiar skin. He had an unexpectedly erotic picture of running his tongue up Ruth's inner thigh and tasting streaks of barbecue sauce or a generous smear of that mint jelly the nearby Irish woman held in its jar like a saint's icon. Everywhere Joseph felt a sensual abandon: the olive-skinned woman who smelled of coriander and curry butting Joseph with her ample bottom; the pretty teenager, her eyes closed in some tight and dark reverie, who fell obliviously against his shoulder; and finally Ruth herself, so luxurious in their subway waltz. Joseph felt bound to everybody as if they were all immigrants in steerage sailing for the New World.

Was this the way Tata felt when he finally left old Europe for New York, his new wife and baby by his side? For a split second Joseph saw the image of two rail-thin refugees, a baby balanced amazingly between them. Then Joseph caught his breath as a sharp pain opened his chest. He could hardly breathe; he had to lean way back from the stirrups and consciously take in air.

Joseph at last then recognized that he was an in-between creature, between worlds, between genders. Betweenness was in his blood. He was, in fact, an orphan. He belonged to no one, to no place. Not to his father, whom he alone survived; not to Brooklyn, where other people now lived and where his childhood was buried. It was terrible to feel so alone inside his body, inside this crowd and this speeding train. How many people knew they were utterly alone? Lauren didn't. She was consumed by her family; she carried the crowd of them everywhere. Ruth didn't suspect, because she was so bent on having a baby that already the idea of it filled her up inside more than any man could. Did Daniel know? Or was his lifetime love with Hella some deep protection?

It didn't matter, Joseph thought. He knew *he* was an orphan; he also felt he could never again love just one person, because when that person left, there was a devastating, complete aloneness. Without Tata, he had no one. Of all the Girards, he had survived, but to what purpose? Alone of all his kind and unable to claim any one person to love, there was one thing he could do: divide himself. He knew he hedged his bets, that by not committing to any one person he'd never win big—but he'd also never have to endure loss: a loss, mostly of himself.

"Are you all right, Joseph?" Ruth reached up with one hand to touch his face. With the other she expertly balanced the latkes she'd made according to Hella's precise recipe.

"Sure... fine," Joseph said faintly, and was surprised at her smile. It was tender and kind; it was the way she'd looked at him in the very beginning of their affair—as if he were a brand new and beckoning land.

In this dim, undulant light she also looked new. When was the last time he'd really kissed her? Joseph wondered. Then he wanted nothing more than that—to feel her mouth against his like another way of breathing. He would kiss Ruth as deeply as he might on a first date in the shifting light of the Number Two to Brooklyn. It would be more chaste and more tangible than anything of himself he'd ever offered.

There in the subway, Joseph did kiss her. The light dimmed and Joseph felt their train nearing the Brooklyn Heights stop. Everyone around them shifted, anticipating arrival. It was on this collective, unconscious wave of excitement that Joseph leaned over and sought Ruth's soft, surprised mouth. He bit her lips, sucking her breath into his lungs. At first she didn't respond, shy and decorous. The subway lights flickered off and then Ruth leaned into him, her head thrown up, taking his tongue between her teeth.

As lovers, they had never kissed like this. Now that they so rarely made love, they kissed with a tenderness that startled them both.

"Hmmmmmmm," Joseph whispered. "What was that?"

"Oh, my... ," Ruth said softly, as if to herself. She was looking down at her shoes like a schoolgirl. Her face was blazing, and Joseph felt her heart beating fast even through all those layers of expensive Sunday linen.

She was alarmed, and marvelously aroused. Ruth struggled with herself because now only the thinnest veil of propriety held her back from Joseph. She swayed close, laying her head on his shoulder. He felt her breathing quicken. Then the lights blared back on, and the brakes screamed.

"I remember this... ," he breathed, and kissed Ruth again in the bright, wavering fluorescence of the car. It was a lighter kiss, but it felt as if they'd finished something between them. Her face was soft, slanting upward still, her eyes quiet, deeply moved. Joseph believed this moment that he could share in Ruth's—what to call it?—nothing less than her reverence. For herself, for him, for what they had shared.

Doors slammed open, they were shoved out into the world. They hardly had to walk, moved on as they were by casserole dishes and warm skillets like prods against their backs. The Chinese man edged valiantly up the platform steps, carrying his Easter turkey toward some distant goal.

Joseph luxuriated in the slow walk up the streets, part of the Easter Sunday parade of pink dresses and somber suits. Against their flushed faces, the Brooklyn Heights harbor wind was a cool slap-slap.

After ten more blocks, Joseph stopped before an elegant brownstone on Henry Street. "Here we are exactly one hour late," he announced, glancing at his note. "I hope we're not too late to pick up Daniel."

They took the steps two at a time and Joseph rang the doorbell with a flourish. Joseph recognized Ruth's eagerness, her yearning as they both stood waiting side-by-side. Only a year ago Ruth's tether to her father had been slashed, too, Joseph realized, and since then she'd been more alone than ever in her life. Ruth was an orphan, too. Why hadn't he felt the weight of her loss before this? Joseph reached out a hand to take hers.

Still they stood waiting. Daniel did not answer his door.

"Maybe he went out for something at the store," Ruth ventured, and though it was a mild evening, began to shiver. "Or he went on ahead without us."

"No," Joseph said, anxiously peering inside through the curtained window. "He wouldn't have left his stereo on." Joseph jiggled the doorknob. The door swung open.

As they entered, Joseph felt a blast of radiator heat and immediately tore off his suit jacket and threw it over Daniel's thin leather office chair. "God, you'd think it was still winter in here the way he's . . . " Joseph began.

He stared into Daniel's office. "Mr. Sorenson . . . ?" he called, throwing back his head to listen. *"Daniel . . . ?"*

Joseph felt Daniel's presence in the house, so why didn't Daniel answer? "Where . . . ?" Joseph began, and then his stomach lurched as if he had just stepped off a cliff into air. "Oh . . . no . . . ," he found his way toward the hall.

Sweat ran down Joseph's armpits and his white flannel pants flapped against his knees as the furnace below heaved heat up through the hallway vents.

"Daniel . . . ?" Joseph whispered at what he guessed was the bedroom door. "Let me in."

Slowly he opened the door and found Daniel lying face down on the gray carpet. It looked like Daniel had just fallen from a great height, his legs askew, his face flat against the floor. Joseph knelt and pulled Daniel's sweat-drenched head into his lap. Daniel's face was translucent blue skin imprinted with swirling patterns of the rug.

"Ruth!" Joseph yelled, but she was already running past him into the room for the bedstand phone.

His eyes blurring, Joseph dug his fingers into Daniel's face, working the clammy cheeks, the cool dents under each glassy eye. Daniel's pupils were so dilated they looked like bullet holes.

As Joseph pulled Daniel closer to him, Ruth knelt down and laid her ear on the man's chest. "Yes," she said, "but it's so faint . . ."

"We're here, Daniel," Joseph breathed, and rocked the old man, "right here."

They heard sirens from somewhere coming closer. Ruth was crying, one hand on Daniel's chest, the other on Joseph's shoulder.

Joseph felt his own breathing go quite shallow. But he held the image of Daniel's dear face in his mind so fiercely that at last he felt the pulse in Daniel's throat deepen.

"Badź spokojny, shhhh . . . " Joseph chanted, hardly knowing what he said. *"Ja kocham Ciebie* . . . please stay, stay with me . . . stay . . . "

There were other people tromping into the room, yelling, prying Joseph's arms open.

"Know him?" someone barked at Joseph, and jerked him to his feet.

Joseph nodded, but he couldn't focus his eyes. "Father . . . " he whispered softly.

"Who?"

"Daniel . . . friend—we're family," Ruth answered for Joseph.

"Ride in the ambulance then, both of you," a man ordered.

"No!" Joseph shouted as they carried Daniel's body away. "You can't take him!"

Ruth reached out and took Joseph's hand. "We can stay with him," she was saying as they climbed into the ambulance beside Daniel.

All Joseph saw was the old man's face. It was so small under the death clasp of the oxygen cup, so far away. Daniel was there and he was not there. He was somewhere else—perhaps somewhere with Tata?

"I forgot this time, too," Joseph said.

"What?" Ruth's voice was in his ear as the ambulance swerved around a corner, the siren deafening.

"I could have carried him myself," Joseph said, and leaned against her. "I could have carried him."

COMING TO THE COUNTRY

HELLA STEINHARDT stood in the hallway of her Brooklyn apartment and met her husband's eyes. "Samuel...," she began softly.

"Give my love to Daniel," Samuel said simply. "And don't be away too long."

As Samuel stood in the doorway while she rang for the elevator man, her husband looked to Hella as he first had when they were medical students together in Vienna before the war, before the first time she left him for America. With him abided Hella's childhood, her old country, what was left of her family. Yet she had never for a moment thought that her sibling-like loyalty to Samuel was deeper than her love for Daniel Sorenson. How silly, she thought, as she waved goodbye and took the elevator, how silly to be leaving home to go to another lover and have one's husband stand there in his faded blue robe and tattered slippers, looking sweet and rumpled and somehow boyish.

At Port Authority Hella boarded the Greyhound bus to Binghamton and the summer family home she had bought with Daniel. Had bought against the thought of just such a devastation as Daniel's heart attack and convalescence.

How terrified she'd been that Easter afternoon to arrive at the hospital and find Daniel almost translucent, his face slack, the only life in him flowing from his hands, large and trembling and strangely cool even as he struggled to take each breath. How did a man so near death have such life in his hands? Hella had wondered. She'd thought that hearing was the last to go, but with Daniel it would be touch.

She kept this in mind all during the journey and even found herself smiling faintly at the prospect of simply touching Daniel again. Did it ever die, passion? The young were so sweetly prudish about their elders' bodies, horrified to imagine them embracing, entering one another through so many more openings, now that their bodies were so thin-skinned, so ready to shatter and open—their spirits like seeds splitting their shells.

Daniel's nurse was young and very professional, and she shook hands with Hella so firmly the older woman winced. Power was not in the strength of òne's grasp, Hella thought, again remembering Daniel's hands, but real power was the capacity to feel deeply what one touched.

"I've left instructions, and the local doctor will be on call if you need him," the nurse informed Hella brusquely. "But I think it's just a matter of quiet and no excitement...." Here the young nurse eyed Hella suspiciously, as if she were here for a weekend tryst.

"Thank you for all you've done, dear," Hella dismissed the nurse, and couldn't help but smile at the young nurse's mistrust.

Daniel was sitting on the wide back porch, a white Fedora rather rakishly tilted to the side of his head as he slept, book in hand. Beyond him was the lake where sailboats glided like gulls. The porch was surrounded by early May color: fuschias, azaleas, and the soft flounce of rose-colored dogwood and tulip trees. Hella was so glad to see Daniel that for a moment she forgot what she was here for and confused this trip with the hundreds of trips over the years when they'd met just like this in her family's house for weekends of work and lovemaking and true reunion.

Habit was half of love, Hella thought now as she quietly put down her bags and crossed to the porch. Everytime she saw Daniel it was as if she embodied the deepest habit of her heart, the way her heart had of turning toward him with a constancy that continued to astonish her.

She stood near Daniel, letting him sleep, then turned her back to him and still saw him perfectly: the angles of his face slack and supple, the faint color in his cheeks that was not health but sun, borrowed radiance. Yet his eyes, when they opened, would be radiant enough, their light so familiar.

It seemed to Hella that she and Daniel had loved each other many lifetimes. Now at the age of sixty-five, Hella found herself wondering about the future. What would it be like? Just exactly *where* would it take place? In some sort of shuttle between Samuel and Daniel? What of when she grew too old to keep up such a commute?

"You're finally here." A soft voice behind her, and Hella turned to greet Daniel.

"Don't we look like retired folk?" she asked Daniel with a smile. She tilted her straw sun hat to match his.

"How long before you go back to the city?" Daniel asked.

"As long as we like. After all, I can work here as easily as there...." Hella frowned. "Easier." She looked at him and her gaze was steady.

"We can't stay here forever."

Then Hella had to laugh. "My dear, we don't *have* forever!"

At this Daniel smiled, too, and his hand instinctively went to the hidden snake-like incision over his heart. "Of course, we don't." After a moment, Daniel added, "We never did."

"It is amazing how long it took us to figure that out."

"Yes," Daniel said slowly, as if he felt the word in his entire body. "Amazing."

"So we'll stay here a while, you and I . . . ," Hella said; then she glanced across the lake where soft, dark clouds were rolling up over the water like waves. "If the weather holds."

"How long did you tell Samuel you'd be away?"

Hella paused, leaning against the white porch rail, her back to the water. "I didn't say. Samuel doesn't know whether I'm leaving him or not."

"And are you?" Daniel asked, his voice taking on that flat tone he used when what he said mattered most.

She meant to say what she'd told Samuel—*Of course, I'm not leaving you.* But when she opened her mouth, she said instead, "I don't know, Daniel... I don't know if I'm leaving him." This shocked Hella and, it seemed, a little current of electricity went through his body, too. Nothing could move in Daniel's body when Hella was near without her feeling it, too. "Oh, my dear...," she tried to make light of it, "here we are talking like teenagers running away from home. Let's do be sensible and for once act our age."

"My body seems to be doing just that," Daniel smiled drily, and very slowly stood up.

She did not move to help him; he did not really need her help and until he did, Hella supported him by not offering. How uneasy this felt, this *not* offering. If they were not living under a shadow, if Daniel had simply broken his hip or foot, she would be there at his side instantly. She had not expected this physical separation to become a way of expressing her deepest intimacy. But then, it had always been true between them that when they were the most autonomous they were the most intimate. It's why their love had lasted.

"Did you ever expect...," Hella began, walking alongside but some distance from Daniel into the dayroom, where they settled onto the couch together, "to be so... well, surprised by our age... surprised, I mean, by *ourselves?*"

"No," Daniel answered. He reached for her Chesterfields and then, without a word, put the pack down. "You can smoke," he said quietly.

"I will," Hella said firmly. "Outside on the porch."

Daniel snorted and shook his head. "Are you also going to refuse to sleep with me?"

Hella turned to him and took off his hat. His hair was thin, curling around his ears like a Southern gentleman farmer. It had gone white early, like hers. She could remember a time when Daniel's hair was so thick and silver it was like ruffled Siamese fur. Now it was fine as baby hair and curled around her fingers.

"How I've missed you," she said very softly, and now their bodies stood together as if by mutual command and they supported one another walking into the bright bedroom.

It was a big room furnished with an old-fashioned canopy bed inherited from Hella's mother, a cedar chest, and a beige lampshade whose dents were as familiar to Hella's hands as the dips and indents of Daniel's body.

They undressed one another patiently as if preparing for a spring afternoon's nap, as if they had nothing more on their minds than to lie naked on the worn blue chenille spread and let the sun warm them. They lay on their sides, facing each other, and Hella traced with one finger the red, raised slash running from Daniel's shoulder blade round to his belly. It had been almost a month since the surgery. Triple bypass, the doctors called it. It looked like those engineering wonders of highway design, but it felt under her finger like a seam of skin cinching together two sides of Daniel's body. Did only one side now belong to her?

As Daniel embraced her, caressing the familiar slopes of her back, pausing almost absently to pop a vertebra he knew would be slightly out, to probe a soft spot on her shoulder, Hella felt a bolt of jealousy quiver in the muscles of her back. What other body were Daniel's hands touching like this? Her father had been right all those years ago: she *was* a savage. Hella sat up in bed and faced Daniel. "Do you truly love him, then?" she demanded. "Do you love your young Joseph?"

"Once you said you'd be ashamed of me if I didn't," Daniel answered, and with one hand touched her mouth, which was stretched wide in a savagely thoughtful frown.

"Yes, I said it and I meant it. But that was before I thought I'd lost you, before your heart gave out on you . . . on me. . . . " Hella hesitated and was surprised to feel tears flowing freely. She allowed him to take her in his arms and rock both of them gently. For a long while she cried, cried as she had not all during the week in the hospital when Daniel had lain attached to machines instead of to her; when he had called her name but not recognized her.

"I'm here now," Daniel said tenderly.

"Yes," Hella breathed. "But now I know something you don't

yet know. I understand what it's like to be in the world without you."

"Is that why you're jealous?"

"I want," she began slowly, as if not knowing herself what she would say, "I want *all* the time we have left together. Finally, I can bear it."

"Bear what?"

"Being with you."

His eyes flashed opened once, then fell hooded and hawk-like again. But he had heard her. He even felt movement in his chest that was not pain but expansion; it was how his heart had felt moments before the attack, as if it were bursting wide open, blood gushing up in a geyser to his head.

He wondered could he at last bear being with this woman who had always required so much of his soul to be near? All their lives together, he and Hella had kept a careful privacy, a distance that was his home and hers. They'd traveled toward one another joyfully, like expatriates recognizing someone from their homeland, but always returning then to others for their day-to-day lives. Could they finally take up residence together?

Daniel thought of all that stood between him and Hella—his family, her husband, his affair with Joseph, his own loss of Cowley and Pelzner. After a lifetime together, they had as much to sort out between them as any young couple. How strange, Daniel thought, that the dance never ended, just changed.

"It's not my wife and daughters," Daniel began slowly. "Nor Cowley and Pelzner, nor even Joseph—because he doesn't just love me, he's simply found another way of loving through me, a way I think he might choose again. There is nothing between us, you and I, my dear, but what's always been there—fear, our fear."

"Of one another," Hella said, and it was not a question.

"Yes, of one another."

"Do you think," Hella had to smile, "that I'll be the death of you?"

"Not physical death," Daniel said, "but losing my life all the same."

"Losing it?"

"To you, dear," he said in a low voice, and turned away.

"Does Joseph frighten you as I do?" Hella asked.

"No," Daniel admitted, and met her steady gaze. "Joseph helps keep fear away." Daniel shifted in the bed, then lay alongside her and propped his head up with one hand. "That's why I'm not seeing him now. I'm guessing he'll turn to you."

"To me?" Hella said, but again there was no question in her voice. She sighed and shook her head.

"Will you help the boy find his way, Hella? Away from me, I mean?"

"You ask a lot of me, my dear," Hella said.

"And you of me," Daniel said with a faint smile. He sat up and reached out to cup one of Hella's breasts in his hand. It was round and fallen and familiar, with wrinkles running through the blue-veined skin. His hands knew every scar and detail of her body. He'd held her foot when it was broken and felt sharp bones poking under his palms; he'd held her abdomen, already criss-crossed with a Caesarian scar, when she'd lain in the hospital bed after appendicitis. Her body seemed as familiar to Daniel as his own.

Once long ago when they'd made love Daniel looked into Hella's face and saw a hundred changing faces, as if beneath him were many people he'd loved before, not in this life. But perhaps it had always been Hella in all those other bodies, those other eyes. Daniel hadn't paid much attention to such notions as reincarnation, but he'd always remembered that moment of recognition. It had shocked him so much that he'd sought refuge in Gerald Newland. He was doing the same thing thirty-five years later. Recognizing Hella—and running from her.

"I don't think I can, Hella," Daniel began very slowly. There was a stillness to his body and hands. "I don't think I can do it . . . even now."

Hella nodded and turned away in a gesture so final it took his breath. "What you don't know, dear," she said softly, "is that I am also afraid of you."

At that moment Daniel reached out and held her face between his hands. Her eyes were closed, but as they opened she was unboundaried, as if he gazed into an expanse of water as far as his eyes could see.

"Hella," he whispered, "close your eyes. Close your beautiful eyes." And then he was inside her, hardly moving at all, although he had never filled her so deeply.

He barely touched the maze of wrinkles running everywhere around her eyes, to feel the world within her. He barely had to move his hips to begin their old tremblings. Inside her and himself he was coiling round and round. He was in the exact center of someplace so deep, Daniel knew he'd never been here before. He was circling through the most ancient parts of himself. Hella was with him, too, and there was only the slightest separation—skin, old skin. So old and so used up, it sloughed off with crinkling sounds like snake skin.

Once, in Egypt, Daniel had watched two snakes entwining, and when he asked his guide if they were fighting or mating, the man smiled a toothless grin and answered, "Neither, not so, Sir. These snakes, they sometimes work together their bodies like this so to help each other shed skins. See?"

All his life Daniel had wanted out of his skin, but now he wanted to stay here, with Hella, with himself. Soon enough he would leave this skin; already it barely held him back. Daniel opened his eyes and saw Hella's face turned to the side, her gray temples beaded with a light sweat as the sunlight fell across their bed, their bodies. They sunned themselves as Daniel lay beside her, his arm cradling her head. Her breathing was so light he almost couldn't hear it and had to watch the pulse in her throat to reassure himself she was still here. Suddenly he saw quite clearly that it was Hella who would leave first. He would survive her. The grief, the surprise of this intuition was so great that Daniel sat up in bed and stared down at her.

"Stay with me," he asked. Below him on the bed she looked so separate from him. Her solitude, like her death, was distinct from him. "I'll stay with you as long as you want me," Daniel said.

"Until I die," she said, and sat up to embrace him. "And then you'll know what I've learned—what it is to be in the world without one another."

"Yes," Daniel said, and wrapped his length around her, then pulled Hella under the light spread with him. His body circled around hers as they lay on their sides.

"It is terrible," Hella said, and stretched. Shadows fell across them with a warm breeze from the lake.

"Yes," Daniel breathed, "terrible."

And then they slept as if they'd been together every night for years and were just settling comfortably. Each body shifted slightly against the other.

One of them—who knew which?—snored slightly, an old rasping, a rattle, a simple shedding of skin.

Part V

SPRING

13

BECOMING THE ENEMY

AT THE END OF a long workday in mid-May, Ruth looked up from her manuscript and was glad to see Lauren leaning against her office door. "That time?" Ruth asked, and noticed that Lauren's lovely white damask slacks which this morning had seemed so crisp and summery were now criss-crossed with wrinkles.

"What a day... ," Lauren breathed. Ruth took note of her friend's weariness. The past month's strain of Daniel's heart attack and Joseph's leaving them to live alone in his uptown studio was finally beginning to show on Lauren, too.

"What happened?" Ruth asked.

"Hella put through her final edits on that dinosaur book. But I don't think we'll ever make the typesetting deadline. Then to top it off, who do you think I just saw being banished from the ladies' confidential lounge?"

"One guess?"

"Right," Lauren frowned, and thumped the doorjamb with the flat of her hand. "I don't understand it. Even the messenger boys are hustling Heather Jaynes out of C&P like she's some bag lady. That's not right, Ruth. Heather belongs here."

Ruth shook her head. The latest editorial memo had read: *Mr. Mercer requests that you politely escort Miss Jaynes to her hotel whenever she enters our premises. She is NOT to be encouraged.*

"Of course, Lauren, it's not right. But Heather can't just keep living in the bathroom."

"Why not?" Lauren shot back, and Ruth was struck by how personal Lauren's anger seemed, as if she were not talking about Heather at all.

"Would you like to ask Heather to live with us?" Ruth tried to take up a teasing tone. "Other people here have taken her in, you know, and Heather always winds up back in the office. Really, what can we do?"

"I guess you've taken in enough strays for one year," Lauren said so quietly that Ruth gave her a questioning look.

"You *did* have a difficult day, didn't you?"

"Sometimes...." Lauren at last entered the office and sat down heavily in the chair across from Ruth. For the first time Ruth noticed that Lauren had gained a little weight recently. "Sometimes this city makes me sick. I wonder how I ever loved it?"

"Let's not cook tonight, Lauren," Ruth suggested. "Let's just make something light... a salad?"

Lauren looked at Ruth with another frown and Ruth wondered if this were deeper than a bad mood. But before Ruth could ask, Lauren said, "Heather was such a fine writer. It's terrible to see her like this. I mean, it makes me wonder what's the point? We work so hard to make books... and for what? Daniel's dismissed, Heather's cast aside like trash, and Hella can hardly keep Peabody from rejecting her authors in favor of self-help books...." Lauren threw up her hands, "And what about the writers themselves?"

"Well," Ruth said softly, "you could all stop writing." Ruth meant it as a silly suggestion, one they might both laugh over. But Lauren stood up abruptly and crossed to the other side of the office to make herself tea. Ruth noticed that Lauren didn't offer her a cup. Was this pointed? Ruth wondered, or was Lauren simply forgetting about her because she was so deep in her own funk?

Sitting at her desk, Ruth stared at Lauren. Yes, definitely she'd put on a little weight. But it was not unbecoming; it made her womanly body even softer. Ruth made a mental note to remind herself to compliment Lauren on this by way of apologizing for her remark about stopping writing.

"We could always go out and eat tonight, if you'd rather," Ruth suggested.

"No, not hungry," Lauren murmured. "Besides, I might meet Adrianne for coffee later on. She's got an idea for a new ending to the last chapter. But...." Suddenly Lauren shifted nervously from foot to foot. "Oh, I don't know what I'll do. I'm tired, that's all."

"You certainly don't have to babysit with me night after night, Lauren," Ruth said lightly. In her loneliness this past month at having discovered that she was not, after all, pregnant, in having lost Joseph at home, and Daniel at C&P, Ruth couldn't help but feel somewhat abandoned now by Lauren, too. She added with a tinge of resentment that surprised her, "And how is Adrianne?"

"Fine," Lauren said, still not turning around from the tea table. "She thinks her editor at Harper & Row might accept my manuscript with some revisions."

Ruth sat up straight. "Really? Why didn't you tell me this before? We should celebrate."

"Don't know, didn't seem right to celebrate. Bad timing."

Ruth found herself unaccountably upset, but she tried to make light of it. "Really, Lauren, we're not the Bobbsey Twins, you and I. Just because I've had a rough month doesn't mean I couldn't celebrate with you over something so wonderful as—"

"I guess I just wanted to keep it to myself for a while," Lauren said quietly. "But now you know."

Yes, now she knew, Ruth thought; and why wasn't she wholeheartedly delighted? Ruth had to chide herself. Was this competition on her part? Could she really begrudge her friend? Or was it something deeper?

Suddenly Ruth remembered a last night with Carl before they separated. He'd told her, "The problem with you, Ruth, is you don't admit equals. What if I weren't a drunk as well as a goddamn good poet? What if I could meet you eye-to-eye without one shot of liquor in me? What if I saw you at your worst, in *your* drunken, dark night, and still loved you—what then, Ruth?"

She had stared at him and felt not anger, but complete terror, as if she were losing herself, falling into his black eyes. She'd drawn back from him. "I don't know what you're talking about," she'd said in her mother's chilliest voice. Ruth knew Carl couldn't bear her coldness; he'd never survive her Ice Age.

"Why, then . . . ," Carl had poured another drink with a trembling hand, "then you'd leave me. Because I came too close, because I could see you and recognize you as my true peer. Then you couldn't hide, you wouldn't be an only child anymore."

"Leave me alone!" Ruth had found herself shouting at him.

"Yes," Carl had said, "that's what you do best. Being alone. You may be in goddamn graduate school when it comes to taking care of people, Ruth, but when it comes to loving you're a beginner."

Now Ruth turned to Lauren, who had just finished her tea, and said softly, "I'm glad for you, about your book. I'm a little jealous of Adrianne being your editor, but it means we can be better friends, you and I, if I am not your editor and you my writer." Ruth paused. "I mean, there's less distance now, isn't there?"

For the first time Lauren turned to face Ruth with a faint smile. "Yes, less distance."

Ruth sat back in her chair, relieved. "Lauren . . . ," she began in a confiding voice, "speaking of your dinosaur book . . . , did I ever tell you that as a child my imaginary friends were . . . well . . . !" Ruth broke off with a laugh. She felt suddenly very shy. Maybe Carl was right, maybe she really was a beginner when it came to intimacy. How could she explain to him then, and to Lauren now, that like her parents before her, she'd learned to give love the way a philanthropist gives a grant: expecting no equal return on her investment, writing it off as a kind of gift, that is to say, as a loss. There had to be another way to love, though Ruth couldn't yet imagine it. Ruth turned to Lauren and summoned her courage: "I've never really told anyone this, but . . . " Ruth stopped when she saw Lauren's face, which was suddenly flushed and distracted.

Was Lauren embarrassed for Ruth? She crossed her arms and said, "Something's terribly wrong, Lauren. It's not just that you've had a hard day. Tell me, what is it?" When Lauren also crossed her arms and stood across the office silently, Ruth continued, "I can see that you're upset. Please talk to me."

"You're upset, too," Lauren said.

"Yes, but you go first." Ruth waited and Lauren opened the coat closet door, taking out Ruth's blue linen jacket. She crossed over to Ruth and laid it on her desk.

"Look, Ruth, let's not try to out-nurture one another . . . not tonight."

"Nurture?" Ruth coolly picked up her jacket and stood up, gathering her things. "I doubt we're in danger of that."

Without another word they walked together out of the office, Lauren tripping slightly on the old linoleum. It was so uncharacteristic for Lauren to stumble, she who was so graceful from years of gymnastics and practically made it a point of pride to dodge in and out of crowds in the street. Ruth had often remarked upon her friend's "street-dancing," as Joseph had called it. But now as they wove between people on the way to the Number Two stop, Ruth saw Lauren trip several more times. The thought struck her: had Lauren been drinking? Surely not. She had no tolerance for liquor, part of her Indian genes, no doubt. As they stood at the corner of 57th waiting for a light, Ruth leaned near to see if she smelled alcohol on her breath. No, nothing but that clean-smelling apricot lotion Lauren always used.

When they arrived at the bus stop, Ruth was startled to see that Lauren showed no signs of waiting with her.

"I've got to pick up some things," Lauren said brusquely.

"For the salad?"

"No," Lauren actually snapped and Ruth took a step back. Standing in this bus crowd with Lauren, Ruth had the sudden sense that they might be perfect strangers. She might just simply turn away from this young woman with the unmanageably curly hair as if she were no one she knew or claimed. After all, she did look rather primitive—like someone you wouldn't want to quarrel with on the streets. "I got some things at the dry cleaners."

Then Ruth remembered. The lavender cashmere sweater and skirt Lauren had borrowed for the night Joseph had taken them all to see *The Magic Flute*. It was his Easter present. That night she'd sat between Joseph and Lauren and believed herself completely content. Joseph, too, had seemed utterly happy. All the way home, he kept announcing that this was his favorite opera. He said it as if complimenting Ruth and Lauren on composing it. That was the last night they'd all three been together before Joseph moved out.

Ruth now turned to Lauren and saw the cool wind off the East River had blown Lauren's hair into a dark tangle barely held intact by the small, tortoiseshell barrette that had been a present from Ruth for Christmas. Ruth felt remorse for ever thinking this woman might be a stranger. She recognized her, of course she recognized her.

Taking Lauren's arm, Ruth said simply, "Is it so hard to confide in me, Lauren? I mean, is it easier to talk to someone like... well, like Adrianne for example?"

"Yes," Lauren said. "About some things it *is* easier to talk to her. She's not as close to me as you are."

"I see," Ruth said.

"I don't think you really do," Lauren said with a tone that sounded to Ruth like real regret. "It's like I have to draw a line... a demilitarized zone. And you have to *not* cross it before I can trust you."

"Cross it?" Ruth heard herself say in the chilliest of tones. "I wouldn't think of trespassing." Ruth stepped back, peered down Madison Avenue for the Number Two and then rummaged in her briefcase for her manuscript. She took out her red pencil and made a mark in the margin. Then she said without looking over at Lauren, "And must you always use war imagery? Really, Lauren, it is trying."

Lauren said nothing, but even without looking at her Ruth knew she was furious. Her face would be flushed and her eyes white like a wolf's. This image suddenly made Ruth realize that

Lauren really was a primitive and therefore unpredictable. She was quite astonished to find herself afraid.

"Sometimes . . . ," Ruth began, not knowing what she was going to say, "sometimes I wonder if Joseph has the right idea. I mean, moving out."

"Are you saying you want to live alone, Ruth?"

Ruth sighed. How could Lauren not understand what she meant? Before Joseph left it had seemed that Lauren practically read her mind. Now she seemed purposely obtuse. "I mean only that I'm thinking of giving up my apartment, too. There's too much left over from other days . . . other people."

"I was happy there," Lauren said, but her tone was angry.

"Was?" Ruth asked sharply. Then she said nothing. "Well," Ruth began again, her own anger rising, "I don't really think I was happy. I think I just made it all up, our happiness, the way I imagined I was pregnant. Like I've imagined a lot of things in my life . . . even my friends."

"You think we all only *imagined* ourselves happy, you mean?"

It frightened Ruth to see Lauren so angry. She didn't want a scene right here on the street. Then Lauren added with an uncharacteristic bitterness that reminded Ruth of Joseph, "So you believe we were just your imaginary friends. Right, Ruth?"

Ruth decided the subject was closed and turned away. "When is your coffee with Adrianne?" she asked in a polite, dismissing tone, the tone that had worked for years when her own mother used it on Ruth.

"I don't know . . . after supper, I guess."

"After *dinner?*" Ruth couldn't help but correct.

"Yes, Ruth, after *dinner*," Lauren said.

Then she surprised Ruth by picking up her leather satchel and walking away. She called back, "I'm taking the subway. I'll pick up salad fixings on the way."

Ruth frowned and made a pretense of going through her briefcase to avoid any stares from the crowded commuters around her who might have witnessed her argument with Lauren. Then she stopped herself. What did it matter what these strangers thought?

What kind of etiquette was it that showed more concern for good manners than for a friend's feelings?

How well Ruth remembered all her childhood years of perfect manners; but under cover of chill smiles, her parents were really denying one another and themselves love. For the first time since Joseph moved out, Ruth found herself relieved that he was gone. She missed him, certainly there was the physical longing. But there was no longer the lie—that they were truly together, partners in creating another life or a life with one another.

As the Number Two at last lumbered up to the stop, Ruth found herself feeling an extra surge of energy, as if something of herself was returned to her. Straphanging alone she decided now that she would take a hot, luxurious bath as soon as she got home. A good book, some French bath oil, and perhaps even a tall glass of iced coffee. Yes, Ruth closed her eyes and swayed against the other passengers—being left alone was not so very terrible, if one were left truly with oneself.

When Lauren entered sometime later she found Ruth singing a sailor's ditty, her arms elbow-deep in stiff white suds as Ruth washed a big brown wool bundle.

"Hullo!" Ruth called to her friend. "I've made us a coffee. After supper, as you say, I'm going to ice it and take a bath. Are you hungry now?"

Lauren's face told Ruth that all this time she'd still been seething.

Lauren hurried past Ruth mumbling something indistinct. Ruth sighed. All right, this moodiness she would accept, too. Lauren needed it. Perhaps this was what she'd meant by her demilitarized zone. After a half-hour when Lauren was still ensconced in her study, Ruth called down the hall, "Are you going to make the salad at your desk?"

"No," came Lauren's muffled reply.

"Lauren," Ruth sighed, perching her pink gloved hands on her hips. "Would you like me to make dinner?"

"Forget it, Ruth." This time Lauren's voice was sharp again, like Joseph's. "I said I'll do it and I will!"

"At least let me make the salad dressing . . . ," Ruth began.

"No, ma'am, I'll make that myself, too."

Exasperated, Ruth said, "Is there anything you'd like me to do, Lauren?" But her tone said, *Is there anything you think I could do right at this moment?*

"No." Lauren at last entered the kitchen. She set about unloading the grocery bags. "Just . . . just do whatever you were doing. . . . "

"I was washing Joseph's robe," Ruth said. "He forgot it and it's time I let go of it. I'll return it to him by messenger boy at the office."

Lauren flinched as she stared across at Joseph's robe. It floated now in cold, white bubbles, its brown wool bloating up here and there in the sink.

To Lauren it looked just like a dead man drifting down the Hudson. She'd seen one once, a dead man floating face-down in the river—or she imagined a man in the water with a hat, drifting beside a big brown lump, a tiny death barge down the wide, dark river. Lauren thought again of the confusion she'd felt after she'd accepted Joseph's invitation this morning in the elevator. He'd seemed so sad and troubled when he'd asked her to come visit him in his studio. But Lauren was more troubled now by herself than by Joseph. She felt out of control. As she slowly tore the shards of red-leaf lettuce, she realized that she was most disturbed because she didn't herself know what she was going to do.

Miserably she tore the spinach leaves to mix with the red-leaf. Then she had an idea. "Want me to . . . ?" Lauren struggled to make her voice casual. "Want me to carry that robe up to Joseph, Ruth? I can drop it off on my way to see Adrianne."

"No," Ruth said firmly, "you don't have to be a go-between anymore, Lauren." She turned to Lauren, who avoided her eyes. "Thanks for offering, but I really think we should wait for Joseph to come back to us. I don't think we can make any assumptions. He'll know when to reach out."

"Will he know to whom?" Lauren asked before she could think better of it.

Ruth stopped wringing the bulky robe. "Yes," she said quietly, "he'll know."

Ruth was thinking of Daniel. She had a good hunch that when Joseph was finally ready to ask someone besides Hella to be with him, he would call on Daniel. Joseph's strange openness to only Hella this past month was a mystery to Ruth. When she'd questioned Hella about it, the older woman kept her own counsel.

"You're right," Lauren said, and suddenly seemed quite subdued, all anger drained. "I shouldn't get involved."

Ruth gathered up the dripping robe in her arms and went to the bathroom to dry it flat on the tile. When she returned to the kitchen Lauren flinched. Ruth saw it and a wave of something like resentment or perhaps pity overtook her. What in the world was going on that made Lauren behave toward Ruth as if every move or word were somehow a violation? It really was too much, Ruth decided, especially here in her own kitchen.

"Lauren." Ruth stood so close to her friend that she could see fear reflected in Lauren's pale eyes. *"What* is wrong?"

Lauren sidestepped Ruth and made for the sink, where she vigorously began scrubbing the rings of brown lint with cleanser.

"I'm the one who's supposed to clean when I'm upset," Ruth commented, and leaned back against the refrigerator, folding her arms across her chest. "Just tell me what's wrong, won't you please?" For a moment Lauren looked as if she might at last open up, but she shrugged and returned to scouring the sink. "If it's something between you and me, I'd like to talk about it; if not, just say so and I'll leave you alone."

Lauren took a deep breath. "I got to make a decision... now... tonight. I don't know what to do."

Ruth smiled, grateful that at last Lauren was opening up to her. She herself opened the refrigerator door and took out blue cheese, buttermilk, sour cream, fresh chives—all Lauren needed to make her homemade Roquefort dressing. "I'm sure you'll do the right thing, Lauren," Ruth said reassuringly. "Do we want to use fresh pepper?"

"Yes, please... just put it there on the table."

Lauren came over to stand beside Ruth at the kitchen counter. Methodically she began mixing the buttermilk and sour cream with a wooden spoon.

Ruth began slicing radishes. For a few minutes they worked in companionable silence; then Ruth felt Lauren's tension return. To ward it off, Ruth said in her gentlest voice, "And so . . . what is this momentous decision?"

"My book . . . ," Lauren blurted, and at that moment she looked desolate. "It's about the ending of my book."

"That?" Ruth said wonderingly. "Just that? That's what's upsetting you so terribly?"

"What do you mean *just that?*" Lauren took a step back. She raised her wooden spoon for emphasis. To Ruth she looked almost laughable. "You're an editor, Ruth, for God's sake," Lauren burst out when she saw the faint grin cross Ruth's face. "You're supposed to understand how someone's writing affects her life?"

"Someone's . . . yes," Ruth said calmly. And now the smile was gone. In its place was a professional coolness that only infuriated Lauren all the more. "But not yours, Lauren. Remember I was the first to work with you on this book. I know your process. If you were upset about the ending of your book, you'd talk to me, of all people. And if I were no help, you're resourceful enough to find someone else who is. Besides, it's not your work that makes you despair like this—it's your life, and rightly so. At least, in your writing, you tell the truth!"

Ruth hadn't meant to say all that; she shut her mouth tightly and turned away. The moment it was out of her mouth, Ruth knew how much her last swipe would hurt Lauren and felt her friend's pain suddenly as if it were her own. "Oh, Lauren," Ruth began, "I'm sorry, I . . . "

"Forget it," Lauren said, and ripped open the little tin foil square of Roquefort. With both hands she began crumbling the blue cheese into the dressing. "*I* already have," Lauren added in a low voice. She looked like it was the one thing Ruth had ever said to her that she would always remember.

Ruth shook her head and turned away. It was hopeless, just as she'd thought earlier in the office. She should move out of this place. At least then she wouldn't go around hurting the people closest to her. That's all intimacy really was, Ruth thought, people getting close enough to truly harm one another. This knowledge must have been what sent Sister Margaret Magdalene back to her convent, her parents to their separate rooms.

"Do we have a lemon left?" Lauren asked in a voice so full of resentment that Ruth felt it was like her parents right there in the kitchen arguing again.

"I'll see." Ruth opened the refrigerator and retrieved a somewhat dried-out lemon from the vegetable bin. She set it down on the table very gingerly as if hoping Lauren wouldn't think it was a weapon.

It was then Ruth noticed that Lauren was stirring her salad dressing with her fingers. The sight made Ruth physically sick. "Let's forget the salad. I'm not really hungry anymore," Ruth murmured.

Lauren let out a huff. "You've got to eat, Ruth. You hardly ever eat. Sometimes I wonder if you'd just starve yourself to death here alone."

Ruth looked at Lauren in complete astonishment. "I certainly *do* eat!" Ruth said. "I've been taking care of myself for a long time, Lauren—a lot longer than you have."

"That's right, honey. That's why you're so thin," Lauren commented, and her voice was full of rage.

"I am not too thin . . . "

Lauren cut her off. "You're such a stick, you've cut off your own period. I mean, *look* at you, sister! You never lost any baby. You weren't big enough for one person, much less two. Pregnant women get big, they grow. You *lost* weight!"

"How kind of you to remind me," Ruth shot back.

Round and round in the mixing bowl and Lauren's hands came up dribbling chunks of mottled cheese, parsley dotting her fingers, blue globs beneath her fingernails. It made Ruth feel like she would vomit. But she was too furious for that. "Oh, *do* wash your hands, Lauren . . . and try using that spoon, for Christ's sake!"

"Don't you dare talk to me like that!" Lauren turned to Ruth, her hands dripping white. "If you want a child so bad, honey, *adopt* one. Stop treating me like a baby."

"And *you* stop calling me 'honey' or 'sister.' " Ruth snapped. "I'm *not* your sister."

"No, you never was." Lauren ran from the kitchen. Ruth knotted her fists and tore off her plastic gloves, slapping them down against the chair. She had an image of peeling off these gloves and whacking them across Lauren's face in some absurd challenge. Just as Ruth was about to shout something down the hall, she felt a stab of pain in her left eye.

Oh, not this, Ruth thought. She tore off her glasses and myopically glared around the kitchen. Everything was so wrong here. Ruth shook her head as if the movement might make her see better, might stop the pounding that began at the base of her skull. She felt there was that familiar sensation of a jigsaw puzzle ripping apart inside her head. Ruth closed her eyes and concentrated on keeping the colorful, shimmering puzzle pieces together, but the pieces separated into a thousand painfully bright, jagged shapes, as if all her thoughts were flying away from her. It took all Ruth's strength simply to keep the jigsaw hovering nearby. Ruth balanced herself, one hand on the counter, the other against the refrigerator.

Out of the corner of her eye Ruth saw Lauren with her coat on standing in the foyer. Then Ruth's left vision doubled, and she had an image of Lauren's hands on her head, healing, massaging. It seemed years ago.

"Where are you going?" Ruth managed to ask, and the sound of her own voice was so loud it echoed inside.

"Out . . . that's all," Lauren said, face buried in the collar of one of her military surplus peacoats, its buttons hanging by a shred.

"You know, Lauren," Ruth heard her own voice far off, "if you can't afford a better coat, at least you might sew those buttons back on tight."

"Are you going to divorce me, too, Ruth?" It seemed to Ruth that Lauren was screaming, and she covered her ears.

"Who's talking about divorce?"

"Like you divorced Joseph?"

Ruth took her hands down from her head and gazed at Lauren's wavering reflection. "Joseph left me!"

"You left him, too," Lauren shouted. She stomped around looking for her purse. "Look, Ruth, two people truly loving each other without protection—from a child, another person, your work, from anything that'll keep the triangle going... I mean, just two goddamn people face-to-face trying to love each other—it's the scariest thing on earth."

"I can't believe you think I only wanted a child," Ruth said. "I wanted more than a baby with Joseph... I wanted someone to share my life, an equal...." Then she stopped, her head pounding.

"That's why you're asking me to move out." Lauren was beside herself. "Go ahead, divorce me, too. I'll be glad to move out of here."

"Are you moving out tonight?" Ruth demanded. She couldn't remember where it was Lauren had said she was going.

"Why not?" Lauren screamed. "Then you can be alone here in this great big apartment. Alone at last. And safe, sister!" Lauren came down heavily on the last word.

Ruth waved a hand. She didn't have the energy to care.

When the door slammed shut, Ruth felt nothing, not even relief. She covered her eyes and worked her way down the hallway to the bathroom. Yes, there was some Fiornal, Joseph's last legacy to her, left in the medicine cabinet. Ruth swallowed the pill without water. She weaved unsteadily on her feet. She wished she could hire someone to massage her head and take this migraine away; or maybe she could call Lauren's grandmother and ask her to sing a lullaby over the phone.

But Lauren's great-hearted midwife grandmother didn't belong in Ruth's family; and Lauren herself had decided not to belong here with Ruth, either. Why had she ever believed any of them? Why had she ever imagined anyone would survive loving another?

If her head hadn't hurt so much, Ruth would have cried. Instead she very gingerly moved toward the bed. Like a blind woman she moved, hands outstretched before her for the silken feel of her comforter. There were so many things she didn't want to see.

"Stop it," she heard her own voice say as she inched toward the bed. "Stop this tiptoeing...."

Then she fell on the comforter and curled around herself in a flexible circle of knee to forehead. She lay like that a long time. Finally, without thinking, without assuming, without wondering if she would survive the night, Ruth gratefully gave herself over to the dark.

14

ONE ROOM, ONE LIGHT,

ONE BODY

"THE FOG COMES in on little cat's feet," Joseph said as he swung open the door for her.

"What?" Hesitating in the hallway, Lauren looked at Joseph askance. She was so exhausted it seemed to her like the middle of the night.

"Or, what is it they say down South—stop pussyfooting around and come on in, y'all?" Joseph finished in a forced tone; but his voice was slurred.

Lauren realized he'd been drinking; it didn't matter how heavily. Joseph was not one to hold his liquor. Even Ruth could drink him under the table. Vaguely, Lauren remembered that it had something to do with Joseph's blood sugar.

Joseph was hurt by Lauren's wary and distracted expression. But, Joseph had to ask himself, what did he expect? Lauren to fly up to his studio on the wings of months of unexpressed passion? No, Lauren didn't have the longing look that had so moved Joseph to reach out to her that morning in the elevator.

Dispirited, Joseph stepped back from the door and let Lauren wander into his studio at her own speed, which was considerably slower and even more wary than any of the alley cats he'd seen up here in his Spanish Harlem neighborhood.

Lauren sat gingerly on the slim sofabed Joseph had covered with a red wool plaid blanket. She was careful to avoid a spring poking up through the cushion.

"I realize it's not the style you've grown accustomed to,"

Joseph commented, and waved his arms around the small, mostly bare studio, "but certainly you have relatives who live like this... you know, fridges and old Chevies rusting in the front yard. Well, just think of me as one of your kinfolk, honey, except I don't even have no front yard." Joseph slumped in the hardback chair across from Lauren and picked up a bottle of Scotch that stood on the snap-tray serving as his endtable. He held it out to her. "Sit yourself a spell," he murmured, "drink your fill... or, swill your swig—whatever they say down..."

"Will you shut up about down South?" Lauren said, surprising herself with her vehemence.

"Ahhhh!" Joseph's grin was his first real greeting. "The fog burns off."

"And another thing...," Lauren continued in a softer, but still firm voice, "I don't think *I'm* being particularly foggy tonight!" She nodded to his fifth of Scotch.

Joseph laughed; it was a real laugh that had the effect on him that finally clearing one's throat has on a chronic cough. He took a deep breath. "Join me, then?" He held out the bottle and with a look of drunken mischief reached behind his chair and handed Lauren a yellow-flowered Dixie cup.

"No comment," Lauren said, but she couldn't help smiling.

"No editorial remarks? Not even any cogent criticism?"

"Nothing," Lauren said softly, her smile fading. "Nothing to kill the pain."

"Then," Joseph gazed at her, "... then, why are you here?"

"You asked me here."

"Ah, yes, now I remember... just another elevator incident...." He faded off and took a drink. Joseph fixed her with a deep frown. "You shouldn't have come. You should have known better, Lauren, than to answer my invitation. I didn't mean it. Besides, if I do remember asking anything, it was asking you *up*. And are you up?"

"Are you down?" Lauren countered. She watched him and felt her anger rising again in spite of herself.

What was wrong with her tonight, anyway? Lauren had to

wonder. First she'd lashed out at Ruth, and now here she was furious with Joseph. Of course, another part of her stood up for her: Ruth was throwing her out of the apartment and Joseph— what was he doing? Drunk and disorderly. Then another little voice reached Lauren. It asked simply, *And what are you doing?*

"I really don't remember inviting you up here, Lauren," Joseph was saying now, but he had his mocking smile as if to say, *We both know why you're here, why you're finally here with me.*

Without thinking, Lauren snapped, "Don't be a jerk, Joseph. Of course, you remember," she faltered and then found herself adding in a low tone, "and so do I."

There was something unleashed in Lauren this moment, and Joseph recognized it. It thrilled him. "I remember," he began. "I remember that the first time I met you in that elevator, I wanted to—"

"Don't say it," Lauren commanded. She looked now like a compact, dark bull, head lowered to charge him if he came at her too directly—as directly as she faced him.

"Why not?" Joseph asked quietly. "Why shouldn't I say it?" Suddenly he started laughing, he hardly knew why himself, or what he'd say next. "And just what is it you think I'm going to tell you, Lauren? Do you think I'm going to proclaim undying love for you?" Joseph couldn't stop laughing. "Undying love?"

Lauren's eyes filled, but Joseph could plainly see it was more from fury than pain. For a moment he thought she might rush at him, just like a little bull, head bent to ram him with all her might. Lauren did bow her head, but only to master herself. After a long moment, she at last said, "No, Joseph, you know better."

Abruptly Lauren stood and walked toward the door. She swung it wide open without looking at him. Joseph noticed for the first time that she hadn't removed her coat. Was it too chilly in here for her? Though it was spring the night was unusually cold. "Is it too cold in here?" he asked, just as Lauren was walking out the door. "I have a heater," he called after her.

He waited several moments. When Lauren did not reappear,

Joseph shrugged. He could barely see straight to pour himself another drink. He glanced back at the open door to see Lauren still standing there. She looked like she hadn't slept in days. Joseph understood this about her, and in accepting this weariness he suddenly acknowledged his own.

Coming into the studio, Lauren shut the door behind her. "Where's the heater?" she asked, taking off her coat.

Joseph gestured to the closet where Lauren found the dilapidated space heater. She looked around for someplace to plug it in. There was an outlet by the bed and one near Joseph's chair.

"Either I'll have to come sit by you or you by me," Joseph said.

"I'll plug it in and put it in the middle . . . there between us." Lauren pointed to a throw rug equidistant between them.

When she turned on the space heater it whirred and the quartz filaments glowed bright orange. For a while that was all they listened to—that, and the sound of street noises far below. The studio was now warm and there was the aroma of baking bread wafting up through the window. They both heard one another's stomachs growl.

She sat on the sofabed, he on the straight-backed chair. They stared at the space heater as if mesmerized.

At last Lauren said, "Do you really believe, Joseph, that I don't know anything about what you're going through? About what you've lost in leaving Ruth, or in Daniel's abandoning you?"

"You don't know what I'm going through," Joseph said flatly. "You've never been through it yourself."

"You're sure about that?" Lauren asked in a low voice. There was no sympathy in her face now, simply a direct gaze. "You have some guarantee written down that Joseph Girard is all alone in this? Why did you leave?"

"Stop trying to understand. You just don't know."

Lauren studied him, then her eyes went back to the quartz heater. "All right," she said quietly, and threw up her hands. "I give up. Just hand me the Scotch."

Joseph stood up and crossed the room slowly. He could barely balance himself, and the liquor coursed through his veins so that he almost heard it whooshing in his ears. He was a regular tidal wave, he told himself. Better watch out.

"You don't really know me at all, Lauren." He stood above her with the bottle. For just a moment he'd had the oddest desire to call her *smarty-pants*, as if they were in fifth grade. God, he told himself, steady now. Don't get juvenile. There was nothing more certain to repel a woman than a man abandoning himself—going backwards until he was so small he'd lose himself in her. Women had nothing but contempt for a man's vulnerability, though they always seemed to encourage it.

Well, he wasn't weak. He was strong. With a great effort of will Joseph reached down and handed Lauren the Scotch. It took almost a superhuman sense of balance for him to pivot, stop, then walk across the room to his chair, where he was safe, away from Lauren's pull on him.

"I don't understand you, Joseph," Lauren began after a long sip of her Scotch, "simply because you don't want me to understand. If I did, you'd have to admit it."

"Admit what?" Joseph demanded.

"That . . ." Lauren quavered and was furious with herself. Was she here to comfort and protect Joseph or herself? Her mission was becoming less and less clear. With the loss of clarity Lauren felt she was losing everything else solid about her, too. "Others are hurt, too," Lauren managed to say, her lips trembling.

"Like you, Lauren?" He waited for her to break open so that he might allow himself to relent—to hold her, to be held.

Instead Lauren gathered herself together and announced stoically, "Ruth, I mean, mostly."

"And what are you? For God's sake, Lauren!" Joseph exploded. "Invisible? A neutral or buffer state? You're in this, too, down in the muck and the mire like the rest of us. What do you think all of this is, if not a *civil war*?" Joseph stood up and faced her from across the room. "I mean, goddammit, Lauren, this is what happens when your precious Gray Ghost Brigade finally realizes just who the enemy is or that there's no enemy, just us civilians trashing and burning one another. And you're in the thick of it! You're here to trash me *and* Ruth, then move on. I know it — you think we're replaceable, that you can just leave us and find others. But let me tell you something, Lauren, that Tata for all his *mishegas* taught me — we're all *rare* and we won't find the likes of each other again...." At this Joseph whirled around and slammed the thin plaster wall with his fist. Then he broke down and sat on the floor in a heap. "We let everyone we love slip through our hands and we can't stop it... we don't really want to stop it." He clasped his hands and rocked himself.

Lauren crossed the room and was leaning near him when Joseph rose and swayed unsteadily to his feet. He grabbed hold of her wrist and yelled, "You come up here like Miss Sweetness and Light to shine on poor little old me. But I tell you, it's false this light you keep shining. It's not real. You're so busy trying to rescue me like some brave little soldier, you don't know whether you even *like* me or not. Loving with you is just a... a reflex. You try to please. You're not choosing. You're so uncommitted; you don't even know why you're here, do you, Lauren?" Joseph began laughing wildly, holding onto her. "You're just like me... in between, in between everybody!"

"Shut up!" Lauren screamed at him, and jerked her hand free. Then he took her by the shoulders and Lauren shoved him back with all her might.

Joseph fell against his chair with such force that he knocked it over and then lay sprawled on the floor.

Lauren yelled with surprise. But Joseph was grinning at her from ear to ear. The moment she realized he wasn't hurt, Lauren began to cry. "Oh, honey, I'm ...so... sorry...," she said between sobs.

"We're all sorry...," Joseph said, making no effort to get up from the floor.

"But I... I attacked you...." Lauren wiped each eye on her sweater cuff. It was her starving-writer's sweater, Joseph remembered, one that he'd almost borrowed. "Do you... do you think I'm..."

"A monster?" Joseph filled in for her. "Now you know what

men feel all the time." Joseph spread out his arms and laughed softly, deeply. "You brute," he said after a grin. When Lauren just looked down at him, as if taking his words to heart, he added, "You're supposed to say, 'Don't play the victim with me! Get up.' "

"Ah," Lauren said, "But I *meant* to hurt you."

"And I you," Joseph said, sitting up. "So that makes two humans here." He reached up and touched her cheek. "But you didn't kill me, did you, Lauren?"

She looked over his body as if checking for some gaping wound. "No," she admitted at last. "I guess I didn't."

"It's because we're the same size," Joseph said, and there was a tenderness in his voice that surprised them both.

"Yes," she said. "I reckon we are at that."

For a long while their eyes rested on one another. Neither broke the gaze; it was not fond. It was frank and clear and level. He held up his hand to her and she hesitated only a moment before helping him up.

"I remember why I asked you here," Joseph said quietly, still holding her hand. He stood now very close to her. "I want what I wanted the first time I ever saw you."

Lauren backed up a step, then crossed to take her place again on the daybed. For a long while she was silent. She lay one hand flat on the red wool blanket as if to steady herself, though it was Joseph who stood weaving in the center of the room.

"Ah," he said. "I shouldn't drink." He shivered, moved toward the space heater. Before its murmuring glow he held out his hands. "Can't hold my liquor." He was aware that only a foot or two above him hung the naked light bulb. He felt its incandescent heat cup his head like a big hand. Suddenly it was very hot in this studio, so hot that Joseph bent and snapped off the space heater. He stood in the middle of the room, his body aching with the lingering heat. "Can I hold you?" he asked her.

"It's not really me you want, Joseph," Lauren said evenly. "Or I you."

"Don't lie," Joseph answered. Still he made no further move

toward her. "You're lying to me, just like you must have lied to Ruth to get out of the house and up here tonight. What did you tell her, anyway? Meeting with your new editor? Working at the library on another draft of your last chapter?"

"Oh, can't you stop it, Joseph?" Lauren asked, hunching her shoulders. "Let's both stop now."

"No," he said. In a moment he was beside her on the single bed. "We're not going to fight again, Lauren, you and I. We're going to make love. Because . . . " Joseph sat beside her on the sagging daybed, but he still didn't touch her. He simply stared straight at her. " . . . Because that's the only thing that makes sense sometimes."

Then Joseph knew how Daniel must have felt, as Lauren faced him now for a long moody moment. Slowly she let her arousal, her anger and resistance show, just the way Joseph had when Daniel finally came to him. Lauren's eyes darkened, changing colors from pale to the sullen gray of lake water. With a deliberate, overcast expression, eyes still level with his, Lauren began unbuttoning the metal snaps of his Levi's. As she felt his swelling, Lauren's eyes widened, the pupils dilating to take him in. Now her eyes seemed as black and deep as Joseph's own.

They plunged into a darkness that even the single bulb above could not illumine; they dove into depths together that neither alone would have dared. It was as if they discovered a dark, moving river that flowed between them, but underground.

He dove into her body, but it was Lauren who felt herself entering him. She entered him as she might a surging body of water that swirled and rushed around her and though they moved against one another with more force than she had ever believed herself capable of containing, there was an eerie stillness of being underwater with one another, but with distant sounds—the far-off, inhuman cries of gulls or whales or people going down.

This made perfect sense: that was all Joseph could think, though he didn't understand it at all. Lauren was slick with their sweat as she eased herself up and down on top of him, all the while staring into his eyes as if she saw something moving there. Joseph realized that it made perfect sense to Lauren, too, though now she began to cry. She rubbed a fist in each of her eyes and leaned way back. Then she embraced him, wrapping her arms and legs around his body, calling out to him before she fell against him like something washed ashore onto his chest, her face tasting salty, stinging his mouth.

"I keep..." Lauren was panting heavily as she lay exhausted. Joseph's skin was so warm and she could feel life rippling through him, up and down his long body. "... Doing these horrible things." Lauren breathed. She wept a moment more, then let out a hiccough.

"That's because you're such a monster," Joseph said, and smoothed her hair, stroking it softly. "Shhh," he said, "shhhh."

"It's awful what we've done," Lauren said, but now she buried her face in the crook of his neck as if it were a cave, a hiding place.

"Yes... awful..." he nodded faintly, staring out at the lights across the rainswept street. Flamini's Fish Market kept flashing its blue and bright yellow sign: *If it swims—we sell it*. Joseph adjusted her weight atop him and said, "Maybe you and I should run away, Lauren. Tata left me a little money. I've been thinking about going to Europe—Poland, maybe. You never know, there might be more Girards left there just like me, God forbid, and Hella will be over there for a month or so; she said I could stay with her in Germany if I want to work on my book."

"Oh, yes," Lauren said lightly with a mock-serious smile. "Run away together... that would solve everything."

He was not used to this tone in Lauren, but Joseph liked it. It reminded him of himself—though in Lauren the irony was lighter and more playful somehow. He reached out an arm and pulled her nose to nose. "Maybe I'm in love with you," he whispered, as if there were someone else in the room who might overhear.

"Maybe not," Lauren said, and lifted herself to sit straddling his chest. Gazing down at him, her direct, candid expression held him closely. "Maybe it's someone else."

"What do you mean?"

"Who else do you make love with like this . . . right here on this bed?" Lauren asked him. "Not Ruth, I know that. But I can tell you've made love here many times with someone else." She shifted her weight and leaned over him. "Who?"

"You," Joseph managed a smile, but his eyes were startled. "In my dreams."

"Me and who else?" She paused, then asked softly, "Daniel?"

Joseph turned his body so that she almost fell off him onto the floor. He said nothing.

Joseph felt a bolt of physical alarm running through his body. It lasted just a moment, but it was unendurable, galvanizing him. This was pure grief. It took him, lasting only fifteen seconds or so, but it left him as weak as if he'd just been electrocuted.

Exhausted, trembling, he lay back beside Lauren, curled near her, his face buried against her back. Lauren adjusted her body to his. They lay like this, intertwined.

They lay a long while, limb to limb—very still. Then Joseph knew that for this moment he was released. He felt cool and tall and supple. Nothing brittle. Nothing broken. Still living.

"It does make sense," Lauren said softly, "it does."

"If you were my friend," Joseph began, his voice a whisper, "if you were just my friend, I'd tell you all about it . . . about Daniel, I mean . . . about Tata—about everything. It would make better sense."

"I am your friend," Lauren said softly.

Though she made no move to distance herself from him physically, he felt her become somehow more distinct from him.

"No, you're my lover now," he said.

Lauren raised herself on an elbow and pulled herself almost luxuriously away from him. She put her hand on his knee. She seemed to be considering him body and soul. Then she decided, smiled, "You're my friend first."

"So . . . ," Joseph laughed and gestured to his naked darkness, "so what's all this then."

"This sometimes happens between friends," Lauren answered softly.

Lauren wrapped her bulky sweater around both of their shoulders. "You're my friend first," Lauren repeated very softly and reached for his hand. "I don't want to lose you."

Everything in Joseph relented. He laid his head on Lauren's shoulder and was quiet for a long while. He felt they were two primitives, just learning how to recognize each other and themselves as human beings.

"So," Lauren began in a low voice, "tell me. You love him, don't you?"

Joseph struggled, then at last said, "I've never loved anyone very long, except my father. I've trashed and burned—it runs in the family."

"The human family," Lauren suggested.

"I think... ," Joseph spoke with difficulty, "I think I do love Daniel. In a way I thought I'd never love, not again. I don't know what this will mean for me, whether I'll go back and forth or make some choice. If I do choose to love only men it will simply be so I won't get too confused. Because the truth of it is... ," he turned to her and brought this out with a sense of wonder at himself, "that I *am* in between."

"Like the Grand Central-to-Times Square shuttle," Lauren smiled faintly. "We need shuttles, too, not just separate tracks—the BMT or the IRT."

"But don't I need to choose, I mean to claim my side?"

"Only if there's a war," Lauren said, and now she did smile. "If you're a civilian, as a dear friend keeps trying to teach me, you simply choose who it is you love—no matter the sex, no matter the North or South of it. I mean, there's no right way of loving. I guess the point is just managing to love at all."

"To keep holding something in our hands, even if those hands have been ruined," Joseph said softly. "My father did that. I never realized because he always let me know how hard it was for him to stay. But he did stay. He didn't let me slip through his hands. He held on—he finally kept hold of someone." Joseph abruptly turned to look at Lauren. "You're not ashamed of me?"

Shoulder-to-shoulder they sat on the bed, exchanging a long

look. "I'm only ashamed of myself," Lauren said.

"Why?"

"I've betrayed a friend."

"And found another," Joseph reminded her.

"Rather have you both," Lauren said.

"Oh," Joseph said sadly, "I wouldn't understand that at all. You know, Lauren, I think we spend our whole lives trying to figure out just *who* we all are to one another. I mean, how we should love one another, what form that will take. I also think we have so much to choose from that we can't choose. Somehow everything including ourselves becomes expendable. That's why we trash and burn because we think there's always someone else. There isn't."

Lauren touched Joseph's face. "We're—how did you say it?—rare." She let go of touching him and in that moment completely claimed him. "You're rare, my friend."

"I'm not your red-hot lover?"

"Yes, honey," she murmured, "real red hot... and a one-night stand to boot."

He nodded, "One night, one light, one room, one body—everything else..."

"Everything else we'll just have to figure out come morning," Lauren finished for him. Then she felt very tired.

"You'll sleep with me?" Joseph asked. "Just sleep." He stood up and turned off the light bulb.

"Been a long time since I've slept with anyone," Lauren said as if just realizing it now. "Yes, I'd like to sleep for a little while. Let someone else keep the duty watch. I'm gone," she said. "Off-duty."

They pulled the old comforter over them. They were so close on the slim sofabed, there was no need for embracing. Lauren's arms rested on Joseph's side, her cheek against his back. And then they rested on one another like children, like civilians.

LEAVES OF ABSENCE

As she waited outside the sturdy wooden door of the Steinhardts' apartment, Ruth listened to the light footsteps hastening toward her voice; she felt the wonder and surge of well-being that a newborn knows when her cries at last summon that soft woman who moves across the darkness, to bring the whole, bright world back into being.

Last night Ruth had felt utterly abandoned. All night she wandered the apartment, her hands resting briefly on this oak chair or that familiar glass table. She felt no sense of possession—of self-possession—which her own home usually lent her. Instead, it seemed she had died there and was haunting herself. Everything was out of place, though she herself had arranged it. Ruth cleaned, played old records, even sat ramrod-straight at the piano for an hour of rigorous scales—but nothing shook the world back into place. At last she emptied the Chemex of its hours-old coffee and trundled off to bed. She hadn't slept at all.

"You look tired," Hella commented as she opened the door. "Come. I've made coffee."

The older woman was still in her plaid-flannel robe. Her flat leather slippers made a whoosh-whoosh on the hardwood floor as she led Ruth into the wide bedroom where a little yellow table was set with two big blue porcelain cups, a crystal bowl of marmalade, and toast. Nearby, Hella's bifocals lay atop a scribbled manuscript.

Ruth smiled; it was a familiar scene, not only because she had met Hella many times for a working weekend breakfast, but also because the scene was so much like a breakfast Ruth herself might have offered.

Ruth felt morning sunlight warm her shoulders as she took her seat, as if someone had fondly draped a shawl over her.

"Do you want me to turn on the lamp?" Hella asked as she sat down across from Ruth.

"Oh, no," Ruth smiled, remembering that Hella took her breakfast here at the windowseat, always by natural light. "This is just right."

Ruth took a deep breath. She had stopped shivering. Her hand trembled once as she reached for the coffee, and though Hella noted this she said nothing; she simply waited for Ruth to begin.

"Your coffee's twice as strong as mine!" Ruth said after a sip; she held the oversized mug in both hands, warming them.

"I'm twice as old as you," Hella smiled.

It was a fact that Ruth had always taken for granted. But this morning she felt the weight of those years: Hella had all Ruth's successes, losses, and longings doubled. This morning it seemed impossible that anyone could survive all that twice over.

Hella asked softly, "So, will you be leaving, too, my dear? Is that what you are here to tell me?"

"Leaving?" Ruth was stunned.

"You have the look . . . ," Hella began slowly, not bothering to disguise her scrutiny, "the look of someone who is leaving."

"It's not me who's leaving, Hella," Ruth said. She was grateful at least that Hella had bypassed the small talk. Ruth already had waited all night long to talk to someone. "It's I who've been left," Ruth added.

"Same thing."

"No," Ruth hastily brushed away a tear in the corner of one eye. "I don't believe that."

Hella smiled tenderly at the younger woman, then waved her hand. "Believe what you like, my dear. But I can tell you that people don't leave one another so much as they change."

Ruth looked down, her lips trembling. Then she began with an unfamiliar bitterness. "First it was my father," she said, "he changed all right—he died. Then it was Daniel... being forced out of Cowley and Pelzner... what kind of change is that?" Ruth did not look up for Hella's answer, but continued in a rush. "Then it was Joseph and now—now Lauren's off on her own. She never came home last night from Adrianne's. I think she's planning to move out, too."

Hella sat back, sipping her coffee. For a long while she said nothing, simply waited as the younger woman struggled and then succeeded to hold back her tears. When Hella saw that Ruth would only sit stoically and drink her coffee, she began in a musing voice, "You know, my dear, I didn't have children until very late in life...."

Ruth looked across at Hella curiously, as if to say *What does that have to do with anything?* But Ruth was too miserable or too polite to interrupt Hella's reverie. Hella's face seemed to smooth out, unwrinkle like silk under an iron.

"And until my own children came along," Hella continued, "I'd always found others to take care of—my writers, friends, even dear Samuel. Then, of course, Daniel and I have always looked after one another. All these years..." Hella paused, poured herself more black coffee. She took a long sip, then said, "We Germans are raised with rules; well, I once thought there was a rule to loving: if I love well enough, I will not be left alone." Hella looked straight at Ruth. "But, you see, my children and then Daniel's heart attack have at last taught me this: I begin alone and end alone. Who, then, can leave me? Or whom can I leave alone? I would simply be leaving someone to his or her own essential nature—and own work." Hella sipped her coffee. "That is not so bad a thing."

"It sounds pretty grim to me," Ruth said.

"Only if one doesn't survive oneself," Hella said and then laughed softly. "And even then—well, who knows?" Hella leaned over and touched Ruth's hand briefly. For a minute Hella rubbed Ruth's hand between hers. Then she let go and sat back, studying Ruth with a look of familiarity and fondness. "You remind me of my grandmother, Ruth," Hella said. "She was like you, full of beliefs and wanting to do the whole world good. If she'd been in this country she would have been one of your suffragettes, or maybe a nun."

Ruth winced slightly at this, but then found herself almost smiling because Hella's face was alive with memories and her tone was so good-natured it carried Ruth along with it.

"Well, my grandmother—we called her *Nanu*—had many children, all of whom grew up exactly like her—true believers. Of course, no one got along. They each had their own exact way. When they all finally left Nanu's home for their various lives, Nanu told me she believed them terribly ungrateful . . . just running off to all parts of the world. But you see, she raised them to follow their beliefs. And follow they did—right out her door!"

"Do you think she did a good job?"

"Yes," Hella nodded firmly.

"Did no one come back to Nanu? Was she always alone?"

Hella smiled indulgently, "Yes, Ruth, she was always alone."

Ruth paused, opened her mouth, then fell silent. Something moved behind her eyes, and then at last she nodded. "Oh," she said, "oh." She shook her head at herself, then added, "You'd think I'd know that by now . . . being an only child."

"No," Hella said gently, "some things have to be taught us over and over and over." Hella fell silent, then began again. "Nanu was simply the first to teach me." Hella made as if to smile at Ruth, but her face was sad.

"Did you ever go back to Nanu?" Ruth asked very softly.

"Yes," Hella said, "I made my own way back to her just before she died. It's funny, you know, but none of her children or grandchildren had really spent much time with Nanu. Of course, there were fewer of us to come back after the war. Still, some made a yearly pilgrimage to London, where Nanu had exiled herself long before the Nazis, disliking most things German. Nanu was always a free spirit. But in her last days she was far from free. She was really quite, quite stricken, you see . . . "

"Ill?"

"Well, there was that certainly . . . her body was so old, rotting away actually, as if she were no more than vegetable matter disintegrating." Hella placed her hand next to Ruth's and without a word Ruth compared the two—her hands, like her father's, strong, finely veined, and Hella's, large and translucent. Hella continued very slowly, "There comes a time when all the body can do is lean toward light—like some sort of plant life. It's very simple. The husk is dying like so many corn stalks in September sunlight—have you ever heard a field of them whispering? While what was inside is gone, or going, or struggling to go?" Hella paused, and when she spoke again her voice was hoarse. "Nanu was like that. I can still hear how her dress crinkled like those husks moving as she lay on the sofa. She did not look the slightest bit familiar to me—and I was scared. I was also young, younger even than you, Ruth, if you can imagine that . . . "

"I can, Hella."

"Nanu simply looked straight up at me and at last I was not afraid anymore. She was so *present* with me that I could not bear the idea of her leaving. I bent down beside her and laid my head on her shoulder and sobbed. She did not touch me—the simplest movement could unhinge her back. But I had the feeling of all of her embracing all of me. Then Nanu said, 'Yes, *Liebchen*, we won't be seeing one another again for awhile, my darling. So what I want you to do is when you leave, let the door be open behind you. Don't close it. I want to listen—I want to listen to your footsteps as you go. . . . ' " Hella stopped. Her face was suddenly very young, younger than Ruth. Ruth felt as old and dark and simple as Nanu. "Left or leaving, changed or changing," Hella said softly, "we see one another out."

They were both quiet a long while, then Hella passed Ruth the plate of toast.

Ruth held up her hands. "No, thanks. I'm not hungry."

"Your mother should have taught you how to feed yourself," Hella said. It was a statement made so gently that there was no judgment. Instead Ruth felt comforted.

Hella put the plate back on the table. She took a piece of toast for herself, buttered it generously and then dropped a large dollop of marmalade on top.

"Hella," Ruth began at last, "I called you this morning because . . . well, I hope this doesn't sound silly, . . . but because I felt so odd last night."

"Sad, you mean."

"Well, yes, sad, I guess . . . like I didn't fit anymore in my own apartment."

"Even the snake leaves its skin," Hella said, then laughed abruptly. "My father was always saying that."

Ruth nodded vaguely, then continued as if she hadn't heard. "Hella, have you ever felt . . . displaced?" Ruth's indiscretion made her blush. "Oh, I'm sorry, I . . . "

"*Ja*, well. . . . " Hella shrugged and took a great bite of her toast. "It wasn't so bad being ordinary."

"Ordinary?"

"Like everybody else . . . with no difference, with nothing really obvious like money or class to distinguish ourselves one from another."

"That can hardly describe you, Hella."

Hella looked at Ruth good-naturedly and slowly chewed her toast. "Are you hungry yet?" Hella asked.

Ruth idly took a piece of toast. She buttered it, decided to do without the marmalade, and then thought she might take just a little.

"I have a whole jar of it, you know," Hella said, smiling at the small portion Ruth allowed herself. "My niece makes this marmalade and ships it to me, jar after jar, as if I didn't have any of my own teeth left so why worry about sweets?"

"Does she live upstate?" Ruth asked, careful to avoid Hella's eyes.

"You're asking does she live near my summer house?"

"Yes."

"Where Daniel is staying?"

Ruth leaned near and impulsively laid a hand on Hella's. "Oh, I miss him so much, . . . more than anybody."

Hella clasped her hand over Ruth's. "And he you, my dear."

The idea of Daniel missing her had never occurred to Ruth. During his last months at the magazine Daniel had been so cool, so distant, as if he'd already abandoned her. Ruth felt tears start in her eyes and this time allowed them to stream down her face. "I don't believe that!"

"Ah, you and all your beliefs. This is not something to believe. This is something you already know to be true—you simply won't accept it. Most things that are truly important are like that. We know them already, we just don't accept."

"Don't lecture me, Hella," Ruth said, and angrily wiped her eyes. "Why should Daniel suddenly miss me now?"

"Because as long as we live, everything is negotiable," Hella said quietly. "Even death doesn't really stop us going through this give-and-take with one another."

Then something inside Ruth was moving. She let the tears run down her cheeks.

"You matter to Daniel a great deal," Hella began slowly, speaking directly to Ruth's bent head. "And he has hurt you." Hella's voice faded off. "But these are things he will tell you himself . . . when he can."

Ruth felt a stirring within her stomach and she realized she was ravenously hungry. All she'd had last night was that bit of salad she'd forced herself to eat in her middle-of-the-night wanderings, and this morning nothing. She reached for the toast and covered it with marmalade. "Will you leave, too?" Ruth asked Hella the question she'd not known was on her mind. "Will you go to Daniel now for good?"

"Yes," Hella said softly. "We will see one another out, Daniel and I."

"And Samuel?" Ruth asked.

"Samuel is part of us. He'll stay in the city and visit Binghamton when he can. Even at my age, I can begin again." She looked straight at Ruth. "Daniel has, too."

"How?"

"We're starting our own publishing house—a very modest one. We have put together at least enough for the first years." Hella laughed out loud. "We are rich in some ways: we have our writers and our friends, all of whom are *very* hard workers."

Ruth returned Hella's smile with a warmth of her own. "And these hardworking friends—are they just as ordinary as you?"

"Exactly." Hella nodded. "And yourself."

"Shall I quit Cowley and Pelzner and join you and Daniel?"

"Do what you want," Hella said. "But my advice is to stay here in the city for a while. Until we can pay you."

"But you must know I want to work with both you and Daniel again. The money is not the issue."

"Let Daniel ask you himself," Hella suggested.

"Hella," Ruth said. "Just tell him to ask."

RUTH RETURNED from the office that night and still felt out of place in her own apartment. Lauren sat downcast at the kitchen table. She still wore her peacoat, as if any minute she might bolt again.

"Back for your things?" Ruth said coolly.

Lauren said nothing as Ruth walked past her, making for the refrigerator.

"You know, Lauren," Ruth was on her knees to clean the refrigerator, "I've been doing more thinking about last night." She pulled a large black plastic bag from its roll and dumped old, shrivelled vegetables from the bin into it. "This apartment just won't do anymore, though of course I'll still keep it . . . perhaps as a workspace." Ruth glanced across the kitchen at Lauren, who barely seemed to be listening. Perhaps she'd even nodded off. With a certain annoyance, Ruth said, "We were speaking of this last night before you bolted out of here so suddenly."

"When will you be moving out?" Lauren asked, rousing herself. "I've already begun looking myself."

"So you *are* leaving?" Ruth said, and angrily crammed some wilting buttercrunch lettuce into the garbage bag. "I guessed as much."

"Guessed?" Lauren said, bewildered. *"You* were the one who *asked* me to leave."

Ruth stared at Lauren in confusion. "I only asked you to look for another place with me, Lauren. But that didn't seem to interest you in the slightest. You ran out of here—"

"What?" Lauren asked. "What are you talking about? You never asked me to move anywhere with you. You just told me you wanted to live alone again."

Ruth sighed and turned to the metal shelves. She saw on the bottom shelf at least ten little containers with gnarled tinfoil tops. Ruth tossed them into the trash without a glance. Only then did she turn back to Lauren. "I can't imagine how you got that idea, Lauren," she said. "Is that why you ran out of there like someone was after you?"

Lauren looked down. For a long while she fingered the salt and pepper shakers, picking up one, then the other, so deliberately that it irritated Ruth. "It wasn't the only reason."

"Lauren," Ruth began, exasperated. "Last night I thought I made it perfectly clear..."

"The only thing you made clear last night was that I needed to sew the damn buttons back on my coat!" Lauren burst out, then just as abruptly fell quiet. At last she added in a very low voice, "And you asked me to stop lying."

Ruth was quiet for a long while, too. At last she remarked, "Have you?"

Lauren looked directly at Ruth, kneeling before the open refrigerator, whose harsh bulb shone on Ruth's face. In this light, Ruth looked frail and older. But Lauren didn't have the first notion of how to reach out for her. "Well," Ruth finally said, "did you at least have fun last night?"

"Fun?" Lauren asked dully.

"At Adrianne's?"

Lauren's face fell. As she stared at Ruth it seemed they were not in a kitchen at all, but outside in the woods standing on opposite sides of a circle someone had drawn in the dirt. Neither could move toward the other; they could only circle.

Slowly Lauren stood up, and from her side of the kitchen Ruth also stood, her arms crossed. Lauren cast about for some story to tell Ruth, although, she thought, surely her friend must know, with the uncanny instinct of all betrayed lovers.

Lauren opened her mouth to lie, and then she noticed that Ruth's hands in their pink plastic kitchen gloves were trembling. This was not someone Lauren had to fend off, fight, protect herself from. Here was someone she herself had hurt.

Only then did Lauren cry. She cried like she had cried last night with Joseph. As a child she remembered holding her head up, letting tears splash down her cheeks. But she had always kept her eyes open, watchful, on the lookout. Now she simply sat back down and put her elbows thump-thump on the kitchen table. She covered her face with both hands and sobbed.

Be like water, that's what her father always said. Well, she'd done just that, hadn't she? She'd let all the passion and unacknowledged depths rise up in her, and look what had happened, look at all she had destroyed. At last Lauren met Ruth's gaze as steadily as her tears allowed.

"Your eyes change color when you cry," was Ruth's only comment.

"How?"

"They're darker," Ruth answered.

Lauren could barely see Ruth's expression because now her eyes were swelling. Nevertheless Lauren at last faced her friend and said, "I have something to tell you."

"Does it make a good story?" Ruth asked. Her eyes, too, were now full and level with Lauren's.

"No," Lauren began, "it's not a good story."

Part VI

BEGINNING AGAIN

FALL 1973

16

SURVIVING ONE ANOTHER

"Daniel," Ruth called from the window, "do you think it's time to bring the bonsai inside?"

Across the spacious front room of the brownstone they'd converted into the Brooklyn office of their Pleiades Press, Daniel Sorenson was just reaching for a book from his shelf. As he stretched he felt the familiar tightness of the scar running across his chest. Months ago the cinch of skin so near his heart might have made him cross his palms over it in a gesture so like one of the dead that it would have frightened him; now the pull and tug of new skin was oddly comforting.

"A bonsai belongs outside," Daniel answered.

"But I worry the first frost will kill it." Ruth opened the window and protectively pulled the delicate blue-potted tree inside.

"Save that mothering for Sarandon's manuscript." Daniel turned back to his bookshelves. "I think his novel needs a deep revision and God knows he'll need a good midwife. Sarandon has such a difficult time with revision. Even at C&P...." Here Daniel stopped, not to frown but more to smile at himself. It was the first time he'd referred to Cowley and Pelzner all week.

"Remember our rule," Ruth laughed, and shook a warning finger at him. "If you mention C&P once more this week, you'll buy cocktails."

"That old place does have a hold," Daniel commented.

"What and who doesn't, Daniel?" Ruth said, and with a sigh

replaced the bonsai in her windowbox. "I *will* bring the geraniums in," she announced, "come the first frost."

Daniel didn't answer, distracted now by the morning mail. For a long time they worked in silence, he reading over the manuscript that had just arrived with foreign postage and Ruth poring over the galleys of their first book of essays by one of Daniel's long-time authors who'd followed him from Cowley and Pelzner to Pleiades.

There was only the soft, steaming sound of the kettle, and from the outside alcove drifted the voice of the intern they'd hired to help with phones, correspondence, and their spring catalog. Though Hella still consulted with Cowley and Pelzner, she was more and more a part of Pleiades. This week she was upstate in the house she shared with Daniel, editing the first Pleiades fiction—a translation of a Spanish novel Hella had long admired but despaired of ever publishing in this country.

When she took a break from her galleys to make herself another cup of English Breakfast, Ruth made her daily call to Hella.

"Oh, it's you, dear." Hella's voice always seemed so near.

Ruth found herself first asking, "Don't you think we should bring in the bonsai tree, Hella?"

"I can see the press is being swamped with calls from booksellers," Hella laughed. "I was under the impression that we were running a publishing house, not a nursery."

"I've had two bonsai trees die on me," Ruth explained, "and I just don't want—"

"That was your Cowley and Pelzner windowbox," Hella gently reminded her. "This is a new windowbox, much closer to the ground—maybe the rate of attrition is less."

"Yes," Ruth said slowly, "some things survive, Hella, don't they?"

"Let your bonsai brave a Brooklyn winter," Hella suggested. "It might very well thrive. Now, what about the mechanical for the Cecilia book cover? Is that back from the printer yet?"

"I'll give you to Daniel on that," Ruth said, and signaled for him to pick up his line.

As she went back to her work, Ruth was aware of Daniel's voice. Had it gotten deeper, more throaty since the heart surgery? Ruth was always slightly concerned for him, though he had made a complete recovery. In fact, Ruth had to admit, glancing at him across the office, Daniel Sorenson was more vibrant than she'd seen him in years—certainly since last year at this time. Though the office was still warm from the late autumn afternoon sun, the thought of last winter made Ruth shiver. She glanced again at her windowbox, where geraniums still bloomed; her bonsai's miniature juniper branches were so pungent she could smell them through the crack in the window. Soon winter would come again —the season that in the city had always scared Ruth. But perhaps Hella was right; this Brooklyn winter might be kinder.

Joseph had always said that Brooklyn was Manhattan's poor, comic cousin, not the tragic hero, just the guy who survives: lacking grace to fall from, just getting by on wits and a sense of personal smallness in the scheme of things. "Brooklyn laughs at itself," Joseph said; "Manhattan takes itself seriously."

Unlike the subject of Cowley and Pelzner, Ruth and Daniel very rarely found themselves speaking of Joseph Girard. But today was different, and perhaps that was one of the reasons Ruth found herself making such an issue of the bonsai. She'd seen the foreign envelope with Joseph's familiar writing. Unlike most Pleiades Press mail, this was unopened by their intern or by Ruth; it was left to Daniel to receive Joseph's first communication since he'd left for Europe several months ago. Ruth was not so much uneasy for herself: since her break-up with Joseph she'd felt a freedom that her marriage and affair with Joseph had never allowed. No, she was worried that Joseph's presence might again put a rift between her and Daniel.

Forgiving Daniel for not telling her about his love for Joseph had been easier than forgiving Daniel for all those last months of coldness toward her at Cowley and Pelzner. Sometimes even now she had a flash of sheer fury at Daniel; Ruth recognized this anger as a deepening in her devotion to him. Nothing was simple: she loved Daniel sometimes like a father; other times, she was delighted to work alongside him as the full partner he insisted she be at Pleiades. But there were those times when she railed against him in her heart because he had left her, because he would leave again. So it was true—Ruth now thought, looking at her bonsai, so beautiful and small—it was true, as a writer had told her last week: "We also hate the people we love. That's why so few people ever let themselves be truly penetrated by love."

"Do you know what Hella thinks we should do?" Daniel was asking Ruth now, as he crossed to pour himself tea.

"I know what we should do," Ruth said suddenly, not even knowing herself what she was about to propose. "I think the three of us should simply buy this place."

"The entire brownstone?" Daniel asked, surprised.

"Every inch," Ruth said firmly.

"Even if the three of us could afford it, there'd be—"

"Ever heard of the Littlefield Grants to the Arts?" Ruth raised her eyebrows and smiled. "I might be of some influence with the board."

"But the press hasn't proved itself yet," Daniel countered.

"Neither has my bonsai," Ruth said. "But Hella thinks we'll all brave the Brooklyn winter just fine."

"And what would we do with all the space? Fill it slowly with books?"

"Well, I could sell my Park Avenue apartment and take the top floor." Ruth stood up. She was so excited she began pacing the floor—a habit that reminded Daniel of himself. He smiled at the sight and sat back in his chair, enjoying her.

"Yes, and would we have rent-paying lodgers to help us with the mortgage?"

"What about a studio on the second floor for a writer? For example, Sarandon hates revision and can hardly bring himself to the typewriter.... Why not offer him a workplace here for a time so we could help him finish the book?"

"Most writers shun editors over their shoulders," Daniel laughed. "But perhaps a translator in-residence or a writer here during the editing or a room of one's own for one of our own?"

"And if not a writer," Ruth continued, "why not one of us?" She paused mid-step and sat down on a stool near his desk. "When I was a child I used to imagine a place for all my friends. Perhaps it was because I was the only child, but there would be so much room for people to live here, too." Ruth dropped her voice, "Once," she admitted, "once I envisioned that we'd all—you, Hella, me, Joseph, and Lauren—all live together in a large house and somehow work together, too. We wouldn't all have to be in-residence at once, of course, but the little apartments within the big house would be there... open to us. It would be... well, like a tribe of individuals. We could come and go and somehow still be together."

"Always the utopian," Daniel said in his best Brooklyn accent.

"That accent would make even Joseph laugh," Ruth said, and then realized that it was the first time since their long, difficult reunion that she'd brought up Joseph's name between herself and Daniel.

His reaction was to give her a direct, level look and then nod as if something between them were sealed. An agreement, an opening, an ease. "Speaking of Joseph: here." Daniel handed Ruth the foreign envelope. "I'd like you to take a look at the manuscript he sent me today."

Ruth took the envelope tentatively and noticed the personal letter was still enclosed. "You can read his letter, too," Daniel said. "And tell me what you think." Daniel turned back to his own work and she to her desk. Just as she was beginning Joseph's letter, Daniel added, "And Ruth..."

"Yes?"

"I'll speak to Hella about your idea."

"Are you for it?" she asked, and met his eyes evenly.

"Yes," he said softly, "I'm for it."

"Then it's settled," Ruth said, and turned to the letter and its enclosed manuscript. "The bonsai will stay outside." Then Ruth read:

Munich, Oct. 10, 1973

Dear Daniel,

Hella gave me your letter when I met her here in Munich. I was so glad to hear from you after this long silence. Sometimes, in my worst moments, I believed you'd never see or write me again. And I've missed you, more than I can say.

Hella says that you are almost completely healed, enough for you both to begin your own publishing house. She's asked me to send you "Survivor," the new first chapter of the novel on which you and I worked for so long. You'll see Hella's hand in this, too. In fact, with my father, and you, and Hella, the story seems at last to be telling itself.

Thank you for all you've given me, Daniel. This story is my small way of trying to give something back to you. I don't know when I'll be in the States again. It's fitting that I should spend Tata's inheritance writing this book that has so much of his spirit in it. It has yours and Hella's spirit, too, I hope. When I've got a rough draft of the manuscript, I'll come back to Brooklyn, to my home, to my—I hesitate to even say it—to my family.

Please let me hear from you. Hella tells me the story of her own parents who, though separate and living in opposite districts of Vienna, still wrote one another letters every day, using their children as couriers on bicycles. Perhaps you and I can begin again working together from opposite sides of the Atlantic. I think of you with such deep affection and gratitude.

Love,
Joseph

P.S. I've located a few members of my mother's family who survived and even flourished after the war. One of them, a distant cousin, Karl, has offered me a place to stay for as long as I need. Karl and I are very close; he reminds me of you, Daniel. I'll be bringing him home with me when I come back to the States.
P.P.S. My love to Ruth and Lauren.

Ruth looked across the office to see Daniel just gathering his coat to leave.

"Lunch?" he offered, and in his tone was all that was unspoken between them—all the complexities to come, the difficulties past, the healings.

"No, thanks," Ruth answered. "I've got a manuscript to read."

Daniel gazed at her from the doorway. He straightened his hat, his expression fond, familiar. "Do tell me what you think, my dear," he said.

"Yes, Daniel." Ruth adjusted her glasses, picked up her red pen. "Always." And without another word, she leaned over the manuscript.

Survivor

Chapter 1.

—by Joseph Girard

What can my children mean when they say "I wouldn't want to survive a holocaust?" What of life have they already annihilated when they say in their hearts, "No, I would rather die"? Who, then, will tell the stories? No one, you say? No one because there will be no one left to hear?

Oh, my dears, in spite of the enemy, in spite of oneself, someone always survives. Look at me, a survivor from another holocaust, an old woman whose bones were bent, not by age, but by my youth.

Those of us who died in Auschwitz—my mother, my husband, my small son—do you call them heroes simply because they left such a world? Is the survivor who tells the stories not a hero, too? What about those of us who still stand in the shadows of the stage at the end of the tragedy and cry, "O world! world! world!"?

In the world of Auschwitz there was no ground zero; it was a slow descent, a terrible, vegetable dance backwards. We did not die instantly, but first had to retreat through anthropological time: we stripped ourselves of children and future, of mates and love, of possessions and tools. Genderless, we became creatures again. We did not reflect or dream. We shuttled back and forth in the mud, in the barracks, in the killing factories. Our only thought was food. To eat was to live. Like the Germans, we became things. We still buried our dead. It was what made us human, like the Neanderthals. But who will bury all my children in the next holocaust? Who will tell my story?

When I first came to this country, I was very young. Death was second-nature to me. Sometimes I even missed it. America was too new, like magazine advertisements. The war went on and on in some people's minds and I was, after all, German. The fact that I was a German Jew straight from the Prague displaced persons camp, my father and I the only survivors of our once huge family —this didn't make us any less the enemy there in that little town in upstate New York. It was 1947 and everyone here seemed to have a washing machine and a big car. I was astonished. Had war bonds made America so rich?

My father died in hospital with such clean white sheets. I saw on my father's face —this man who had been put to work as a doctor in Mengeles' "hospital" in the children's ward —I saw my father's relief. He would not have to live or remember one minute more. As I took his arm, he whispered with a fierceness that shall always haunt me, "Grete, find your twin. Live for him."

Of course, I had no twin. Now I had no father. I felt like I was the last person left on earth, and in a way I was. I was the last of my kind. After I buried Father —I would *not* have him burned— all I wanted was to sleep. That was something I never got enough of in the camp. I didn't want to dream. But I did.

I dreamed of my friend Samuel. He was a violin student. He sang me entire symphonies there on the arrival platform as we waited for the trains of deported Jews. We took their possessions and never breathed a word of what else would be taken from them. We walking shadows were called "Canada" after that rich country because what we took from our fellow Jews made the Nazis rich. Samuel, before his deportation from Hungary, had played third violin in the Vienna Youth Philharmonic.

"You have to imagine the rest of the orchestra," Samuel would tell me, "just like you have to imagine that there is, outside, another world."

Ten days before the Allies came, guards took Samuel to Killing Factory Number 2. I watched him be led off. His scalp was sore from ringworm and his legs were bowed from malnutrition. Samuel joked that he had, at last, become his own instrument. He asked the guards as they thrust him into the shower to make a violin bow out of *his* hair. . . .

Well, that was Samuel. The day I took all my father's sleeping pills, I dreamed first of Samuel, and I did hear music, *his* music. It was so beautiful, it broke my heart. When my neighbor found me I was already almost one with the music that held Samuel, my father, my son, my all. I was unconscious, but still humming aloud —something from "Die Zauberflöte," or what you in this country call "The Magic Flute." I'd hummed as far as the Queen of the Night's aria, O *zitt' re nicht, mein lieber Sohn.* When my neighbor called the ambulance some part of me was aware and damned her; this was no rescue. I wanted the dark queen.

Those first days in the American hospital were so quiet; it reminded me of the last week in Auschwitz. Everybody there was just waiting, too. At night, when I came out of the sedative, I held my breath, remembering a woman who slept next to me in those filthy wooden bunks. One night Maria just announced she would die: not one more day would she survive the horror. I lay listening to her breath. And it did stop. Maria was gone; she willed it so.

But when two years later, I tried to will myself dead in a clean American hospital, my body breathed on, fierce and greedy, like a baby. I realized I would have to work to die. I began believing then that if I could just sing my way through the entire "Magic Flute," I would disappear like Maria. Music, too, has a will of its own. It is hardly human. So was I, hardly human.

I began singing softly to myself. I refused all food. In my singing I got as far as the duet between Pamina and Papageno and then suddenly I forgot what came next. Me, a once distinguished opera student! Much praised by my peers. But then, my peers were all dead. What could they tell me?

In desperation one morning at breakfast, I stole a fork and later gouged my wrists. A young psychologist about my age—his name was Frank—put my in solitary, like a common prisoner. He took me off the sedatives and said to call him when I was tired of keeping company with killers. Pretty strong stuff, wouldn't you say, for a kid psychologist? He was probably too young, even, to go to war. What did he know? The only thing I liked about him was his impatience with me. That I had to admire, as well as his lack of sympathy. Locked in solitary, I was impatient, too; and I certainly had no sympathy for myself.

I told myself that this was exactly what I wanted—to be left as alone as I knew myself to be. No visitors. Who would come? Only young Frank. And if he thought for a moment that I would fall for that "killer" routine... well, I was a very smart young woman. I had gone to university; I was a woman of talent and passion, the best that Europe—after all *its* attempts at suicides—could offer. Who was this Frank fellow? A naive and wrongheaded American who couldn't know that the world had gone mad outside his sleepy little upstate hamlet. He was as bland, arrogant, and deluded, this blond, blue-eyed boy, as any Nazi.

I was even embarrassed for him one day. He was whistling. Light and breezy as if nowhere in the world was there still any suffering. But he was a fine whistler. I wondered if he had perfect pitch, like me. I almost thought he did, listening to him as he whistled down the hall outside my cell. Then it occurred to me that

Frank could help me with my plan to disappear. Perhaps he knew "The Magic Flute," or perhaps he could help me finish singing it?

As I said, there is a great will in music; it comes out of nothing, like air that goes in and out of our bodies. I was so intent on remembering my opera that I barely noticed the nurses floating in and out with their feeding tubes. I did drink water, because I needed it for my voice to work. I also noticed Frank, because sometimes I heard him pick up snatches of an aria I was singing softly. He'd walk away down the hall whistling it absently. But one day I heard him do more than just mimic me: he actually whistled the rest of that duet I'd forgotten! I burst out laughing. It hurt my throat and split my lips, but I didn't care. Soon I would be gone and Frank would help execute me.

Then this Frank comes the next morning and takes me from my cell into a playroom. Ungodly bright, it was painted yellow, a terrible luminous yellow like sunlight. It was a room meant for a child, not me. Frank sat down near me and said in his light, nonchalant voice, "You're wrong about that duet, you know."

I was indignant! *"Bei Männern, welche Liebe fühlen?"* I demanded, and hoped my high German might throw him off. "I know that duet perfectly well, young man, I *performed* it."

Frank sat back and smiled at me. I thought I saw contempt in his grin. "No," he said, "listen...." And then he began singing, in my language, a beautiful, perfect German. But it wasn't his facility with my language that struck me to my core, it was his voice as he sang first Pamina's part and then Papageno's. I, who had always sung Pamina, heard those lovely notes sung by a man. It was like hearing the opera for the first time. I cried and that made me furious; Frank pretended not to notice; and because of that and his voice, I almost let myself like him. But when I asked him to bring me a record player and the opera, he flatly refused. I truly hated him.

"But I will do one thing for you," Frank told me, and in his tone was the contempt I had seen in his smile. It made me so angry; but I said nothing, then when he was silent I finally had to ask,

"What's that? What can *you* do for me?"

"Sing with you."

"Sing what?" I asked suspiciously. Could he know of my plan?

"*Die Zauberflöte*, of course."

I almost choked at that. Never in my life had I wanted anything so badly as what this man was offering; but I had to be so careful not to show my need. If I showed anything to make me human, this careless stranger might take it away.

He had the power to blot me out, to utterly cancel my existence. I had somehow given him that power. Well, I assured myself, we both wanted the same thing now: we both wanted to destroy me.

"All right," I said slowly, trying to assume Frank's own nonchalance. "I'll... I'll sing the opera with you; but we must sing it from beginning to end. I don't want to repeat passages, though you might need some help. Why not bring the music along?"

"No," he said simply.

"The libretto, then?"

"No, I don't need it, do you?"

I could hardly reply. A wave of nausea and dizziness moved over me and for a moment I felt faint. Again, he didn't seem to notice, and again I was grateful. He knew what a thing I had become. It was no secret. Of that I was sure, and my relief was remarkable. "Of course, I don't need anything. The music is in my head." I had recovered myself completely, and Frank nodded.

"Well," he said, "that's settled. We'll begin it tomorrow, here in the playroom."

I made a face at that word—*playroom*. These Americans are so juvenile. But I let it go because Frank, unknowingly, was going to deliver me to my death. Oh, how he would mourn! How he would rue his helping me disappear. It might even ruin his professional reputation, just as the Nazis ruined my father's.

"One thing," Frank said as he was leaving, "you'll have to play a game with me." He shrugged and made a face as if to say "rules are rules." Then he nodded toward the outside and I understood he was not as much in control here as I'd believed. He was, after all, as young as me, and there were his elders to be pleased. I understood this. "But first we can sing."

I, too, shrugged. "*Ja*." I found myself slipping into my own language—a thing I had not done in this young, self-congratulatory country.

Every noon he would drop by with his bag lunch and eat awful white bread sandwiches, a slice of cafeteria pie, and an apple. I told him, if he thought the sight of *that* made me hungry, he was wrong. But he didn't take offense; he ate his lunch as if it were manna from heaven. I suppose that's because his young wife made it every morning and somehow Frank couldn't separate the Wonder Bread from her pretty, smooth body which he left standing half-robed in the kitchen every morning. I guess he believed his wife was offering him her heart and soul in those greasy bag lunches. I didn't like to hear him speak of his wife; when he did his face lost its contempt and nonchalance and took on a gentleness, a candor that frightened me. There were times I thought he might start talking to me with that same tenderness in his voice—and that I could not have endured. I did like his voice, but only when he was singing.

He sang beautifully for an American, an untrained talent. Once I made the mistake of asking him, "What are you doing in this hospital?"

"What are *you* doing here?" he immediately responded, and I recognized that I had slipped up. I had made the mistake of starting to talk to him. Once that started, he would have the advantage. So I remained silent, except for singing.

One lunchtime Frank showed up with his bag lunch and a little cardboard tube. He popped open the lid and threw out its contents. All these little plastic sticks, brightly colored. At first I thought they were long tiny forks, and I was amazed at Frank's indiscretion! Didn't he remember my wrists?

"Well, this is the game we have to play," he said, almost apologetically. He rolled his eyes and again nodded outside at "them," whoever these authorities were who insisted upon such nonsense. "Do you know it?"

I shook my head stubbornly. But I understood that Frank was just doing as he was told. Besides, we were already half-way through the opera.

"They're called pick-up sticks. It's a child's game, really."

"Yes," I said impatiently, "for children."

He shrugged and then explained it all to me, how I had to pick up each stick individually by color without disturbing the pile. Child's play, indeed. But for a half-starved girl whose hands were always shaking it was a terrible task. Frank explained that for each time I successfully completed my task, we could sing another bit of the opera. So now I had to earn our singing.

It was so laborious, these sessions in the playroom playing pick-up sticks. I had to start eating just a little to build up my strength and coordination, because by the time I'd finished picking up those sticks, I had no stamina left for singing. It was all very, very hard work and sometimes I dreaded it.

How long we went on like that, Frank and I, I don't recall. I do know that one day, toward the end of the opera, my wrists suddenly wobbled during our game and the pile toppled crazily all over the floor. But that wasn't the problem. *The problem was the pain.* It was the most hideous thing I have ever felt, as though my skeleton had collapsed and I was just broken bones poking up through my skin. I was splintered into a million pieces and it was . . . it was shocking, that sorrow could be so physical. I fainted. When I came to, there was Dr. Frank calmly playing pick-up sticks, ignoring me. I could hardly speak, my body hurt so badly. It was the first time I had had any feeling since I could remember. My wrists felt as if I'd just then slashed them, and I held them up to Frank like some kind of creature who's chewed off his own paws to escape the trap.

"It's your turn, Grete," Frank said and met my eyes. He would not take my hands in his. He would not comfort me. "Your turn to play."

At that moment this man was completely monstrous to me, inhuman. Here I was so terribly hurt, and he, a doctor, would do nothing.

"Look!" I cried, and held my wrists up to him. "Look!"

"It must hurt," Frank said, but not kindly, more as if he were looking at just anyone's wrists, as if I had nothing to do with him. "It must hurt, what you did . . . ," he said and then seemed very distracted by the pick-up sticks. He ignored me completely and began playing the game without me.

I stared down at my wrists and saw there were thin, raised scars, still red and ugly, but healing. It should not hurt so. The pain was unbearable. Tears streamed down my face as I held each wrist with the other hand.

"Do you realize we have only one duet left?" Frank asked me, pausing in his game. "Papageno and Papagena . . . it's my favorite . . . "

"That's not the end," I protested. "I've got to sing the Queen of the Night's death scene and then you'll sing Sarastro lines and we'll both do the final chorus."

"Melodramatic fluff," Frank said, as if I were the most sentimental of women and he the realist. He seemed embarrassed for me as I knelt beside him, trembling, holding my wrists. Perhaps he was even ashamed of me, I thought. What was very clear was his contempt. I was useless to him. I couldn't even play this stupid child's game! "I said, it's your turn, Grete." Frank waited for me to bend over and, with hands that shook as if electric tremors pulsed through my arms, I began plucking the blue pick-up sticks from the pile.

It took every ounce of my strength. Each movement set off in my body a shudder and waves of pain so intense I almost blacked out. But now I knew that at last I was dying. And even though my wrists were slashed and bleeding, I sensed that I would be released from this pain, from this hospital prison camp.

As I worked on the last stick, I could already hear the strains of the Queen of the Night's demise coming back to me perfectly: *"Zerschmettert, zernichtet ist unsere Macht, Wir alle gestürzet in ewige Nacht."* . . . Shattered, sundered is our might! We all shall plunge to endless night!

It took all my will, but I did pick up those last sticks without disturbing the pile. With a child's triumph, I turned to Frank. "Now we sing the ending!" I almost shouted.

Frank was quiet. He stood up and stared down at me as if all along he had known what I was up to.

"Go on . . . " I demanded, "you have Sarastro's first part."

"I don't want to take my turn in *this* game," Frank said simply, and turned away. "You'll have to do it alone."

"Alone?" I cried, and that one word annihilated me; it ached in my wrists and throat like a last pulse. "But you have to help me ... help me go."

"No," Frank repeated. "No one gets to kill herself in this opera." He moved to cross the room toward the door. I caught his pants leg and groveled as I never had in my life—not even to the Nazis. "Please," I begged, "it hurts too much.... Please ... "

"No," he repeated. "Just let it be."

And his *no* was all the no's I had ever heard or said. His great *No!* boomed out like a darkness to swallow me.

I didn't think. Still holding that pile of pick-up sticks in my hand, I jumped up and caught Frank by surprise. I stabbed him again and again in his broad chest.

He didn't even flinch.

You see, those pick-up sticks had no sharp points on them. I'd never noticed. Frank stood with his arms flung out and let me batter him with my little sticks until at last I slid down, exhausted. I wrapped my arms around his legs and buried my face against his knees.

I have never sobbed like that—before or since. Then I felt his arms reach down to pull me up, and when I was at last eye level he was again the Frank who sang arias and talked tenderly about his wife.

"Grete, *Liebchen*." He shook my shoulders gently. "You didn't kill me. And you didn't kill them." He touched my face. "All those bodies ... you've picked them up now, haven't you? You've buried each and every one. They're not here anymore. But you are. Grete ... will you stay?"

Oh, you see how long I've stayed. How very long. Sixty-some years—long enough for another holocaust to come round. Now I am old and want to live; then I was young and wanted to die. I don't blame the young for wanting to die, for saying to this lethal world the old have made for them, "No, I don't want to!" I don't blame anybody.

I don't blame. I'll bury all the bodies that nobody killed. I'll pick you up, every broken bone like so many little burned sticks. I'll bury all my children with their toys and stories like playthings for the beyond. I'll be here, I'll abide, I'll bury all our dead—all we did. I'll begin again to make us human.

17

SMALLER THAN LIFE

THE SNOWSTORM had sent much of the Cowley and Pelzner staff scurrying home early this evening. That was always these New Yorkers' response to the first snow, Lauren thought, sitting at her desk in Holden's Harbor listening to the sleet loudly pelt the window. Then she smiled at herself. It had been just over a year since she'd come to New York, and she was making assumptions as if she'd lived here half her life.

"You'll be the last one left," called Mrs. Holden from the doorway. She was so bundled up in muffler, heavy mittens, and galoshes that she reminded Lauren of a child in a snowsuit.

"I can use the quiet," Lauren smiled, and waved to her. Lighting a cigarette, Muriel made her way down the hallway like a homebound express.

Now the office was Lauren's own. There were no phone calls, no slow-motion messenger boys wandering in and out, no office intrigues; just the murmuring tea kettle in the corner and the softer sounds of the storm leaving whimsical white splotches against the dark window.

Lauren welcomed this reverie, to gather herself before taking the train to Brooklyn and her first meeting since early summer with Ruth Littlefield. So many months had passed, and so much silence, that Lauren was seized with a kind of terror at the prospect of seeing her old friend. Lauren felt that when she at last did meet Ruth again, all would fall into place, the way a jigsaw fits together from the moment one finds the sky piece, the border piece.

Lauren strolled down the hall to the ladies' confidential lounge for cream from the small office refrigerator. As she opened the door, feeling for the light switch, she was startled by the sound of a cooing and warbling, then the invisible whoosh of small wings. *Bats in a cave*, was Lauren's first thought, and she instinctively ducked, covering her head. The coffee mug crashed to the floor, hot liquid pooling on her new shoes. Now she'd have to dry her nylons and shoes on the radiator before braving the slush on the streets outside.

"Damn!" Lauren burst out, and groped for the light.

"No light!" a voice said from the corner of the ladies' confidential lounge.

"Who . . . who is it?" Lauren crouched, did not make a move for the light. She'd read about bag people and wild-eyed crazies who lived in skyscrapers at night, or subway tunnels, when all the office workers went home. Sitting in the subway just last week, she'd looked up from reading *War and Peace* to be mesmerized by a *Daily News* article entitled "New York at Night: Human Cockroaches Come Out of Woodwork and Into Your Office."

"Don't be afraid." The voice spoke so knowingly it was as if it were inside Lauren's own skull. Vague memories of *The Secret Sharer* made Lauren uneasy, and she realized that she was often more afraid of stories she'd read than of anything real happening to her.

"Who are you?" Lauren demanded, but her voice was very small in the dark.

The antique Victorian lamp on the bedside table glowed suddenly, and in its rosy shadow sat a woman Lauren was slow to recognize. For nothing about Heather Jaynes was familiar, except perhaps the vague, colorless eyes which did not dart, as Lauren remembered, but fixed on her with a stranger's calculated disinterest. Perhaps Heather had been living in the subways so long that her face had taken on the permanent expression of a New Yorker in the underground.

"You don't like the subway anymore, do you?" Heather demanded now.

Lauren was so taken aback by Heather's clairvoyance that she couldn't speak.

"Well, sit down, . . . sit down," Heather said in a perfect imitation of Muriel Holden, complete with the wild sweep of her hand toward the cozy overstuffed chair next to the chaise longue where Heather lay buried underneath the sherbet-colored comforter. "Don't break your head over it."

It was as if Heather had lost her own core and instead accumulated every gesture, voice, and thought of those she'd lived with so long at Cowley and Pelzner.

"Yes, I'm here at last," Heather said, once again intuiting Lauren's smile, her thoughts. "What a long summer it was under the stairs, underground; . . . but I knew come winter Charlie would let me in. He does, you know, every weekday evening now. It's only during the day that he follows Mercer's orders and escorts me out. But he promised me when the weather changed, I could come home again."

"Home. . . . " Lauren said. "Yes, I'm glad to see you after all this time, Heather."

She was, Lauren realized. Without thinking Lauren reached for the shortbread tray. But it was no longer there. It was only Heather's reappearance that triggered Lauren's memory of the sweets.

"And so you're the only one of your little group left here, are you?" Heather asked, and she was polite as could be.

"I can't stay long, Heather," Lauren said, remembering her dinner with Ruth. The dim light, the hush of the snow outside, the open window with its warbling pigeons—all gave Lauren a sense of being out of time.

"Why not? I'm staying on, you know . . . so will you."

In the light of the first snow falling, Lauren's eyes adjusted to the dark enough for her to really see Heather: she was wearing woolen gloves with the fingers cut out, but the impression she gave was more of a Victorian lady than of a bag lady who'd spent all summer living in subway tunnels. Heather also wore tiny, leather lace-up boots, again like a petite gentlewoman, though

Lauren did note that the tip of the left boot was bound in brightly colored rags.

"You know, Miss Meyer," Heather now began, and in her tone was a courtesy and depth, as if the underground had transformed her. Lauren was moved by Heather's womanly softness, her yielding and generous contours even under those filthy clothes. Heather's face in this lamplight was ravaged, very old, and kind—the mercy that comes most from mothers. "You know," Heather continued, "I've begun to think of everything, not in terms of survival . . . but as surrender, one to another."

"Surrender?" Lauren asked.

"Did I ever tell you that in the war I drove a double-decker bus in London during the Germans' worst air raids?"

"No, never, Heather," Lauren said. She remembered reading one of Heather Jaynes' early novels. It was set during the second World War and told the story of those harrowing air raids. Was it a real event in her life that Heather was remembering, Lauren wondered, or was she simply recalling one of her own stories? Did it matter? "Tell me. Please."

"Well," Heather sat back, poured herself a delicate cupful of whiskey and began, "during the Blitz I was in this perfectly lovely sanitarium when Chamberlain made his pretty little speech. But it was war he was declaring, we all knew that. Mother cabled me to come back to New York, but I was having such a good rest right there in Climpton Wood. Cross House was green and quiet; they even let us troop out every now and again for theatre. But when the Blitz began . . . well, who of us loyal lunatics could rest? I tell you, though, it wasn't simple patriotism that got me into the driver's seat of those buses . . . it was my vast experience. After all, for me the sky had *always* been falling." Heather broke into peals of laughter. "You see, my normal life was a rain of terrors, so why not drive a bus through blazing streets, air-raid sirens howling, all the rubble and dusty brick and even bodies underneath? Sometimes people just froze in my way like deer in headlights. 'Come on, my pickled pears,' I'd say, and hustle them safely aboard my bus and then drive like a demon to the nearest shelter...."

Heather paused, and in that moment Lauren saw how very beautiful she once had been, pale and aquiline like one of the wax figures Lauren had seen in the London wax museum—was it Anne Boleyn, poor beheaded queen of Henry VIII? Or was Lauren remembering the jacket photo she'd seen on one of Heather Jaynes' own books?

"I read your first book," Lauren ventured now, but shyly. She knew it was bad form at Cowley and Pelzner to talk about the early work of an author who had fallen into literary silence. But Lauren violated this office rule because she believed Miss Jaynes herself was long past rules. "I liked it very much."

"More than you like me," Heather Jaynes said without skipping a beat. "Most people do."

"Not at all," Lauren protested.

"If I were only as good as my books, you see," Heather mused, "I might have made my way in the world with a little more... well, more balance. Because you can't *live* in a book." Heather gazed at Lauren and her eyes then fixed on her with a clarity Lauren had not witnessed before. "You see, I believed my ordinary self *expendable*... like many artists. I gave over everything to my books until, well, until I was so personally small I slipped through the crack in the world." Heather paused and then began laughing softly. "I was... well, smaller than life."

"It's hard, isn't it?" Lauren heard her own voice, though she had no idea what she was going to say. "It's hard being so big and so small at the same time."

At this Heather Jaynes looked straight at Lauren and studied her in silence for a long while. Under the woman's scrutiny, Lauren bowed her head—not in shame or shyness, but with a sense that she was glimpsing some truth that she herself needed if she were going to navigate her way in the world and not end up like Miss Jaynes.

"I keep having a dream," Heather said slowly, "and I'll tell you so someday you might tell others. I dream that I am in a castle with a beautiful woman painter. All her portraits are hung in the castle, yet something is terribly wrong with the family. Slowly they are being executed by a murderer among them. I see a connection here. The moment the woman paints a portrait of someone in her castle, that person is murdered. I keep watch over the young girl I know will be the next victim and, sure enough, in the middle of the night a man emerges from the woodwork to attack. I fight him physically but he is very strong and magical. He and I fight without weapons—only words and bodies. I know I will never kill him, nor he me. This is a very old battle between us.

"When I have him down on the ground, my hand to his throat, he begins weeping and I suddenly can hear his thoughts. I realize that it is the beauty of the paintings versus the reality of the subjects transformed that torments this murderer. He sees the paintings as perfect, the people as flawed. When the painting is done, he believes its human subject must then be destroyed because somehow the person's imperfection competes with or undermines the beauty of the art."

Lauren could say nothing; she had the urge to run away, not only from Heather Jaynes but from Cowley and Pelzner, which too much resembled Heather's castle. Hadn't this publishing house maintained its cherished literary reputation at the cost of the very people who had made it great? Hadn't they sacrificed the best—Daniel Sorenson, Hella Steinhardt? Maybe she, too, should leave, Lauren thought. As soon as she signed her book contract, she could leave Holden's Harbor.

"No, don't leave," Heather said softly, and Lauren couldn't tell whether the woman had again read her mind or was responding to Lauren's backing out of the door.

"Do you want me to stay a while longer here with you, Heather?"

"Don't leave Cowley and Pelzner," Heather said. "Stay inside the castle, fight the murderers. No more human sacrifices. It's not what God wants . . . never did, really. But we are always offering, don't you know, because there's something in all of us that yearns so to give back, give everything back. We are not expendable, I tell you. We may be mortal, but we are not expendable."

Lauren stood very still in the doorway. Outside the snow fell like another layer of white down on the very tops of the pigeons' heads as they perched on the open windowsill and pecked from Heather's upheld hands. Lauren had no idea why, but tears welled up in her eyes and she stood with her head bent, as if only this woman could give her the benediction she needed to leave.

"A long time ago," Heather said by way of letting Lauren go, "I used to take daily walks with a man from my sanitarium. He was a shellshocked soldier dragged reluctantly from the Blitz rubble. When we walked round and round the green he'd breathe so oddly, great exhalations like those of a breeching whale. When I finally asked him what he was doing, he answered, 'I've breathed too much of the world's air, and now I'm giving back some so you won't suffocate.' 'Oh, my poor pickled pear,' I told him. I loved him for just being here with me, for walking nearby and breathing." Heather paused and let go of Lauren's hand. "And I've never been able to love anyone else as I did that man who walked with me on the green. Have you?"

Lauren was very still. At last she said, "No. I don't think so."

"That's why we have long lives," Heather said, and her face was so dark, so unfamiliar, she could have been any old woman. "Leave the door open when you go," Heather said, and sat back in the chaise longue, weary at last.

Lauren stood quietly letting the whoosh of the radiator wash over her like the rhythm of an ocean. Outside the snow was so thick she'd be glad to descend into the subway, surrender to it and let the downtown express deliver her to Brooklyn Heights and Ruth's office.

"I'll see you again soon," Lauren said by way of taking her leave.

"Perhaps, my pickled pear," Heather Jaynes murmured.

And Lauren left the door to the ladies' confidential lounge ajar.

BETWEEN PEERS

Aftera hot, slushy ride on the Number 2 downtown express—imagining that she saw Heather Jaynes in every underground hideaway—Lauren entered the Brooklyn duplex with the door marked *Pleiades Press.*

"You're not late." Ruth Littlefield looked up from her wide desk and met Lauren with a composed smile. She did not get up from her chair or come to greet her.

Immediately Lauren saw Ruth was drawing most on her professional manners, the cool and gracious distance that at any moment might well change into a crevasse between them. Taking a deep breath, Lauren said directly, "Hello, Ruth I'm glad to see you again."

For a moment they exchanged level glances and Lauren was reminded of reading once that in the first moments between people, everything is decided. But what about first impressions after long separation or betrayal?

Lauren found herself a seat in an overstuffed chair and took off her wet leather pumps.

"New shoes?" Ruth asked, and for just a moment there was a fondness in her voice.

"I wanted to make a good impression," Lauren laughed nervously.

"Well," Ruth said, "you certainly didn't succeed. Where are your galoshes?"

Lauren frowned. "I don't wear galoshes, Ruth. That's for city folk. I don't mind getting my feet wet."

For a moment she thought Ruth might laugh aloud, delighted to be so met and countered; but Ruth looked away and said nothing. In the silence Lauren studied the office. Books lay piled atop the mahogany desk which Lauren now recognized as having been Daniel's at Cowley and Pelzner. Everywhere in the room were signs of him: oak cabinet files; his bronze lamp; and many of the manuscripts strewn across Ruth's desk were scrawled over in Daniel's precise hand. Discovering Ruth so comfortably self-possessed among all of Daniel Sorenson's things gave Lauren much hope. Perhaps Ruth would forgive her as she had Daniel?

"Can you believe this blizzard?" Lauren asked.

"Yes," Ruth said, and the coldness in her voice made the room seem less safe than the storm outside. Ruth turned to Lauren. "There's much I've had to believe lately."

Lauren lowered her head as if she'd been physically rebuffed. For her one night with Joseph she had lost both of them and her home. Now she was to lose the future: Ruth would not be her friend. This was simply a formal transaction, Lauren realized: she must ask Ruth's forgiveness; Ruth's civilized politeness must grant it; then they would part. Silence would harden into uncommitted courtesy.

"It's cold in here," Lauren heard herself say in a small voice.

"Daniel believes if we stint on heat, we'll have more money for the writers and production," Ruth commented. Then she added in a less formal tone, "But I've bought a space heater and I run it when Daniel's not around. Why don't you take off your coat—you must be soaked—and warm yourself?"

As Lauren obligingly unburdened herself from the heavy woollen embrace of her overcoat, Ruth noticed that she had finally sewn the metal buttons back on tight. No longer did they hang on strings in a way that had outraged Ruth one evening long ago: that summer night when Lauren had left Ruth and gone to Joseph, the night followed by the next day, the confession, the final break-up of housekeeping. So often these past months Ruth had gone over it all in her mind. Alone in her childhood apartment, watching the seasons change, longing for the sound of voices to counterpoint hers, Ruth had finally decided to sublet her parents' Park Avenue apartment. Now she kept a modest studio apartment upstairs in this Brooklyn brownstone above the press. Hella and Daniel stayed here, too, when they were in the city and had taken a loan to remodel part of the basement into a separate apartment.

"I'm fine, really," Lauren assured her, but Ruth saw her friend plainly shivering.

"Well, I'll turn up the space heater and maybe it'll reach you way over there."

Lauren was quiet a moment and Ruth couldn't read her face. Was it resentment she saw there? Surely not. After all, they were here to make it up, one to another, weren't they?

"How is your work?" Ruth asked, seeking safe ground. Her question only deepened Lauren's frown. "And your family?"

"Both good," Lauren answered, her eyes lowered. "I've signed a contract with Harper & Row and my sister Clare visited me this summer. Also, I've decided to stay on at C&P . . . fight from the inside."

"So everything is just fine with you. You weren't disinherited after all?" Now Ruth was feeling some resentment of her own, though she couldn't quite figure out why.

She was alarmed at how poorly things were going now between them. In all these long months of absence, and without the actual presence of Lauren or Joseph, Ruth believed she had truly forgiven them both.

Now Ruth wondered about that. She had a moment of panic and thought about asking Lauren to just leave, that she wasn't yet ready for this, face-to-face; that all the mercy was in her mind, not her heart; that she still needed time to simply see Lauren for brief periods and actually work her slow way toward forgiveness. This discrepancy between her imagination's ability to forgive or heal a wound and her ability to be near the actual deliverer of that wound confused Ruth so much she, too, lowered her eyes and fell silent.

"No, I wasn't disinherited," Lauren took up. "At least not by my family." Lauren fell quiet.

Ruth noticed that habit her friend had of scanning with her eyes when she was most lost in thought. And the sight of this familiar expression made Ruth smile. For the first time she felt real pleasure in Lauren's presence. But she kept still, waiting for Lauren to continue.

"Do you know who I met right before coming here?"

"Who?"

"Heather Jaynes."

"Oh, my!" Ruth exclaimed. "You're always running into her. Once I swore I saw Heather myself in Port Authority in one of those awful tunnels. I told myself it couldn't be her, I'd rather see Heather dead."

"Too bad they don't have a morgue for writers like they do for their books," Lauren said, and the look on her friend's face startled Ruth. Rarely had she seen this bitterness in Lauren. "Or at least a sanitarium."

"Didn't you ever used to dream of a white plantation house all lost in green with libraries and tea and nothing to do but rest?"

"They sent Heather someplace like that during the war . . . ," Lauren began.

"And do you still believe there's a war on, Lauren?"

This question stopped her. She recovered herself and glanced at Ruth with a frown that slowly changed to a grin. "Yeah, honey, sometimes I surely do. A cold war."

Ruth smiled, too, and though they were laughing there was little warmth in the room. "Well, what do you expect? The whole world is on the brink of blowing up . . . ; we're just acting it out between ourselves."

Lauren looked down at her hands. "You know, my father was very poor. Still, he's always fixing things long after they seem no earthly good, fixing and puttering and putting things back together even if they're not right. He still just puts them somewhere in the house so we can at least look at them, keep them in our daily life."

"We always bought new things," Ruth said softly. "The Littlefields replaced their car every year with a new model. I don't think I ever saw anything outlast its usefulness."

"Think our friendship has outlasted its usefulness?" Lauren asked as she at last took off her coat. "Want to replace it with a new model?"

"Would your father even try to put us back together again?" Ruth countered.

"We done broke bad, honey," Lauren said in a low voice.

To Ruth, Lauren seemed so familiar, and she remembered Lauren's hands, how skillfully she had worked to ease the pain of her migraine.

Lauren continued, "Heather told me something I didn't understand until just now."

"What was that?" Ruth leaned forward, unaware that Lauren noted this and leaned forward herself.

"She said something about surrender... yes, that was it... surrendering, one to another."

"And what did she mean?" Ruth asked, then added softly, "What do you mean?"

Lauren was quiet a long time. Then she stood up and crossed the room. She squatted on her knees near Ruth and held up her hands to the old-fashioned space heater. It was unlike Joseph's. It was an imitation radiator filled with water that now steamed and breathed as if it were another warm presence between them. The heat it lent them was more diffuse than Joseph's fiery quartz heater: somehow it seemed feminine. "I'm so sorry, Ruth," Lauren said, head bent, palms held to the heater. She looked up at Ruth. "I'm so sorry I hurt you."

Ruth met her friend's eyes. "We'll have to do this slowly... because... well, because it means a different kind of openness now between us—one that is conscious, between equals, knowing full well our great capacity to do harm as well as help one another heal."

Lauren turned back to the heater, nodding slowly, almost rhythmically, her whole body moving in a kind of slow dance in her long squat. Yes, she thought, this was what long friendship would be like, long lives and a slow, measured opening—not the opening of a wound, but of a heart's territory that must be respectfully explored, cherished, worked, not abandoned or trespassed. "Maybe that's what we can do with one another," Lauren at last suggested.

"What?"

"Maybe we won't even try to fix it all between us now . . . ; we can just keep ourselves in each other's sight. I mean, see each other in an everyday kind of way . . . so we won't believe we're so broken. So we can mend."

"I've noticed you've done quite a job of that on your peacoat buttons." Ruth stood up and crossed to the kettle. "Tea?"

"Yes, ma'am."

"You know," Ruth began, musing in the habitual way she had of combining a simple chore with her most telling comments, "I've missed our teas." This made Lauren smile. She suddenly remembered Ruth, in all her daily habits. These movements, this tone of voice, this tilt of the head while Ruth delicately poured the loose tea into the strainer—no one in the world but Ruth made tea like this. There was no one in the world like Ruth, Lauren thought now, no one like Joseph or Hella or Daniel, no one like herself. No replacements. And that's what Heather must have meant. God didn't want human sacrifice. Not when everyone was so precious.

"Joseph once told me . . . " Here Lauren winced at the name between them, but she had to say it. "He told me that I think we spend half our lives wondering just exactly who we *are* to one another."

"And who am I, do you think?"

"My friend," Lauren said without hesitation.

"And Joseph?"

"Friend, too."

"Do you hear from him?" Ruth asked. "Does he write you as he does Daniel?"

"Yes."

"And when he comes home, what will he be to you then?"

"My friend," Lauren said again firmly. "That's all."

"Perhaps that's everything." Ruth studied Lauren a moment and then at last nodded as she set the teakettle back on its cooling coil. "Joseph and I are still not talking."

"Did you ever... really?" Lauren offered this almost shyly, but as if it were her right now to see so deeply and say so.

"Not really, no," Ruth admitted slowly. "I think Joseph and I helped one another through a sad time... fatherless children. I think we were often kind, instead of passionate."

"Maybe kindness is true passion," Lauren said.

Ruth received this in silence. She gazed out the brownstone window to the streetlamps now lost in a flurry of snowflakes. It was so still that she could hear Lauren breathing. This simple sound comforted Ruth more deeply than anything Lauren said.

For a long while they were silent, listening to the steaming space heater, the teakettle, the hush of whiteness outside. Soon they would venture out in search of some sustenance, some supper they might share with each other.

At last Ruth murmured, "I was just remembering something...."

"What?"

"Something the nuns used to teach us about first snow."

"Is it a good story?" Lauren asked with a faint smile.

"Yes, it is," Ruth answered.

"But first, Ruth," Lauren sat up in her chair and balanced the teacup on her knees, "first, I want to hear another story."

"And what's that?"

"I want to hear all about them... you know, your imaginary friends."

Ruth sipped her tea and nodded slowly. Then she laughed out loud. "Well, I'll violate all laws of storytelling. I'll have to tell you the ending first."

"They survived, didn't they?" Lauren said. And then she met Ruth's eyes over the brimming rim of her teacup. "Even now, you have them with you?"

"Yes," Ruth said softly, "they're here. Right here."

ABOUT THE AUTHOR

A transplanted Southerner and graduate of the University of California at Davis, Brenda Peterson has worked for *The New Yorker*, lived on a farm near Denver, where she was a fiction editor for *Rocky Mountain Magazine*, and taught at Arizona State University in Tempe. Now an editor and environmental writer, Ms. Peterson makes her home in Seattle. Her first novel, *River of Light*, was published in cloth by Alfred A. Knopf in 1978, and reissued in paperback by Graywolf Press in 1986.

COLOPHON

The dust jacket image is by Yvonne Jacquette, "Tip of Manhattan," a woodcut from Experimental Workshop.

Text and cover for this book were designed by Tree Swenson.

The Aldus and Optima types in this book were set by the Typeworks.

Book manufactured by Edwards Brothers.